He traced a wa_____ve of her
cheek and then_____s if he'd
never seen anyth___ as fascinating. "I'm feeling a powerful urge to kiss you again."

Then he did, this time brushing his mouth so softly
over hers that, for a moment, she wasn't even sure if he
really had kissed her.

But he had, there could be no doubt.

She knew because a flurry of tingles rippled through
her again. They spilled from her kiss-swollen lips right
into her belly where the startling sensations twirled wickedly before tumbling ever downward until she was quite
sure her toes must be curling.

He'd changed greatly.

And much as it annoyed her to admit, she almost preferred the brutish ox she remembered. What that said
about her didn't bear consideration.

Either way, she was in trouble.

⚜   ⚜   ⚜

PRAISE FOR
SUE-ELLEN WELFONDER

"Few writers can bring history to life like Sue-Ellen Welfonder! For anyone who loves historical fiction, the books
in the Highland Warriors trilogy are a true treasure."
—**Heather Graham,** *New York Times*
best-selling author

SEDUCTION OF A HIGHLAND WARRIOR

TEMPTATION OF A HIGHLAND SCOUNDREL

SINS OF A HIGHLAND DEVIL

"4½ stars! Top Pick! The first installment in Welfonder's Highland Warriors trilogy continues a long tradition of well-written, highly emotional romances. This marvelous novel is rich in love and legend, populated by characters steeped in honor, to make for a sensual and emotional read."

—*RT Book Reviews*

"A richly enjoyable story. Welfonder is a master story-teller."

—ARomanceReview.com

A HIGHLANDER'S TEMPTATION

"[Welfonder] continues to weave magical tales of redemption, love, and loyalty in glorious, perilous mid-fourteenth-century Scotland."

—*Booklist*

SEDUCING A SCOTTISH BRIDE

"4½ stars! Welfonder sweeps readers into a tale brimming with witty banter between a feisty heroine and a stalwart hero...The added paranormal elements and sensuality turn this into an intriguing page-turner that fans of Scottish romance will adore."

—*RT Book Reviews*

BRIDE FOR A KNIGHT

"Once again, Welfonder's careful scholarship and attention to detail vividly re-create the lusty, brawling days of medieval Scotland with larger-than-life chivalrous heroes and the dainty but spirited maidens."
—*Booklist*

ONLY FOR A KNIGHT

"4½ stars! Enthralling…Welfonder brings the Highlands to life with her vibrant characters, impassioned stories, and vivid description."
—*RT Book Reviews*

WEDDING FOR A KNIGHT

"A very romantic story…extremely sexy. I recommend this book to anyone who loves the era and Scotland."
—**TheBestReviews.com**

MASTER OF THE HIGHLANDS

"Welfonder does it again, bringing readers another powerful, emotional, highly romantic medieval that steals your heart and keeps you turning the pages."
—*RT Book Reviews*

DEVIL IN A KILT

"A lovely gem of a book. Wonderful characters and a true sense of place make this a keeper."
—**Patricia Potter, author of** *The Heart Queen*

TO DESIRE A HIGHLANDER

SUE-ELLEN WELFONDER

FOREVER

NEW YORK   BOSTON

Copyright © 2015 by Sue-Ellen Welfonder
Excerpt from *To Love a Highlander* © 2014 by Sue-Ellen Welfonder

Forever
Hachette Book Group
1290 Avenue of the Americas
New York, NY 10104

www.HachetteBookGroup.com

Printed in the United States of America

First edition: August 2015
10 9 8 7 6 5 4 3 2 1

OPM

Forever is an imprint of Grand Central Publishing.
The Forever name and logo are trademarks of Hachette Book Group, Inc.

The Hachette Speakers Bureau provides a wide range of authors for speaking events. To find out more, go to www.hachettespeakersbureau.com or call (866) 376-6591.

The publisher is not responsible for websites (or their content) that are not owned by the publisher.

ISBN 978-1-4555-2628-4

In loving remembrance and to honor three very special souls: Tricia Heintz, my longtime reader and friend. Tricia was always upbeat, a trait displayed by her email by-name, Sunshyne. A great joy to all who knew her, she was fiercely devoted to her family and friends. She left us way too soon, but her beautiful light shines on, undimmed in the hearts of all who loved her.

Dan Phillips was the husband of another longtime reader and friend, Cathy Phillips. Rarely have I known a couple more in love and devoted to each other. Cathy and Dan were the stuff of real romance, not the fiction kind. I wish they'd made their 40th anniversary, but they had 39 beautiful years and a love so strong, it will live on forever.

And for my darling wee Em, with the whole of my heart. You shared my desk chair through the writing of all my books, beginning with *Devil in a Kilt* and you almost made it through this one as well. I would need to write a new book to say how much you meant to me. I will love you forever and miss you so much. But we will be together again. Until then, wait for me, my little friend.

Acknowledgments

From the beginning of my writing career, my world has been blessed by beautiful readers who, like me, appreciate all the wonder of medieval Scotland, Highland magic, animals (real and mythical), meddling crones, and—of course—big, bold Highland heroes and the strong and proud heroines who love them. You've shared my belief that reading a book is actually opening a portal and being swept away to wherever or whenever your heart desires. Thank you so much for your love, enthusiasm, and support. It has meant and means so much to have you on this journey with me. A thousand blessings and all my love to each one of you.

As always, to my very handsome husband, Manfred, who gifted me with a standing suit of armor early in my career (in celebration of a book release). He is my true knight in shining armor, always was and ever shall be. Also for my dear wee Jack Russell, Em. My brightest shining star for so many years, and still. I miss you so, little man.

TO DESIRE A HIGHLANDER

All good women should know that a Highlander's smile is as dangerous as his sword, perhaps even more so.

—Roag the Bear, a master of the art

The Legend of Laddie's Isle

❦

In distant times when Scotland's Western Isles and the Hebridean Sea were young and largely empty, few men were brave enough to sail such wild and treacherous waters. Fearsome beasties could dwell there, lurking beneath the white-capped waves, lying in wait for the unwary. All knew the gods and their minions held sway in this far-flung, untamed place. Such powerful deities didn't look kindly on those who'd dare to claim what was theirs.

Even so, some men tried.

These brave souls were Highlanders, known to be bold and adventurous.

No scaly-tailed, boat-swallowing serpent or even an angry, trident-wielding sea god could dissuade them. Strong, hardy, and fearless, these warriors sailed their galleys deep into this vast and magnificent world of islands and islets. They looked in awe at the many sheer cliffs and soaring peaks, the sheltered coves of gleaming white sand. Their oarsmen rowed with skill and power, the ships flashing across the dark blue swells. Not to be outdone, well-practiced helmsmen guided them expertly past glistening-black skerries, the jagged rocks kissed by luminous sea spray.

Wherever their galleys took them, the splendor of this place known as the "Isles on the Edge of the Sea" only grew greater and greater.

Men's hearts beat faster at the beauty.

Many were consumed by a burning wish to grab a piece of this glorious seascape for their own.

Sadly, such fierce craving is dangerous.

Otherwise sensible men forget themselves, greed and desire driving them to carelessness. Wits often evaporate when temptation is so great.

When that happens, doom soon follows.

Yet the lure of the Hebrides is potent and powerful.

Men who've looked upon such grandeur are forever changed, their souls ensnared. For they've breathed the chill, peat-scented air, and felt the rush of cold, sea-borne wind, the magic of the Isles, entering their blood. Such men are never again free, escape impossible.

Truth be told, they wouldn't leave if they could.

Some such adventurers lost their lives trying to stay.

And so it came about that one of the most remote corners of this watery world harbors a long-uninhabited islet and its half-ruined keep.

A rocky spit of land said to be home to no more than wild winds and stronger currents.

The tower doesn't have a name, for it was never intended to be anyone's refuge. Its origins reach far back in time to days no longer remembered. Even so, some whisper that the keep's first stones were laid in memory of a wee laddie who washed ashore there after his father's galley splintered on a nearby reef during a storm. All men were lost that day and many of their women perished as well, dying of broken hearts when they learned of the tragedy.

Storytellers say that men built a cairn in the boy's honor, setting stones to mark his last resting place on this earth.

Seamen, being a superstitious, good-hearted lot, allowed no ship to pass without dropping anchor so that a few stones could be added to the memorial.

This gesture of respect was carried on for centuries.

In time, the cairn grew into a tower. But the passing years dimmed memories and so the nameless keep began to crumble, its once-proud walls falling shamefully apart. Seabirds claimed the cold, dank stones and the hall echoed with the howl of gales and the lashing of rain. Soon, the wee isle, so rock-hewn and windswept, also bore the taint of being haunted. Men sailing by stayed clear, no longer willing to stop in honor of the lost laddie.

But now the island had a name.

Hebrideans call it Laddie's Isle and claim the boy walks the island on stormy nights when the clouds slide away from the moon. Witnesses swear that the lad glows. That he wears a torn plaid and carries a small, luminous dirk that he points toward the deadly skerries that damned his father's ship. He is credited with saving more than a few lives in rough and terrible seas.

Even so, because of the reefs and the ghost, many men hesitate to speak the name Laddie's Isle.

Until the day the Scottish King sends a man to claim the crumbling keep and use the island to perform secret duties in the royal name.

This newcomer is as big, bold, and daring as a rogue adventurer can be. He fears neither wild winds nor huge, tossing seas. To be sure, he isn't worried about ghosts and ancient legends. Indeed, he's a man who laughs in the face of danger, even welcoming trouble. Little does he know how much he's about to get...

Chapter One

❧

Laddie's Isle
Spring 1400

Lady Gillian MacGuire knew the moment the gods abandoned her.

They'd fled as soon as she'd set foot on this much-maligned island. Even her brothers had made the sign against evil as they'd climbed aboard their father's ship. Good men didn't sail these waters.

Not if they valued their lives.

The currents were too strong; the seas wild and rough. Unpredictable winds blew always, cutting as knives and colder than hell.

Gillian glanced about the bleak and fearsome shore-line, chilled already.

No one could blame her long-lost betrothed for leaving the place. Shivering, she drew her cloak tighter. She could almost believe the tales that the rocky little island was haunted. That it was cursed because of its dark and sad history. But now there was word her betrothed was returning after five years away—to reclaim his home and to take his bride.

Gillian stepped closer to the water's edge. Behind her, sheer cliffs loomed high and black. Everywhere else, the sea boiled and churned, lashing against the jagged shore. The spray dampened her skirts and misted her skin. Above her, seabirds wheeled and cried, and the chill air smelled strongly of the sea. The salty tang quickened her pulse, stirring her Hebridean heart even as her world threatened to crash down around her.

But tears and pity weren't for her, a chieftain's daughter. She preferred to stand tall, shoulders squared and chin high. A brave young woman with long centuries of noble blood in her veins, she prided herself on her strength.

She was equally proud of her by-name, the Spitfire of the Isles. Secretly, she'd also believed she held the gods' ears.

That they even favored her, looking on her kindly and guiding her in times of trouble.

Now she knew differently.

Somewhere beyond the horizon, Donell MacDonnell was making his way home.

Gillian didn't blink as a wave broke over the rocks, the icy water sluicing her feet. She had other concerns of much greater importance.

She was the MacDonnell's bespoken bride.

Yet wedding him was the last thing she wanted.

While not quite an ogre, he was many summers her elder. She doubted he'd ever washed his great black beard, which was bushy enough to house at least three nests of mice. His arms and legs were thicker than trees, his girth immeasurable. Worse, he suffered onion breath.

His meaty hands bore scars, something she'd admire and honor in most warrior chieftains.

After all, a leader unwilling to fight beside his men wasn't worthy of his status as a commander. Regrettably, Donell's hands weren't just marked by battle. The skin around and beneath his fingernails was black with grime. If his breath smelled of onions, his flesh reeked of things she didn't want to name.

She shuddered, a chill sweeping her despite her determination to remain calm.

A passing galley had dropped anchor at her father's island home, Castle Sway. The ship's crew begged, and received, hospitality for the night. Plied with generous viands and free-flowing ale, and warmed by the hearth fire, the seamen spoke freely, sharing news from afar.

These tidings included their meeting with Donell at a well-visited seafarers' tavern on the mainland coast.

Unaware that their words chilled Gillian's blood, even upending her world, they claimed he was journeying back to his isle. That he'd vowed he was eager to resume his duties as chieftain of his watery domain.

His arrival was imminent. Or so Castle Sway's friendly and loose-tongued guests had asserted.

Gillian fisted her hands, clutching the folds of her skirts. She welcomed the chill numbness of her fingers. Focusing on the bone-deep cold and the sharp needle pricks racing up her wrists and along her arms kept her from thinking how opportune it would be if Donell's galley were to spring a leak, sinking into the sea.

She might not want to marry him, but she didn't wish the man ill.

Even so...

She bit her lip, remembering how his big, dirty-nailed hand had gripped hers on the day of their betrothal. He'd lifted her fingers to his lips, his greasy beard tickling her skin as he'd kissed her knuckles.

The hunger in his eyes as he'd done so, the way his gaze had swept her head to toe, was a memory she wished she didn't have.

His slow smile, which revealed the yellowish stain of his teeth...

"Mother of all the gods." Gillian lifted a hand to her brow, peering out across the sea. To her relief, there was no sign of Donell's galley.

That didn't mean he wasn't coming.

The mist was thicker near the horizon, spoiling her view. He could be out there now, his ship slicing through the waves, his crew's well-plied oars speeding him toward the steep-sided spit of rock known as Laddie's Isle.

Tamping down her ill ease, Gillian reached inside her cloak and slipped her hand through a slit in her skirts. She curled her fingers around the small leather pouch that hung from a narrow belt slung about her hips. She took comfort in her secret treasure's solid weight and bulk, the hope its presence gave her. Perhaps she could still buy her way to freedom.

"Eager for his arrival, are you?"

Gillian jumped, whipped her hand from within her cloak, and spun about to face her oldest brother, Gowan.

He stood less than a sword length away, towering over her. He'd crossed his arms over his chest and planted one booted foot firmly on a seaweed-draped rock. His deep russet hair, the same rich red as her own, blew about his shoulders, and he was eyeing her intently, peering at her as if she'd grown two heads.

"You startled me." Gillian lifted her chin, ignoring his question.

"And you surprise me." He flicked a glance at the sea. "I wouldnae have thought you were so keen to greet the man."

"You think I'm here to welcome him?" She tossed her head, knew her cheeks were flaming. "Could be I'm hoping his galley doesn't appear."

"You ken it will, lass." He stepped closer, set his hands on her shoulders. "That's as sure as the morrow's dawn. No' liking it will change naught."

Gillian drew a tight breath, saying nothing.

She kept her chin high, hoping Gowan—her favorite among her eight brothers—wouldn't hear the racing of her heart, the dread churning in her belly. He might sympathize with her, to a degree. But as a man, born and bred of the Isles and with their ways and traditions carved into his bones, he wouldn't understand her displeasure.

"Anything is possible if the will is there." She stood straighter, forcing herself to believe her words. "The highest mountain can be torn down if you take away one rock at a time."

"Aye, and by the time you're done, you'll be so auld and addled, you'll nae longer remember why you started such a fool's errand."

"It's no' foolish to me."

Her brother frowned, shook his head slowly. "You dinnae ken what you're saying."

"I do." She did.

She'd empty the sea with a thimble if doing so would keep her from becoming Donell's bride.

"All lasses must wed, as well you know." Gowan lifted a hand, tucked her hair behind her ear. "That is just the way of it, how life here has e'er been and aye will be. You could do worse than the MacDonnell. He has his own isle, small though it is. His tower will be sound enough, once repaired. The prospects are grand." He swept out an arm, taking in the endless stretch of the sea, the shimmering mist. "Magnificent enough to swell the heart of any Hebridean."

"I've nothing against Laddie's Isle." Gillian spoke true. "It's Donell I cannot abide. You weren't at Sway when he came for the betrothal ceremony. None of you were there," she reminded him, sure that if her brothers hadn't been away at sea, and had been home, in their father's hall, they'd have argued against the match.

"He is a toad." She raised a hand when he started to protest. "He's also ancient, a graybeard."

"Lass..." Her brother took her hand between both of his own, his grip warm and firm. "Donell MacDonnell is no more than ten summers older than you. That much I know. The last five years have fogged your memory."

"I wish that were so."

"I'm sure it is."

"Did Father send you to find me?" She slipped her hand from his grasp, suspicious.

Wasn't it in their sire's best interest to be rid of her? A good enough natured man, but much too lusty for his age, Mungo MacGuire had a new young wife. Lady Lorna wasn't even as old as Gillian. If the clan tongue-waggers were to be believed, she was just as hot-blooded as her adoring husband. It was whispered that she'd vowed to give him more sons than the eight he already had.

Lady Lorna also didn't much care for sharing her new home with her husband's daughter.

Gillian frowned, her blood heating even more.

Gowan angled his head, watching her with eyes that missed nothing. "Da is too busy ordering our brothers about, making them ready the keep for MacDonnell's arrival. He didnae send me to look for you."

"If he did, he needn't have bothered. I'd almost rather stay here." She glanced toward the cliffs, the nameless tower that claimed the promontory's best vantage point. "What awaits me at Sway, but Lady Lorna's peevish glares and taunts? I'm hard-pressed to say which ill is worse. Sharing a hall with a shrew or being shackled to an ogre."

To his credit, Gowan looked embarrassed.

But he held his tongue, still not siding with her.

"You should've stayed in the tower, enjoyed a few ales with our brothers." Gillian held his gaze, seeing no reason for anything but the truth. Perhaps she should have also remained at the keep. She could be sitting by the fire with her beloved hound, Skog, stroking his scraggly fur, rubbing his bony shoulders, wishing them anywhere but this bleak isle, dreading Donell's arrival.

Instead, she'd picked her way down to the rocks, drawn here as if by an unseen power.

Even now, she felt the fine hairs on her nape lifting, stirred by a tingling sensation that also rippled down her back and along her arms. She shivered, hoped Gowan wouldn't notice.

She took a breath, attempted her most level voice.

"I know you have my best interests at heart. But there's nothing you can say or do to make this day a good one."

"Aye, well." Gowan glanced again at the sea, then to her. "Could be you'll find Donell to your liking." He sounded hopeful. "The ship's crew spoke highly of him. They said he wore a fine mail shirt and more arm rings than the Viking warlords of old."

"Indeed?" Gillian was sure they were mistaken.

Gowan nodded. "They sang his praises after you retired for the night. Had you still been in the hall, you'd have heard them."

"They must've been in their cups when they met him." She could think of no other explanation.

Her onion-breathed, great-bellied betrothed could never be likened to a Viking warlord.

Gowan frowned. "Will you no' give him a chance?"

Gillian flicked at her sleeve. "Do I have a choice?"

"In truth, nae." Gowan gave her a long look, somehow managing to appear both sympathetic and annoyed. "You're duly promised to him, oath-bound. Such a pact is binding, cannae be easily undone."

"That I know." Gillian turned to the sea, another truth giving her strength.

She took a deep breath, pretended to smooth the folds of her cloak so she could touch the small, heavy pouch hidden beneath her skirts.

"I will greet Donell MacDonnell as is expected of me." She forced the words, her hand resting on her secret treasure. "I shall take his measure then, and no' before."

"I am glad to hear it." Gowan sounded relieved.

Gillian didn't say that she already knew how the dice would fall.

She'd seen the hunger in Donell's eyes the day of their betrothal ceremony.

To be sure, he'd looked at her in lust. Even young and innocent as she was, she'd recognized the male need burning in his gaze.

More than that, she'd seen the blaze of greed.

However much she might have pleased him, her father's riches, so proudly displayed in Castle Sway's great hall, had impressed him more.

Donell MacDonnell desired coin above all else.

The knowledge helped her summon a smile. "All will be well." She reached to squeeze her brother's arm, hoping to reassure him. "But I would like to be alone now. I need the fresh air and sea wind to prepare myself to meet my future husband. You surely understand?"

Gowan looked at her sharply, perhaps not so easily fooled as she'd thought. Then he stepped back and flashed a grin, once again seeming relieved.

"As you wish." He glanced off into the distance, toward the still-empty horizon. When he turned back to her, he leaned forward, his gaze piercing. "Dinnae think you'll e'er be alone, lass. Your brothers and I sail past here often enough. We'll look in on you, make certain the MacDonnell is treating you right."

"I know you will." Gillian didn't doubt him.

She just wished she'd be sailing with them, as she'd done so often in years past. They even praised her, claiming no one beat the ship's gong better, that her rhythm surpassed that of any seaman in these waters.

When need arose, she'd even taken the great steering oar.

Sailing the seas with her brothers let her spirit soar, was an exhilarating freedom she loved and needed. Never had she dreamed she wouldn't accompany them, but would only see them plying the waves, flashing across the shining waters to watch over her, ensuring her well-being.

In her new life as bride to a man she found repulsive.

But she loved her brothers, especially Gowan. So she sought to ease his concern. "I know you'd never fail me, none of you."

"I am glad to hear it." Gowan nodded once, then reached to pat her shoulder comfortingly before he turned and started back up the steep cliff path.

Gillian watched him go, her hand still on her hidden treasure. She rubbed the lumpy pouch, grateful for its bulk and weight. The silver coins and cut-up brooches it held. The armlets and rings she'd gathered with care, ancient bits and pieces of a Viking hoard her great-great-grandfather had discovered buried in a riverbank, in his youth. Riches well preserved in a lead-lined chest.

The portion in her leather pouch was all that she could claim.

Her share was enough, she was sure.

Wealth untold, which she hoped would buy her freedom.

She wouldn't be given to a man she abhorred, whatever tradition and duty demanded of her.

Resolve cloaked her like a shield and she could feel her pulse slowing. The racing of her heart returned to a strong, steady beat as she pushed her worries away. Her breath came easier and the cold began to leave her bones. She was strong and brave, courageous. She wasn't called the Spitfire of the Isles for nothing.

She'd stand against Donell MacDonnell.

She'd walk away the victor. The silver in her secret pouch would pave the way for her escape.

But then, as if the gods resented her boldness, the wind quickened, blowing harder. The gusts shrieked, whipping her hair and tugging at her cloak. Not to be outdone, the sea rose, turning angry, as white-capped waves hissed past the rocks, flinging icy spray onto her. Salt stung her eyes and she blinked, rubbed her fists against the burning. It was then, as she struggled to see, that chills raced through her, prickling her skin. A terrible cold swept her, worse than a dark winter night before the onslaught of a blizzard.

"By all the gods..." She shivered, still blinking furiously.

In truth, she didn't want to clear her vision.

She knew what would greet her when she turned her gaze on the sea.

Even so, the shock slammed into her, her eyes widening at the sleek galley racing toward Laddie's Isle. The ship cleaved mist and waves alike, seeming to fly across the water. A fierce dragon's head glowered from the prow, minding her of Viking ships. Despite the distance, she could see that the twin banks of oars were lined with big, powerfully muscled men. Their mastery of the oar-blades sent up plumes of white water so that the serpent-headed ship didn't just appear to bear down on her, but to froth in hunger.

Most alarming of all was the huge warrior at the prow. *Donell MacDonnell.*

His dark hair blew in the wind, and mail glinted at his broad, plaid-draped chest. He was every inch as big as she remembered. Only now he looked even more formidable.

Thick-bearded and frowning, he could've been Thor swooped down from Asgard to strike fear into the hearts of mortal men. Most surprising of all, his girth had somehow shifted so that rather than a great ale-belly, what now drew her eye was the width of his shoulders and the many silver rings lining his muscular arms.

A great bear of a man, he looked stronger than six men. His scowl—a dark one surely aimed at her—left no doubt that he wasn't a man to cross. She could see him whipping out his sword in a heartbeat, swinging with deadly skill. Without doubt, he was the fiercest, most masculine man she'd ever seen.

She'd been raised among Highlanders, warriors who wielded their weapons as easily as they blinked or quaffed ale. But some men were bolder than most, able to claim the very air around them with only a glance.

Somehow, her betrothed had become such a man.

For a beat, she felt sure she might sway on her feet. She knew her pulse was racing, tried hard to ignore the fluttery sensation in the lower reaches of her stomach. She pressed a hand to her throat, finding it difficult to breathe.

In her memory, carrying such a great blade as the one strapped to his hip would've winded him. He'd have huffed and puffed, his face turning red with the effort.

Now...

The five years away must've hardened him.

Gillian inhaled tightly, not knowing what to think.

She could feel his gaze slamming into her, branding her, the shock and disbelief stunning her.

Their gazes locked, the impact intense and disconcerting. Her breath caught again.

Before she could lift her chin, showing she wouldn't be intimidated, the sea mist thickened and billowing sheets of gray swirled around the ship's prow, hiding Donell and his galley from view. But she could still hear the creak and splash of the oar-blades, the beat of the gong as the ship sped closer.

Any moment, it would flash up onto the landing beach. She could almost feel the sand trembling, the cliffs shaking with the fury of Donell's arrival.

She also knew, deep in her bones, that he was more than a changed man.

She'd only caught a glimpse of him, but it'd been enough.

He wouldn't be bought.

He'd claim her and seize her pouch of ancient treasure. He'd devour her whole and spit out her bones. Laughing, he'd crack his knuckles and glance about for his next victim. She could almost feel his pleasure in the triumph, see the gleam in his eye.

His ruthlessness left her with one choice.

She'd have to be even bolder.

Chapter Two

❧

"Ho, Roag! Were we no' making for Laddie's Isle?" Conn of the Strong Arm, braw helmsman of the *Valkyrie*, raised his deep voice, his amusement ringing. "It looks to be a place of women."

"You err," Roag the Bear called back to him. He stood high atop the ship's prow-platform where, until just moments ago, he'd been in a good temper, enjoying the cold winds and steep running seas. In particular, he'd been admiring the isle's soaring cliffs and rugged headlands. He appreciated wild places and was eager to reach his new home.

Now he wore a frown, his brows drawn together as he tried to peer through the thick wall of mist that had swept up out of nowhere.

"There are nae women on that rocky spit of land, be sure of it!" Roag lifted his voice above the wind, willing it so. "Some say a wee laddie walks the isle, a boy thin as air and easy to gaze through!" He glanced over his shoulder at the men on the oar-banks, flashed a grin. "The poor mite gave the isle its name, so the legend.

"For sure, the stories of him scare folk away." He turned back to the sea, the whirling mist that only seemed to worsen. "I cannae think of any women who'd dare risk meeting him."

Some of the men behind him chuckled, clearly of the same opinion.

"I saw a lass, I say you!" Conn argued, belligerent as always. "Right fetching, she was. Well-made and with a fine set of—"

"You saw rocks and mist, you arse." Roag glanced up at the dragon-head above him, prayed to the gods that his friend was wrong, his mistake caused by a trick of the mist or, more likely, all the ale he'd quaffed the night before.

"Think you I cannae tell a wench from stone?" Conn thumped his chest, his mirth making the others laugh again. "I haven't yet seen a curl o' mist that made my fingers itch to grab it."

A smile twisted Roag's lips despite his annoyance. "Then its ale fumes bewitching you, letting your eyes see what's no' there. The mist hereabouts isn't like other mist. It drifts and dances, some say it even has a soul. Could be a curl of it thought to tempt you?"

His men sniggered.

Conn roared, his laughter echoing across the waves. "'Tis smooth, hot, and wet female flesh that maddens me, as every man here knows.

"And there be naught wrong with my eyes." He fell quiet then, and Roag knew he'd be nodding his shaggy, red-bearded head, looking round for sympathy.

Roag just hoped his sight had deceived him as well.

He'd also glimpsed a shapely, flame-haired female on the islet's rocky shore. She'd looked right at him, her eyes blazing with fury, her hands on her hips as if by sheer will she hoped to blast him from the sea.

Then the wretched fog swept in and she was gone.

Unfortunately, he could still feel her out there, staring at him with fire in her eye, wishing him ill with a ferocity that scorched his gizzard.

She could only be a siren, a selkie, or a sorceress.

As she clearly despised men, he didn't care to discover which.

If he was lucky, his own aching ale-head had conjured her.

He and his men had knocked back a few ales too many at the Saucy Wench inn and tavern before they'd set sail for the last stretch of their journey, a foray of great importance that didn't need the distraction or interference of females, mythic or otherwise.

For that reason, he'd made certain that his men enjoyed themselves to the hilt, as it were, with the big-hearted, light-skirted lassies at the Saucy Wench.

He peered again into the mist, this time catching another glimpse of the island's rugged and precipitous coast. It was hard to tell for sure, but he'd almost swear he could make out the square keep and its curtain walls, high atop the jutting promontory.

Of the wild-haired, blazing-eyed siren was no sign.

He should be glad.

Instead, his jaw tightened and he found himself narrowing his eyes even more, searching the rock-strewn shore for a flash of her fiery-red hair.

"Have done, you fool," he snarled at himself beneath

his breath, now wishing he'd joined his men in airing a few skirts at the Saucy Wench.

Had he indulged—and for some inexplicable reason, he hadn't been in the mood—he'd now be watching for Laddie's Isle's landing beach instead of a maid of mist who likely didn't even exist.

He frowned again, tried to tamp down his irritation.

He'd gone mad, for sure. Women had no place in his mind just now.

"The tales were true, eh?" Big Hughie Alesone climbed up on the prow-platform, his steps surprisingly light for such a giant of a man. A tireless oarsman and even better with a sword, he was one of Roag's most trusted warriors. "This is the last corner of the Hebrides, perhaps the end of the world."

He came to stand beside Roag, hooked his thumbs beneath his sword belt. "I'd no' have believed your isle would prove as blighted as we heard, just a rocky spit o' land, home to nae more than wild winds and stronger currents. It's a cold place, dark and godforsaken."

"So it is," Roag agreed. "My gods would love it for just those reasons."

He could, too.

And that was troubling. He had reason not to fall under the island's spell. After all, he wouldn't be there a day longer than was required of him. Duty sent him to Laddie's Isle, and the same responsibilities would call him away again when his business was done.

"You didnae come up here to tell me what I already ken." He slanted a look at Big Hughie, well aware that the oversized Highlander always skirted what was really on his mind. "What's bothering you?"

Proving Roag had guessed right, Big Hughie rocked back on his heels, his ruddy face turning an even brighter shade of red. "It was what Conn said," he admitted after some moments. "About the maid o' mist he saw."

"There was nae such female." Roag hoped he spoke true. "Conn has Erse blood. The Irish aye see sprites and faeries everywhere. They have that from their ancestors and cannae help it."

Big Hughie shook his head. "I dinnae think so."

"Say you?" Roag cocked a brow.

"Aye." This time Big Hughie nodded. "I saw her, too."

"Well, she's no' there now." Roag didn't know why, but the strongest feeling told him that nothing in his life would ever be the same again if she was. As he couldn't allow such an upheaval, he looked again at the steep-sided little isle, relieved to see nothing on the rocky shore but seabirds and the shattering waves.

"She could've gone somewhere else." Big Hughie spoke what Roag didn't want to consider.

"If that is so, and we find her, we'll send her away." That, Roag could do.

He had ways of seeing his will enforced.

Every man onboard the *Valkyrie* knew it. So did many others. When he wanted something, no one and nothing could keep it from him.

Turning to his friend, Roag placed a hand on the big man's shoulder. "There's a fine north wind blowing." He used the code that would alert Big Hughie he was about to say something bitter earnest.

His own face sobering, Big Hughie glanced at the drifting mist. "Is there, indeed?" he returned, in kind.

"Aye, and it'll worsen before the day is o'er." Roag

tightened his grip on Big Hughie's shoulder, releasing him after speaking the final phrase.

Big Hughie stilled, waiting.

Roag was direct. "There's no place on this mission for womanizing. We left such pleasures at the Saucy Wench. Any man who forgets himself, should a female cross his path, will soon be sorry.

"Go now, and remind your shipmates. Make sure they also remember my name is Donell MacDonnell." Roag nodded once, watched the big man return to the oar-banks.

Alone again, he cracked his knuckles and then lifted a hand to rub the back of his neck. Already suffering a hellacious ale-head, he could feel an even worse throbbing starting in his temples.

Donell MacDonnell was the only part of this journey that soured him.

He was Roag the Bear and aye would be.

But as a member of the King's Fenris Guard, a secret band of highly trained warriors prized for their fearlessness and loyalty, he was oath-bound to embark on whatever mission the crown gave him.

This time that meant assuming the identity of a long-absent, newly dead Hebridean chieftain who'd also served the King. For years, the MacDonnell had passed on observances about the activities of unruly, disloyal island clans. Information gleaned thanks to the strategic location of Laddie's Isle, which made its keeper privy to all ships passing through these waters and to their business, often shady dealings that the King wished reported to him.

Regrettably, the rough-hewn and querulous MacDonnell hadn't been as discreet as his position demanded.

He'd landed in a Manx dungeon cell where he'd wallowed for years, then drowned off the Island of Man when he'd finally escaped.

After three of the King's royal ships had been attacked and plunged to watery graves far beneath the waves, Roag had been charged with the same duties as the late Donell MacDonnell.

Except that he was expected to do more than note and report disturbances.

He was here to end them.

And he would.

Of all the Fenris, he worked best in chaos, sauntering in like the bear he was named after and overpowering any opposition with the sheer power of his indomitable presence. His size and muscle also didn't hurt.

His loyalty was unbending.

Roag loved the tight and oath-bound brotherhood named after Fenris the Wolf in Norse mythology. Fenris was a troublemaker, believed to be the son of Loki, the trickster. Established by King Robert III's brother, Alexander Stewart, the notorious Wolf of Badenoch, the Fenris Guard's men were troublemakers equal to their legendary Nordic namesake.

They did the King's dirty work, plying their trade where more fastidious men wouldn't venture.

Roag and his crew were more daring than most Fenris.

But they had a weakness for women.

Roag was also susceptible to shapely ankles and well-rounded hips that swayed invitingly. High, full breasts that bounced and jiggled, and like any hot-blooded man, he couldn't get enough of the dark, more intimate shadows that beckoned betwixt a comely wench's parted thighs. The lass on the rocks offered all that and more. Even as she'd scowled across the water at him, clearly wishing him ill, her boldness had attracted him.

He knew she'd been there.

He also loved a challenge.

Nor could he deny the truth. She'd made his loins tighten, causing his manhood to twitch with appreciative, ever-growing interest.

The same thing was happening now, much to his annoyance.

Laddie's Isle was dead ahead.

Through a break in the mist, he could even see a fine and shallow bay cut deep into the headland. The slant of the sand and shingle offered an ideal landing beach for the *Valkyrie*. A cascade of white waterfalls spilled down one side of the cove, and lush green grass beckoned from the top of the shadow-slashed cliffs. The beauty took his breath, and his pulse quickened. On the wind, he could smell the cold freshness of the falls, the isle's earthy-rich peat. He inhaled appreciatively, and then released a low whistle. For sure, he'd never been anywhere so grand.

"Take heed, men! Behold our new home, for howe'er long we're needed here. And remember"—he flashed a glance at the rowers on the crowded oar-banks—"as soon as we've beached the *Valkyrie*, I'm Donell MacDonell."

His words raised a chorus of laughs from his men.

Then he flung up an arm, signaling them to slew the ship toward the cove. The men responded at once, his helmsman using the long steering oar to swing the craft round even as the others began back-watering the strakes. Any moment, they'd rush up onto the shore, arriving in a showy flourish, as was his crew's style.

Pride should be swelling his heart, the promise of a new and intriguing mission for the crown whetting his appetite for adventure.

Instead, he could only stare at the golden-sanded landing beach, amazement sluicing him.

The maid of mist had returned.

She was just stepping into view around a bend in the coastline. Her flame-colored hair spilled free and wild, a gleaming mass that tumbled to her hips. Her rich green cloak blew in the wind, the shimmering fabric molding to her curves, revealing her to be even more stunning than he'd believed. She was a temptress, indeed.

And she'd brought friends.

A small army of huge, grim-faced Highlanders marched behind her onto the beach. Each one bristled with steel and looked eager to greet Roag and his men with their sword-points and ax-blades.

Only one man in the party looked pleased.

He was an older, bushy-bearded lout with the same vibrant red hair as the siren. Clearly a chieftain, the man grinned like a loon as he strode to the water's edge, even lifting a hand in greeting. There could be no doubt he was the maid's father. And something about his exuberance shriveled Roag's liver.

Worse, the lass's narrowed, angry-eyed stare warned that he wouldn't like whatever this unexpected welcoming party had to say.

What a shame that the girl's prickliness only intrigued him all the more.

He meant to discover what put such fierceness in her gaze.

After that...

He didn't know. Whatever happened, he hoped it would involve her full breasts crushed against his chest, her melting sweetly into him, her soft, warm lips parting beneath his own as he kissed her, and more.

That was his desire.

However unwise.

Chapter Three

⚜

He's arriving in style, eh?" Mungo MacGuire, Hebridean chieftain of great-hearted but rascally renown, smoothed the plaid slung proudly across his broad, barrel chest. His red-bearded face split in a grin, his gaze fixing on Donell MacDonell's fast-approaching longship. More accurately, he kept his eye on the big, dark-haired man on the ship's high prow-platform. "Laddie's learned to handle a galley, he has! Belike the years away have been good to him."

"Perhaps he's enjoying his flourish so much he'll sail on to impress a more appreciative audience." Gillian was sure she wouldn't be so blessed.

She also knew her father hadn't heard her.

It scarce mattered that he stood right beside her.

He never paid her any heed when in the throes of one of his passions. Showy sailing and swift galleys topped his list of obsessions. Seeing her wed and out of his care ranked nearly as high. Donell's display held him in thrall.

Her brothers, standing in a small group closer to the water's edge, appeared equally enraptured.

"It's bluidy bold seamanship." Andrew, her youngest brother, glanced round at her other siblings, who bobbed their heads in agreement. "No' many can cut across such a wicked current."

"Aye, no' like that." Ross, one of her middle brothers, stepped onto a tidal rock, watching appreciatively as Donell shouted orders to his oarsmen. "It's no' easy beaching a craft here."

"We arrived without mishap." Gillian advanced on them, their enthusiasm annoying her. The formidable hulk of a man at the ship's prow irked her even more. Feeling her face heat and her pulse quicken, she stopped at the surf line, set her hands on her hips.

"The tides weren't running so strongly then," Gowan reminded her, ever the peacemaker.

"We've put ashore in worse." Gillian knew that was debatable, but felt a need to be contrary.

Truth was they'd used a smaller, less accessible landing spot on the isle's far side, chosen because it allowed an easier landward approach to the keep. Beaching there was a nod to the mass of supplies they'd brought along.

Skog, her aged dog, had been another consideration.

She wished the great beast was at her side now rather than up at Donell's keep, for Skog was fiercely protective. Though old, he snarled at the first hint of a threat to her. She was sure he'd despise Donell on sight, giving him his still-fearsome growl. Unlike her family, Skog wouldn't be impressed by a flashy show of reckless seamanship, the waves breaking along the proud ship's keel.

Gillian turned her gaze back to Gowan. "A man would have to be full mad to sail so close to thon skerries, to fly in here so fast."

A slow, men-aye-stick-together smile curved Gowan's mouth. "MacDonnell doesnae look worried."

"You'd think he'd have made for the site we used." Gillian tilted her head and considered her eldest brother. "Surely he'll have cargo?" She glanced down the shore, to the steep and winding track to the keep on its jutting promontory. "It'll be hard carrying goods up the cliff path. Can it be Donell has grown addled? How can he have forgotten the easier ascent on the other side of the isle?"

"Could be he's eager to arrive." Gowan defended him, just as she'd expected. "Rounding the island would take longer and mean sailing through the worst skerries. We came from that direction and ken those waters well, the dangers of the submerged rocks out there."

"The reefs have ever been here."

"So they have. Like as no' Donell wished to avoid them."

"This is his isle." Gillian wouldn't back down. "He should know these waters better than we do."

"Have done, lass. You're showing claws."

Gillian angled her chin, challengingly. "Wouldn't you, in my position?"

Ignoring the look of reproach Gowan shot her, she shook back her hair, letting the wind blow the long, unruly strands about her shoulders. With any luck, she'd resemble a wild-maned, untamed fury. The kind of prickly, difficult female no man would want as a wife. Lifting her chin, she fixed her gaze on Donell, willing him to slew about, speed off into the mist, never to be seen again.

The longship held course.

Gillian's heart began to pound, a terrible instinct warning her that the man about to sweep so boldly into her life would change it forever.

She'd have to be strong if he wasn't to break her.

So she hoped there was a fierce gleam in her eye, visible from the sea.

She also drew herself up, glad for her height, and the sense of purpose that let her squelch any show of weakness. She stood as still as stone, memories of her last encounter with Donell giving her the daring to stare back at him as his gaze roamed over her.

Even through the fanning sea spray, she could tell.

He was assessing her, boldly and with arrogance. His perusal made her entire body flush hotly. She burned with agitation, her blood roaring in her ears. But she'd sooner grow hooves and a tail before she'd capitulate and look aside. Worse, hide behind her family.

Traitors whose glee was scarce contained.

Her father kept some measure of dignity, waiting a bit back from the shore. But her brothers, including Gowan, were now scrambling to join Ross on the rocks so they could observe Donell's approach.

Gillian was only annoyed.

Her unwanted future bore down on her from the sea she loved so dearly, Donell's sleek, dragon-headed longship racing ever nearer in a froth of high-splashing white water and fast-beating oar-blades.

The craft's wake glittered silver, a relentless arrow pointing her way.

Any moment the ship with its great square sail and shield-hung sides would flash up onto the landing beach, coming to a swift, shuddering stop even as her own world met an equally abrupt end.

Her long-lost betrothed was home at last.

And she meant to greet him with all the soft, submissive charm of a hellcat.

So why had her mouth gone so dry?

How could her nerves fail her so badly, her palms dampen as she dug her fingers into her skirts? She didn't know, but looking at him, there at his prow, made her shiver. And not in the way she would've expected.

She turned her face into the cold, salt-laced wind, refusing to acknowledge the whirl of fluttery emotions awakening inside her.

Donell wasn't a man to ignite such a reaction.

Yet...

She narrowed her eyes, studying him. He'd grown harder, appearing almost twice the size she recalled. More than that, he'd gained a rugged appeal she would've admired in any other man. He was also better groomed. His black hair gleamed as it blew across his shoulders, his beard was still full, but neatly trimmed. No longer looking like a haven for lice, fleas, and the remains of his dinner. It galled her to admit, but he'd turned dashing in a devilish way. His stare stayed on her, his dark eyes fierce. Raw male prowess rolled off him, his boldness heating her skin as their gazes locked.

Gillian kept her expression cool, intent on remembering who he was.

She didn't want to find him attractive.

She'd been so sure a few costly trinkets would dissuade

him, buying her freedom. Now, a gut feeling told her he'd throw back his head and laugh at her offer. That he'd claim her and her treasure.

Come what might, she'd press for the advantage, using skill, wit, and wiles, to bargain with him. She just hoped she could do so in the proud, self-possessed manner she'd intended. The well-thought-out plan she'd laid for him.

Trouble was she'd expected the Donell of old.

Now...

Already, her heart thudded against her ribs, hammering almost as loudly as the clang of his ship's gong, the thunder of its lightning-quick oars, and the hiss of the waves along the hull.

Proving he must be half-crazed as well as much changed, Donell didn't order his rowers to keep back-watering the sweeps as the longship sped closer. Far from it, he signaled his men to give one last great pull on the oars, a bold maneuver that sent the ship shooting up onto the landing beach in a spray of foam and pebbles.

Gillian tried not to be impressed.

Her brothers fell back, calling encouragement, belting a few whoops, cheering as one.

His gaze still on her, Donell leapt from the prow before the ship juddered to a halt.

"Ho, there!" He looked away from her to wave at her brothers, then he made for her father. His stride was long and purposeful. "What honor do I—"

"Donell MacDonell, I greet you!" Mungo met him halfway, grinning ridiculously. "The pleasure is ours! My sons and I welcome you with all the hospitality of Clan MacGuire. My daughter is most pleased." He thrust out an arm, indicating Gillian. "She awaits you gladly."

"Indeed, I do." Gillian nodded once, not saying that her eagerness was only to make him a deal he couldn't resist. That all she anticipated was bidding him farewell, watching him and his wee isle disappear beneath the horizon as she sailed away on the tide.

The image strengthened her.

So she remained where she stood, refusing to rush forward with her brothers, who formed a half-circle around him and her father.

To her relief, and inexplicable irritation, Donell didn't encourage her to join them.

Instead, he greeted Mungo like a friend, returning the older man's grin with a broad smile of his own.

"Mungo MacGuire!" Donell threw an arm around her father's shoulders, embraced him as if they'd been the closest of allies. When he finally released him and stepped back, he was still smiling. "I am well pleased to see you, and your family." He turned to Gillian's brothers, moving along the line of them, clapping a few on the shoulder, giving one or two a friendly punch to the arm.

"Sakes! We thought you'd sailed off the world's edge." Blackie, Gillian's most dashing brother, spoke what she wished had happened. Named for his dark good looks, so unlike her other brothers, Blackie welcomed Donell with a grin as wide as Mungo's. "We set sail as soon as word of your return to Laddie's Isle reached us.

"Where were you?" Blackie glanced round at his brothers, looking again to Donell when they all nodded, showing equal curiosity.

"Ever sailing these Isles, I was." Donell glanced at the horizon, his face sobering. "A storm damaged my ship and carried us into Manx waters, where we weren't greeted kindly." He shrugged a big shoulder. "The good folk of Man accused us of spying and tossed us in a pit. I only just escaped, gathering a new crew and ship on my way home. Sadly, my other men are no more."

Gillian edged closer. Curiosity compelled her to hear his explanation. That, and the surprising awareness that sprang between them when he caught her gaze again, smiling this time. The smile made his eyes twinkle and the wind riffled his hair, tossing the gleaming black strands. Gillian's pulse raced, looking at him. He had a disturbing effect on her, something about him taking her breath, drawing her forward even when she didn't wish to go.

Rough and bearlike he might be, but he'd turned much too handsome.

And she was much too aware of the change.

"I didnae expect a welcoming party." He addressed Mungo, but kept his attention on her. A frank gaze that swept from the top of her head to her toes and back up again. "I'd forgotten how swiftly word spreads in these isles. It is good of you to greet me."

"Aye, well…" Mungo hooked his thumbs in his sword belt, oblivious to the tension crackling in the chill air. How Donell's smile widened, his gaze not on Mungo, but steady on Gillian.

She could scarce breathe. Try as she might, she was unable to look away from his dark eyes. Had they always been such a rich molten brown, so blatantly male, and disturbingly sensual? His smile made them crinkle, a small detail that only heightened the good looks he'd gained in his absence. Gillian wished he'd scowl; anything to banish the dimple just above his beard. She also tried not to notice how his nearness almost made her dizzy. For sure, she didn't like the shivers that his bold perusal sent rippling all through her.

"We've brought supplies, readied your hall." Mungo rocked back on his heels, blethering on. "Seeing as you've been gone all these years. It was the least we could do, almost family as we are—"

"Indeed." Donell nodded, but said no more. He rubbed the back of his neck, some of the warmth going out of his eyes, his smile fading.

He seemed taken aback, not sure what to make of her father's words.

Watching him closely, Gillian thought she'd seen confusion flicker across his face, but the look was so fleeting, she couldn't be sure.

He'd turned away, glancing to where his men were still scrambling off the longship. A few were already unloading spears, swords, and armor, while some shouldered great rolls of fleeces and large sailcloth satchels that surely held clothes and bedding. Several of her brothers had climbed aboard and were helping to heft crates and barrels onto the shore. From the smell drifting on the wind, the cargo was salted herring and dried meat.

"I've brought a shipload of provisions." Donell turned back to her father, slinging an arm around the older man's shoulders. "But my men and I thank you for your generosity. For truth, your Castle Sway kitchens produce more appealing fare than our meager goods.

"You'll join us for a homecoming feast this night?" He again looked at Gillian, but then his gaze flicked to the large square keep so high above the rocky shore. Swirling mist almost hid it from view, but the tower's ruinous state was apparent. Salt and sea wind had bleached the window shutters still in place, turning them as gray as the crumbling stone. A few gaps in the walls warned nights within would prove as cold as on the rocky shore.

Donell gave her father a self-deprecating smile. "Then again, as things stand..." He flashed another glance at Gillian. "I cannae promise my hall is fit for a lady—"

"Pah!" Mungo waved away his objection. "My gel is no ordinary lass. As your betrothed, she'll put the place to rights before you can blink. Gillian has a way with housekeeping, she—"

"That I ken." Donell didn't miss a beat, heading over to her, coming fast.

The glint in his eye, the hard set of his jaw, made her forget every word he and her father had just exchanged. Indeed, even her reason for standing here almost slipped from her mind.

She saw only Donell, the slight narrowing of his dark, intense eyes.

She held up a hand, hoping to halt him.

He kept on, ignoring her objection. "You needn't assure me of her talents." He tossed the quip to her father, not breaking stride. "Lady Gillian is as renowned for her skills as for her beauty."

"See here..." Gillian couldn't finish, needing a steadying breath more than arguments. Sparks leapt between them, the very air shifting. Heat rose around her, warming her skin despite the racing wind, the day's bitter cold.

He was almost upon her and she felt more than saw his displeasure. He'd caught himself quickly, even before her father finished speaking. If he'd been shocked by the implications behind praise of her housekeeping talent, he'd again seized the advantage. He wore a wickedly devilish look that jellied her knees.

She bristled.

He might be roguish, even wildly attractive, but she wouldn't bat her eyelashes, allow him to fluster her. There were surely enough women who did. And she wasn't about to join their ranks.

She wasn't so easily charmed.

So she lifted her chin, willing a steely glint into her eyes. She knew with feminine instinct that he wasn't pleased by her father's reminder of their betrothal.

Perhaps he'd met another woman during his years away, wished to marry her?

One could hope.

She wouldn't mind releasing him from their ties, freeing him to claim another.

Unfortunately, the closer he came, the more she discerned an entirely different intent. As he loomed before her, his towering presence blocking her family and even her view of the landing beach, she knew she wasn't mistaken. Especially when he set his hands on her shoulders, a slow smile spreading across his strong, bearded face.

He meant to kiss her.

She frowned, hoping to dissuade him.

"It's too late for posturing, sweetness." He shook his head, the thick raven silk of his hair teasing his broad, plaid-draped shoulders.

"I did no' expect to see you again." Gillian straightened, flicked at her sleeve. "No' this day, no' ever. In truth, I scarce recognize you."

"Then I was gone too long, I'm thinking." He caught her hand, linking their fingers, bringing her wrist to his lips. The warmth of his mouth against her skin and the light brush of his wind-chilled beard sent a rush of tingly sensation along her nerves.

Even the thin scar that arced across his left cheekbone made her breath catch, her insides quiver. Obviously a knife-slash, and a mark she didn't recall, the scar enhanced his appeal, giving him a roguish air she was sure had most women melting into puddles at his feet. Inexplicably irritated by the notion, she stiffened, hoping he couldn't tell how much he unsettled her.

Chill mist swirled around them, but she'd have sworn the air held enough heat to singe them.

She could feel the blaze, hot and searing.

Worse, a terrible tingly warmth spread across her most private places. Intense, and shockingly pleasurable, the rush of intimate sensation was unlike anything she'd ever felt.

She kept her chin raised, sure even the blood in her veins had turned to flame. "I understand if you have regrets about our betrothal. If you'd rather—"

"My only sorrow is that I left you on your own, all this time." He straightened, still grasping her hand. His own was warm and firm, calloused. "It was an unavoidable mishap that I must remedy to the fullest. Indeed, I shall put the task above all others," he said, a slow smile curving his lips. "You, fair lady, deserve nae less."

Gillian bristled, not missing the irony in his voice.

She was certain he hadn't meant a word.

The tingly ripples between her thighs began to lessen, the unexpected and shocking heat cooling.

"I, sir, am the least of your cares." She leaned around him to peer at his ship; the men still unloading his cargo.

Some of them threw looks at Donell that showed they were amused by his encounter with her. One or two ignored him, their gazes boldly traveling up and down the length of her. She turned back to Donell, pretending not to have noticed. "You have much work to do. I do no' wish to intrude, though I would like to speak with you."

He inclined his head. "I am honored."

Gillian narrowed her eyes at him.

Honor was the last thing on his mind. She hadn't been raised in a castle filled with men not to recognize when she was being teased. Or, as with this man before her, being played for a fool.

"You are honored I wish us to speak?" She lifted a brow of her own. "That is all?"

"Nae." He looked amused by her challenge, which only heightened her annoyance.

"We shall enjoy more than talk." He squeezed her fingers and smiled again, the intimacy of his tone sliding over her as softly as the whirling mist. "Surely you ken how much I've missed you?"

She didn't, not at all. "I find that hard to believe."

"Then you know little of men." His gaze slid over her, appreciatively. "You are no' a maid easily forgotten."

Gillian felt heat inching up her neck. She was also aware of her temper rising. Any moment he'd push her into proving why she'd earned her by-name, Spitfire of the Isles. But she didn't trust herself to speak, not now. How could she when he was looking at her as though he might devour her whole?

"You have not seen me in five years." It was the best she could do.

Just standing so close to him hampered her wits, making it hard to find words. He was simply too big, too bold, and entirely too confident.

She didn't care for his swagger.

"It has been a long time," she gave him the same argument, the intensity of his gaze unnerving her so much she could think of nothing else.

"Nae man could gaze upon you and no' desire you." He touched her hair, letting his fingers trail lightly over the wind-mussed strands. "Such a man would carry your image with him always, nae matter where he journeyed or how long he was away. He'd yearn for you in his waking hours, suffering the loss of your presence, and he'd dream of you at night, longing for you through the empty darkness.

"Think you I am different from other men?" He arched a raven brow, held her gaze.

"I believe some men are gifted with silvered tongues." She wouldn't have thought it possible, but he seemed to possess such a talent.

"Indeed?" He again employed his deeply seductive voice, so much smoother and richer than she remembered.

Worse, as though he'd read her thoughts and wished to bedevil her, he leaned in so close that their faces almost touched. His eyes narrowed on hers, steady and deliberate. His breath flickered across her lips, soft, warm, and intensely disturbing.

"So you are familiar with men's tongues?" He arched a brow again, his tone laced with a hint of amusement. "The skills of mine might shock you."

"Nothing you do surprises me." Gillian stood straighter, not about to show how much he unsettled her.

His words, and their scandalous implication, made her heart beat faster and sent tingly awareness coiling through the lower parts of her belly.

"Aye, well..." He lifted one of her curls, rubbing the strands between his thumb and forefinger. "For sure, you caught me unawares, being here."

"My father is responsible." She saw no reason to lie.

She also felt feverish, certain she'd sway any moment if he didn't step back, giving her air. Already, her heart raced crazily and she heard a strange, high-pitched buzzing in her ears, as if a herd of maddened midges swarmed right behind her head.

"Then I am in his debt. You were much on my mind, lass." He shifted his gaze to the sea, where the tide ran strong. The wind was picking up, the cold air full of brine and the scream of gulls, the reek of wet rock and seaweed. It was a heady blend to any Hebridean. Clearly appreciative, he closed his eyes, inhaling deeply.

When he turned back to her, a wicked smile came to his lips. "I did miss you."

"I do not see why." Gillian spoke as levelly as she could, successfully extracting her hand from his grasp. "We only saw each other once, when we were betrothed at Sway."

"All the more reason to waste nae further time." He seized her hand again, nipping her fingers with his teeth. Pure devilry glinted in his eyes, as if he wished to fluster her. "Do you no' agree?"

Before she could respond, he pulled her to him, whipping an iron-hard arm around her so that she was crushed to his broad, mail-clad chest. From a great distance, or so it seemed, she heard her brothers—or Donell's men?—cheering and shouting encouragement. Despite their tumult, or perhaps because of it, he clutched her even tighter, capturing her lips in a hard, rough kiss that swept her with a current of scorching heat. With his other hand, he gripped the back of her head, holding her in place as he plundered her mouth, kissing her deeply. It was a kiss unlike any she'd ever imagined and its boldness stunned her, leaving her breathless.

Shaken and rattled, beyond repair.

When he finally set her from him, his flashing grin once more in place, it was clear that every man on the landing beach had watched. Worse, the approval on their faces proved they'd found masculine delight in seeing her long-lost betrothed claim what was his.

Too bad she felt otherwise.

Brushing down her skirts, she met Donell's amused gaze. "I am not a tavern wench to be ravished so scandalously, before all men and—"

"There is nae shame in a man eagerly greeting his wife-to-be." He looked round at the others, her father and her brothers, his own crew, who'd stopped their work to stare down the beach at them.

"You could have waited." She followed his gaze, immediately wishing she hadn't.

Every man present returned Donell's smile, the lot of them grinning like fools.

"Nae, I couldn't have done." As if he wished to vex her even more, and entertain their audience, he traced a finger down the curve of her cheek and then along her jaw, studying its path as if he'd never seen anything as fascinating. "By Thor, I'm feeling a powerful urge to kiss you again."

And then he did, this time brushing his mouth so softly over hers that, for a moment, she wasn't even sure if he really had kissed her.

But he had, there could be no doubt.

She knew because another flurry of tingles rippled through her again. They spilled from her kiss-swollen lips right into her belly, where the startling sensations twirled wickedly before tumbling ever downward until she was quite sure her toes must be curling.

"Kisses are a fine thing, eh?" His tone was wicked. The way his eyes twinkled proved he knew what she was feeling.

Gillian stood frozen, sure her outrage made her glow like a balefire.

If she'd thought she was unsteady on her feet before, now her knees had weakened and spirals of shockingly pleasant heat persisted in spinning through the lowest regions of her female parts, warming her in places that shouldn't respond to him no matter how masterfully he kissed.

"That, good sir, wasn't necessary." She met his gaze, more sure than ever that she'd need more than a few silver coins and Viking baubles to be rid of him.

He'd changed greatly.

And much as it annoyed her to admit, she almost preferred the brutish ox she remembered. What that said about her didn't bear consideration.

Either way, she was in trouble.

Chapter Four

✤

"Sweet lass, I disagree powerfully." Roag used his most charming tone, aware it would annoy her. No one else on the landing beach would hear, but he knew they were observed. So for good measure, he also rubbed his thumb across her lower lip. "Kisses are aye needed, perhaps even life-sustaining. I cannae think to forgo such a delight."

"I would call it otherwise." She gave him a long, deliberate look, irritation sparking in her lovely emerald eyes. "It wasn't enjoyable to me."

"Is that so?" Roag smiled at her.

Her chin came up, the movement treating him to a delicate waft of lavender, a scrumptiously light and feminine scent that sent a rush of heat straight to his groin. "I didn't like it at all."

"I dinnae believe you. For myself, I couldnae resist kissing you." He was also sure that she was the work of the devil.

Stepping back, he braced his legs apart and crossed his arms as he eyed her up and down. For sure, he had the rights of her. Only the fiend himself could craft such a bewitching enchantress. Lushly made, possessed of a fiery temperament, and with her coppery curls in wild abandon, she'd tempt the most hard-hearted man. Even one who'd sworn that he'd gone off women, something he, as a well-lusted, hot-blooded sort, certainly hadn't done.

He appreciated women.

Nae, he craved them like the air he breathed. Perhaps even more so.

What a shame Lady Gillian was such a botheration.

But she was, so he kept his most roguish smile in place, hoping it was bold enough to send her running home to her cozy hearthside at Castle Sway. An island keep he thanked the gods he'd taken the effort to learn by name as the Clan MacGuire stronghold.

Truth was, he'd spent days studying a list of the Hebridean chieftains he might encounter on this mission. He'd learned their titles and by-names, the location and names of their island homes, their allies and enemies, how many ships and men they commanded, and even their peculiarities if they were known to have any worth noting.

He'd passed hours holed up in a little-used chamber at Stirling Castle, questioning the few men who'd met Donell MacDonnell, learning all he could about the rascally, skirt-chasing chieftain.

There'd been no mention of Lady Gillian MacGuire.

And he was going to have strong words with Alexander Stewart, King Robert III's notorious brother, commonly known as the Wolf of Badenoch, and undisputable leader of the secret order of warriors known as the Fenris.

A clandestine brotherhood of trust that the Wolf had now breached beyond repair, sending Roag to this spit of rock in the windiest, coldest corner of the Hebridean Sea without warning him that the man he was supposed to be, by all the hamstrung, cross-grained gods and their minions, hadn't just been a lecherous scoundrel of a hot-blooded wenching blackguard, but a fine lassie's betrothed.

It was an inexcusable oversight.

He'd been assured he'd find Laddie's Isle deserted, empty of all but weed-draped rock, the roar of the sea, and the bite of cold, salty air.

The isle wasn't supposed to be occupied by a siren.

Nor had he thought to meet such a vixen's father and brothers, men clearly eager to foist her upon him.

He required peace and solitude, a quiet place to work in stealth.

Lady Gillian stepped hard on his toe and poked a finger into his chest, reclaiming his attention and proving she was just the hellion he'd imagined. "We are betrothed, not wed or even handfasted," she declared, her eyes blazing. "More restraint would be appreciated."

"Dinnae push me, lass." Roag pulled his foot from beneath hers and scowled at her. "My patience has already been tested this day, more than you ken. So have done and be glad I'm no' of a mind to do more than kiss you.

"For the now," he added, just to rile her.

Vexed himself, he glanced over his shoulder at his men, at her family. They were at the far end of the cove, making for the steep cliff path up to the ruined tower. Some were already climbing the harrowing track. He watched them for a moment and then turned again to the iron-gray sea, the freedom of its tossing waves.

Annoyance sluiced him. His damned head still throbbed, the ache even worse now. Closing his eyes, he pulled a hand down over his bearded chin.

Hoping to brace himself to better handle what was fast becoming the worst day of his life, he took a deep, fortifying breath of the cold sea air—only to hear the sudden swish of skirts and the unmistakable crunch of hastening female footsteps on the pebbled shore.

Roag swore and snapped open his eyes.

Lady Gillian was striding away from him, hurrying down the beach toward the others. The straight set of her back and her shoulders, along with her swift gait, screamed her perturbation to anyone who might see her.

"Prickly she-witch." Roag frowned after her, his mood darkening even more when he saw that the men were now halfway up the cliff, about to turn a curve that would hide them from view. The great bulk of the headland would also prevent them from seeing the lass picking her way up the steep stone steps behind them.

A light rain was falling now and the path, little more than a perpendicular goat track, would be more slippery than ever.

If she fell, plunging to her death . . .

Roag took off at a run, pounding after her. A thousand thoughts went with him, clouding his mind, making him crazy. Dark, angry, and disturbing notions, riding him like a demon, urging him on.

Never in his world could he allow her to storm up such path in haste, in caution-blasting ire. Yet there she was, her skirts hitched high, her shapely legs and trim ankles carrying her much too quickly up the rain-wet cliff.

"Bluidy hell!" He ran faster, his heart almost stopping

when she slipped, flailing her arms before she caught herself and hurried on.

"Ho, lass, wait!" He reached the start of the path, launched himself up the rough stone steps, hewn out of the cliff centuries before. "Stay where you are, hold—"

The wind gusted, carrying away his shouts. The fool maid climbed on, one hand on her hip and the other at her brow, surely in a futile effort to keep her windblown hair from whipping across her eyes.

Roag doubted she could see at all.

The thought chilling him, he hurried on, taking the steps three at a time. He also swore, though his curses couldn't be heard above the wind. Never would he have believed his arrival on Laddie's Isle would be such a disaster.

He didn't deserve the complication that was Lady Gillian.

He had enjoyed kissing her. In truth, he was almost sorry they hadn't met somewhere else, under different circumstances. He could still taste her lips, feel her soft, warm body in his arms, held tight against him.

That was most irksome of all.

Not because he regretted kissing her, but because he wanted more.

Chapter Five

❧

*P*rickly she-witch." Gillian repeated Donell's slur to her-self on an angry huff. For sure, it was good if he despised her. But she'd been raised with too many brothers not to know he'd only hoped to goad her. She suspected he enjoyed deviling her, that he viewed her agitation as a game, a challenge to amuse him. Rough and uncivilized as he was, he'd seek to tame her, bending her to his will. And he was the sort who'd not leave be until she'd capitulated.

A shame for him; she'd hold her ground.

Determined to thwart him, she hitched her skirts higher, hurrying up the rocky path.

He erred if he thought to break her.

It was just a pity that her temper had set wings to her feet, sending her scurrying much too quickly up the slip-pery track. Her pride wouldn't allow her to slow her pace. She could feel his stare boring into her back. She also thought he'd called after her, shouting for her to wait, but the wind and crash of the sea made it hard to be sure.

Not that she cared.

She wouldn't give him the satisfaction of seeing that she recognized her recklessness as she ascended to his ruined keep. A cold, stony tower better suited as nesting place for seabirds than anywhere good men should attempt to carve a home.

Knowing she daren't look down, she did risk a glance upward. Heavy bands of dark clouds raced overhead and thick mist swirled everywhere. The wind was sharper at this height and carried the chill, wet smell of rain.

Any moment the heavens would open.

A pity such weather hadn't swept in before Donell spotted the island.

The mist and clouds might've hidden Laddie's Isle from view, causing him and his men to sail onward, sparing her this unwanted reunion.

But the gods truly had deserted her.

And the higher she climbed, the more she cursed the leather pouch of Viking treasure swinging from her belt. She'd swear the goods within tripled in weight with each step she took. Breathing hard now, she pressed a hand against her hip and leaned into the wind, not wanting to think what would happen if the ever-heavier silver coins, cut-up brooches, armlets, and rings caused her to lose her balance again. The track's steepness was harrowing enough, the slippery stones a danger on the fairest of days.

And this day, though glorious in every way that usually thrilled her, was anything but mild.

Knowing she shouldn't, she cast a quick glance at the rocky shore and the stormy, white-capped sea so very far beneath her. Wishing she hadn't, she hurried on. If only Donell hadn't kissed her, sweeping her with emotions

she'd never expected to feel for him, igniting her temper
and causing her to flee.

Now...

One false step and her life would be ended, dashed
to nothingness before she'd had a chance to truly live, to
taste the excitement, adventure, and passion that had to
be more than the sweet words spun by bards before the
hearth fire on chill, dark nights.

"Damn the bastard," she seethed, nearing one of the
worst turns of the track. A spot where the cliff's rough
black shoulder reared into midair, the thrusting rocks
home to swarms of wheeling, crying seabirds, and nary a
one looked willing to let her pass.

Indeed, several swooped right at her, clearly aiming to
maim.

"Gah!" She flung up an arm, dodging the attack. The
birds veered away, screaming angrily. But her foot slipped
on a loose stone, the world tilting as rock, sea, and sky
merged into one, spinning crazily.

Strong hands grabbed her from behind and swung
her against the cliff face. Before she could blink, Donell
leaned in so close she could scarce breathe. He held her
in place, his palms braced on the cold, wet rock on either
side of her shoulders. He was breathing as hard as she
was, his bearded face wearing a fierce, dark scowl.

"Have you nae wits, lassie?" His eyes glittered dangerously as he pressed closer, so near that the sheer strength
of him almost overpowered her. His mail-covered chest
kept her pinned where she was, his hard-slabbed muscles
and the steel rings of his mail shirt as immoveable as the
stone behind her. "Only a fool would tear up a track like
this. Or can it be"—his lips brushed her ear—"that you

were so eager to share my bed, you couldn't wait to reach my keep?"

Gillian bristled. "I'd sooner lie with a drooling dotard than suffer more of your attentions!"

His eyes narrowed for a moment, his gaze searing. "Then, my beloved betrothed, mayhap you should've dissuaded your father from bringing you here. Seeing you now, what a beautiful woman you've become in the years I've been away, I cannot help but to desire you."

He kept his gaze locked on hers and she could see the force of his will, his steely command. "For truth, I may tell your father to leave you here, that I'd forgo the formalities of proper nuptials and a lavish wedding feast.

"Why wait"—he took her chin in his hand, tilting her face to catch her earlobe between his teeth—"when the taste of you on my lips is already maddening me?"

"You were mad before you left this isle." Gillian jerked her head free. "Now you're even more crazed."

"So some men say." He straightened, something in his tone making her shiver. "Even so, I'm no' so depraved that I'd stand by and see a foolish lassie plunge to her death. Truth be told, I'd kill the man who would."

"Your chivalry is admirable." Gillian kept her chin raised, hoped he wouldn't notice the tremors rippling through her. "You are much changed."

"No' that much, sweetness." He leaned in again and pressed his lips to the curve of her neck, first nipping her sensitive flesh, then licking her, slowly and leisurely as if savoring her. When he finally lifted his head, he fixed her with such a fierce intensity she was sure he must hear her heart knocking against her ribs.

She searched for something to say, anything to hide

how much he unsettled her. "I do not remember your scar," she said, glancing at the thin, silvery line arcing across his left cheekbone. "Indeed, I scarce recognize you at all. You are so different from—"

A howl cut her off, keening and mournful, its distress rising above the wind.

"Skog!" She broke free, ducking under his arm and darting around the bend in the path. Her mind whirled with a thousand terrible images of her ancient dog, cold and confused in a strange hall, his cloudy eyes searching for her. She hiked up her skirts again, quickening her steps, the beloved beast's panic her own.

Donell MacDonnell forgotten.

Until he pounded up behind her and caught her hand, whirling her around before she could charge up the last, most steep and treacherous bit of the track.

"I'll no' have you hurtling to a watery grave!" Once again, he hauled her right against him, clamping her to him with an iron-banded arm about her waist. He glared at her, the fury in his voice, terrifying. "No' so long as you're on my isle, in my care." He started forward, keeping her clutched tight, guiding her past the great black rocks, as he pulled her up the path. "The day hasn't dawned and ne'er will that I carry a woman's blood on my hands."

"So noble." Gillian didn't believe a word.

"No' at all, sweetness." His voice was hard, his tone cold. "I'll no' have you ruin my homecoming."

"You bastard." Gillian put all her loathing for him into the slur.

A glint of humor lit his dark eyes. "Sheathe your claws, vixen. You'll need more than name calling to insult me."

Gillian glared at him, outraged heat rushing to her cheeks. "Let go of me!" She tried to pull away from him, her efforts futile. "That was my dog howling, you fiend. He's old and half blind. He'll be—"

"He should be home at your Castle Sway." He spoke in a casual tone, but she heard his reproach. "Old dogs have nae place on ships, especially in rough waters. They need a hearthside and quiet."

"Skog needs me." Gillian spoke as levelly as she could, not about to let him see her weaken. "You saw him at our betrothal. He was aged then. Now he's frail and cannae be left to himself. Skog goes where I go."

"Your devotion is admirable." He urged her forward, helping her up and over the wet and glistening edge of the cliff, not letting her glance down at the vast sea beneath them. "Dare I hope you'll develop such an attachment to me?"

"You may hope this farce finds a swift end." Gillian didn't care if he saw her irritation.

He wasn't looking at her anyway, bent as he was on dragging her across the cliff-top toward his half-ruined home, so bleak and barren on its rocky, sea-lashed crag. But halfway there, he glanced at her, his determined stride underscoring his dark, almost predatory stare.

"I've nae room in my world for foolery or prickly females," he warned, quickening his pace as they approached the tower's torchlit door. "I do enjoy a challenge.

"And you, Lady Gillian"—he flashed a wicked smile—"are proving a most delectable one."

Chapter Six

✦

Roag held the tower door wide for his unwanted betrothed, his first glimpse of his new home proving as much as the lass herself that he'd lost control of his world. Instead of the great empty hall he'd expected, a place likely filled with birds' nests and vermin, men bustled everywhere. Some were aligning trestle tables and benches, others hurried about lighting the iron-bracketed torches that illuminated the huge, cavernous space.

No one was idle.

Someone had even swept the stone-flagged floor, though no new rushes were spread as yet. MacGuire's and Roag's own men pitched in, Gillian's sire standing in their midst, shouting orders and looking benevolent in a way that curdled Roag's liver. He wanted naught to do with beaming fathers of brides, most especially when the maid in question was apparently promised to him.

He wasn't the marrying sort.

And he had no intention of joining such blighters.

He crossed his arms and surveyed the scene before him. A man needed to know the lay of the land lest he step into a rabbit hole and find himself sprawled facedown in the mire. Things were mucky enough already.

Some of the men were now settling in at the tables, looking eager to dig into generous helpings of bread, cheese, and jugs of ale. One or two walked about with lit tapers, touching them to the wicks of oil lamps hung from the ceiling rafters on iron chains. The hall boasted two hearths, and a haunch of venison cooked on a spit over one, its fat dripping into the flames. The delicious smell made Roag's mouth water. At the hall's far end, some- one had thrown a white tablecloth across one of the long, rough tables; the many heaped platters of roasted meats and other feast goods, along with ewers of mead and wine, marked it as the tower's high table.

As did Lady Gillian, who stood a few feet away, her stiff posture in no way detracting from her startling beauty.

Roag frowned at her, wishing she truly was the mythi- cal sea siren he'd first thought her to be.

She was certainly seductive enough.

Unbidden, he felt a strong tug at his loins, his body's reaction to her only fueling his annoyance. She was more than a wench to keep a man's bed warm. She'd claim a man's soul if he let her, branding his heart, ruining him for all others, and bleeding him dry before he could say his name, if he even remembered it.

Such females were dangerous.

And Lady Gillian, with her gleaming mass of flame- colored hair, emerald eyes, and luscious curves, would be the death of any fool she opened her legs to, an image that sent another bolt of desire straight to Roag's most susceptible, already tightening male parts. He could well imagine the pleasure of her, the glossy deep-red curls that guarded her sleek, female heat.

Her spirit also made her memorable, the high color on her face leaving no doubt that she wasn't a woman to trifle with, and that she possessed a temper.

Roag appreciated hot-blooded bed partners.

A shame she wasn't a tavern wench.

And hadn't he treated her like a saucy light-skirt? By Odin's bleeding elbow, he'd dealt with her more ignobly than any woman to ever cross his path, high- or lowborn. It scarce mattered that his words and actions were justified. That he was on a secret mission for the King and not come here to take a wife. His coarseness was meant to frighten her away, send her fleeing with her sire back to her own Hebridean fastness, never to darken his door again.

Yet something about her called to him. Her voice, soft as a spring breeze; the fresh, clean scent of her, so feminine, with a hint of lavender; the sparkle of her deep green eyes and the thickness of her lashes. Even the slight crease between her brows fascinated him; the rapid beat of the pulse at her throat, showing her irritation, proving her strength and backbone.

She deserved better than a life tied to an oaf like Donell MacDonnell. Nor did she need someone pretending to be the long-dead lout.

However just his reasons; regardless of how high a hand commanded him to commit such a folly. In his duties as a Fenris Guard, disguises were often necessary. It was why he'd perfected a variety of dialects. There were times when life or death, the very weal of Scotland, depended on his ability to appear as someone he wasn't.

But he'd never donned the role of an innocent maid's betrothed.

He didn't like it at all.

Bile rose in his throat and his gut twisted, his appetite of a moment before vanquished.

Across the hall, Lady Gillian shifted so she stood near one of the hanging oil lamps, its soft glow limning the shape of her, taunting him with her lush, ripe curves. The glossy sheen of her hair made him imagine those shining tresses spilling about her naked shoulders, her bared breasts, as he drew her under him; or perhaps as she sat astride him, riding him to their mutual release.

That she'd be a passionate, fiery lover stood without question.

He had an eye for such things.

Just now, he set his jaw and pulled a hand down over his chin. Even the glimmer of a thought to take her to his bed was madness.

What he needed was to be rid of her.

His mood worsening, he tore his gaze from her, turning instead to the hearth fire at the opposite end of the hall. Unfortunately, what he saw there, before the roaring fire of peat and driftwood, riled him as much as the temptation that was Lady Gillian MacGuire.

Her beloved dog, Skog, lay sprawled before the fire. Huge and shaggy, his thick gray coat couldn't hide his bony haunches or the telltale whiteness of age that marred his great head. His cloudy eyes also made no secret of his ancientness, and Roag knew from long years of loving dogs that Skog surely only moved with stiffness and pain.

No such beast should have endured the rigors of a sea voyage.

And neither should the wee lad kneeling beside him, stroking the old dog's shoulders. Clearly ailing, the boy's color was unnaturally pale and his clothes were torn and ragged. Such neglect was a sad stain on Clan MacGuire for not looking after the sprite better, even if he was a kitchen laddie. Roag knew well how rough a road such boys traversed. Hadn't he once turned roasting spits and hauled water, trudging up endless stairs with buckets larger and heavier than himself?

Those were days he didn't care to remember.

No lad would suffer them under his roof.

Leastways not for as long as this crumbling pile of stone stood under his care. If he was to laird it here, he'd begin now.

He had started forward, making for the boy and the dog, when a firm grip to his elbow caught him back. Wheeling about, he nearly collided with Conn of the Strong Arm, the *Valkyrie*'s helmsman. A huge, great-bearded man with a shock of red hair, Conn wasn't a man to cross, and little slipped by him. He also wasn't a man of many words, speaking only when he had something to say, usually a matter of import.

"Aye?" Roag waited, doing his best to ignore the ill ease that plagued him on seeing his friend's grim-set face. "Dinnae tell me more ships are landing," he lowered his voice, careful that no one else heard, "this time bringing brides for each one of you."

"Nae, nae, the seas are empty." Conn's tone was equally cautious. "But something's no' right. Two of MacGuire's men were seen carrying goods up from the landing beach on the far side of the island."

"That's no' surprising, seeing how they've readied this

hall. Still…" Roag considered. "We'll set a few men to watch MacGuire's ship. Better yet, to take a peek onboard, have a nosey at their cargo, if any." He paused, pulled on his beard. "The man's brought enough supplies to sustain us if we were under siege for a year. My gut says he's just a deep-pursed chieftain, hoping to prove his strength with a show of generosity."

Conn shook his head, looking troubled. "I dinnae think so."

"I do. Though we'll sure keep an eye on him. There are enough scoundrels who can lie with a smile, do worse once under a man's roof." Roag cast another glance at Lady Gillian's dog and the wee lad. He didn't care for the boy's baleful expression, the way his pale skin almost shimmered in the glow of the hearth fire.

Turning back to Conn, he placed a hand on the big man's shoulder. "If MacGuire proves false, our swords will make him regret it. I've already dealt with his daughter. She'll be wanting nae part of me after they leave." He leaned in, close to Conn's ear. "I say she'll beg her father to sail now, before we even sit down to the feast they've prepared for us. And if not"—he shrugged, not liking the twinge of guilt that jabbed him on recalling how crudely he'd treated her—"you can be sure we'll be gone before any nuptials can take place."

"I dinnae trust the man." Conn remained adamant.

"He's a Hebridean chieftain like them all." Roag released Conn's shoulder and stepped back. "Mungo MacGuire is boisterous and proud. He nae doubt sings and tells tales, fights and drinks, beds women, and has more children than even his well-filled coffers can feed." Roag knew such men from Stirling's court. Chieftains, lairds, and nobles were aye the same, no matter if they were Highlanders, Islesmen, or Lowlanders.

Conn frowned. "He's up to trouble, I say you. Truth tell"—he grasped Roag's arm again, pitched his voice lower than before—"I think he means to attack us when we sleep. You ken he'll no' be sailing away till morn. There's a reason—"

"Aye, he wants his daughter wed," Roag said. "I dinnae see him as a murderer."

"Then why did I see his two men hiding crates in the heather?" Conn slid a glance to where the MacGuire chieftain now sat at the high table with a few of his sons and his daughter. "It was up on the high moors, it was, and the men weren't his sons, but hard-faced oarsmen. The crates"—he turned back to Roag—"were just the right size to hold a stash of swords and axes."

"Then we'll have men scour the moors at the same time others have a look at the ship."

Roag glanced aside, his attention caught by a movement across the hall.

There where the wee serving laddie crouched beside Lady Gillian's ancient dog.

Only the boy was no longer kneeling. He'd stopped stroking the beast's bony shoulders.

He'd stood.

And his bare feet hovered several inches above the floor. The faint shimmering Roag had noted earlier was more pronounced, the boy's entire slight form shining as if lit from within. The strange light showed the ragged tears in his plaid, the tiny dirk glowing at his belt.

He was the ghost boy of Laddie's Isle.

Roag stared at him in disbelief, watching as he faded to nothingness.

Glancing at Conn, he saw that his friend hadn't seen aught. He was staring across the hall, a suspicious eye turned on Lady Gillian's sire. For all Conn's size and might, he feared bogles. If he'd seen the ghost lad, he'd already be halfway back to the *Valkyrie*.

The pleasure had been all Roag's.

He frowned, not surprised.

Somehow he seemed the only one this wee, dismal isle wished to torment. But he could give as good as he received, so he'd pretend he'd seen nothing. He suspected he hadn't. The long, arduous sea journey and the annoyance of arriving to discover an unwanted bride-to-be were simply taking a toll.

No more, no less.

Conn edged closer, his gaze still on the MacGuire chieftain. "There's little a man willnae do if enough coin crosses his palm. Could be MacGuire and his tribe o' sons are lying about the betrothal. Belike he's using his gel as a reason to come here. Then he and his lads will have done with us in the night, before we can expose their crimes against the crown, our good King's ships and men."

Roag frowned. "I hope you're wrong."

"Most times, I'm no'." Conn's chest swelled a bit.

"MacGuire isnae our man." Roag was almost sure of it.

He couldn't say why—Conn rarely erred—but this time...He flashed a look at MacGuire. Try as he might, he just didn't see the laughing, big-bearded chieftain as anything but a gregarious windbag.

He also knew when to trust his gut.

Over the years, his instinct had saved his neck many a time.

He also couldn't ignore the chill swirling around him. He cast another glance at Lady Gillian's dog, sleeping soundly, and alone, before the hearth fire. Of the wee bogle there was no sign. Even so, gooseflesh rose on his nape. An eerie silence filled the hall, a stillness he'd wager only he heard. Outside, a damp mist descended, likely causing the gloom. The day was just turning colder and darker.

The hall—his now, he daren't forget—was clean and warm, the murkiness chased by torchlight.

Roag rubbed the back of his neck, relieved when his ill ease began to lessen. The bustle and din of the hall resumed; the odd stillness no more. Unfortunately, one sound stood out above the mutter of low voices, the scraping of benches, the clatter of ale cups and eating knives. It was the unmistakable lightness of a female's footsteps, and there could be no question of her identity.

"Some might say you're a lucky man, *Donell*." Conn's expression lightened, the appreciation in his eyes confirming the lass's approach.

Steeling himself, Roag turned to face her. She was coming right toward him, her back as straight as if she'd swallowed a sword, her shoulders squared, primed for a fight. Her flame-bright hair glistened in the torchlight and a becoming flush stained her high cheekbones. Her great emerald eyes flashed, sparkling like jewels.

Agitation became her.

But her determined stride warned of another troublesome encounter.

Just to bedevil her, Roag gave her his darkest, most wicked grin.

"My lady, can it be you yearn for my nearness?" He took her hand when she reached him, pressed a kiss to her palm. "I am flattered. I didnae expect such devotion."

"You surprise me as well." She snatched her hand from his grasp, her chin rising. "Your men"—she flashed a chilly look at Conn—"appear equally ill-mannered. I wouldn't have believed it, but the years away have lessened your appeal. I dislike you now even more than before."

Conn turned aside, disguising his chuckle behind a cough.

Roag kept grinning, silently cursing Donell Mac-Donnell for inadvertently tying him to such a spitfire. "Then I shall enjoy the pleasure of wooing you anew," he promised, secretly admiring her nerve when she glared at him through narrowed eyes. "I'm right fond of challenges."

"He is that, fair lady." Conn made her a gallant bow, not at all perturbed when she ignored him, her gaze remaining on Roag.

"I know well what he is," she returned, the color on her cheeks deepening.

"And I thought you'd be enjoying your father's fine fare about now." Roag did his best not to notice the creamy skin displayed above the deep cut of her gown's bodice. Much as he enjoying riling her, his duties here would be better served if he placated her, keeping her and her family unsuspicious until they sailed away on the morrow.

Never, he hoped, to be seen again.

To that end, he nodded appreciatively toward the high table. "Are you no' hungry?"

"No." She angled her chin. "For some reason, my appetite has fled."

"A pity, that." Roag assumed a look of sympathy, secretly amused when she matched it with a glare. "Your father has laid out quite a feast, but then he's known for his openhandedness."

"My father has a reason for all he does."

"So does everyone." Roag let his gaze roam over her, from head to toe and back again. Another quick smile came to his lips when she stood straighter. Her high-spiritedness fascinated him.

He'd never cared for timid women.

He could see this one writhing beneath him, her legs locked around him and her nails scoring his back. Her sweet, husky voice crying her pleasure...

"Speak plain, lass." He pushed the thought from his mind, not wanting to imagine her spent in his arms, her lush nakedness hot, smooth, and slicked by sweat.

He failed miserably, a rush of intense heat roaring through him.

"I just did," she told him. "I wouldn't have sought you out otherwise."

"My lady, I am wounded." Roag clapped a hand to his chest, trying to look grieved. "I'd hoped you'd come to beg more of my kisses."

She stared at him. "You are mad."

"Aye, so I am." He'd not deny it.

He just wasn't of a mind to say why. He never would've believed such a difficult lass could intrigue him. Indeed, he couldn't think of any he knew who'd possess the boldness to challenge him—especially after he'd kissed her so soundly.

Regrettably, she wore her ire well.

Her emerald eyes shone like jewels and high color stained her cheeks, while her wild dash up the cliff path had tangled her hair, letting the flame-bright tresses appear as they might if she'd just been bedded.

And that was a direction he didn't care for his thoughts to go. If they did, he'd be sorely tempted to seize her again, crushing her to him so he could plunder her lips once more, taste her sweetness.

What had come over him?

He didn't know, or want to.

So he stepped back from her and crossed his arms, annoyed that her lovely lavender scent wafted around him, worsening his desire.

She narrowed her eyes, studying him as if she could see right into him. "Whether you are crazed or not, I would speak with you."

"Can we no' do so at the table?" He didn't need to stand here with her, the play of torchlight and shadow only making her all the more beautiful. Conn lapping up every word, clearly amused.

Roag shot him a glare, hoping he'd saunter off. But he only leaned back against a stone pillar, looking much too interested to leave.

"See here, Lady Gillian," Roag couldn't keep the edge out of his voice. "It was a hard journey and I'm hungry. That roasted venison—"

"I'd have words with you now, before you join my father." She held his gaze, her voice strong. "What I have to say ought not be heard by anyone else."

She turned a look on Conn, apparently having more power over him than Roag, for the big man pushed away from the pillar, shrugged, and then strode away, disappearing into the smoky murk of the hall.

"So now we are alone, my lady." Roag waited, watching

her carefully. Everything about her warned he didn't want to hear her pronouncement.

He glanced out over the hall, made a sweeping gesture. "There is nae one near. Leastways no' close enough to catch your words."

"Perhaps not, but there are too many eyes."

"You should've thought of that before you sailed here with half your clan."

"You said everyone has reasons for what they do." She returned his earlier words. "Perhaps I had my own for coming here."

"And they weren't to welcome your long-lost betrothed?" Roag already knew the answer.

"They were not, no." She didn't lie.

"Then I am most eager to hear them." He wasn't at all.

"I shall present them to you after the feasting." She held his gaze, her tone cool and calm, confident. "You can come to me in the room off the stair's first landing. It's been readied as my sleeping quarters."

Roag almost choked. "I dinnae think that's wise."

He wasn't about to tell her why.

"I disagree," she said, not surprising him at all. "My bedchamber is the only place I can be sure my father or brothers won't disturb us."

Roag shook his head. "I'm thinking you should tell me whate'er troubles you, here and now."

"That isn't possible." Annoyance flickered across her features. "You don't understand my intent."

"Then explain yourself better."

"As you wish." She lifted her gaze to his. "I wish to make you an offer. Doing so requires revealing treasures I can only show you behind closed doors."

Chapter Seven

❧

Mercy, had she lost her wits?

Had she truly asked him to her sleeping quarters? Aye, she had, and she suspected she'd sorely regret it—necessary as it was to meet with him alone.

The trouble was that just his presence in the vast, yawning great hall proved almost overwhelming. Facing him in the confines of her tiny bedchamber would cost her greatly. In truth, she didn't know how she'd suffered through accepting his arm and letting him escort her across the crowded hall. She'd heard the thunder of her pulse in her ears every step of the way, knew her face had flamed.

Now, having taken her place at Donell's high table, she drew on all her strength to hold herself as tall and proud as was possible while seated. It wasn't easy. Not just because of her betrothed's huge, black-bearded self across from her. The way he'd locked his dark gaze on hers, so challengingly. She refused to flinch, and neither would she shiver. She'd sooner eat pebbles from the shore and fill her wine chalice with seawater, before she'd admit discomfort.

But...

She was freezing.

The air was chill and raw, despite the hall's fires and the many iron-bracketed torches and hanging oil lamps. Outside, a damp mist clung to the tower, saturating the stones and penetrating every crack in the ancient, crumbling walls, bringing the kind of cold that seeped into bones.

Still, she wouldn't fetch her cloak.

Doing so felt like an insult. Not to Donell. She doubted he'd care. Glancing round the table, at his men and even her family, she imagined few men would understand what weighed on her heart, troubling her deeply.

She pitied the tower, little more than a half-ruined pile of stone and sorrow, if one believed the tales of its tragic origin.

She did, aware that all legends were spun of more than a grain of truth.

So she held her peace, respecting the keep's age and dignity, if not her unwanted betrothed.

Faith, but he unnerved her!

Just now his gaze was flicking over her bodice. "Will you no' have some uisge beatha?" He reached beneath his plaid, producing a silvered flask that he offered to her. "Finest Highland spirits, this is. A good long draw will warm you well, chasing the cold."

"I am comfortable, thank you." Gillian gave him a tight little smile.

"So be it." He tucked the flask back beneath his plaid. But his gaze flicked again to her breasts, the exposed skin above her gown's low-cut edge. "I would've sworn you're feeling the hall's chill."

"I'm fine, I assure you."

"Hiding your feelings isnae one of your strong points, my lady."

"I am not hiding anything."

"Nae?" He lifted his ale and took a long drink, his dark gaze watching her over the cup.

"So I said."

"Then admit you're cold. You're awash with gooseflesh." Donell looked round at the other men, his gaze lighting on Gowan. "I wouldnae see your sister take ill. This is a drafty auld keep, no' fit for weans or lasses."

As if to agree, the wind racing past the tower quickened then, howling louder than ever, even banging a shutter somewhere above them. Donell cast a look at the largest hearth, the one where Skog sprawled before the fire. He narrowed his eyes at the hearth's rough, blackened stones, as if he expected a gale to race down the chimney, blowing soot and smoke into the hall. Then his face cleared, and he turned back to Gowan.

"My years away haven't been kind." He threw another glance at the hearth, the shadows there. "The tower is scarce habitable."

"Heigh-ho!" Gillian's father slapped the table. "That's your problem, laddie. This place needs a woman's hand and a score o' fine chubby bairns to warm its moldy old heart."

Ignoring him, Gowan set down his eating knife. "Gillian is no ordinary lass." He held Donell's gaze. "She thrives in wild weather, loves the sea, and is cold-hardier than many men. She's a great prize, my friend."

"She is, indeed." Donell glanced at her, his gaze intent.

Gillian tried to ignore how her heart beat a little faster, her pulse quickening. Whether it pleased her or not, he stirred a heightened awareness in her. She had to resist the urge to smooth her skirts or worry a fold of the table linen. Never had a man so unsettled her.

Worse, his mouth curved as if he knew.

Keeping her chin raised, she sought composure. Deep inside, she secretly wished that the wind would indeed rush into the hall, catching him up in its chill embrace and sweeping him away. Anywhere but here with his dark good looks and savage masculinity making her feel more vulnerable than she would ever have believed, as if her body responded to his maleness, even clamoring for his attention.

She inhaled deeply, half surprised she could even breathe in his overpowering presence.

She knew he was watching her. He'd hardly looked elsewhere since they'd taken their seats. She tried to ignore him, sipping her wine and forcing herself to eat. But at times, she suspected he was smiling at her. His lips slowly curving in a disturbingly knowing manner.

Yet each time she snapped her gaze to his, he only lifted a brow, his face expressionless.

It was quite maddening.

And all the while, everyone else ate, drank, and blethered on, unaware of her turmoil.

Andrew, her youngest brother, leaned around Gowan then, catching Donell's eye. "Our Gillian is a better hand on a galley than any of us!" he boasted, pride in his voice. "No one beats a gong better. She keeps perfect rhythm, and can even take the steering oar in a pinch."

"That is true," Gowan confirmed. "She's sailed afar with us, unafraid of rough journeys and no' even blinking at the danger of places few men have seen and fewer know exist." He leaned toward Donell, his face earnest. "Wild winds and rough, cold seas make her soul sing. She is a maid unlike any other. Her brothers and I, our whole clan, demand you treat her well."

"So I shall." Donell lifted his ale cup to Gowan, drinking only when Gowan returned the salute. "When I come for her, to make her my wife, she'll lack for naught. You have my word, before your family, and my own good men who shall guard this keep with me."

"We are glad to hear it." Blackie, Gillian's swarthiest, most good-looking brother, pointed his eating knife at Donell, then stabbed a choice piece of roasted venison as his brothers voiced agreement.

"She's waited long for happiness," Boyd, another brother, declared.

"So has our lord, dinnae doubt it." A shaggy-maned, red-bearded man at the end of the table nodded, ignoring the dark look Donell tossed him. Conn of the Strong Arm, as Gillian knew he was called, turned to her. "Lady, I am the *Valkyrie*'s helmsman," he told her. "Ne'er have I heard of a woman on a warship. By the gods, no' manning the steering oar.

"'Tis a sight I'd like to see." His blue eyes held interest at learning of her skills, softening Gillian's heart, chipping at her defenses.

She could like this man.

And her betrothed clearly didn't want him to admire her. He'd returned his attention to his roasted meat, his face set like stone.

Ignoring him, Gillian smiled at the big helmsman. "Perhaps you shall see such a wonder. In the morn, when we sail for my home, the Isle of Sway. I shall take the steering oar if my father and my brothers agree." She glanced at them, her spirits lifting to see the love and warmth on their faces.

Only her father didn't look pleased.

Indeed, he avoided her eye.

Donell MacDonnell appeared even more annoyed than before. No longer tearing into his venison, he now watched her over the rim of his ale cup, his gaze piercing. Gillian thought a muscle jerked in his jaw, but she couldn't be sure because of his beard.

Either way, Conn of the Strong Arm's congeniality vexed him.

Unable to resist rubbing salt into the wound, Gillian took a breath. "You see, Sir Donell," she addressed him formally, her tone as strong and proud as she could make it, "we do things differently in the Hebrides."

"That, I have ever known." He took a long, slow sip of ale.

Something about the intensity of his perusal, the deep richness of his voice, caused a fluttering in her belly. A startling flurry of tingly warmth, surprisingly pleasant, but also troubling because the sensations rippled across places she wanted well guarded from Donell MacDonnell.

He smiled and inclined his head as if he knew.

Gillian hoped not.

She also didn't flinch. She was a chieftain's daughter, however rascally her sire. She carried the blood of many more leaders before him. Her spine was forged of steel, and fire ran in her veins. She'd been born to courage. No one backed her into a corner, certainly not the huge, dark-eyed, hard-muscled man sitting across from her. If a thrill of excitement ran through her just looking at him, such feelings were surely caused by knowing she'd soon see the last of him.

She was certain of victory.

Hadn't his eyes lit at her mention of treasure? A prize so precious, she could only show him behind closed doors. He'd looked at her in lust, revealing he'd misunderstood. He'd suspected she'd strip before him, using feminine wiles to see her will done. He'd expect to bed her in exchange for breaking their betrothal.

Gillian glanced at the hall's high-set windows. The sky was gray and slightly luminous, swirly mist drifting past the narrow openings.

Soon, evening would be upon them.

Her rendezvous with the man who thought to put his hands on her naked flesh, possessing and ravishing her, taking her innocence as his due.

He thought to breed with her.

Gillian could feel a flush heating her face. She knew he wanted her. She'd seen the same look on her brothers' faces when they were out sailing and they'd dropped anchor near a shore-side tavern. The kind known for lusty, eager-to-please serving wenches, always ready to air their skirts. Donell clearly planned to get beneath hers.

She'd also heard scraps of gossip about him over the years. Shocking tales, whispered in Sway's kitchens when no one knew she was about. Rumor was he had an unhealthy interest in bosoms. Hadn't he devoured hers with his gaze, just moments ago? Gillian felt loathing unfurl inside her. She wasn't about to bare her breasts for him, perform the spectacles Sway's serving wenches swore he craved so hungrily.

A shame her breasts were full, firm, and round. The sort she knew men appreciated. How she wished they were better covered now, hidden behind a shawl or shapeless gown.

Above all, she hoped Viking silver and gold would prove of greater value.

Not liking the cold knot sitting so heavily in her stomach, she clasped her hands on the crisp white table linen and did her best to appear calm. She straightened her back a bit more, hoping her cool mien and stiff posture would dampen Donell's amorous ambitions.

His slow, lazy smile said that wasn't so.

"Are you no' hungry?" He arched a brow, a hint of amusement in his peat-brown eyes. A dimple flashed above his beard, making him dangerously attractive in a bold, roguish way. He reached to tap the tip of his eating knife to her plate, his hand brushing her forearm. "You havenae touched your venison."

"I have now." She snared a piece of the perfectly roasted meat, popping it into her mouth, chewing carefully. She also tried to ignore how his warm skin lighting against hers sent an unexpected swirl of hot tingles across her female parts. How could such a known beast stir such a reaction? Furious, she forced herself to swallow the meat.

It tasted like muck.

She knew the venison was delicious. Her father's cook had preroasted the haunch at Castle Sway, seasoning it with secret spices. Then he'd prepared the meat for the sea journey so that her brothers needed only to place the haunch on a spit and stoke the fire.

"Such a delicacy is a rare delight." Donell spoke low, provocative. His gaze was even more disconcerting, steady on hers. "Such a feast should be savored, each succulent taste celebrated to the fullest. Do you no' agree?"

Gillian didn't answer.

She knew he wasn't referring to the venison.

"You are observant," she owned, meeting his gaze. Then, summoning every ounce of steel she possessed, she took a long, slow sip of wine. "I truly have lost my appetite. It could be something here doesn't agree with me."

Donell smiled wickedly. "All the more reason for you to eat. A good meal will replenish you." He took a large bite of venison, chewing appreciatively. "My hunger has increased since arriving here. Indeed, I am ravenous." His eyes gleamed, his gaze roaming over her. "I doubt I can get enough."

Gillian looked at him pointedly. "Then do not let me keep you from your meal, sir."

"Donell."

"As you wish, Sir Donell."

To her annoyance, he laughed. "I am well-pleased with Lady Gillian's spirit," he declared, turning to her father. "In the Manx prison these last years, the only woman I saw was the toothless crone who brought me meals of moldy bread and soured ale.

"Your daughter, MacGuire, is a refreshing change." He punched her father's arm, good-naturedly, and then went back to his meal, cutting another generous piece of roasted meat. "Lady Gillian is as welcome as this venison after the sparse rot I endured in my lonely cell."

Some of his men chuckled, but the red-bearded giant, Conn of the Strong Arm, frowned. "Enough, my friend," he said, an odd note in his voice. "Have done, and let's no' speak of troubled times."

"Indeed!" Donell raised his ale cup to his helmsman.

"You do not look as if you've subsisted on such a foul and meager diet." Gillian smiled sweetly at him.

At the end of the table, her brother Gowan cleared his throat. "I've heard the lords of Mann work their captives hard," he said, ever the peacemaker. "There are tales of men treated like slaves, forced to row ships without sleep, split trees and rock, and even fight bears for the nobles' nightly entertainments. Nae doubt, Donell—"

"So it was, my friend." Donell glanced at his own men, each one except the helmsman nodding agreement. "I ought to thank the bastards." He leaned back, slapped his flat, mail-covered abdomen. "Ne'er in all my days have I been in such form!"

"That is certainly true." Gillian took another sip of her wine, watching him carefully.

He didn't look anything like the ogre she remembered.

If her father had better eyesight, he'd agree.

She kept her cup against her lips, no longer drinking. She did observe Donell across the rim, not trusting him farther than the cloth-covered width of the table. "Some might say you are a changed man."

"So I am! Be that as it may, my wish to wed you is stronger than ever. By the gods, I'd hasten our nuptials!" He glanced at her father. "'Tis now spring. What say you we marry at Castle Sway by summer's end? That will allow your family to plan the ceremony and a proper feasting. Guests from afar can make the journey."

"That would please me." Relief sluiced Gillian. If all went as she hoped, she'd be well rid of him long before then.

Turning to her father, she plied her most gracious tone. "Lady Lorna would welcome such a date." Her step-mother would appreciate Gillian's plans more. "She'd have ample time for preparations, and I'd be gone before the birth of her first child. My rooms are close enough to yours to make a fine nursery.

"Summer's end it is." She lifted her cup to Donell, her smile even genuine.

The slow upward curve of his own lips said he saw through her. "Your eagerness flatters me, my lady." He reached across the table, knocking his cup to hers. "After all this time, I wouldnae want a greater delay."

"I've a better proposal!" Her father stood, slapped a hand on the table. "I say this poor man has waited too long already. Seeing as he's endured so much, I'm accepting his original offer!"

Gillian blinked. She didn't have any idea what her father meant.

She did know his levity boded ill.

His face had split in the grin he wore whenever some-one stumbled into a trap he'd laid for him. Cunning as he was, few then escaped.

Donell clearly recognized the danger, his smile no lon-ger reaching his eyes. For a moment, he looked perplexed. On another day, in a different world, Gillian might have felt sorry for him. As things stood, she knew her father's scheming would affect her in a worse way.

"You are a good man." Donell's face cleared as her father stooped to pull a worn leather sack from beneath the table. "I wouldnae have thought you'd remember, or be so generous."

"You erred, eh?" Mungo tossed him a grin, even winking.

Gillian watched her father intently. She didn't care for the great ceremony he made of plunking the bag on the table, untying its strings with a flourish.

She felt cold, almost light-headed. "What's in there?"

"What we need!" Her father thrust his arm into the old leather bag, retrieving a silver-and-jewel-rimmed mead horn that he waved over his head. Gillian knew the famed drinking vessel, and it answered all of her questions. It also iced the blood in her veins.

"The Horn of Bliss," she said unnecessarily, feeling herself blanch.

"To be sure!" Her father grinned. "A good thing I thought to bring it along."

Gillian stared at him, at the mead horn, as the meaning of his words sank in. She still held a handful of honeyed nuts, but dropped them now, letting them fall onto her plate. Several slid into her lap, then rolled to the floor. She couldn't speak, could hardly breathe. The horn's silvered rim gleamed in the torchlight. Its sheen taunted her, trapping her in a disaster she couldn't believe was happening.

The Horn of Bliss changed everything.

"A fine piece." Donell eyed it appreciatively. "Worth a king's ransom."

"'Tis priceless, aye!" Mungo nodded, looking proud and benevolent. "Old as stone, it is, or so some say. The horn has been passed down through MacGuire chieftains for o'er five hundred years, perhaps longer. A great Viking warlord gave it to one of my forebears in exchange for his youngest and most beautiful daughter. The poor man had—"

"His own gains at heart," Gillian cut in with her opinion of her ancestor's motive.

She stood, scarce hearing her voice for the roaring in her ears. From somewhere distant, she thought she caught her brothers' protestations, the mumblings of Donell's men, and poor Skog's barking.

She couldn't tell for sure because the hall had dimmed before her. The walls and tables and torches blurred, swimming together as the floor tilted beneath her feet. One of her father's men was approaching, a large jug in his hand. He stopped beside Mungo, deftly pouring rich, golden mead into the Horn of Bliss, Clan MacGuire's most sacred heirloom. According to legend, the relic would ensure carnal bliss and many children to every man who partook from it. Drinking from it would seal a handfast. But would Donell remember such after so much time away?

MacGuire chieftains saw the Horn of Bliss as a secret weapon, believing its power guaranteed such alliances went as wished, with a wedding after the pair's year and a day of couplings.

Gillian didn't want to breed with Donell.

Not this night, and for sure not for such an interminable length of time.

"Wait!" She darted around the table, intending to snatch the horn. "Don't touch it!" She lunged, reaching out. "Don't let him give it to you."

But she was too late.

Already, her father was presenting the relic to Donell, grinning broadly as her unsuspecting betrothed lifted the horn to his lips, tipping back the silver rim and drinking deep of the mead within.

Gillian stared at him in horror, watching as he unwittingly sealed their handfast. Whatever followed didn't matter. The Horn of Bliss was tradition and no MacGuire would deny its validity.

Even Gillian couldn't.

The deed was done.

Chapter Eight

❦

You fear your father would poison me?" Donell looked at Lady Gillian as he placed the emptied drinking horn on his new hall's high table. He had no idea why she hadn't wanted him to sample her father's mead, but damned if he didn't enjoy riling her.

He liked the color that then stained her cheeks. "I didnae think you were that fond of me."

A smile curved his mouth. He couldn't help it.

He shouldn't be amused at all, not seeing her agitation. But she drove him to feel and do things he couldn't explain, as if she'd bewitched him.

He looked away, then back to her. "I'm honored."

"You shouldn't be." She glanced at the discarded horn, her breath coming fast from her sprint around the table. "You have no idea what you've done!" Her green eyes flashed, blazing like jewels. "Drinking from the Horn of Bliss seals my clan's handfasting ceremony, binding a pair as surely as a priest mumbling sacred vows."

Roag's smile faded. "A handfast—"

"Aye, that's what this is. My clan has ever been known for them."

"Handfasting?" Roag stared at her.

He couldn't think. His mind whirled, a sick feeling spreading inside him. "My original offer..." He turned to her father, letting his words trail away, hoping the fiend would enlighten him.

"As you wished, my boy, as you wished!" Mungo pulled a dirk from beneath his belt, began slicing a narrow strip from his plaid. "To be sure, I wasn't for accepting a hand-fast back when you proposed it. The gel was too young." He swelled his chest, cocky as a rooster. "Seeing as you've waited so long to claim her, I'm thinking you deserve her now." He grabbed Lady Gillian's arm, swiftly looping the tartan around her wrist, thrusting her hand in Roag's direc-tion. "No need to wait months for a wedding, no' when she's here, ready and willing to be yours."

"Indeed." Roag forced a grin, cursing the rascally bas-tard in silence and his own rashness for landing in such a position.

Refusing wasn't an option.

Not if he wasn't to reveal his true identity and risk the King's mission, earning his justifiable wrath. Fenris never failed. If they did, they didn't live long enough to regret their mistake.

"Then let us be on with it." Seeing no choice, he grasped Lady Gillian's hand, linking their fingers. He didn't blink as her father bound their wrists with the plaid strip. He even ignored the urge to punch the grin off the older man's ruddy, red-bearded face.

Roag might love his King, but he appreciated breath-ing more.

Life was too good, generally, to lose it because of the machinations of a wily Hebridean chief and his admittedly desirable daughter. Already the lout was reciting the ancient words, a sacred ceremony Roag had witnessed once or twice, never believing he'd fall prey to one.

"...you are entering a hallowed bond, here within this circle of kith, kin, and friends, and blessed by all the powers of the Old Ones," Mungo's voice rose, drowning out the scraping of bench legs on stone, the shuffle of feet as Lady Gillian's brothers gathered around them.

Roag's men joined in, their eyebrows nearly as high as the ceiling's smoke-blackened rafters. Not one of them protested, no doubt knowing their own Fenris necks rested on their compliance, the damning pretense that Roag was Donell MacDonnell.

"Do you enter this union freely?" Mungo slung another band of the cloth about their wrists. "Are you prepared to stand together always, on days of fair winds as in nights of hard rains?"

Lady Gillian ignored her father, pinning Roag with a glare as sharp as emerald ice. "Aye," she vowed, unblinking.

At the edge of the circle of men, Big Hughie Alesone began to cough. Roag sent him a look and Big Hughie turned aside, bending double as one of Roag's other men slapped his back. The oaf was clearly laughing, and Roag made a secret vow to have harsh words with him as soon as this farce ended. There wasn't anything amusing about his plight.

More important, he had no intention of keeping false vows.

Fenris sometimes suffered for Scotland, and he'd never been one to shun duty.

He wouldn't start now.

So he stood straighter and put back his shoulders, giving his bride his fullest attention. He even summoned the semblance of a smile. "Aye, I will stand with Lady Gillian on fair days and in rain."

"Will you honor and respect one another?" Mungo made another loop around their hands. "Sharing laughter and sorrow, easing each other's pain and seeking to replace it with gladness?"

"Aye." Lady Gillian's agreement came cold and clipped.

Roag was sure the floor was opening beneath his feet. He could feel himself sliding into an abyss, a dark and suffocating place of no return. Somehow he nodded, even voiced his assent. "So be it, aye."

"The bond is made!" Mungo MacGuire grinned, securing a third loop around their wrists. "As your hands are now joined, so are your bodies, hearts, and spirits from this moment onward for a year and a day. Should you then choose to part, any child bred of your union shall be honored as your legitimate heir and..."

Roag closed his ears to the old chief's droning.

He knew the words, and their portent.

He wouldn't be held to a bride not his own; a wife bound to a man he wasn't.

What a shame the anger of the old gods worried him more than the disdain of a monk or priest. But their ire couldn't be helped. He wouldn't fash himself over something so unavoidable.

In his place, King Robert would have done the same.

Without question, his King would also lift the maid's skirts, sampling all she had to offer him. Roag felt a coil twisting deep inside, a cold, iron band turning slowly, squeezing the very life and breath from him.

He wasn't a marrying man.

"Donell, I accept you as my handfasted husband," his bride spoke the ceremony's final words, "from this day onward, so long as our union pleases us."

Roag fumed. Little would suit him less.

"I take you as well, my lady." He didn't dare glance at his men. "I make you the same vows," he added, sure he would have killed Donell MacDonnell slowly and with his bare hands if the craven wasn't already stone cold dead.

"So they are one!" Mungo untied the tartan binding with a flourish, slinging it around Roag's shoulders. "Hail the happy twain!"

"Hail Lord Donell and Lady Gillian!" Every man present shouted the chorus. Some thumped fists on tables, while others stamped their feet. "Long life and many bairns to them! May the gods e'er hold them in their hands!"

Roag tipped back his head and stared up at the ceiling, the age-blackened rafters and the wisps of curling blue smoke drifting everywhere. He was not a "lord." And he damned sure didn't care to be any woman's husband, handfasted in the ancient pagan ways or bound by the stricter laws of church and state. More than that, he didn't care for the last part of the ceremony.

The kiss he was obliged to give his bride.

Never had a woman looked at him so fiercely, especially when he was about to kiss her. And damn him to hell, but he didn't like it at all.

He wasn't an ogre.

Many women had sought his kisses…and more. This one tempted him in a worse way than any lass before her. Already, his blood heated, his loins tightening. Her sparking eyes intrigued him. A challenge he couldn't resist.

At the moment, he found her so appealing, he didn't care that she was trouble.

"A kiss, a kiss!" Men kept up the cry, clapping their hands. "Have done, lad! Kiss her!"

Conn alone moved away, striding from the hall, closing its half-warped, iron-shod door behind him. Not a man to be indoors for long, he surely sought the briskness of the sea wind. Or would have on any other night, Roag knew. As things stood, Conn was showing his displeasure, well aware that Roag wouldn't refuse his bride a kiss.

How could he?

"A kiss, a kiss!" The shouts grew louder, several of MacGuire's men wending their way through the throng, handing out well-filled cups of ale and brimming mead horns. Plain, unadorned drinking horns, not intended to maneuver men into Roag's pitiful quandary.

Somewhere a musician grabbed his pipes and gave a few long, high-pitched skirls before launching into a rousing tune, blowing gustily as he strutted about the hall. Near the fire, Skog sat up and started to howl, the ancient beast keeping time with the blaring pipes.

Lady Gillian ignored the ruckus, her face closed.

But her eyes glittered in the torchlight, her gaze showing her fury.

Roag stepped closer, leaning in to place his lips to her ear. "I could demand to see you naked, my lady. It's an old custom, and my good right before this goes any further." He kept his voice low, deliberately wicked. "When I kiss you, you'd best make me think you're enjoying it or I'll peel that gown off you here and now, taking my time to look you over, to see if I want you."

"You wouldn't dare!" She seethed, nipping his fingers when he brushed his knuckles along her jaw.

"Dinnae push me too far, lass." Roag made no attempt at gallantry. "There isn't much I won't do, especially when provoked by a woman clearly in need of a man's attentions."

"You bastard," she hissed, her eyes blazing.

"Perhaps I am." He gave her a frank look, entirely too pleased by her spirit.

He wasn't about to undress her. Seeing her bare-bottomed and in all her lush, smooth-skinned glory would set him like granite. He'd want her in ways not good for him. And he wasn't that kind of a fool.

"A kiss, a kiss!" The men were roaring now, some leaping onto benches for a better view.

Lady Gillian stood rigid, her hands fisting at her sides.

Roag glanced at the men, the warriors crowding the hall. He saw a sea of big, bearded men in leather, mail, and tartan. They all cheered, and in the haze of drifting smoke, it was hard to tell his friends from MacGuires. He did know they'd keep up the din until he kissed the lass. Then they'd quaff ale, wine, and mead, eventually slumping across the tables or sliding onto the cold, stone floor.

He'd spend the night in his bride's quarters.

Not bedding her, much as the notion aroused him. But to make sure she didn't stir mischief.

He didn't trust her.

Worse, she was sharp-witted. And that left him no choice but to protect his mission the only way he knew how. There were certain things no woman could resist, and he'd mastered them all. Kissing was one of his greatest talents. When he tore his mouth from Lady Gillian's, she might still despise him, but she'd tingle to the core and she'd crave more.

Roag started to smile, the prospect making him think of even more wickedly delicious ways he'd love to excite her. For all the women he'd bedded, he'd never had the pleasure of initiating a virgin in the delights of carnal passion. Awakening Gillian MacGuire's lust was an almost irresistible temptation. He could tell she was born to be passionate, wildly uninhibited once she'd tasted a skilled man's loving. He wouldn't mind touching her as he kissed her, using his hands to show her how quickly a lusty woman thrilled to questing fingers, knowing explorations of sensitive places.

He could make her writhe, gasp in wonder...

If only she were someone else.

Regrettably, she wasn't.

And neither was he. So he did what duty demanded and pulled her to him, claiming her lips with a hunger that was all too real. He kissed her long, deep, and with enough tonguing to sear her with such heated intimacy she'd forget every reason to doubt him. She went pliant in his arms, her hands coming up to grasp his shoulders, her fingers clutching his plaid.

She swayed against him, her breasts pressed to his chest. "You shouldn't..."

"I cannae help myself." He spoke true, and then deepened the kiss in a fierce openmouthed onslaught. Raw need, and something about her, made him ravenous. He couldn't pull away if he wanted.

She did, looking at him with furious eyes, her cheeks flaming. "Everyone is staring."

"So they are." He tightened his arms around her, not ready to release her. "I'm mad for the taste of you," he said, his voice deep and rough. He caught her nape, lowered his head to kiss her anew. "Your father has given you to me. Nae man here wouldn't claim such a prize."

"Many are my brothers. I don't care for them watching."

"Think you they do no' kiss, and more? Men will be men, whoe'er they are."

"But—"

"Nae." Roag brushed his thumb over her lips, their soft, moist ripeness doing terrible things to the part of him he should ignore. He inhaled deeply, knowing he should pull away, unable to do so.

He didn't care about staring, long-nosed brothers. He wasn't bothered by the whoops, foot-stomping, and table-slapping of his own men.

Let them gawk if they wished.

Besides, it'd been too long since he'd kissed a woman so thoroughly. The one in his arms served a need, no more. She slaked his lust, making him hard, giving him pleasure he couldn't deny. Especially in the name of Scotland.

If he wasn't enjoying himself so much, he'd set her from him and throw back his head to laugh.

He'd just added liar to his many sins.

His roaring need to possess her had naught to do with his dearth of bed partners in recent times. Truth was that he'd aired so many skirts, sating himself on an endless succession of tavern wenches and other willing, lust-driven females, that he'd grown weary of the deed. Yet his loins had twitched just spotting Lady Gillian on this bluidy isle's rocky shore, her hair all tangled and windblown, her eyes blazing green daggers at him.

She could ensnare him so easily.

So he did what he must, leaning in to press his forehead to hers as he nipped her cheek, flicked his tongue across her petal-smooth skin.

"I would savor every inch of you, sweetness." He made the threat above her ear, swirling his tongue there. "I'll devour you whole, not stopping until I've tasted the darkest, sleekest part of you."

"You are mad!" She drew a sharp breath, outraged.

"Aye, and I'll give you pleasure you've ne'er dreamed." He chose words to shock her, but damned himself voicing them.

"A stone would have a better chance."

"Aye, well, now you've challenged me. I have nae choice but to prove you wrong."

She drew back, staring at him narrow-eyed.

"Indeed, I must." He smiled, making sure it was the one that always won female hearts.

It was just disturbing that he felt his own beginning to pound.

Yet how could he help himself . . .

She smelled like a meadow of lavender, warmed by spring sunshine. Her skin was smooth and creamy; her lips temptingly lush, so untried and innocent.

And he was a bastard! The sort he'd never thought he would be.

Half wishing she was a grizzled, wart-nosed crone, he cupped the back of her head, thrusting his fingers into her hair, determined to kiss her so recklessly she'd run from his hall, leap into the sea, and swim all the way back to her Castle Sway. He wanted to unsettle her so roundly she'd never again come within a hundred sea miles of him.

Instead, she trembled and clung to him, even returning his kisses. A sigh escaped her, and fool that he was, he kept on twirling his tongue over and around hers, savoring how their breath mingled, each in- and exhalation soft, warm, and dangerously intoxicating. Molten flames consumed him, searing him as if they were intimately entwined, skin to skin, their naked bodies joined as one.

He imagined parting her legs and gliding into her, feeling her slick, female heat clench around him...

It was more than he could bear.

He growled, a deep rumble in his chest that broke the spell, the maddening way she'd made him forget reason. At last, the thunder of his blood in his ears receded as the din of the hall once again swelled around him. Grateful, he tore his mouth from hers. Breathing hard, he looked down at her, so fetching with her flushed cheeks and angry eyes. He gripped her wrists and lowered her hands from his shoulders, thrusting her from him. Not quite as gently as he should've done, but she'd shaken him to his bones.

So he dragged his sleeve across his beard, then stepped back, hooking his thumbs in his sword belt as he looked round at the ranks of men.

"That, my friends, was five summers without a woman!" It was all he could think to say.

Brash words he was sure would've spilled from Donell MacDonnell's lips.

That they made him feel like an arse didn't matter.

What did were the chuckles of manly commiseration, the nods and lifted ale cups. Few men could go so many years without a woman. Hardly a one wouldn't sympathize with a wretch so deprived. Only Roag's companions knew his claim wasn't true. And like him, they played their part, coming forward to clap him on the back, congratulating him on gaining such a fine and fiery bride.

"She will make you a good wife." Mungo beamed, his big chest swelling. "There isn't a maid in these isles as fair, or as capable. She'll mate well, giving you—"

"She will sup now." Roag stepped between the lass and her father, not about to discuss her fertility. He was more inclined to punch the old fox in the nose for putting his daughter in such a position.

Not that it was Roag's fault.

He was equally wronged, perhaps more so.

Still, the maid was beneath his roof. She needed to eat. If the gods held any pity for him, she'd overindulge and fall into a deep, long-lasting sleep. Better yet, before she wakened, her father would decide Roag was unsuited for her. That he was too bold, too wild and rough-hewn for his precious daughter, who shouldn't be shackled to a great-bearded fighting man of iron and steel with little use or desire for a highborn, virginal wife.

Unfortunately, Mungo's grin was even wider now.

His eyes glinted with the satisfaction of a man who'd just achieved the outcome he'd wanted. It was all Roag could do not to glower at him. He did turn to his bride, catching her wrist when she would've spun about and hastened away. Knowing he shouldn't, he brought her hand to his lips, turning it, to press a kiss to her palm.

Something pinched and twisted deep inside him, a small part of himself that he shouldn't acknowledge. But he did, tightening his grip on her hand as he straightened. He stepped closer, let his face clear, giving her one brief glimpse of the man he truly was.

"You needn't join us at the feasting, lady." He leaned in, pitching his voice for her alone. "Say you're tired and go abovestairs. I'll meet you there later, as we agreed, in your quarters."

"In hell, you mean." She yanked free of his grasp, glaring at him before sailing away.

Roag stared after her, not surprised when she made for her scruffy old dog, Skog. The beast still slept before the fire. And once again, he wasn't alone. The wee ghost lad hovered beside him, glowing brighter than before as he stared at a nearby arrow slit. He held one arm outstretched, his small, luminous dirk pointing at the sea.

Lady Gillian kept on, unaware.

Indeed, the bogle was already fading as she reached her dog. She leaned down to waken Skog, stroking his bony shoulders before leading him from the hall and into the dimly lit stair tower.

Roag frowned, his misery complete.

He'd never wanted a wife. Worse, was being bound to one who belonged to another man. And he certainly wasn't pleased about the wee ghostie. He'd heard the tales about the bogle. Legend claimed the lad pointed his dirk at the sea when trouble was coming.

Roag almost snorted. For sure, the sprite had the rights of it, except for one minor flaw.

The problem was no longer at sea.

She'd already arrived and was mounting the keep's turnpike stair. Worst of all, before the night ended, he was obliged to follow her.

It was the last thing he wanted to do.

He refused to acknowledge how much he was anticipating it.

Chapter Nine

✤

Good lad, only a few more steps and we shall have our peace." Gillian praised Skog as they rounded the last turn of the narrow stair and the shadowed landing finally came into view. The old dog's slow, careful gait made the breath lodge in Gillian's throat. It hurt to see her once robust and powerful companion so feeble. Even so, she kept her voice bright, didn't let her sadness show. She owed that to Skog's pride, always doing what she could to maintain his dignity.

Hurrying ahead, she opened her door so he could enter the small room without her needing to fumble with the rusted iron latch.

She'd struggled with the door earlier, the delay causing Skog to sink down onto his haunches to wait. With his back legs and hips so age-weakened, even the simplest movements could pain him.

Stepping aside, she watched as he trundled past her and made for the bed of soft plaids and furs she'd prepared for him near the chamber's only source of warmth, a tiny coal-burning brazier.

Guilt clawed at her for exposing him to the rigors of the sea journey. Now he had to suffer the dubious comforts of this half-crumbled tower.

But it couldn't be helped.

She didn't trust her stepmother, Lady Lorna, to take proper care of Skog in her absence.

Having him with her was better for them both.

Especially now, trapped here as she was, little more than a captive, while her family sailed home to Sway without her.

"No matter, sweet one, this, too, will pass." She followed Skog across the room's wooden floor, knelt to pull his favorite fur covering about him after he circled a few times and settled himself on the plaids. "We shall enjoy an evening of quiet before we're disturbed. Then"—she smoothed a hand over Skog's head, smiled into his cloudy eyes—"we shall be away again soon.

"Not to Sway, but somewhere better." She pushed to her feet, brushed down her skirts. "A grand place with many people, great houses, inns, and shops, more ships and bustle than we've ever seen. There's even a magnificent cathedral. You'll find plenty of dogs to keep you company, perhaps a few cats as well. For sure, there will be butchers offering the finest meaty bones. We'll have a new home with my mother's uncle. He'll greet us gladly..."

She let the words trail away as Skog had fallen asleep, his snores already filling the darkened room. Their small, sparsely furnished chamber smelled of old stone, rain, and the sea, and that was infinitely more appealing than the great city of Glasgow ever would be, much as she'd put on a brave face for Skog.

She didn't want to live in Glasgow.

Such a place would suffocate her.

Yet now, suspecting what she did, she also had little desire to return to Sway.

Sadly, it was important that she didn't.

At least, for the now.

Hoping she was wrong, she set a hand against her hip—she was exhausted—and took a closer look at the two large crates she'd spotted as soon as she'd opened the tiny room's warped, rusty-handled door. Unfortunately, even as tired as she was, she'd seen rightly.

The crates were from Castle Sway.

And as she hadn't seen them anywhere aboard her father's galley on the voyage here, she could only surmise that they'd been hidden from her.

Indeed, she was sure of it.

She also had a strong sense of what the crates contained.

And who'd packed them.

"Oh, Skog…" She glanced at her sleeping dog, her heart clutching to see how the light from the brazier and the room's one oil lamp picked out the sparse patches in his once thick and shining coat.

Praise the gods she'd brought him with her.

Poor, sweet Skog wouldn't have lasted a sennight in her stepmother's thoughtless, unwilling care. Lady Lorna wasn't fond of animals. Except beastly ones on two feet who desired only to keep her on her back, ravishing her all the day and night, or so the Castle Sway tongue-waggers swore when the lady wasn't within hearing. That was often, as Gillian's father was just as hot-blooded as his young, high-spirited wife, a lust-driven she-vixen who had no interest in old dogs or her new husband's similarly aged daughter.

Lady Lorna desired only to lie abed, though certainly not for sleeping.

Gillian's father worshipped her, his duties and family largely neglected as he strove to keep his new young bride happy and satisfied.

Gillian was as welcome at Castle Sway as a pebble in a princess's shoe.

Her only hope was persuading her newly handfasted husband to accept her treasure in exchange for safe passage for herself and Skog to the port of Glasgow. Once there, she'd appeal to her late mother's uncle, a shoemaker who'd made a good living and name for himself by once repairing the late King Robert II's boots after he'd damaged them in a fall on the slick cobbles outside Glasgow Cathedral. Impressed by the young shoemaker's work, the King had sent him trade, his royal endorsement sealing the cobbler's fortune.

If he yet lived, he'd help Gillian.

If he'd died, he'd have family remaining who'd surely aid her. No Scot would turn away blood kin.

Gillian just needed to reach Glasgow.

Hoping she could, she went to where a low, rough-hewn table had stood earlier. Centered beneath the room's only window, the table had held a plate of oatcakes and cheese, along with a jug of wine.

Someone had shoved the table into a corner.

In its place, the two Castle Sway crates loomed beneath the tall, narrow window. Ignoring the view beyond—wild, empty desolations, especially watery ones, were her favorite places—she worked the first crate's bindings and lifted its lid, her heart sinking as she looked down into the large, well-filled chest.

Her dread confirmed, she stared at what was surely half of her worldly goods.

She didn't bother to open the second chest.

A fool would know it contained the rest.

Her departure from Castle Sway and her life as she'd known it had been more rigorously planned than she'd have ever imagined.

Until now, she'd wanted to hold on to the hope that her father hadn't brought along the Horn of Bliss to maneuver Donell into a handfast. She'd told herself that her boisterous, proud, and attention-seeking father only sought to impress her much-traveled betrothed.

Now she knew the truth.

Including why two of Lady Lorna's hard-faced guards had joined them on the sail to Laddie's Isle. Something they'd never done.

They'd been tasked to secrete the crates onboard and bring them to her quarters.

Except...

Gillian looked again at her much-loved dog, this time frowning. Not that her scowl had anything to do with poor, hinky-hipped Skog. Far from it, he was again proving her salvation, helping her in ways even faithful, obedient Skog didn't realize.

She was about to prove to Donell what he should've known before hoisting his sail and setting forth into the great Sea of the Hebrides.

The carved-in-stone truth that Hebridean women weren't fools.

*   *   *

In his own corner of the room, wee Hamish Martin hovered near the iron stand that held the chamber's only true illumination, a brightly burning oil lamp. He might be young as mortal men reckoned years, but he'd been about for so long that he was surely as wise as any earthly ancient. Leastways, he hoped that was so. Either way, he was quite certain the oil lamp would help him stay hidden from the lovely lady he already admired greatly.

He'd learned over the centuries that some people did see him.

Most didn't, which suited him fine.

Those who did glimpse him swore he glowed.

So he hoped the lamp's light would outshine him. He wanted to know why the lady was upset. He also liked dogs. No, he loved them. Before he and his father had set forth on the ill-fated journey that brought him to this state and this place, Hamish's father had promised him a pet. After the voyage, Hamish was to have his choice from a litter of puppies born to the bitch of a neighboring laird. Hamish had loved the mother dog and looked forward to claiming his new puppy once they'd returned home.

Sadly, they never did.

And he hadn't seen a dog on this isle in all the long years he'd been here.

So he couldn't help drifting close to this dog, even though the beast was anything but a wriggly whelp. He was very old, Hamish knew. He could also tell that the dog could see him. And that he was kind. That he loved and belonged to the pretty lady.

His brow furrowing, Hamish peered at her as she knelt before two large crates, one of them opened. She didn't look happy about the beautiful gowns and fine lengths of embroidered linens that seemed to fill the chest. Indeed, Hamish was sure her eyes were glistening wetly. And even he knew that a lady crying is never good.

He wished he could say something to help her.

A soothing word, or two, might be welcome.

If only she might hear him.

But he didn't want to frighten her. That happened sometimes. He'd seen grown men faint because they chanced to catch a look at him. Not that their fear should surprise him. Wasn't his plaid torn and stained? Sometimes seaweed clung to his legs and arms, sticking fast no matter how hard he tried to brush it away. Worst of all was his glow, especially when his dirk lit up, shining brighter than the stars. Blessedly, that was a rare occurrence.

He shouldn't complain.

Those were times he knew to warn people about something.

The skerries that sank his father's ship, the tides, when they ran so fast and furiously, and other dangers he often didn't understand.

He'd just know folk needed to be wary.

Which was surely why his dagger was turning blue around the edges now, shimmering with a dazzling brilliance that increased the longer he peered across the dimly lit room at the lovely lady.

Something, or someone, was approaching her, bringing anger. Hamish could feel it rippling and darkening the air, and that worried him. Then he recognized the tread of the man coming up the steps.

It was the big, black-bearded man who'd seen him in the hall. The one with the scarred cheek and black hair as shiny as a raven's wing, he was the leader of the men in the second boat that had arrived that day.

He was the warrior who'd kissed the lady.

Hamish liked him.

He reminded him of a man who'd worked as a smithy at his father's keep. He'd carried Hamish on his strong shoulders, telling him tales, and sometimes laughing so hard that Hamish was sure the trees in the wood shook. This man didn't seem to laugh much, but Hamish liked him all the same. He knew he wouldn't hurt the lady.

As for her...

Hamish's heart squeezed and his eyes started to sting, his cheeks growing damp. The lady reminded him of his mother. Leastways, how he imagined she would have been at a younger age, before he'd been born.

He did miss his parents.

So who could blame him if he was curious about this pair who seemed to dislike each other so intensely, yet who kept seeking out each other like the breakers raced to shore?

Who would mind, anyway?

Scarce a soul took note of him.

He was aye aware of everything. He also knew to slip away now, leaving them to fight their battles alone.

So he threw one last longing glance at the dog and then sifted himself onto the landing, not surprised to see the big, black-bearded man striding purposefully for the lady's bedchamber door.

Hoping good would come of their encounter, Hamish allowed himself a smile.

It was his first in centuries.

Determined to savor it, he stood a bit straighter and

pulled his ragged plaid closer about his shoulders. He also
lifted his beardless chin. A shame, that, for he would've
enjoyed growing a beard someday.

But he was feeling rather fine.

That was something.

Then, knowing the lady and the warrior wouldn't
appreciate his lingering, he slipped deep inside the tower's wall, drifting down, down, down, to the hidden place
where he'd sought shelter so many years before.

So long as he was able.

Roag stepped into the tower's smallest, meanest room,
not knowing whether he should be annoyed or pleased by
Lady Gillian's choice of quarters.

Any other time, he would've knocked. But she'd riled
him beyond all restraint with her perfidy. She stood by the
window, her back to him, the fog-shrouded night limning
her. Gallantry demanded he clear his throat, give her a
slight bow when she turned to face him. What a shame he
wasn't of a mind to be so chivalrous.

She didn't deserve niceties.

Still, he had his honor.

And he'd not tarnish it just because she and her family
were a band of conniving plotters, full of deceit.

Even so...

He was duty-bound to get to the bottom of their scheming, to protect his mission for the crown. He suspected her
father simply wanted to unload his prickly, unmarriage-
able daughter. But he couldn't discount that the ploy to
leave her here might have deeper, more nefarious roots.
After all, Conn was already suspicious of the man. The
lass could be a spy for the English for all he knew, a

companion-in-evil to the men attacking and sinking King Robert's ships.

He doubted it, but had to consider the possibility.

Men in the throes of lust were known to spill secrets along with their seed.

Such a trick was older than time.

So he remained near the door, closing it softly behind him. When necessary, Fenris moved with great stealth, an ability that benefited them well. It was also a talent that had saved his neck more than once. Just now, he wasn't concerned with staying alive. He wanted to know the contents of the two crates beneath Lady Gillian's window. They had to be the chests Conn mentioned; claiming he'd seen MacGuire's men hide them up on the moors.

Duty demanded he observe her behavior regarding the chests.

So he stood quietly, letting the shadows cloak him. He also lowered his breath, even slowing the beat of his heart, so that he could blend into the gloom, becoming one with the murky chamber.

That accomplished, he studied his bride.

To his surprise, she didn't appear scheming.

She simply peered down at the crates' closed lids, her stance and everything about her warning that she wasn't happy. Were the chests filled with treasure? The secret goods she wanted to show him? Valuables so precious she was loath to part with them?

Roag frowned.

He'd expected her to greet him in a loosely tied robe, nothing underneath. In the hall, he'd learned her by-name, Lady Spitfire. He'd wondered if she'd earned such a title not just by her peppery tongue and supposed daring, but by a wild and abandoned thirst for passion. Desires of a decidedly earthy nature that—he couldn't deny—he wouldn't mind indulging for her.

However unwise.

The last thing he needed was to surrender to the baser urges she stirred in him. She was a lady of quality, more trouble than she was worth. She also held the power to ruin a King's mission, perhaps endangering the whole kingdom.

That was a threat he couldn't allow.

He fought back the urge to swear, his mind whirling with conflicting emotions. He was angry for lusting after her, yet he also felt a reckless desire to spend the night naked and sweaty in her arms. He'd enjoy sating himself on her charms, and giving her equal pleasure. He'd been so sure she'd fling off her wrapper, present herself in all her tantalizing glory, tempting him to do whatever he wished with her, however long it pleased him. On the condition, of course, that he'd break their vows afterward.

She'd challenge him with a trade—brazen, outrageous, and so wantonly irresistible—he wouldn't be able to refuse.

That's what he'd expected.

Instead, she wore a heavy woolen cloak, its hem dragging on the floor, the hood raised to hide her glorious hair and her lovely face that so easily stole his reason.

She wasn't dressed for seduction.

She'd armed herself against the room's bitter cold.

His scowl deepening, he took a soundless step forward, his eyes adjusting to the room's dimness. Little more than a cell, it could have been a rude stone hovel, ancient and roofless, thrown together to shelter the hermit monks who once plied these cold, lonely seas.

He gazed about, not liking what he saw. The poor

lighting shaded everything in gray and black, from the rough-hewn bed to the equally crude table with the meager repast she hadn't touched.

Only the small red flames of a coal brazier broke the gloom, their lurid glow more like a chink-sized glimpse into hell than any semblance of comfort.

No woman of breeding should spend even a moment in such grim quarters. No gently-born maid should know that such bleakness existed.

If he could shape the world, no lass would, regardless of station.

Chill air blew in through the window then and he caught the alluring scent of her perfume, fresh lavender, light and delicate. The fragrance reminded him of a spring meadow after a soft, cleansing rain.

The fine, surely costly scent underscored how out of place she was in a room without even a scattering of rushes on the floor, or wall tapestries to lessen the bite of the cold, wet night.

Again, he slid his gaze over her, puzzled.

A larger, more habitable room loomed at the top of the tower.

It was his laird's chamber, or would be once he'd claimed it. The King's spies at Stirling had described the room to him, insisting that its hearth held a good fire, and that the four well-made window embrasures offered sweeping views in all directions, a boon for his mission. He'd been warned not to expect the comfort of his quarters at Stirling Castle, but that he'd find the room tolerable enough for the brief duration of his mission.

He'd have thought Lady Gillian would've pounced on the keep's best chamber.

By rights, he ought to be glad she'd taken a room so dismal, set in the perfect corner to catch the worst rains and fiercest gales.

She'd find no succor here.

For reasons he couldn't explain, that irritated him.

A greater annoyance was that, despite her shapeless woolen cloak, and how she'd shielded her lustrous red tresses, something about her roused him unreasonably. Raw, raging need pounded through him, desire so fierce he'd almost swear he was once again a beardless youth—hot-blooded, overbold, and bursting with eagerness to plunge into the sleek female heat of his first lover.

Roag drew a tight breath, aware that if ever he touched Lady Gillian in such ways, she'd own his soul, possessing him as no other lass could ever have done.

Determined to resist the Hebridean spitfire, he crossed the room on silent feet and stepped up behind her, speaking above her ear. "Did you no' tour the keep before I arrived?"

"Gah!" She jerked around, her eyes furious in the shadows of her hood. "Do you never announce yourself? How dare you sneak up behind me!"

"I dare much, lady." He took her hand, bringing it to his lips.

"To be sure, you do." She snatched her fingers from his grasp, glaring. "Be aware that I am just as bold." She smoothed the folds of her cloak to reveal the unmistakable hilt of a dagger hidden at her waist. "We ladies of these parts do not look kindly upon men who would take us by surprise. Such cravens soon regret their folly." She flicked a glance at a most unruly part of him. "Some even walk away leaving their best bits behind."

"You were no' so fast just now." It was all Roag could do not to grin.

He did love a woman with spirit.

He couldn't keep a corner of his mouth from easing up a bit. "I'm no' missing any parts."

She angled her chin defiantly. "I was distracted."

"By what, my lady? The sumptuousness of this room?"

"I am not your lady. My mind was on matters that do not concern you."

Roag stepped closer, shaking his head. "You err. You are now much more than 'my lady,' and I've an interest in everything you do. So tell me, did you no' explore the tower before choosing this benighted room?"

"We went through the keep, my family and I." She glared at him again. "We cleaned as best we could. You surely know it was necessary. Seabirds had nested in some of the rooms and their messes needed clearing. We lit the hearth fires, the torches and oil lamps, and also searched for vermin. Rats, mice, and any other—"

"You viewed each room?" Roag was sure she hadn't.

"We did." She gathered her cloak tighter, her annoyance tangible. "I told you—"

"I should've spoken more plainly." Irritated himself now, he gripped her chin and tilted her face upward. "Why this chamber? There's a much grander, more fitting one at the top of the tower.

"I'd have thought you'd wish more comfortable quarters." Lowering his head, he brought his mouth toward hers. So near that his beard grazed her skin and their breath meshed, just as when they'd kissed in the hall. "A place more fitting for a fine lady's deflowewing? That is what you planned, is it not? So why this poor cell, with its lack of—"

"This room suited me." She broke free, her face coloring. "If you weren't such an onerous, unfeeling blackguard, you'd know why."

"Well, I dinnae, so speak." Roag ignored her insults, moved closer to the crates beneath the window. "Why would a chieftain's daughter, accustomed to finery, choose a small, bitter cold—" He whirled, throwing open the lid of the first chest. "Enough of this nonsense, for here is the proof." He scooped up an armful of gowns and undershifts, tossing them onto the room's only chair, a small, three-legged stool. "Your men were seen hiding these crates up on the moors. They were later observed sneaking them in here."

He opened the second chest, slamming it shut again as soon as he'd seen the damning contents. "For truth, you were so certain of victory that you brought along all your worldly possessions."

"They are that, yes." Rather than look guilty, her eyes blazed with anger such as he'd never seen. "Everything I own is in those two chests."

Rather than admit her scheming, she placed a hand on the rough window ledge and leaned toward the opening, inhaling deeply as if she needed air. When she turned back to him, she appeared more composed, though disdain was etched all over her lovely face.

"I had good reason to choose these lodgings." She made a sweeping gesture with her hand. "I selected this room because it's on the first landing."

Roag stared at her, sure she was daft.

He also didn't believe her. "That's why you shouldn't be here." He glanced at the window. The dark, wet night, and the cold, wild sea, so near the waves might as well have been tossing inside the room's dank walls. "In a gale, waves will surge right in here."

"That I know." She didn't blink.

Roag felt his patience thinning. "Say you?"

"I just did." Her tone should've frosted the air.

Roag blew out a breath, pulled a hand down over his beard. Rarely had he exchanged words with a more stiff-backed female. Nae, he'd never had the displeasure. Not once in all his days.

To be bound to her by a handfast, however unjust and unbinding, was a punishment he wouldn't wish on his most reviled enemies. She clearly felt the same, watching him from narrowed eyes, as if she plotted to slip her dirk between his ribs when he slept.

Barely contained fury seethed inside her. He could feel its blaze scorching him.

Had he truly believed she'd greet him naked? Baring her charms almost as soon as he'd crossed her threshold? Instead, she engaged him in barbed and ludicrous converse that made no sense; an unpleasant sparring of words that she appeared to be winning.

Proving it, she moved to stand beside her sleeping dog. The beast slumbered deeply, not even snoring, and he was so heaped with old plaids and furs that Roag had completely forgotten the poor creature.

He remembered now.

And something about Lady Gillian's icy glare would've made his liver quiver if he were a lesser man.

"I only thought to sleep here once," she said, her tone as chilly as her stare. "The weather signs didn't indicate a too-fierce night and"—she glanced at the mound of plaids and furs covering her dog—"had a gale blown in,

Skog and I would've sought shelter elsewhere. This room offered the easiest access for him."

Roag blinked. A terrible rushing noise rose in his ears and he was quite sure the floor dipped beneath his feet. Or perhaps it was his stomach dropping, the awful knowledge of what an arse he'd been.

"You took this room because of your dog?" He saw the truth in her eyes.

She looked at Skog again, her face softening. "His hips are weak, and his back legs. He has a hard enough time crossing a hall. It's beyond his ability to climb a turnpike stair to its topmost room, however well-appointed such a chamber might be. Leaving him to sleep alone elsewhere wouldn't work. He whines and howls if I am away too long.

"I would also suffer." She lifted her gaze. "Skog and I are inseparable."

"So I recall." It was all he could think to say. "I ken what he means to you."

"You do? Somehow that surprises me. You paid him scant heed at Sway, the day you came to secure our betrothal."

"I saw enough."

"So have I." She looked at him in a way that gave justice to her by-name. "More than enough, actually."

"Sheathe your claws, lass." Roag spoke more harshly than he'd intended. "I didnae come here to spar with you."

"So you didn't, I'm sure."

"See here," Roag tried not to growl, but she really was riling him. "Have you forgotten it was you who desired this meeting? I'd understand, as there was much excitement in the hall this e'en." He stepped closer, swore beneath his breath. "A handfast, sealed by your own sire, should it have slipped your mind."

"My memory is excellent." Her chin came up. "There is little I forget."

"I'll no' be forgetting your dog again." Roag sought to lead her in another direction, not liking how she'd bristled at his mention of the handfasting ceremony, as if she held him responsible.

Yet she and her wily father were to blame.

So why did he feel like such a craven?

Furious that he did, he slid another look at her dog. The aged beast had shifted beneath his heap of plaids and furs, freeing a tattered ear, floppy and bearing scars. Worst of all, one milky eye was now fixed on Roag. It was a stare more curious than agitated, the dog's apparent trust only deepening Roag's guilt.

He loved animals.

He, too, would've lodged the dog in secure quarters, easily reached.

Leastways, he would've done if Skog's prickly, high-strung mistress hadn't scattered his wits. Regrettably, she did that and more. Just now she paced about the chamber, the hem of her silly woolen cloak trailing behind her, and something about her furrowed brow twisted his gut.

He always trusted his instincts, and they were screaming alert.

Hoping to regain control of this ill-begotten evening, he leaned against the rough stone wall, crossing one ankle over the other. He aimed to appear as at ease and at home as the black-hearted scoundrel, Donell MacDonnell, surely would've felt in this miserable room.

Deliberately, he kept his gaze off Lady Gillian's stiff-legged, half-blind pet.

He gave Lady Gillian his fullest attention. "Your dog will be seen to, you have my word."

She tossed a look at him as she passed the window arch. "Your concern for him is most noble."

I am anything but that, he almost snarled.

Instead he cleared his throat, preparing to give her a peace offering. "I will carry him up and down the stairs whene'er you seek or leave this room."

It was an easy enough boon.

He'd help the dog whether it pleased her or nae.

"If I am no' about, my men will be ordered to do so." He watched her carefully, not surprised to see nary a flicker of appreciation on her face. Far from it, she straightened her back and went to the window, where she stared out into the night's darkness.

She held herself so erect that if he hadn't been watching her, he'd have sworn she'd swallowed a spear. Her stance, and the air of righteous disdain rolling off her, was the reason—one of many—that he'd always avoided entanglements with ladies of high birth.

They were too icy when the world didn't run their way, the cold water in their veins chilly enough to freeze a man at a hundred paces.

Keeping her back to him, she placed a hand against the edge of the window, drew a visible breath. "Thank you for assuring me Skog's needs will be addressed," she said, the reproach in her voice belying her gratitude. "As I told you at Sway, I've had him since the day he was born. His mother died having him, his litter mates with her.

"He is everything to me." She turned to face him, her chin raised. "I appreciate any extra care shown him."

"He shall have it." Roag nodded.

"I should also appreciate knowing who you are." Her eyes narrowed as she looked him up and down. "You aren't Donell MacDonnell."

Roag didn't blink, hoping he'd misheard.

Unfortunately, the murderous look on her face said he hadn't.

"To be sure I'm Donell," he bluffed, using all his Fenris skill to keep his tone convincing.

She only lifted a brow. Then she crossed to him and plucked at his plaid, slid her fingertips across the shining steel links of his mail shirt. "Donell MacDonnell never wore a clean plaid in his life and his mail never saw a polishing rag."

She met his gaze, triumphant. "What have you to say for yourself?"

"Five years in a cell changes a man." Roag chose the only excuse he could think to give her. "I've come to appreciate cleanliness."

"Hebridean women aren't fools." She spoke calmly, a victorious smile curving her lips. "Say me your true name."

Roag frowned, knowing doom was upon him. "I am Don—"

"No, you are not." She went to stand beside her dog, set her hands on her hips. "If you were, you'd know I lied when I said I've had Skog since his birth. He wasn't even at Sway five years ago. He came to me a year after your visit, a full-grown dog already.

"And you, sir . . ." Her emerald gaze pierced him. "You are a liar."

Chapter Ten

✦

Have done with this nonsense, whoever you are." Gillian stood in her dank, half-crumbling bedchamber and fixed the man before her with all the righteous indignation she could summon. "Your claims about remembering Skog prove you are not Donell MacDonnell." She drew herself up.

"And I, good sir, do not suffer falsehoods."

"Nor do I," he had the gall to state.

"Somehow I have trouble believing you." She held his gaze, not caring if he saw her displeasure. Indeed, she hoped he did. "I'll hear your real name and your purpose."

"Was it no' you who bid me here?" He braced his hands on the stone wall, either side of her shoulders. "You wished to show me something of great value," he said, leaning in. "A treasure you couldn't reveal except behind the closed door of your privy quarters."

He brought his lips to her ear. "Have you forgotten?"

"You question me?" She nipped under his arm and

whirled about, setting her hands on her hips. "You cannot recall your name. Or can it be you do not have one?"

"Sure, and I do," he said, his voice low and hard. "You've heard it and can use it."

Gillian's chin came up. "The name you've given me isn't your own."

"You'll stop provoking me if you're wise." He didn't deny her claim. "Have done."

"I will not."

"I've nae time for shrews, lass."

"Liars have no place in my world."

"'Sakes, but you're prickly." He looked her up and down, frowning. "Even a lass born and bred in the wilds of the Hebridean Sea should have some wits." He came closer again, his tall, broad-shouldered menace towering over her. His dark eyes glinted in the dimness, as did his mane of black hair and his thick, full beard. Even the silver Thor's hammer at his neck gleamed threateningly, catching the red glow cast by the brazier.

His long sword hung at his hip, and he wore two dirks, one at his waist, another tucked in his boot. Gillian let her gaze flick over him, sure he had at least two other unseen weapons on him. He looked rough and uncivilized enough to cut a man's throat at his own high table, his good looks dark and savage.

The thin scar that arced across his left cheekbone added a hint of wickedness.

But it was his swagger that made him dangerous.

He could've been the Devil's own man-at-arms.

She didn't care.

Desperation was an instructive bedmate and she'd learned her lessons well.

So she kept her chin raised, her gaze locked on his. "I have sense enough to know your kind."

"Then you'll ken that nae good comes of poking your nose where it doesnae belong."

Gillian squared her shoulders, prepared to challenge him. "I say you should know that those who dwell in wild, empty places, carved by rock, sea, and wind, view the world more clearly than men who walk on cobbled streets. Isolation sharpens our senses, the remoteness showing us things missed by folk like you."

A corner of his mouth hitched up. "Folk like me?"

"Especially like you."

Gillian held her ground, doing her best to ignore how powerfully the atmosphere had shifted in the little room. Even the air seemed charged since he'd strode up to her. Now he leaned back against the wall and crossed his arms, his dark gaze fixed on her. She felt her face heat, her attention caught by the Thor's hammer at his neck. The amulet gleamed silver in the moonlight, marking him as a pagan.

She shivered. An ancient awareness rushed along her skin, warming her, even though the room was filled with the night's cold.

She knew something of the old ways.

Her family even had ties to a great cailleach. A far-famed crone who, according to legend, gave a special boon to the clan after a long-ago chieftain aided her. Gillian looked more closely at the Thor's hammer, noting the smooth edges, as if it'd been held and rubbed often. Something inside her responded, her blood racing.

She'd always admired those who honored the ancient gods, especially Norse ones.

She was drawn to their strength.

The man before her was also bold. He claimed the space around him, and being near him stirred sensations she'd never known, even making her breath feel almost locked inside her.

He was still watching her, his gaze intense. "So what am I?"

"You are not from hereabouts." Gillian knew it in her bones. "I doubt you've ever been to the Hebrides before now. You're a town man, perhaps from someplace even larger. Not Edinburgh…" She angled her head, studying him. "You have a raw edge I wouldn't expect from there. Edinburgh is too grand, the folk there too fine. If I were to wager, I'd place you from Glasgow. To be sure, you speak with a hint of the Isles in your voice. But that is something you could've learned."

"Say you?"

"I know it is possible." She did.

"I'm thinking you know many things." He was mocking her.

"Perhaps I do. When I was small, a wayfarer called at my home." She remembered him well. "He traveled as he could, criss-crossing the land, even these fair isles. He claimed no clan, not even a wife, saying his feet aye itched, and so he roamed."

"A wise man."

"He was also greatly talented. Skilled in ways I never forgot, so impressed was I by his astonishing gift."

"What might that have been?" He pushed away from the wall, his expression guarded.

"He had a way with tongues."

For a beat, Gillian thought he was going to choke, but he caught himself at once.

"Indeed?" His gaze pierced her, his face revealing nothing.

She watched him as closely. "He could cast his voice to sound as if he came from anywhere in Scotland, even Ireland, England, or Wales. If he had a bit too much ale, he could be a Frenchman. He entertained us for days, telling us tales from afar, always rendered in the local dialect."

"A great gift, aye." He strode away then, crossing the room to the table with her evening repast of oatcakes, cheese, and wine. He took the jug and poured two measures of wine, offering her one.

Shaking her head, she declined. "I do not believe the traveler was unique, though he was the first with the skill to call at Sway."

"I have ne'er heard of such a talent." Her handfasted husband lifted the cup to his lips, draining it as swiftly as if the costly Rhenish wine had been home-brewed ale.

Gillian watched him reach for the second cup, not missing the slight jerking of a muscle in his jaw, barely visible beneath his beard.

She went to stand beside him, sensing victory.

She waited as he drank, slowly this time. "I believe, sir, that you have the same skill as the wayfarer."

He finished his wine, returned the cup to the table.

"I should enjoy such a gift." He wiped his mouth with the back of his hand. "Alas, I am no' so blessed."

Gillian didn't bother to argue.

There was no need.

She'd maneuvered him into a corner with Skog. She was sure even without his admission that she'd guessed rightly.

"I have known all along that you couldn't be my betrothed." There, she'd said it. "No man changes so greatly in five years."

"You know so much of men?" Again he avoided a direct answer.

"I have many brothers. Sway is also home to my uncles and cousins, and"—she felt her body tighten with tension—"a sire who has forgotten to act his age. He—"

She broke off, heat blooming on her cheeks. She hadn't intended so say that last bit, but her temper had the best of her. If he was angered by her father's craftiness, she was furious.

"My father is a good man." She looked away, at the window arch again. Despite everything, she did love her father. For sure, he was wily. He could be thoughtless. But she cared for him deeply, and that only worsened her dilemma. "His head is easily turned by ladies." That was probably more than she should say, but annoyance was riding her hard. "He's had many wives. When he takes a new one, he becomes distracted.

"His wits then fail him." She went to the brazier to warm her hands.

Images of Sway rushed across her mind, squeezing her heart, ripping her soul. After the death of her former stepmother, she'd acted as lady of the keep, enjoying her duties, even daring to hope her father wouldn't wed again. Yet he had, and Lady Lorna didn't suffer two females of high standing under one roof. There were other things she didn't tolerate, or so Gillian suspected. And they were damning enough to make this nameless keep's dank, crumbling walls seem as warm and welcoming as a fine summer's breeze.

She drew a breath, resenting the heat pricking her eyes, the sudden tightness in her chest.

Sway had once been a pleasant place. Good cheer was ever found in its hall and there'd never been a need to cast furtive glances up and down corridors before choosing which path to take. No one in the household had merited such precautions.

All was at peace.

Until the arrival of Lady Lorna.

Gillian dashed at her cheeks, as discreetly as she could.

"My father has much on his mind." She turned back to the room, hoped the shadows would hide any telltale sheen in her eyes. "He does forget himself."

"He was clever enough to bind us this night."

"He has a way of turning things in his favor. Some say it's the MacGuire charm. All our menfolk have it, a gift to make people do what they wouldn't otherwise. Men and women fall over backward to please them, doing their will without even knowing."

She waited as a gust of wind wailed past the tower. "They charm everyone."

"They did no' charm me." He gave her a hard look. "For sure, no' your father."

"I do not believe he set out to win your esteem." She didn't say the aim was to be rid of her. "The MacGuire charm works in many ways. Some call it the MacGuire luck. How else would my father hold the affection of his new young wife? Lady Lorna is younger than I am, yet she stays abed with him for days, and—"

Gillian drew a sharp breath, heat again surging up her neck, onto her face. She couldn't believe she'd voiced such intimacies. Or that she'd allowed herself to be led so far off track. Perhaps Devorgilla of Doon, the half-mythic cailleach legended to have bestowed the MacGuire charm on the clan so many centuries ago, had also gifted the scoundrel before her with a magical allure?

An ability to fuddle female wits!

Many swore the great Devorgilla aye lived, so it wouldn't surprise her.

"If you were no' an innocent, you'd ken that even a man of age is capable of satisfying a woman." He came toward her again, so much dark, masculine ruggedness rolling off him that her heart beat wildly.

He gave her a slow, roguish smile, as if he knew. "Truth is, the greater a man's experience, the more pleasure will be enjoyed by his bedmates."

"You, sir, are overbold." Gillian was sure he knew all about satisfying women.

He had that look about him.

"Bold, and..." *Magnificent enough to set a girl's heart aflame, to haunt her dreams forever.* She released an exasperated breath. "Too filled with swagger, too fond of drawing that sword at your hip."

"That may be true." An edge returned to his voice, his smile fading.

Yet even with such a hard mien, he stole her breath. His face was strong, his scar so appealing it was almost a secret weapon. Something about his dark eyes made her heart race. She'd felt the astonishing power of him when he'd crushed her to him, his hard-muscled chest like unyielding steel, so much caged restraint thrumming through him. When he'd whispered against her ear, she'd shivered. Just now, her fingers itched to stroke the gleaming silk of his thick, black hair. Regardless of who he was, or wasn't, everything about him quickened her pulse. Even his scent, so warm and rich, with hints of the sea, clean wool and leather, and the cold night air, stirred feelings that set her insides aflutter.

He was unlike any man she'd ever met.

And so like everything she desired.

What a shame he was so false, empty as a hollowed tree.

She lifted her chin, glad she'd seen through him.

"Why did you lie about remembering Skog at Sway?" She held his gaze, determined to have answers. "You haven't denied it and can't."

"Did you ne'er think I had more on my mind than the dogs slinking about your father's hall?" He stepped closer, slid his thumb down her cheek, over her lower lip. "Even so young, you tempted me."

Gillian bristled, the lie a slap in her face.

She narrowed her eyes, not suspiciously, but accusingly. "Are you still saying you're Donell MacDonell, Laird of Laddie's Isle?"

"I am keeper of this place, aye." He didn't blink.

"Any marauder could drop anchor here and make such a claim."

His expression hardened. "I am nae common thief, lady."

"You could be worse." Her tone was cool. "A broken man without a clan, an outlaw, even a murderer, a traitor to our land—"

"See here, lass." He gripped her shoulders, made an irritated sound. "Even here in the Hebrides, sheltered from the rest of the realm, you surely ken things are no' always as they seem?" He looked into her eyes, his gaze fierce. "There are matters I cannae tell you. Nae, things I willnae tell you."

"I only ask your name." Gillian broke free and stepped back, holding out her arm to stop him when he again started toward her. "Why you are here, claiming—"

"I have every right to this isle."

"Skog's full name is Skogahverfi." Gillian glanced at her pet, glad he still slept. It wouldn't have been good for him to witness her agitation.

"Your dog has naught to do with this."

"He does." She turned back to him, annoyed that despite all she knew, she still felt so powerfully drawn to him. "Skog is why I know you're lying. He is called after his home in Iceland, for he was the sole survivor of a shipwreck at Sway.

"He washed ashore with a seaman who only lived long enough to let us know that the downed ship hailed from Skogahverfi. I gave Skog that name and nursed him back to health, caring for him day and night. He was no whelp, yet you didn't blink when I said I'd had him since he was weaned.

"That proves you are a liar." She could feel her indignation rising, living outrage inside her. "You are not Donell MacDonnell."

For a long moment he just looked at her, taking in her words.

"See here, lass. I ne'er set out to mislead you." He pulled a hand down over his beard. He sounded grieved, but his tone quickly hardened. "There are matters—"

"Pretending to be my betrothed is not a 'matter,' it is willful deception." She poked a finger into his broad, mail-covered chest. "Who, and what, are you?"

"I am myself." He looked at her in a way that sent chills rippling through her. "You and your father schemed to see us paired, and so you stand under my care. All that you now do concerns me."

"It needn't. I had no part in this."

"Everything I see says differently, including your too-large, moth-eaten cloak." He flicked a glance over the mantle. "Had I known, I'd have given you a better cloak from my own supply stores."

"I don't want another." She didn't need this one.

She did adjust its heavy folds, knowing the cloak's voluminous length served her well, shielding her from the stranger before her. The mantle was Gowan's, an ancient but well-loved garment he used on sea journeys. He claimed he'd inherited it from his great-grandfather, hence the mantle's worn wool and frayed edges. Gillian meant to return it to Gowan's travel pouch as soon as the man claiming to be Donell left her room.

But he was walking slowly around her now, appearing anything but ready to make an exit. "You shall receive a new cloak all the same," he said, casually as if they were discussing the weather. "I've done much in my life. A few things I'm no' proud of." He threw her a look, his gaze sharp. "I'll no' have the freezing death of a chieftain's daughter added to my sins."

"I wouldn't freeze if the seas rose around us and this very tower turned to ice." Gillian stood straighter and put back her shoulders. "Gowan told you true. I do love raw weather, in all its bracing forms. I've no need of a two-finger-thick woolen mantle to warm me." She glared at him, her pride stinging. "A long, noble lineage doesn't mean one's blood thins.

"We of the Hebrides are of good, sturdy stock. We have stout hearts and we thrive when cold winds blow, when the sea churns." She wished she could draw herself up even taller, but Gowan's cloak was too heavy.

"Such a spirited lass, and blessed by such hardihood." He who wasn't Donell strolled over to her, touching his fingers to the pulse at her throat. "Yet you drape yourself in—"

"Not lies." Gillian stood her ground, ignoring how her heart thundered. The way his caress slid through her, sending tingly awareness across her skin. "You're maneuvering away from all that matters."

She met his gaze, knew her eyes were blazing. "I'd have your name. That's the least you can give me, if you refuse to say why you're here."

Chapter Eleven

❧

Roag went to the little chamber's window and braced a hand against the cold stone of its thick-walled edge. Lady Gillian truly had chosen the tower's bleakest room. He stared out at the dark water, wishing she wasn't here at all. But, she was. And he couldn't ignore her. Or the complications caused by her presence.

They were many.

Worse, he didn't know what to do with her.

"I'm waiting to hear your name," she said behind him, her tone impatient. "Better yet, I'd appreciate your reason for this farce."

Grinding his teeth, Roag left the window and went back to stand in front of her.

"I didnae come here for a handfast, that's certain." He scowled at her. He could feel his temper building, struggled against an eruption. He wasn't a man to unleash his anger on women. But the minx had him in a corner. And he loathed feeling so trapped.

How could he tell her his name?

He couldn't.

Indeed, he was oath-sworn to his King not to. He'd agreed to swear he was MacDonnell even if his sealed lips meant his death.

For sure, he daren't reveal his reason for sailing to Laddie's Isle. His life wasn't his own when he embarked on a Fenris mission, King and Scotland always weighing heavier than any personal need or wish. Vows had been made, his honor at stake.

Still...

"Damnation." He tipped back his head, stared up at the ancient, rough-stoned ceiling. He could almost feel it swooping down on him, joining forces with the room's barren walls to press in upon him from all sides, squeezing his heart and soul. An inescapable vise that squashed all he believed, leaving him in a chill, dark void. The kind that would plague him for all time coming, always reminding him that he'd broken the one tenet he held above all others.

Honor women, always.

Never in his life had he distressed one.

It didn't sit well with him to do so now.

Even so, he gripped the vixen's chin. A muscle jumped in his jaw and he hoped to the gods she didn't see. "Trust me, sweet. You dinnae want to hear my name or my business."

"You err. I am most interested."

Releasing her, he shook his head. "You'd regret the knowledge."

"Then tell me of the man you're claiming to be." She held his gaze, her tone challenging. "If I've to expect the real Donell MacDonnell to come seeking me, I'd rather know now."

"He poses you nae threat." Roag spoke true. "Your betrothed drowned trying to escape the Isle of Man."

She didn't blink. "So you admit your deception?"

"I'll own I am no' Donell MacDonnell, aye." Roag glanced at the window arch, the sharpening wind seeming to scold him. The half-moon followed suit, glaring at him through the clouds, accusing him of becoming all the cravens he'd ever reviled for their callous handling of women.

He despised liars.

Until this moment, his duties had never made him feel like one. Hadn't he acted for Scotland's greater good? The false names and cast-voices were necessary tools to see the King's will done, his various roles chosen carefully by the King's own brother, Alexander Stewart, the Wolf of Badenoch and leader of the Fenris.

No man could fault him, or would dare. Not if he loved his country.

But a woman?

Roag set his jaw, clenched his hands at his sides. His next words would change his world forever, dashing everything he'd worked so hard to build. The reputation he'd never dreamed to achieve, having been born a lowly court bastard, spending his boyhood nights on a pallet of straw in a corner of Stirling Castle's kitchens. Yet he'd crawled and struggled and fought his way to the top, earning a place in the kingdom's most elite secret order.

The Brotherhood of the Fenris was his life. He served well, was one of the few ever invited to the Wolf's own lair, far away in the northern Highlands.

Such trust wasn't given lightly.

And he appreciated every bleeding ounce of it, was sure he also held the earl's friendship. More than once, the King had placed his life in Roag's hands, knowing he was a man of his word, his loyalty unbending.

Never had Roag defied him.

Doing so was unthinkable.

When a man was stripped bare, his honor was all that remained.

Now he was about to soil his, irrevocably.

Yet when he looked at the lass before him, seeing the spirit, and hurt, in her lovely green eyes, he had no choice.

Not if he wished to sleep at night.

Lady Gillian, his handfasted bride, by rights or nae, was about to learn who he was and why he'd left Stirling to sail to this blighted spit of rock in the middle of these even more forsaken waters.

It was an admission that would be her damning.

"I am Roag, my lady." He made her a slight bow, some of the weight sliding from his shoulders.

He'd abhorred deceiving her.

"Only Roag?" She tilted her head, looking at him suspiciously. "Have you nae clan name?"

"For sure I do." He gave her what he knew was one of his most carefree smiles. "But unlike most men, I'm no' aware of whose blood to claim. I am a bastard. The baseborn get of a nameless mother and father, born and raised at the fine court of Stirling Castle.

"So Roag it is, and ever shall be." He shrugged, comfortable as aye in his name and station. "Some folk call me Roag the Bear."

Her gaze flicked over him. "Because of your size?"

"So it is." Roag inclined his head in acknowledgment, unable to keep the pride from his voice. "The by-name is also for my brawn." He drew back his plaid, showing her his powerfully muscled arm. The silvered bands that graced them had each been a gift from the King for a particularly difficult feat, royal rewards for acts that could only have been accomplished by a highly skilled, well-trained warrior of immense strength.

"So you wear warrior rings. Your overlord values you." She didn't look as impressed as he'd have hoped.

Instead, she paced back and forth, tapping a finger to her chin as she rounded the little room. "Can it be, Roag the Bear, that you stole those armbands?"

"Can it be, lass, that your father wanted rid of you because of your peppered tongue?" Roag yanked his plaid into place, brushed at the folds.

Not even flinching, she held his gaze, her expression cool as spring. "Perhaps you heard of Donell MacDonell's demise and came here hoping to profit from his uninhabited tower, his title as laird and keeper of this isle? Fierce warrior that you are, you didn't expect anyone to oppose your claim."

Roag almost snorted.

She'd nearly guessed his mission. She just didn't realize that his guise wasn't aimed at lining his own purse, but at serving Scotland. He was here to protect the weal of every man, woman, and child in the kingdom.

She rounded on him, beside her sleeping dog. "It must've been a great shock to find a bride and her family waiting to greet you."

It was a disaster. "That is true."

"How terrible for you to have your plans snarled before you even set foot in the tower you came to steal."

Roag stiffened. "Have care, lass. I am nae thief."

"Then what are you?" She folded her arms, watching him with her bold, green gaze.

"No' what you think." Roag kept his face expressionless.

"I didn't tell you what I think. You heard what I believe."

"What one believes isn't always true."

"Nor are denials."

"Would you trust anything I said?"

"Nae."

"So I thought." Roag rolled his shoulders, aware of a dull throbbing pain between them. "See here, lass. Whatever his reasons, your father bound us this night. He'll sail away at first light, leaving you behind without a care or thought. The truth is that suits me fine."

It did.

Now that he'd given more thought to the matter.

Having MacDonnell's promised bride at his side supported his mission.

The botheration she presented was secondary.

He glanced at the window arch, the thick fog coming in from the sea. "To everyone outside this wee, drafty chamber, you are now my bride." He looked back at her, hoping his tone made her position clear. "You daren't forget that, ever."

"I see." She drew her cloak more tightly about her, clutching its edges in a white-knuckled grip. "You think to claim me, as part of poor Donell's legacy. You intend to go on as if—"

"Poor Donell? I thought you couldn't abide him."

Her chin came up, her eyes sparking. "He has left this world, and so must be pitied."

"Dead or no, so long as your family is here, he lives and breathes. Indeed"—he went to the window, placed his hands on the ledge—"I'd warn that if you give even the slightest indication that I am no' who I say I am, I'll have nae choice but to ensure that your father and his men cannae sail away in the morn. If you dare reveal my true name, they'll no' leave at all." He turned back to her, his expression suitably fierce. "Ever."

Her eyes flew wide. "You would threaten my family?"

Lass, I wouldn't harm them if they all dropped to their knees and tipped their heads to the sides, waiting for the sword blow. I've ne'er raised a blade against innocents and willnae start now. Say her that, you arse. Tell her.

Instead, he gave her a curt nod. "If need be."

She glared at him. "You're heartless."

"That may be." Roag hooked his thumbs in his sword belt, leaned back against the edge of the window arch. "Disregard my warning and you'll find out. I'd advise you no' to chance it."

"If I do?"

He didn't hesitate. "Then you will be as without family as I am."

"So you truly are a bastard." She was still standing near the brazier and its glow flickered around her, edging her with a bright golden sheen.

She looked like an angel.

He felt like the devil.

"A true bastard," she said again, her disdain piercing his heart.

"I have ne'er denied it." He wished he could tell her that all the stars would fall from the sky before he'd harm her or her family, even her rascally sire.

Had Conn's suspicions about her two chests proved true, the man would now be in the tower's dungeon. But for once, the big Irishman had erred.

And so...

Roag only flicked a speck of nothingness from his plaid. "You should ne'er have come here."

"I had no choice." She clasped her hands before her. Then she gave him a look that made something funny happen inside his chest.

He hoped to the gods he only imagined the glitter of tears in her eyes.

If she cried...

He drew a deep breath, steeling himself to remain unmoved if she did.

The truth was, he'd never seen such a courageous woman. Much as he'd rather their paths hadn't crossed, he was drawn to her, powerfully. She could so easily make him forget everything outside these stone-cold walls, narrowing his world so that it held only her.

There was something about her, something that attracted him so strongly, he'd swear he wasn't here to do a King's bidding, but at her behest.

Perhaps the witch-woman she'd mentioned had charmed her as well?

As if she'd somehow called to him, and he needed her, nothing else mattering. And that was the most foolhardy notion he'd ever had.

It was crazed.

So he stayed at the window, glad for the sea wind that

blew his hair, the moon's silvery light falling across his mail shirt, the steel hung all about him. She needed to see him as ruthless. To that purpose, he touched his sword hilt, letting the gesture say words he couldn't because they sat like soured ash on his tongue.

Lady Gillian didn't appear daunted.

Roag knew he looked formidable. His face was deliberately grim, his gaze as cold as only years of Fenris work could hone it. His sword, Havoc, was a well-blooded blade, his casual grasp of her hilt enough to warn anyone that he wielded her well, and with deadly accuracy.

He raised her now, just a few inches to reveal the sheen of her steel. "Lady, if you care for your kin, you'll do everything I say you."

Lady Gillian's brows lifted, her face chilling. "So we come to the pass I expected."

Roag lowered Havoc back into her sheath, waiting till another gust of wind rushed by before speaking.

"Lady, you sailed here prepared to stay on this isle, by whatever means." He didn't want to believe she was part of a nefarious scheme, but he couldn't deny the proof before him. He glanced again at her coffers, each one bursting with her clothes and worldly goods. "You cannae deny that. You laid your own trap."

"I knew nothing of those crates, or that my chamber at Sway was emptied." She met his gaze, anger in her great green eyes. Her hood fell back, revealing her glossy, flame-bright hair. "I do know that you came to my room expecting to have your way with me." She stood straighter, pushed back the hair that was sliding across her cheek. "Why do you think I wore this cloak? Did you truly believe I freeze so easily?"

Any other time, Roag would've laughed. "You thought to make yourself unattractive?"

He should've guessed.

"You shouldn't have made the effort." He strolled over to her, tugged on the heavy woolen edges of her cloak so that it slipped from her shoulders, falling down her back. He caught the mantle with one hand, whipping it off her and tossing it onto her narrow, lumpy-looking bed. "Trying to hide your loveliness is as effective as forbidding the moon to shine. It cannae be done."

"Nor can you sway me with honeyed words."

"That, sweetness, is the last thing I'd wish to do."

She inclined her head, her lustrous hair tumbling to her hips. "We agree about something."

And I shouldn't have disrobed you. Rarely had he made a greater mistake. Even in the dim light, her close-fitting gown drew attention to her full breasts, the slimness of her waist, the pleasing curves of her hips, and the shapely thighs he'd felt pressed against his own when he'd kissed her. She was lovely enough to have been promised to a lord, a man of high rank and standing. To think she might've been shackled to a scoundrel like MacDonnell made his gut tighten and sent bile to his throat.

As if she saw his face darken and mistook the reason, she stiffened. "You have already kissed me, sirrah. You have thought nothing of seizing me, touching me in the most intimate—"

"I had to kiss you." Roag's head felt nigh to exploding. He didn't want to think about holding and kissing her, how soft and pliant she'd felt in his arms.

If he did…

Damnation, already, his best piece was twitching!

Gods help him, but she wakened desires he didn't even know he had.

"Lady Gillian," he began, a little more roughly than he'd intended, "if I'd have touched you as a man lays hands on a woman he desires, I'd still have the feel of you burning my palms, the taste of you on the back of my tongue." He threw a glance at her cloak. "Were that so, nae ratty old mantle in all Scotland would keep me from wanting you."

"Then I am blessed that you do not."

"You have nae idea what I desire, or dinnae."

He hoped that would remain so.

"I will tell you I've no wish to ravish you." He turned again to the window, needing his back to her so she wouldn't see the evidence of his lie. The proof of how very much he did want her. "I'll no' pounce on you, you have my oath. But"—he loathed this part—"if you break your word to me, I'll hunt your kin to the ends of the world, leaving nary a one to—"

"I haven't given you my word." She was on him in a beat, all wild, unbound hair and fury. She grabbed his arm, gripping tight. "If you harm my family, I will see you half-buried in the sand and let the tide drown you."

Roag looked at her, torn between admiration and annoyance. Unfortunately, she had to believe the worst of him. There was no way around that, much as he wished otherwise.

So he eased his arm from her grasp, and carefully chose his words. "You dinnae want to pit your brothers against my men. You're a fine, braw lassie, so you'll tolerate me spending the night in this room. I'll sleep on the floor, beside the coal burner." He nodded at the brazier.

"Then, when we bid farewell to your menfolk at the morrow's dawn, you'll play the happy bride.

"Donell MacDonnell's bride," he reminded her, taking her face in one hand and forcing her to look into his eyes. "A single false move, the merest slip of tongue, and you ken what will happen."

She glared at him, anything but frightened. "I do not care where you lay your head this night, and you needn't threaten me. I will not expose your deceit." For a moment, she closed her eyes, as if composing herself.

When she looked at him again, her voice was steady. "In exchange, I—"

"A trade?" Roag's brows snapped together.

"Of sorts, aye." Her gaze was direct. "I have a deal for you."

Roag took a step forward, everything suddenly clear. "That's the reason you're here, am I right? You seek to bargain with me?"

She flipped back her hair, her gaze not leaving his. "What I have is worth more than any bargain. Indeed, it is a treasure, and one you can't refuse."

"Then show me." Roag folded his arms, waiting.

He didn't tell her he wouldn't consider her trade.

Not even if she pulled down the sun and turned its light into a bottomless hoard of golden coins. A shame for her there were men who could never be bought. Not many, to be sure. But they did exist.

He was one of them.

Whatever she meant to offer him, she was about to be disappointed.

Chapter Twelve

❦

I am aware, Sir Roag, that there are men who value wealth above ravishing women." Gillian looked at him through narrowed eyes, irritatingly annoyed because he'd claimed no interest in pouncing upon her.

Not that she wished such attentions.

Still, his assertion had stung. She'd caught his gaze settling on her often enough since his arrival on the isle. She'd been sure his eyes had held manly admiration, sometimes even lingering where they shouldn't. Now she knew he'd feigned such interest, apparently finding her lacking.

What a shame his darkly rugged looks drew her!

A shame, and a great botheration.

So she flipped back her hair, gave him what she hoped was a very cool smile. "Sir Roag—"

"I am no knight, my lady." He didn't return her smile. "Simply Roag, as I told you," he said, his face an unreadable mask. "I am also a man and the blood in my veins is just as red, just as desirous of women, as any other man's.

"I'll also no' walk away from good coin—if I earn it myself." He closed the distance between them, clamped his hand around her chin. "I am more fond of other things, see you? Keeping my head on my neck, breathing, and living as I please."

Gillian didn't like the way he was looking at her. His dark gaze burned into hers, the heat in them not a sensual fire but one that indicated he thought poorly of her.

"That is clear, sir," she used the title anyway. "No one would argue that you do as you wish."

"So I do."

"Then perhaps my bargain will offer you more ways to pursue—"

"I will no' be bought, lady."

She gripped his wrist, lowering his hand from her chin. "Then perhaps I can appeal to your charitable heart?"

"I dinnae have one." His face closed and he folded his arms, everything about his stance enforcing his claim.

"I see." She did, and her stomach was sinking.

Her mind raced, seeking an alternative way to deal with him. He was clearly stubborn. Yet he also made no attempt to hide that he wasn't pleased by her presence. That was something she could work to her advantage.

So she drew a breath, studying him. *Roag the Bear.* By whatever name, he was tall, broad-shouldered, and as hard-muscled as, if not more so than, her strongest brothers. She found him exceedingly appealing, despite everything she now knew. He might not be Donell MacDonnell, but he looked more at home in this rough-walled, cold and dank tower than Donell could ever have done.

He was also dangerous.

Only a blackguard would abandon all niceties in the presence of a lady.

In truth, she was sure he didn't hold with such civilities in any circumstances.

His stony heart wouldn't allow such softening, no doubt seeing any kindness not as a virtue, but a weakness. Not for a moment would she believe hot, red blood coursed in his veins. He was a cold man, clear to the marrow.

How infuriating that he wasn't the real Donell. He would've scooped up her treasures with both hands, stuffing the hoard of goods into his belt pouch, his boots, maybe even his ears. He valued coin above all else, would have welcomed her offer.

No doubt he'd have also insisted on lying with her—a distasteful stipulation that would've cost her much maneuvering to avoid. But to ensure safe passage to Glasgow, his agreement to leave her in peace, she'd have been more than willing to stretch her wits. He'd been known to drink himself into his cups. A downfall she could have used to her advantage, declaring he'd "done the deed," and it was not her fault if he couldn't remember.

For the weight of her treasure, and perhaps the promise of more from her wealthy uncle in Glasgow, he'd have set sail with her faster than a full moon tide.

She'd have won.

With Roag, her chances didn't look good.

He was a very different man.

Wishing he wasn't so difficult, she moved to the fire, needing its warmth. She also wanted to put as much space between them as the tiny room allowed.

He stood only a few paces away at the window, where

light rain pattered against the wide, stone-cut ledge. Mist blew past the opening, the wild night suiting his dark good looks. Torchlight flickered across him, making his beard glisten, and his arm rings. He apparently possessed enough wealth to afford a swift well-made ship, fine weapons, loyal men, and the richest mail she'd ever seen. Most important, for her purposes, she knew he was as hard as all that gleaming armor.

"So," she began, deciding plain words would work best with him, "we are agreed that you are completely devoid of honor. You are a man not above threatening an innocent woman and her entire clan, to see your will done."

"If need be, aye." He didn't show a hint of remorse.

"So I thought."

"Then why waste your breath stating what you knew?"

"Because I still wish to make a deal with you." Keeping her back straight and her shoulders squared, Gillian held his gaze. Her heart hammered and she hoped he couldn't tell.

"We have already done so." As if dismissing her, he turned to the window, stared out at the rainy darkness. "Or have you forgotten what I've told you?"

"I remember very well." An uncomfortable blend of anger and dread weighed down on her. "The words are etched on my soul."

Her entire world had spiraled down to this cold, dank cell of a tower room. Everything that had happened to her before this moment no longer mattered.

What did was how she presented her trade.

Every man had a price.

Even bold, arrogant, heartless ones, though it might be necessary to dig deeper to find it.

She would.

So she went to the window table and refilled his discarded cup of Rhenish wine. She hoped the potent libation might loosen his tongue enough for him to reveal what would sway him.

"Take some wine," she said, trying to speak amicably.

"I've had enough." He turned, dashing her plan as he slid the cup back toward her. Worse, he stepped right up to her, bracing his hands on the table edge and leaning in, trapping her. "Though"—he had the nerve to smile—"I appreciate your intent. I've aye admired women who are no' just beautiful, but clever and brave."

"I don't care what you think of me." Gillian lifted her chin, hoped her eyes were blazing.

"I think you are as stubborn as I am." He flicked a glance at the wine cup. When he returned his gaze to her, a corner of his mouth hitched up. "You thought to ply me with wine, fuddling my wits and gaining advantage. It willnae work, lass." He leaned closer and stroked his thumb over her lips. "Nothing you say, or do, will make a difference. Spare yourself the effort."

"I was only being hospitable," she insisted. "It is a great tradition in the Isles."

He arched a brow, seeing through her.

"A bastard, my lady, especially one raised in the rough world of Stirling Castle's kitchens, can smell a rat before he e'er leaves his hidey hole." He set his knuckles beneath her chin and tipped back her head, capturing her gaze. "Be warned that I'll no' be tricked. No' by you, or anyone."

Gillian stiffened, relief sluicing her when he lowered his hand.

She refused to acknowledge his small triumph.

Above all, she hoped he couldn't tell how much he unsettled her. He was undoubtedly her enemy, that stood clear. Yet his touch, even spurred by irritation, sent sensation racing all through her, even warming her from within.

Blessedly, his boldness brought him so near that her gaze snagged on the pagan pendant he wore so proudly, the silver Thor's hammer amulet. She'd seen him reach for it a time or two since his arrival on the isle. Once, she'd heard him mutter what sounded like an ancient Norse prayer as he'd rubbed his thumb across the piece, hinting he viewed it as a talisman.

That meant she'd found his weakness.

His price.

Sure of it, she took a deep, steeling breath and straightened, not caring that doing so made her breasts brush against his broad, mail-covered chest. It couldn't be helped. He stepped away from her, moving swiftly as if her touch had burned him.

Good, she was gaining ground.

If she made him uncomfortable, she'd have a better chance of his wanting her gone. Encouraged, she drew a breath, silently asking the gods for guidance.

"The silver hammer of Thor hangs at your neck." She flicked her gaze to the pendant. "It is a handsome piece. Can it be that you honor the old ways? That you look in awe to the Northmen who once ruled these waters?" She saw at once that she'd chosen the wrong words, for his eyes narrowed slightly, wariness stealing across his features.

"The Vikings were marauders." He touched his Thor's hammer again, lightly, as if it meant nothing. "I wear this amulet because it was the first silver I could afford. It reminds me that hard work and perseverance taste better than bread crumbs and poor man's ale."

"You speak like a Hebridean." Gillian didn't believe a word.

She was sure he trusted in the amulet's power.

Either way, she was now certain she'd soon be off this wee islet and sailing for Glasgow. Hoping so, she went to her bed and reached under its mattress for her small leather pouch of Viking hoard goods.

"This is what I wanted to show you." She lifted the bag, jiggling it so he could hear the clink of the silver. "There are enough Thor's hammers in here for the necks of all your men. Also armlets, rings, and cut-up brooches, ample coin to purchase a much grander isle than this one, even to build a great castle."

To her surprise, he said nothing.

So she undid the strings and opened the pouch, upending it so the contents spilled across her bed. "It is a wealth beyond measure," she said, lifting a handful of coins and letting them spill through her fingers. "Surely a fair exchange to rid yourself of a bride you don't desire."

He glanced at her, his eyes glinting darkly in the torchlight. "I said I wouldnae ravish you, no' that I dinnae desire you."

Gillian chose not to answer him.

Something about the way he was looking at her made her feel as if her skin caught fire, a slow-burning warmth that spread all through her.

He smiled a little, as if he knew.

Then he strolled across the room, joining her at the bed. "This is your treasure?"

She nodded. "It is mine, aye."

He picked up a coin and held it to the torchlight, turning it this way and that before tossing it back onto the pile. His second choice was a heavy, intricately twisted silver-and-gold arm ring, a prize that had surely once belonged to a great Viking warlord.

"I've ne'er seen so much plunder." He returned the armlet to the pile, his gaze roaming over the silver pieces. "Where did you find such goods?"

She smiled. "I didn't. My great-great-grandfather discovered a hoard of Viking treasure buried in a riverbank. The riches were well preserved in a large lead-lined chest. He was very young at the time, but even then a far-thinker.

"He told nae one of the find except his father and clan elders, men wise enough to safeguard the treasure to be used for the weal of Sway, and our people." She trailed her fingers over the pile of silver, slid a glance at Roag. "Although he was just a lad, my great-great-grandfather requested one boon of the elders. Clan legend is that he'd seen his favorite sister wed a not-so-fortunate man and then witnessed the hard times they endured, the husband too stubborn to ask for help from either family.

"And so"—she looked at him, her smile brightening—"in return for finding such a prize, he asked that, so long as the treasure lasted, each daughter of our chiefly line be given a portion against ill times."

"And this is yours?" He glanced at the treasure.

"It is."

Confidence swelled in her breast. Pride and the surety that she'd won.

"Sorry, lass—"

She held up her hand. "Say no more—yet." She didn't like the set of his mouth, the hardness in his eyes. "You don't understand, see? These riches can be yours. I am offering them to you. A simple exchange—"

"I dinnae want your treasure." He folded his arms. "I willnae be bribed, my lady."

"That wasn't my intent," she argued, gripping his arm before he could turn away.

He looked at her. "What was?"

"A trade." She released his arm, annoyed by the spark of contact. "You render me a certain service and the hoard goods shall be your payment."

"For what?"

"Passage to Glasgow." She met his gaze, her voice steady. "I want you to take me there, then escort me to the home of my mother's uncle."

He arched a brow. "That is all?"

"It is enough." She pushed back her hair. "You do not need or want me here. I have no desire to remain. My great-uncle is a shoemaker, high in the King's favor. He will have a place for me at his hearth. We would both be well served."

She held his gaze, willing her words to make it true. "I would have a new home."

"You already do, my lady." He flicked a glance about the small room. "My sorrow if it doesnae please you."

"There is more." She wasn't finished. "On thon bed are great riches. Enough coin to fund your adventures for all your days."

"Perhaps I am weary of adventure."

"So you won't take me to Glasgow?" Gillian could hardly hear her own voice for the rushing sound in her ears, the blood beginning to drum at her temples.

"Nae." He shook his head and light from the wall torch fell across his face, illuminating the hard set of his jaw, his stony expression. The other half of him was in shadow, the darkness making him look cold, even dangerous.

She was sure that he was.

But she was determined to be strong, unafraid. Cowering before adversity had never been her nature. She owed it to the generations of brave women before her not to give in to despair. Hebridean females were not hollow reeds, bending in the wind.

They stood tall, always.

And so would she.

"I made you a good offer," she said, pleased by the steadiness of her voice. She glanced at the hoard goods, then back to him. "You are not interested?"

"So I said, aye." He picked up her leather pouch, began filling it with her treasure.

"I see." She drew a tight breath, struggled hard to keep from pressing a hand to her brow.

She couldn't remember her head ever pounding so fiercely. "You would keep me here against my will?"

"Call it what you wish." He turned to her, held out the bag of silver. "By your own sire's deed, you are the hand-fasted bride of Donell MacDonnell. This was his home, where you now belong. Excepting my own warriors, the men below believe I am MacDonnell. I've told you what will happen if you claim otherwise."

"And if I do?"

He angled his head, considering her. "The morrow would see a Viking ship burial. Your father's galley put to flame, his and your brothers' bodies burning inside it."

Gillian's eyes rounded. "You wouldn't dare."

He stepped up to her, pressed the treasure pouch into her hands. "You'd be wise no' to find out."

Chapter Thirteen

❦

So you would keep me here forever?"

Lady Gillian's words made Roag's entire body tighten, and not in a good way. Guilt and annoyance swept him, and he felt a muscle jump in his jaw. So easily, he could smash his fist into the little room's wall. Instead, he watched through narrowed eyes as she shoved her treasure pouch beneath the bed and then straightened, her eyes ablaze, high color on her cheeks.

It mattered not.

There was only one answer he could give her.

"You will remain on the island for as long as is necessary, aye." The words spoken, he went to the window, his future now seeming as impenetrable as the night's cold swirling mist. How had he landed in such a disaster? And what did he intend to do about the sparks between them?

Nothing, he knew.

A grievance that annoyed him more than it should.

Worst of all, he suspected he would have to cause her more pain than he'd already done.

"Who is your mother's uncle?" He braced his hands on the cold, wet stone of the window ledge, hoping her answer would not be the one he suspected. "The shoemaker in Glasgow?"

"Thomas MacCulloch." She spoke the name he'd dreaded. "Many years ago, he had the good fortune to repair the late King Robert II's ruined boots after he'd damaged them in a fall near Glasgow Cathedral. In gratitude, the King sent him trade. His endorsement made my mother's uncle a rich man. He—"

"He is dead, my lady." Roag turned from the window, hating that he had to tell her. "Your uncle's skill as a shoemaker was well known in Stirling. Many nobles visited his shop whene'er they journeyed to Glasgow. So his passing is known to me, Stirling man that I am. Thomas MacCulloch and his poor lady wife succumbed to a fever some years ago.

"If they had children, I'm no' aware." Roag forced himself to tell her true. "Their home and the wee shop now belong to another man. A tailor, last I heard. If MacCulloch was your only family in Glasgow, there would've been nae reason for you to go there."

"I didn't know." Her brow furrowed.

"So I gathered." Roag tried not to scowl. He already felt more like an arse than ever before in his life. Having to dash her last hope of refuge made him feel even worse.

What he'd like to do was gather her in his arms and comfort her, protecting her from whatever it was that had her wishing to go elsewhere than her home.

It was none of his concern why she didn't want to return to Castle Sway.

For sure, he wasn't the man to soothe her cares.

He required her silence, no more.

"I am sorry, lass," he said, gripping her hands before he realized what he was doing.

She didn't flinch, seeming not even to notice—a truth that indicated only, he felt, their powerful attraction. His overwhelming urge to not just band his arms tightly around her, but hold her hard against him and kiss her long and deep, plundering her lips until the last trace of anguish was gone from her face.

"So am I." She drew a long breath, pulled her hands from his. "By all telling, he was a good man, his wife a kind-hearted soul." She paced a few steps and then knelt beside her dog, stroking his rough-coated back. "I shall have to think of somewhere else for Skog and me to go. There is surely—"

"You are no' leaving Laddie's Isle." Roag's tone was gruff, deliberately so.

When his work here was done, he'd find a good home for her—if she still didn't desire to return to Sway.

It was all he could do for her.

"Dinnae trouble yourself making plans, sweet." He took a bit of cheese from the table, leaned down to let her ancient pet take the treat from his hand—a gesture he regretted at once, because she needed to think he was entirely heartless.

Sure she'd cast some spell on him, fuddling his wits, he straightened and brushed his hands.

He also ignored Skog, trying not to see the appreciation in the beast's milky eyes. How he'd started thumping his tail on the room's stone-flagged floor.

"What you must do," he said, knowing his words would make him the greatest gutter-dredge in all Scotland, "is strip naked and climb into your bed. I will do the same—for a while."

She jolted, pushing to her feet. "I will not!" Her voice rose, her face paling. "You said you'd not—"

"And nor shall I." Roag felt his own face heating, anger at himself almost scalding him. He ignored how her dog was struggling to rise, the confusion on Skog's age-whitened face. "No' climb into bed with you, I mean."

He turned aside, pulled a hand down over his beard. "I said I wouldnae ravish you, lady, and I willnae." *Howe'er much I'd like to.* "I will remove my clothes, as will you. You have my assurance I'll no' watch as you do so, nor as you slip beneath the covers. But we will spend the night naked."

"I don't see why." She came round to stand before him, the color returning to her face. "What difference—"

"I arranged for one of my men to bring a small party abovestairs," he told her true. "They willnae stay long, nor even enter the room. But they will peek inside. When they do, they'll see you in the bed. You'll hide your breasts, but I'd ask you to bare your shoulders so there's nae doubt to your nakedness.

"And"—he reached to touch her hair, unable to help himself—"you'll muss your hair, making it look tousled from—"

"Your attentions!" Her eyes narrowed, her fury crackling between them, almost heating the air. "You want them to think you've taken my innocence."

"Lady, you are sheltered, indeed, if you're no' aware that your menfolk already expect that to happen. In

truth, my own men wouldn't be surprised by the sight."
He stepped closer, set his hands on her shoulders. "This
night, in this wee room, the two of us joined on thon bed,"
he told her, the words conjuring images he didn't want to
acknowledge.

"Mating," he added, hoping his frankness would shock
her into believing him the brute he was trying to appear.
"It is what's done on the night of a handfast. Anything
else would stir suspicion and I cannae allow that."

She set her hands on her hips. "So men will come
abovestairs to see me in bed, thinking the worst?"

"They will think no ill." He cupped her chin, lifting
her face. "Your family will be pleased. My men, though
they know fine naught will have happened, will still envy
me greatly."

Her eyes glittered. "I won't do it."

"You will." Roag leaned in, so near his nose almost
touched hers. "Be glad there'll benae viewing. I told your
sire I was already satisfied with you, and my men wouldn't
dare call for the like, knowing what they do."

She shivered, visibly. "That's a barbaric custom."

"Even so, it remains tradition." He released her, stepping back before he kissed her. She riled—and roused—
him that greatly. "If a newly bonded pair dinnae stand
unclothed before each other, assuring themselves and all
concerned of the acceptability of their *attributes,* much
can sour in unions where an heir is required."

"We do not have a union." She smoothed back her hair,
brushed at her skirts.

"Perhaps, nae." He gave her that. "But you are bound
to MacDonnell. He could demand to examine you, lady.
Carefully, at length, and in any way he might choose,"

he warned, aware her prickliness could cause problems lest she feared to rile him. "As a generally well-lusted man, I wouldnae mind carrying out such a viewing of you. Indeed"—he felt his damnable cock twitch—"I'd relish it."

"You, sir, are a beast."

"So some say." He unclasped the large Celtic brooch at his shoulder, tore off his plaid, and flung it aside. Bending forward, he began pulling off his heavy mail shirt, allowing himself a wee surge of pride that he had the strength to do so without the aid of a squire. "If you dinnae wish to see just how beastly I am, you'd best make haste to undress your bonnie self and crawl into bed. I'll be unclothed in an eye-blink and if you aren't, I shall come and do the honors." He straightened, carefully placed his hauberk on the floor.

"You needn't," she returned, disdain edging her voice.

"I would do so gladly."

"A beast and a bastard, then."

"Aye, that, too," Roag shot back, secretly amused by her spirit.

Before a smile could quirk his lips, he reached to tug off his boots, his only boon to his honor being that he kept his back to her. He could hear her undressing. The soft rustling of her clothes as they slid down her body and fell to the floor set him like granite. It was a sight he would spare her. A vexatious condition he supposed would plague him all night.

And who could blame him?

"One other warning, sweetness," he called, now standing full naked near the window. "When my men knock on the door, I'll be answering it naked. If you dinnae want to—"

"I have seen unclothed men, sirrah," she snapped, the sound of bedding being whipped back revealing she was climbing beneath the covers. "I will not wilt if I glimpse one more."

I willnae wilt either! Roag almost declared, half worried he'd remain hard for days.

No female had ever beset him so fiercely.

He'd lost count of how many lovelies had willingly aired their skirts for him, pleasuring him gladly, even begging him to do so again. They'd all been delicious dalliances, their charms abundant and their carnal skills well honed.

Lady Gillian was pure.

Yet she burned with a fiery passion he knew would kindle a blaze that would brand him for life.

If he dared to touch her, intimately.

Nae, if he even caught a single glimpse of that oh-so-tempting part of her.

Sure of it, and that the devil himself had sent her into his path, he waited until she settled in the bed. He risked a peek, relieved to see that she'd rolled onto her side, facing the wall, and with a pillow covering her head.

He was safe for now.

So he did the only thing he could think to do and strode over to the window, hoping the night's chill, damp air would reduce the problem at his loins.

Blessedly, that was so.

But even after he'd stood there long enough to hear Lady Gillian's breath slowing—a sign, he hoped, that she'd fallen into an exhausted, much-deserved slumber—his manhood didn't completely relax. He remained twitchy, his fool piece hanging fine, but so primed the mere thought of her roused him.

So he pushed her from his mind and looked out at the sea, sure he'd never been given a more difficult mission.

Indeed, when he left here he might tell Alex Stewart he was done as a Fenris.

He could take his savings and purchase a small plot of fertile land, become a farmer. Or perhaps he'd invest in his friend William Wyldes's inn, the Red Lion. The sprawling inn with its well-visited public room was a favorite Fenris watering hole not far outside Stirling town. Roag also appreciated the Red Lion's serving wenches. Comely lasses who knew how to please men and didn't set their heads to aching or torment them so fiercely that they stood before the windows of dank and crumbling towers, willing the hard biting wind to chill the lust out of their cocks.

But the night wind was lessening—and his unruly man-piece took advantage, swelling anew.

And not because he'd remembered Wyldes's lovelies.

It was her.

Lady Gillian MacGuire.

Sure he was doomed, Roag stepped closer to the window, not caring if he got wet. But the rain, too, was thinning. The thick fog had moved on and only wisps of mist curled past the tower. As he'd argued with Gillian, being both a bastard and a beast, the night had begun to clear. Moonlight slanted down to make the sea gleam like beaten silver and bright stars glittered high above. From below came the slapping of waves against the rocks, the sound surprisingly soothing, a balm to his weary soul.

It was a night so beautiful that his heart ached.

But its glory couldn't compare to the woman asleep on the bed behind him.

He closed his eyes, drew a deep breath against her allure and the spell of this wee isle.

He didn't want to appreciate either.

He also wondered when he'd become so prophetic. Had he truly told the lass he might be wearying of adventure? He had, and he hoped to all the gods it wasn't so.

Unfortunately, he couldn't shake an even worse notion.

That he wasn't tired of the chase, but embarking on a new gamble: one that went by the byname Spitfire of the Isles and would change his life forever.

Chapter Fourteen

❦

H o, Donell!" A man's voice filled the small room, his call waking Gillian.

Other greetings joined in, her father's and her brothers' voices unmistakable as someone rapped on the door, demanding entry in a jovial, celebratory tone.

"Your friends, they're here." Gillian sat up in the narrow bed, clutching the covers to her breast as she peered into the dimness, searching for the Bear. She saw him at once, for the tiny chamber didn't offer any hiding places.

He was on the floor beneath the window, his plaid wrapped around him, and in the pale moonlight, it was clear to see that he'd slept. His dark hair was tangled and he blinked, as if he'd just been ripped from deepest dreams.

He was also naked.

Leastways he was partially so, his hard-muscled chest and shoulders and his powerful arms gleaming in the moonlight. Dark hair fanned across his chest and arrowed down to his waist where the dark line disappeared beneath his plaid. Gillian wished she hadn't noticed, for the sight made something flutter inside her.

She tore her gaze away, meeting his eyes.

"Your viewing party," she reminded him, keeping her voice low, blessing Skog, who was finally stirring, his ancient ears at last catching the knocks on the door.

The dog pushed slowly to his feet, barking. But his tail wags hinted that he wouldn't bar entry to the intruders.

He surely heard, or smelled, her kin.

Gillian did, too, the ale and mead fumes wafting past the door seams proving that much merriment had gone on in the hall as she'd confronted Roag, her world crumbling around her. She tightened her grip on the bed covers, glaring at him.

"Have done," she urged him, tipping her head toward the door. "Let them peek in and go."

"No' till you wipe that scowl off your face," he warned, at the bed so fast she hadn't seen him move.

Blessedly, he still held his plaid about his waist. But the thick, long-looking ridge picked out by the brazier glow showed that even partially covered, his manhood was rampant.

Gillian bristled. "How can I not frown when you dare come close to me—like that?" She flicked a glance at the bulge, her heart racing madly. "It's unseemly. I am a lady—"

"Aye, so you are." He leaned in, bringing his face so close to hers that his warm breath brushed her cheek. "This night, a well-pleasured one, you hear?" He reached out, mussing her hair, arranging it to spill about her bared shoulders. "Bite your lips a few times, and hard. Then pinch your cheeks. They need to glow as if thon shouting men have just disturbed us."

He didn't need to explain his meaning.

She knew.

And feeling indignant and righteous didn't stop the rush of sensation racing through her as he fussed with her hair. His strong, warm fingers brushed along the side of her neck, then skimmed across her shoulders, each touch sending a new rush of tingles flashing over her skin. The flutters in her belly worsened, even as annoyance stole her breath and tightened her chest.

"Have done, I said." She snapped her brows together, determined to show her fury.

"I would love to." He cupped her chin, his own anger darkening his face. "Now do as I warned, or I might."

Gillian pressed her lips together. No longer frowning, but schooling her features into a smooth, expressionless mask.

At the door, the raps became poundings. And hoots and laughter joined the shouts for "Donell" to let them in. Skog's age-roughened barks accompanied them, the ruckus annoying the Bear so much that he stepped back from the bed and raised his hands, fisting them as if to vent his anger.

His plaid fell to the floor.

"Oh!" Gillian's jaw dropped, her eyes rounding. He was more than *rampant*. He was ragingly so, as the moonlight and the brazier's glow revealed.

"Indeed." He glared down at her, making no move to snatch up the fallen plaid. "And if you're as clever as I suspect, you'll ken that a man in such a state isnae one to rile.

"Now look sated." He stepped nearer to the bed's edge, the whole of his naked perfection only inches away. "Remember if you dinnae, there will be a price of blood to pay—your kin's."

Gillian scooted closer to the wall, felt her face heating with rage. "You bastard."

"So I am," he agreed, already striding for the door.

"Ho, Donell!" the first man who'd knocked called out again, lifting his voice above the others. "'Tis cold and drafty on this landing! Let us see the two o' ye, so we can head back down to the warmth o' the hall and our mead!"

"Or are ye still so busy plowing fertile fields that ye dinnae hear us?" another shouted, his words spurring a burst of laughter and more vigorous door-hammerings.

"The seeds are sowed," Roag confirmed, throwing the door wide.

Two of his largest men stood on the threshold. The red-bearded giant Gillian recognized as Conn of the Strong Arm, the *Valkyrie*'s helmsman, and a man reported to have Erse blood, spoke first. "You ken why we're here, my friend." He clapped a hand on Roag's shoulder, peering past him to narrow his eyes at Gillian. "'Tis tradition in my Irish homeland as well—looking in to see that all's right betwixt the happy twain after a bonding."

Roag glanced back at her, then turned again to his helmsman. "We are well satisfied, be it known."

Gillian heard him, wanting nothing more than to sink into the shadows.

"Aye, sweet?" Roag shot another look at her, a warning in his eyes.

She forced a nod, if not a smile. "I will be tired come morning," she returned, grasping the first response that came to her. *Had this beast truly lain with me, I doubt I'd be able to walk for a week!* She kept the truth to herself, took care not to let the bed coverings slip from her trembling fingers.

"All that was required of us has been done," she added, hoping the hot color staining her cheeks would appear to the gawkers as the flush of passion.

She refused to think of this as a viewing.

It was an outrage.

"So all is well?" The question was directed at Roag and came from the second man, an equally towering figure she'd heard Roag call Big Hughie Alesone.

Perhaps even a bit larger than Conn, but with hair almost as red, Big Hughie's ruddy face shone in the landing's torchlight. The suspicion in his eyes hinted that he wasn't as good at pretending as the Irish helmsman, Conn.

"Is there aught ye be needing?" Big Hughie didn't even look her way, his furrowed brow on Roag. "Fresh sheeting..." He gave Roag a telling look, his gaze flicking briefly to the bed. "I've brought a flask o' uisge beatha for you and the lass—to celebrate the night." He pulled the flask from beneath his plaid, thrust it into Roag's hands, muttering something close to Roag's ear—words so low and indistinguishable Gillian couldn't catch them.

She was sure they wouldn't please her.

"Father!" She leaned forward, raising her voice above Skog's excitement, for the old dog was winding in and out of the men's legs, his thin bark marking his age as he sought to join the ruckus. "Father," she called again, for she couldn't see him in the throng. "I have a wish, if I may?"

"To be sure!" He pushed through Roag's men, his

girth suddenly filling the doorway. "I can see you're well cared for, praise be all the gods!"

Beaming, he swelled his great chest, slid a beneficent glance at Roag before turning back to her. "Name your wish, lass."

Gillian took a breath, her heart knocking hard against her ribs. She didn't want to draw Roag's anger, but he'd arranged this spectacle. So he couldn't fault her if she used it to her advantage, giving her family their best chance of escape.

She had no choice, really.

Moistening her lips, she thought quickly, knowing at once what must be said.

"You know how much I love you," she began, relieved when the words rang clear and strong. She kept her gaze on her father, trying hard to ignore the big, naked man beside him. "How much I love all of you," she added, her heart squeezing as her brothers crowded behind her father, each well-loved face wearing an odd mixture of guilt, hope, and excitement.

They knew she wasn't pleased to be in Roag's bed.

Yet they'd been fooled and thought she should be.

She only cared that they survived the morrow.

So she looked directly at them, pretending she didn't even see Roag's crewmen, who were playing their roles so well. "My loves," she called to her family, "I'd be grateful if you sail away as quickly as possible on the morrow. Perhaps even before first light, if you'd grant me such a boon?

"Truth is, I shall miss you fiercely, and do not want to suffer a long, drawn-out farewell." *I fear if you do not make haste, we will not see each other again in this life.*

Her stomach churned at the thought. She ached to give them a stronger warning. "Please—say you'll do this for me."

Her father blinked, glanced at her oldest brother, Gowan, and Andrew, the youngest, who both stood nearest to him. When they nodded, her father looked relieved.

"Aye, so we will," he agreed, turning back to her. "If the tides are running strong, we'll be away before the sun can break the horizon."

"I am glad." *Sail fast, please.*

"No more than my Lorna shall be!" Her father's face split in a grin and he nudged Gowan with an elbow. "She doesnae like being alone too long, that one!"

"Then hurry home to her." Gillian forced a smile, a light tone that hid her dislike of her stepmother. "Now, please leave us," she added, settling back against the bed cushions, pretending to stretch from weariness.

In their ale-headed state, some of the men might even think she wished more of her new husband's attentions. If so, that suited her fine.

The sooner they left, the faster Roag would snatch up his plaid, hiding his blatant maleness from her view.

Or so she hoped.

In truth, she had a hard time keeping her attention on the men on the landing instead of staring openly at the naked man whose bare-skinned magnificence was burning the backs of her eyes.

She suspected the sight was branded there, his shocking carnality ready to taunt her forever.

No man should hold such power over a woman.

That he did, over her, made her chest ache with an emotion she didn't want to examine.

So she waited until his men and her father and brothers turned away from the door and, one by one, trudged back down to the meager comforts of the tower's cold and drafty hall. Roag the Bear—she now understood why he'd claimed that his by-name had to do with his great size—closed the door only when their departing footsteps stopped echoing in the stair tower.

"You did well, lass," he said, sliding the door's drawbar into place, locking them in the little chamber. He strolled across the room, stopping by her bed to pick up his fallen plaid.

He did not sling it around his hips.

He only dropped it onto the end of her bed as he stood looking down at her. "They believed we coupled," he announced, speaking as casually as if they were both fully clothed and dining at the high table. "If you perform so well in the morning, they may leave in peace, unscathed, and still amongst the living."

Gillian felt her fury rising, rolling through her like waves. She refused to acknowledge his brazen display. "I will hold you to your word, sirrah."

"You have it."

I would rather see you clothed. She hoped her eyes said the silent words.

"A shame I am not sure how good your word is," she did say. Holding his gaze, she flicked a speck of lint off the bed, no longer bothering to appear content and drained from love play.

The very notion sent heat inching back up her neck, onto her cheeks. "You are a scoundrel such as I've never met. An honorless, cold-hearted blackguard who—"

"Dinnae make me keep warning you no' to vex me,

lass." His voice hardened, his expression turning fierce. "You've already caused more trouble than you know."

"What should I say?" She couldn't believe his audacity.

"Only you ken, my lady." He glanced at Skog, his face softening a bit as the beast circled three times and then lowered himself ever so slowly to the floor beside the brazier.

Gillian wished she hadn't seen—the evidence of Skog's stiff joints reminded her of his age. Watching Roag look at her pet in sympathy made her feel hollow inside.

She didn't want to like anything about him.

And much as she was trying not to notice, he was also doing the exact opposite of what she'd hoped—now that they were alone again, he made no move to cover his nakedness.

So she glanced at his plaid, her irritation almost alive. "Are you no' going to put that on?"

"Nae." He didn't blink, his bluntness drawing her attention right where it shouldn't be.

He'd grown larger!

She knew why when his gaze lowered to her breasts and one edge of his mouth lifted in an almost-smile.

The bed covers had slipped, falling near to her waist.

"How dare you!" She jerked up the sheeting, her heart hammering wildly. "You should have told me."

"The covers only just slid down." He spoke as if it were nothing—as if it were every day a man ogled her naked breasts, her nipples that, to her horror, were chill-tightened and thrusting. "I will tell you that you've bonnie teats."

"Bonnie—"

"So I said." His smile deepened, revealing a dimple.

"I'll also tell you that I haven't slung on my plaid because I aye sleep naked. It has naught to do with you.

"What does is making surenae one doubts we've sealed our handfast." He placed the flask Big Hughie had given him on the bed and then bent to pull a dirk from his discarded belt.

Straightening, he ran his thumb along the dirk's blade, nodding once when a bead of red appeared. "I'm no' wanting any questions when we go belowstairs in the morn."

Gillian shook her head, her eyes rounding. "You're not going to cut me." She drew a breath, tried to shore up the strength she was so proud of having. "Even you—"

"The blade is for me, sweet," he said, taking a quick slash across his forearm.

He dropped the dirk onto the bed, and then dragged his fingers down his arm, using the blood to smear the sheets. When he was done, he grabbed the dirk again, this time cutting away the soiled portion of the linen. He crumpled the cloth in his hands and then shook it out, holding it up like a banner.

"A parting gift for your da." He began rolling it up, satisfaction on his handsome face. "No man will dare claim you are no' duly given and bound to the Laird of Laddie's Isle. And your kin"—he pressed the linen roll against the cut on his arm—"will sail away relieved that you're happy.

"So long as you do as required on the morrow." He stepped closer and leaned down to drop a quick kiss on her lips. "Till then, have a sip or two of the fine uisge beatha Big Hughie left for you," he suggested, flicking a glance at the flagon. "Good Highland spirits to help you sleep the night."

"How thoughtful you both are." *You're fiends from the coldest pit of hell.*

She made no move to retrieve the flask. She did want a sip. More like, she'd enjoy several.

But reaching for it would risk having the covers slip again, perhaps revealing even more of her than the breasts the great lout had already seen.

As if he'd heard her thoughts, he took the flask and handed it to her. "Here, drink now."

And so she did, holding his gaze as she gulped down two healthy measures.

She wiped her lips with the back of her hand, but didn't return the flagon. "All I need is for you to be gone."

"As you wish," he agreed, running the fingers of his unbloodied hand down her cheek. "I have aye sought to make the lassies happy. If you'll close your lovely eyes and count to three, I'll be back beneath my window, stretched out in the shadows, before you look again."

He didn't wait for her to do as he bid, simply turned and headed to the window, his plaid clutched in his unsullied hand.

Gillian glared after him, sure a greater dastard couldn't walk the earth.

She should despise him.

Indeed, she did!

But his long, well-muscled legs, his proud back, and—the gods preserve her—his tight, beautifully made ass, were limned silver by the moonlight. Every bold, naked inch of him, revealed to her in all his shocking beauty. And much as she resented and reviled him, he stirred her in ways that made her question everything she'd ever believed about herself.

Could it be she was wanton?

As man-crazed and lacking morals as she suspected her stepmother to be?

Or were all women naturally susceptible to a man in all his naked glory? Even when they'd seen the wickedness that lived in his soul, the falseness of his heart?

She was sure she didn't want to know.

Chapter Fifteen

✦

Roag knew the instant his dreams of slavering hell-hounds and sulfurous brimstone turned real. The howls pierced the mists of sleep, hurting his ears, and the soft, feminine murmurs that accompanied them became disturbingly familiar. The voice belonged to Lady Gillian, and her dog, Skog, was whining.

Pushing up on an elbow, Roag squinted into the gloom of the maid's lodging.

He frowned, not remembering when he'd fallen asleep. His back hurt, and his neck was stiff, his aches and pains leaving no question he'd kept his word—that he'd spent the entire night on the hard stone floor.

His scowl deepened. He was sure he'd crossed the room only moments before, leaving Lady Gillian in her bed, the covers pulled to her chin, her furious gaze burning holes in his back as he'd tossed his plaid onto the floor beneath the window. He felt as if he'd only just made his sleeping place, pulling a length of plaid over him, the warmth from the nearby brazier and Lady Gillian's slumbering dog taking the bite out of the chill night air. He'd barely closed his eyes.

Now...

Another howl echoed in the darkness, more soothing words from the lass.

His wits returning, Roag threw back his plaid.

"Bluidy hell, what's amiss?" He leapt to his feet, his heart racing as his eyes adjusted to the room's deep shadow.

"Nothing," Lady Gillian's voice drifted to him from the maze of black and gray that was just beginning to take form. "All is good, no cause for alarm."

Say you. Roag fisted his eyes, rubbing them. He was too weary to assume the hard look he should turn on her, too sleepy to find harsh, uncaring words.

The dog's cries had pierced him. The worry in the lass's voice sent cold dread straight through him. Much as he needed her to think him a true bastard, nothing moved him more than old dogs and women in distress.

"Where are you?" He took a step forward, still straining to see in the dimness.

"I am here, with Skog."

That I know! Roag tamped down his temper and glanced about, his vision slowly improving.

It wasn't necessary to look far.

The brazier still glimmered, its faint glow showing him Lady Gillian on her knees before him. The great shaggy beast she'd bent over, her arms cradling him as she pressed the side of her face to his shoulder, crooning the soft words he'd heard in his sleep.

Blessedly, Skog was no longer howling.

Unfortunately, he was whimpering.

And hearing his misery made Roag's gut clench. He hoped the beast wasn't ill. He loved all animals, but was especially fond of dogs. He hadn't known this one long, but already felt an attachment.

And that wasn't the worst of it.

Now that he could see better, he could tell the lass was full naked. By the soft glow of the brazier and the thin slant of moonlight yet spilling through the window, the entirety of her charms were picked out in all her lush, well-made womanliness.

Roag closed his eyes again for a moment, pulled a hand down over his face.

For one crazy-mad moment, he prayed to all the gods that when he again opened them, he'd find himself wrapped in his plaid on the cold stone floor.

Still asleep and dreaming.

Not really wanting to, he cracked one eye, and then the other.

Lady Gillian was still naked.

But now she'd scooted around behind her dog, was trying to shield her nakedness with his bulk.

"Have you no decency?" She crouched lower, glared at him over the beast's head. "Turn around!"

"I have already seen most of what you'd hide." Roag didn't budge. "Now I'd have a look at your dog. His howls—"

"Are over," she cut him off, "and you needn't be concerned."

She drew back a bit, glanced at her dog. For a moment, the annoyance left her face and she looked younger than she was, vulnerable in a way that tore at him. She smoothed a hand along the dog's side, leaned close to kiss the top of his head before returning her gaze to him. "We go through this now and then. Skog has fearful dreams. He—"

"He is blessed to have you." The words sprang from Roag's lips, coming from his heart, and too swiftly for him to catch them. He hadn't wanted to sound sympathetic. But he was, more than she'd ever know.

More important, he wanted her covered.

"Here." He snatched his plaid off the floor, swirling it around her shoulders. "You'll catch a chill."

"Thank you!" She clutched the plaid about her, glancing down to adjust its folds so that nothing below her chin or above her knees remained visible. At last, she looked up at him again, a blush staining her cheeks. "You were sleeping so soundly. I didn't mean for you to catch me..."

"Naked?" Roag felt his scowl return, his cock twitching. "That I believe, lady." He grabbed his tunic, pulling it quickly over his head, glad its length would hide what she did to him. "Now tell me what happened."

"I already did." She stayed where she was, stroked her hand down Skog's back. "Sometimes he whines and howls when he sleeps," she explained, speaking with a softness that wound its way right inside him, touching places nowhere near his loins.

Places no woman had ever affected and that he didn't want to allow now.

So he folded his arms, hoped his expression was suitably unmoved. "So he dreams?"

"He does, aye." She blinked, her eyes glistening in the dark. "They frighten him. He's done this as long as I've had him, so I believe he is reliving the shipwreck."

"When this happens, you soothe him." He spoke to have something to say.

He knew the answer.

But he'd rather say it himself than have her speak words that would wrap even more tightly about his chest. He didn't want to hear a truth that would make him like and admire her, a softness and appeal that would undermine his restraint.

In truth, he was a master of resistance.

Never in all his days had he stood fully unclothed before an equally bare-bottomed lass and not ended such a bountiful night without a tumble in the heather. With pleasure he had indulged in heated romps in castle stairwells, or fast and furious joinings on the silken sheets of women who favored luxury. On such occasions, all that had mattered was a mutual slaking of needs, then a cordial parting of ways, both parties depleted and content.

Such had been his life.

And he wasn't after change.

He did frown.

Here he was in the wee small hours, fashing himself over an ancient dog that wasn't even his, and a woman who, however desirable, would no doubt cheer if he fell dead.

"To be sure I soothe him." Lady Gillian's voice slipped through his annoyance, thrusting an even pointier sword into his heart. "Skog had a rough start in life. It is not surprising that he sometimes remembers the dark times.

"It is my hope that each frightening dream will be the last such," she said, rubbing the dog behind his ears before she pushed to her feet. "If I can't spare him the bad memories, I try to give him as many good ones as I can."

"I am sure you do." *Something tells me you are skilled at creating memories to brand a man, even a four-legged one!*

"I hope so." Her tone held a guilelessness that punched him. "Skog's experiences at sea weighed heavy on him."

"Yet you took him on a voyage to this isle, exposing him to—"

"The journey could be the reason for his troubling dream." She nodded, not denying it.

"Then why risk him?" *Lest you knew of your father's plans to ambush me with your clan's fool Horn of Bliss?* Roag glanced at the dog, trying to ignore how his heart twisted to see him sprawled on his side, his legs sticking straight out, his light snores hinting that he was no longer distressed. "You could have been returned to Sway by the morrow's gloaming. Surely, he would have done well enough without you for such a short time."

"Skog goes where I go. It was best to keep him with me."

"Indeed."

"Not for the reason you're thinking."

"What would that be?"

Her chin lifted. "I'd hoped to gain passage to Glasgow. You believe I knew my father intended to handfast us."

"I believe what I see, lady." Roag didn't deny it, welcoming the reminder of her perfidy.

In the chill dark of this room, at such a late hour, her ragged old dog at their feet, and her loveliness limned silver by moonlight, he'd almost felt sympathy for her. He *had* lusted after her.

Now he caught himself.

Her eyes narrowed, sparking like emeralds set afire. "You see what you desire."

"That is so." *Be glad you dinnae ken what that is!*

Roag returned her frown, half inclined to tell her how easily she unleashed his baser urges.

Instead, he rubbed his brow.

His head was beginning to throb—which was a much better annoyance at his temples than elsewhere. "I have men in my crew, lady, who claim to have seen the infamous Blue Men whilst sailing the waters of the Minch near Skye. A few will swear they've spotted the great beastie said to swim in Loch Ness. One is Erse, an Irishman, and he's the worst of the lot, aye telling us that he glimpses faeries dancing in swirls of mist.

"I dinnae hold with such foolery." He let his tone challenge her, knew instinctively that she was keeping something from him. "I trust only in the truth."

"Yet you are here as a liar, pretending to be someone you're not."

"So I am, aye."

"Then you cannot speak of truth."

"Have a care, lass." He stepped closer to her, furious that her words made him feel guilty. For sure, he was here to deceive, but for the most noble reasons and under orders from the highest voice in the land, King Robert himself.

"There are many shades of honesty," he said, struggling to rein in his temper. "How it appears to you depends on the light you're standing in."

She shook her head. "When it applies to you, aye?"

He smiled faintly. "I cannae allow myself to think differently, lass. Matters greater than you or I hang on what I do here."

"What a shame then, that you're so wrong."

Roag scratched his beard, wondering if he was. He hoped not. If so, the maid and her fetching presence would pose all kinds of other problems. The sort he didn't need and would be hard-pressed to ignore.

So he gripped her chin and scowled down at her. "I've warned you no' to rile me. Above all, dinnae forget I'm Donell so long as your kin are yet here. Remember that, and hold your tongue."

"If I don't?" She held his gaze, her own anger shimmering all over her.

"You're a fool." Roag whipped an arm around her, pulling her to him. A mistake he regretted at once, for he could feel the soft fullness of her breasts pressed to his chest, became too aware of her feminine warmth through the wool of his plaid, the thinner linen of his tunic.

"I'm a man of my word, sweet." *How sad that was no longer true.*

He wanted nothing more than to ravish her—and he was of a powerful mind to do so now.

Especially here in the quiet of the moon-washed night, them both naked save for a bit of cloth. By her own father's doing, he had every right to claim her. Even if he wasn't Donell MacDonnell, he was the new Laird of Laddie's Isle. Leastways for so long as his business kept him here.

The MacDonnell's bride, however much he wished otherwise, fell in as part of his mission.

And just now, with her lavender perfume scenting the air, the feel of her pressed against him...

Never had he been so tortured.

Worse, he could tell by looking at her that she wouldn't leave him be this night. The fight stood all over her, the spirit he secretly found so appealing, almost crackling in the scant breath of space between them. He wanted her badly, but he wasn't a man to take a woman against her will. He reviled such men and would never stoop so low. Not even if he desired her so fiercely he could taste his lust on the back of his tongue.

He had to be rid of her.

Send her fleeing back to her bed, hiding her much-too-tempting self beneath the covers.

If she dared come near him again, her sparking eyes and anger-flushed loveliness tempting him, he'd still not touch her. But he would spend the rest of the night rock-hard and miserable.

It wasn't a pleasant notion.

And he could think of only one way to ensure his night's peace.

"I've heard the devil also keeps his word," she taunted then, almost as if she'd guessed his plan. "That doesn't make his evil good. It only proves—"

"There are ways to silence a clacking tongue, sweet." He made no attempt to keep the menace out of his voice. "Dinnae provoke me into—"

"What?" She glared at him. "Kissing me?"

"Damnation!" Roag tightened his arms around her, pulling her even harder against him. He slanted his mouth over hers, kissing her with a fury that shocked him. Hunger such as he'd never known sluiced him as he plundered her lips, devouring her sweetness and drinking her breath, some still coherent corner of his mind warning that he'd rarely done anything more foolish.

She tipped back her head, her lips opening wider, her tongue meeting his. She gripped the back of his head, threading her fingers in his hair, clinging to him as if she enjoyed the kiss—as if she burned for him with the same ferocity.

It wasn't the reaction he'd hoped for.

He'd thought to send her scurrying into the shadows, shocked and furious as she dived beneath her bed covers, never to come near him again.

Instead...

The vixen returned his kiss, her fiery passion sending such intense pleasure through him that he feared he'd spill.

Before he could embarrass himself, he tore away from her, his relief great when he saw the desire in her eyes change into outrage. "That was only a taste, sweetness. If you wish more, a fully intimate sampling offered in full view of your family, then you'll remember my kiss when we go belowstairs in a few hours.

"You'll imagine what would happen if I kissed you elsewhere," he warned, flicking his gaze to the place he meant, despising himself for shocking her.

Disliking himself even more because he would dearly love to give her such kisses!

Instead he leaned in, letting his gaze narrow on hers. "I dinnae like kissing lasses I've nae interest in." *I pray the gods you cannae tell how interested I am in you.*

Feeling more and more like the devil she'd named him, he straightened. "Dinnae force me to do so again. Come the dawn, you'll walk at my side, looking pleased to be there. You'll make nae mention of devils and liars. You—"

"I will curse you to hell!" She hauled back and slapped him, the crack of her hand across his face loud in the tiny room.

Roag didn't care.

Indeed, he welcomed her anger.

Only so would she believe the threats he'd made to her. She'd do as he required of her, and her family would depart in peace, sparing him the annoyance of keeping them all on the isle should she relent and blurt the truth of his name.

So he watched as she finally did as he'd hoped, storming back to her bed.

He waited for a surge of triumph.

It didn't come.

What did was a rise of bile in his throat. His mission here had soured before it'd begun and there was only one way he could think of to regain lost ground.

It wasn't enough that he'd told the lass his name.

If he hoped to sleep of a night, he'd have to reveal his purpose as well.

His honor demanded it.

But only after the departure of her kin.

Chapter Sixteen

❦

Several hours later, Gillian stood fully dressed beside the window of her wee bedchamber and decided the gods were wise to let the day dawn so cold and fog-shrouded. The gloom felt fitting at the hour she must bid farewell to her father and brothers, never knowing if she'd see them again in this life. If her gaze would ever again fall upon her beloved home, the fair and distant Isle of Sway.

What she did see was Roag hefting poor Skog onto his shoulder. Regrettably, his kindness to her dog only reminded her of his promise that he aye kept his word.

And that unsettled her.

No, it terrified her.

Just as he clearly intended to honor his vow to carry Skog up and down the stairs, so would he also slay her kin where they stood if she dared to vex him.

Despite all, she was sorely tempted.

It went against her nature to bow down before criminals—and to her, he was no less villainous.

That he was kind to old dogs meant nothing.

Once, long ago on a wee neighboring island, a half-crazed man had slit the throats of all his four neighbors, claiming their large number ruined the isle's peace.

That man had loved dogs, having over a dozen he doted on.

Roag the Bear had sworn to kill many more men than four. And his potential victims weren't strangers. They were her nearest and dearest kin, blood of her blood.

She took a long, deep breath of the chill sea air, bracing herself to give the performance of a lifetime. To pretend she hadn't just become the handfasted bride of a dead man, but that he'd also taken her innocence, a deed she'd supposedly accepted and enjoyed.

Praise the gods, she'd woken first. It had been no small feat to wash and dress in the dark, and so swiftly as she'd done. But she'd managed. The alternative, tending her ablutions and pulling on her clothes before his wicked eyes, had spurred her on.

He'd taken his time.

She'd positioned herself at the window, keeping her back to the room until he was decent.

Now he was provoking her further, winning Skog's gratitude, and also by pausing at the foot of her bed to retrieve the bloodied roll of bed linen.

She'd hoped he'd forgotten.

"Must you take that belowstairs?" Her cheeks heated as he tucked the sullied cloth beneath his belt.

"Aye, I must." He shifted Skog in his arms, reached to pat the cloth. "Proof that I ravished you."

Gillian leaned toward him. "They'll believe you without seeing a blood-smeared cloth." *With your swagger, no man would dare doubt it.* "It's a barbaric custom."

"And a well-kept one." He opened the door, stepping out onto the landing. "If all such virtue-trophies were laid in a row, there'd be enough to circle this fine realm more times than a man can count."

Aye, a man!

Gillian kept the sentiment to herself and followed him down the winding stair. She didn't have a choice, really. Devilish as he was, if she even hesitated, he'd surely deliver Skog safely to the hall and then return for her, tossing her over his shoulder as he'd done with her dog.

Only he'd use much less care with her.

She frowned and hitched her skirts as they neared the bottom steps. In her wildest dreams, she'd not have been able to imagine such an infuriating man.

He stopped at the base of the stair tower to lower Skog to the floor as gently as if the old dog were made of glass-spun ribbons. Most annoying of all, she could tell he truly cared for Skog's well-being.

And didn't her pet turn adoring, grateful eyes on him?

It was beyond toleration.

Gillian tightened her lips, waiting to see what else he would do. She also needed to steel herself to face her family, to play the role that would save their lives.

She just hoped they still were breathing.

She didn't see them anywhere in the hall and would have been horrified, but not surprised, if Roag the Bear had ordered his men to have done with them as they'd slept.

Squinting to see through the smoke haze that seemed

much thicker now than yestere'en, she felt her nape prickle when she noticed that Roag's men also appeared different.

All big, bearded men with strong faces, some of them—the ones scattered about the hall's perimeter—wore harder expressions. Studying them more closely, she was sure that she caught the glint or bulge of hidden weapons. Swords, dirks, and axes, carefully tucked beneath plaids or cloaks, but noticeable on second glance. Certainly more arms than were needed inside a hall. Especially at a time when men would normally be claiming places at the long rough tables, thinking only to break their fast.

Gillian's heart sank when she spotted two other stony-faced warriors appearing to lean casually against the wall near the tower's main door.

They were perilously close to the many spears and swords propped in a corner of the keep's entry.

"What's the meaning of this?" She turned to Roag, kept her voice low. "Why are some of your men armed like guards? And where is my father? My brothers, and their oarsmen?"

"My men are prepared to act if you forget yourself." He stepped closer, going nose to nose with her, tucking her hair behind an ear as if it was a loving gesture. "'Tis only as a reminder that they're allowing you to see their arms. Your kin will no' notice, as men see only what they expect."

Lowering his hand, he smiled down at her. "Your family are untouched," he said, pitching his voice so that only she could hear him. "They already sit at the high table." He nodded in that direction. "Can you no' see them?"

"No, and I still don't." She frowned, but now understood why she'd missed them.

Even more of Roag's rough-looking warriors stood near the raised dais. Their broad backs hid the high table, as did the combined smoke from the fire and the many wall torches at that end of the hall. A thick haze hung in the air, the smoke almost stinging her eyes. But if she peered around or between the men, she could now see her family. Unless she was mistaken, they were all present.

"Praise be." She pressed a hand to her breast, relief making her almost weak-kneed. "I thought you'd—"

"Killed them in their sleep?" He slanted a glance at her.

"You did say it was possible."

"I dinnae strike any man no' full by his wits and looking me in the eye. My men would tell you the same." He spoke softly, his voice's cold edge chilling her. "Your kin are only at risk if you tell—"

"I won't." She wouldn't.

"Then take my arm," he said, offering it to her. "Come with me into the hall."

"With pleasure." Gillian forced the lie as she hooked her arm through his and he led her forward, straight through his milling phalanx of men. "'Tis a fine morning," she added, even managing to speak lightly should any of his men be particularly long-eared.

It wouldn't surprise her.

He surely had his most vigilant spies trailing them, ready to spring if she made one false move.

So she deigned to disappoint them and turned her brightest smile on Roag, glancing at him with seeming affection.

Some of his men exchanged glances. One or two coughed and looked aside, clearly not knowing what to make of her unexpected fondness for their leader.

A man who was pulling her deeper into the hall, and—she couldn't believe it—who was unfurling the soiled roll of linen and waving it in the air like a banner.

Gillian's smile froze. "You can't do this. Please..."

Beside them, Skog began to bark, his milky gaze on the linen. Either he thought Roag wished to play or he was excited. Perhaps he recalled the banner that always snapped in the wind on Sway's battlements. Skog had enjoyed patrolling her home's ramparts until age made it too difficult for him to climb the tight and winding battlement stair.

"It's a point of pride, lass." Roag leaned in, dropped a kiss on her brow. "The men would demand to see it."

"Your men must know it's not real."

"They know me, so will think it well could be."

She didn't doubt it.

She already knew he was well-lusted. He was also outrageously bold, seeming not to care what society thought of him.

Proving it, he waved the cloth higher, calling out to her father as they neared the dais steps. "MacGuire of Sway, I greet you this fair morn! See here the proof of your daughter's virtue."

A cheer rose above the din of men's talk and Skog's barking. Boisterous shouts and well wishes spread as all present swiveled their heads to watch Roag brandish the cloth. Even his own men played along, those already seated rapping on the long tables with the blunt ends of their eating knives. Others raised balled hands in the

air and stamped their feet. The noise was deafening and
only increased as Gillian's father sprang up and pushed
through the throng, leaving the dais to stride over to them.

"My daughter!" He gripped her hands, beaming.
"How I have waited for this day! To see such a smile on
your face and know you have a man to care for and protect you. One able to keep you happy, always!

"'Tis clear that is so." He turned to Roag, nodding in
satisfaction when he lowered the blood-smeared cloth and
began rolling it up again. "I aye knew you'd be a good
match for my gel. A shame it took so long for you to
return to claim her."

"Indeed." Roag didn't hesitate, his voice sounding so
sincere that Gillian wanted to kick him. "But now I am
here, she is mine, and she shall want for nothing."

He glanced at her and she smiled, hoping her silence
wouldn't annoy him.

If she tried to speak, she'd either scream or cry.

Both possibilities could have dire consequences.

Her grinning sire had no idea of the evil before him.
She knew, and much as it pained her, the love she felt for
her father and her brothers gave her little recourse but to
speed them on their way. They needed to leave before
she became too angry to check her temper. And so that
none of her brothers had time to observe her and her
handfasted husband too closely.

Her father's eyes weren't the best, but her brothers
might notice the distress she was trying so hard not to
show. Their wits were sharp, and that could pose a problem if she weren't careful.

Gowan, especially, knew her better than most. He'd be
quick to sense that all wasn't well.

So she slipped her hands from her father's grasp and stepped closer, cradling his beloved face. "I will miss you so much," she said, pushing the words past the thickness in her throat. "But you must catch the strongest currents, and they will be running now. If you've already eaten, then—"

"You'd have me away so soon?" His smile widened and he flashed it at Roag. "Belike you've already replaced me in her affection, laddie! She wants to be alone with ye."

"I am honored." Roag sounded as if he was, even looking every inch the ensorcelled bridegroom.

Gillian felt ill.

"Wanting you gone doesn't mean I don't love you." She smoothed her fingers through her father's hair, the deep red shade so like her own. "Go swiftly, please."

"You're no' vexed with me?" His face sobered, and a flicker of guilt glimmered in his eyes. "I ken you ne'er suspected I'd hoped our journey here would end in a handfast."

"No, I didn't know." She hadn't. "It scarce matters now and isn't of any import. You chose well years ago, betrothing me to Donell," she added, finding it so hard to speak the name. "He is a good man and treats me well."

Donell is dead and at the bottom of the sea. This man is false, only being nice before you.

The unspoken words danced on her tongue, aching to break free.

She took a deep breath, knew she had to be strong.

"Ours will be a good match. I shouldn't have fashed myself all these years. No doubt I was too young to appreciate him at our betrothal," she reassured him, her insides twisting because Roag had finished rerolling the linen and was handing it to her father.

The two of them were a grand pair, both beaming like longtime friends and allies.

Heat bloomed on her cheeks as her father accepted the cloth and tucked it, most respectfully, beneath his own belt.

It is his blood!

Drawn to fool you, to aid him in his scheme to claim this isle and steal Donell's lairdship.

She tried not to think about what he might yet do to her family. What could happen to her once they'd gone.

Was she the only soul who saw through him?

Apparently so, for her brothers had now joined them and, to a man, they gripped Roag's shoulders briefly, and then gave him a rough but good-natured punch to the arm.

It was a greeting they saved for friends.

Like her father, and even Skog, they were siding with the man they believed her handfasted husband.

Andrew, her youngest brother, proved it by thrusting a horn of warmed mead into the lout's hands. "She's a fine lassie, sir," he offered, looking pleased when Roag drained half the horn. As was custom, Roag returned it to Andrew for him to finish—an exchange of friendship and tribute.

"She's the finest of the fine, I agree." Roag slid his arm around her, pulling her close.

He turned to Gowan, her oldest and favorite brother. "I ken you'll worry about her. Rest assured there is nae need. She will have much to keep her occupied, making this dank, auld tower a home."

On his words, Skog pulled away from them, shuffling a few feet and then dropping onto his bony haunches to stare at nothing. Gillian could hardly bear to watch, his confusion making her heart ache. She glanced at Roag, half expecting him to scoop Skog into his arms again, perhaps taking him back to her chamber. But he only watched the dog, his brows drawing together when Skog gave what could only be called a happy bark and began wagging his tail.

Gillian's ill-ease lessened a bit.

She wasn't ready to lose Skog, and if he stared at nothing, surely such confusion was tempered by his seeming gladness? Dogs on their last legs didn't bark cheerily or wag their tails—leastways, she hoped that was so.

Roag also caught himself, his brief frown gone. He replaced it with a smooth smile as he set a hand on Gowan's shoulder. "I will guard your sister with my life, as will my men." His words rang true, his expression likewise. "She will aye be well-treated."

"See you that she is." Gowan stepped up to her, clutching her tight. When he released her, he kissed her cheek. "Remember what I said, lass. We will no' forget you."

Turning back to Roag, he nodded once. "You have a precious charge, MacDonnell. My family and I shall keep you to your word."

"I ne'er break it." Roag didn't blink.

Gillian tried hard to keep her annoyance from showing.

How skillfully he twisted words, speaking the truth but meaning something else entirely.

He was indeed "guarding" her. And she didn't doubt that his men in the hall had strictest orders to watch her carefully, now and always.

He'd said as much.

Yet her family was falling for his lies. It was beyond

comprehension, but also reassuring, because it meant they'd leave without suspecting him of foul doings. Were that so, they wouldn't leave peaceably.

And as much as it pained her to admit, she knew which side would win in a fight.

"Make haste, for I cannot abide long farewells." She took her father's arm and guided him to the tower's main door. She glanced back at her brothers when they didn't immediately follow. "Come on, away with you all!"

"She speaks true." Roag hurried them forward, his own men parting to free a path through the crowded hall. "A drawn-out leave-taking serves naught. Besides, the tides will be running hard now. You should catch them before they turn."

"So we shall!" Her father flashed another look at her, the brightness of his eyes splitting her heart.

There is more you should catch, she ached to say. But she held her tongue, hoping she'd someday have a better chance to speak the words in her heart.

Time had flown away from her, anyhow.

The morning's fog was still dense, but to the east, a lighter shade of gray marked the horizon, warning that the sun would soon rise. Her family needed to go.

At the door now, Roag took Mungo's hand with both of his own, gripping with obvious enthusiasm. "If we e'er have news that must reach you, be assured it will," he promised, looking every inch the handsome and besotted good-son. "Word will be sent as swiftly as possible."

To Gillian's horror, her father grabbed Roag, hugging him. When he stepped back, his eyes glistened even more and his whiskery cheek was suspiciously damp.

"I'll hold ye to that!" he boomed, regaining a bit of his

dignity by swelling his great, barrel chest. "I did aye look forward to having a grandbaby! The more, the better," he added, turning to Gillian for a final embrace.

"Be quick about it, lassie," he urged, pulling back to give her a broad smile. "Ye ken how much I love the wee ones."

Oh, I do...

She did.

Weren't she and her many brothers a testimony to Mungo MacGuire's belief in having children? Likewise his fervent wish to sire more on his new young wife?

She started to say so, leaving out her feelings about Lady Lorna, but Roag was already ushering him through the tower's great outer door. Her family disappeared down the cliff stair, vanishing one by one into the blowing mist. Then Roag closed the door and slid the heavy drawbar in place. In less than a blink, she was cut off from her departing kin. Locked in a cold, crumbling tower with a man who neither wanted nor needed her.

And for the love of all that was good, she didn't know what to do about it.

About the same time, but in a cold and dark corner of the tower that no one had visited in centuries, another resident of Laddie's Isle strutted to and fro, his thin shoulders straight and his wee chest puffed as never before.

It didn't matter that no one shared his excitement.

Not that anyone could even if they wished.

To his knowledge, no one knew about the hidden place so deep beneath the tower. Half sea cave and half hewn by man, the small round chambers with their low ceilings and black-rocked walls had weathered the isle's storms long before the first stone of the present tower had ever been laid.

An act done to honor him, he knew—for he'd seen the many, many ships drop anchor off the isle's rocky coast, looked on as they'd rowed ashore, each man leaving a stone in his memory. A cairn of caring that had grown into a tower.

How sad that no one kept up the tradition of caring for the structure.

Men are fickle and often fools, easily frightened by what they do not understand.

Fear of him had doomed the tower.

He'd been the cause of its demise, even when it'd been erected to uphold his too-short life.

The world wasn't always fair, he knew.

It was a lesson he'd learned swiftly, simply by observing the folk who passed by, or took time to visit his isle. He didn't think it fine, or just, that men feared him. Truth was that he'd borne much fear himself in the early years.

So he did what he could to spare them other worries.

Didn't he aye warn of danger?

High seas and wicked storms, submerged rocks and wild tides? Those who'd seen him and bided his alerts sailed on to safe harbors, or so he hoped.

As for the others...

He liked to believe they also prevailed, even if they didn't recognize why they might've felt an urge to change course or take extra care when passing the isle.

Even so, it saddened him to be so alone.

Now, this night...

Two new souls on the isle had seen him in the hall!

The old dog, Skog, had looked right at him, barking

happily and even wagging his tail. Seeing the dog's gaze seek and find his had delighted him no end. When the beast had started toward him, his stiff gait only allowing him to come a few paces forward, Hamish's heart had turned over. He'd been torn between great joy that the dog saw, and even liked him and sorrow that his presence might confuse Skog, used as he was to flesh-and-blood men.

Somehow, though, he believed Skog understood such things.

Dogs were much smarter than people, after all.

They ken that a soul is a soul, however solid it does or doesn't appear.

Life goes on, as he now knew.

Skog's acceptance of him set his heart to racing. He was proud to have won the dog's affection.

There was only one disappointment, but even that wasn't too bad.

The man, the leader of the warriors who'd arrived, the one called Roag the Bear, could also see him. That alone added to his excitement. It was rare for more than one person at a time to see him—and he did count Skog as a person.

It just hurt him a bit that the man chose to pretend he wasn't there.

Some folk just didn't want to believe.

Hamish stopped his pacing and sifted up to a narrow ledge carved into the rock wall. It was where he'd slept in the last days of his earth life and he still rested there when the need for a slumber overcame him.

Just now, he stood on the ledge, lifting on his toes to peer through a crack in the wall.

It was his favorite viewing point, sheltered as the chamber was from high winds and lashing seas.

Unfortunately, what he saw troubled him more than ship-sinking weather.

As was the way with bogles, he could do things that no mortal soul could manage. Seeing for great distances and through thick fog was one such feat.

It was how he managed to help as many seamen as he could.

So he wasn't surprised to spot the dark ship racing the tide along the horizon. Rarely had he seen a galley travel at such speed in fog as thick as this morn's. Sadly, his ability to peer into the hearts of men told him that they were evil men. And the wickedness they were about this morn wasn't the first time they'd taken to the seas to spread terror.

A shame he didn't know what that evil was.

He just knew they were bad men.

And, of course, that he needed to alert the new laird of his isle to the danger.

Something told him a lot depended on whether Roag the Bear would believe him.

Worst of all, he suspected the trouble would have something to do with Lady Gillian.

Chapter Seventeen

❧

Roag's fury knew no bounds as he turned away from the closed tower door. He refrained from leaning back against it and heaving a great sigh as he was truly tempted to do. Instead, he ran a hand through his hair and satisfied himself with a single tight breath. And still he wanted to rage and roar.

Seldom had he been so angry.

But he reined in his temper, schooling his features when Gillian went toe to toe with him before he could move away from the just-closed door.

She looked at him through narrowed eyes. "My brothers are excellent seamen. They will be away, far from your reach, before you or any of your henchmen could descend the cliff stair."

"To be sure." *I am more glad to see them go than you, fair lady.*

"I would ask the same courtesy of you—I wish to be alone now," Lady Gillian announced. "To recover from

saying them farewell. And"—her chin came up—"to
have at least a few moments free of your menace.

"If you come after me, I shall forget I am a lady." With
a wave of her hand surely meant to stave off any protest,
she whirled about and strode away, her head high.

Roag watched her go, her anger only worsening his
mood.

His own fury was now seething.

Only he wasn't wroth with her.

His temper was aimed solely at himself. He burned
to release it and there was only one way, as he'd already
decided. She needed to hear the truth, oaths, consequences,
and all else be damned. He'd gladly suffer whatever came
at him.

To that end, he'd even risk riling her further by following
her up the battlement stairs, for that was where she'd gone.
Like as not to try to peer through the morn's fog, catching a
last glimpse of the family she clearly loved so much.

He couldn't imagine such a bond.

Though he did have Fenris brothers he'd walk through
fire for, even facing death for them, if need be. Truth be
told, he'd done the like more than a few times.

And he'd do it again, gladly.

He couldn't stomach her low opinion of him another
bluidy moment.

But when he turned to head after her, two fiercely
frowning friends blocked his path. They were his Erse
helmsman, Conn of the Strong Arm, and Big Hughie
Aleson, one of his most tireless oarsmen and a man who,
despite his great size, fair danced on his feet in a sword
fight, even making his sword sing. These men were the
most trusted of his men, and he loved them like brothers.

Just now they looked ready to kill him.

He knew better than to step around them. If it came to a fight, he'd win.

That wasn't his concern.

It was the knowledge that they were such stubborn loons that, afterward, they'd still follow him wherever he went, even if he'd bloodied them to a pulp.

So he folded his arms and returned their glares, letting them know he wasn't of a mood to be provoked.

Conn didn't care, flicking his gaze over him, shaking his head, disapprovingly. "Run full mad this time, haven't you?"

"Ne'er thought we'd see the day you'd do anything so foolish." Big Hughie stepped aside as another man, one who'd agreed to work the kitchens, hurried by with a large platter of cold venison and two jugs of morning ale.

Roag scowled, ignoring how the tempting aroma of the roasted meat, even sliced cold, wafted behind the man with the tray.

He was ravenous—and not just for the day's first meal.

It was a pitiful state and made it easier to meet his friends' glares with a glower of his own.

He leaned toward them, the back of his neck on fire with annoyance. "What else could I do?"

To their credit, Conn and Big Hughie exchanged glances, their angry faces now looking a bit sheepish.

"I'm no' sure," Conn spoke first, pulling his beard. "I'd have to ponder it."

"Think you I had a chance to do so?" Roag had him there.

"Nae, but—"

"It wasnae right for us to scare the lass." Big Hughie

glanced at several spears propped in the shadows near the door. "Did you see her face when she came in here, saw some of our men bearing hidden arms, enough steel to fight an army of England's heaviest horsemen?

"She believed we'd cut down her kin, she did." Big Hughie's distaste for their deception stood all over him.

None of Roag's men grieved women gladly.

Not at all, if they could help it.

Roag felt the same.

Even so . . .

"It was necessary," he said, the excuse sounding weak even to his own ears.

But his words weren't hollow.

Much as he regretted the morning's charade, the weal of every man, woman, and child in the realm depended on their mission. Their success at ratting out the cravens who were sinking the King's ships, drowning good men, and damaging Scotland's chances of ever again gaining a firm hand on their own crown.

Their work here demanded addressing.

They'd sworn solemn vows.

His anger rising again, this time almost choking him, Roag turned to a crumbling arrow slit and let the cold morning air cool his heated face. He drew a deep breath, wishing that his three favorite Fenris brothers—Sorley the Hawk, Caelan the Fox, and Andrew the Adder—had accompanied him on this foul and benighted mission. Raised court bastards at Stirling Castle, the same as him, growing up in the castle kitchens and stables, they understood him as few other men could, and he loved them fiercely.

Not that he'd ever admit the like.

The truth was the four of them ended up in each other's beards more often than they ever agreed on anything.

But their Fenris work, so oft accomplished together, and always pitting them against great danger and death, had taught him who his true friends were. He valued Conn and Big Hughie almost as much, and he liked and respected the other men with him on this mission. But he missed Sorley, Caelan, and Andrew.

Above all, he hoped they were faring well on their own present assignments. He didn't know where Alex Stewart had sent Caelan and Andrew, though he was sure Sorley had been granted a respite to enjoy a quiet life with his new lady wife, Mirabelle. And to spend time with his newly found father, Archibald MacNab of Duncreag Castle in the Highlands.

Of the four of them, Sorley was the only court bastard to have done so well, winning the love of a beautiful and besotted wife, along with a Highland chieftain sire with a home where he was assured a warm and heartfelt welcome.

Roag frowned and rubbed the back of his neck. He wouldn't want Sorley's fortune even if the gods offered suchlike on a silvered and jeweled platter.

He enjoyed his freedom.

The adventures that kept him journeying about the land, no bonds or ties hampering him as he served the crown, and—it must be said—did as he pleased.

A home and a wife shackled a man.

Already, his wife—better said, his pretend consort—had two of his most-loved men scowling at him.

Worst of all, if he could, he'd glower at himself!

He did close his eyes and press a hand to his brow in a futile attempt to ease his aching head.

It didn't help.

When he looked again, Conn and Big Hughie hadn't taken themselves elsewhere. They still crowded him, their arms crossed and their faces belligerent.

"Bluidy hell!" Roag gave them an equally dark look. "Come in here," he snarled, stepping into a small, round chamber cut into the thickness of the wall beside the door. "I'll no' speak of such matters in the open hall—lest the lass sneak back down the steps to listen from the shadows. She's a clever one."

"She'll no' be coming down anytime soon." Big Hughie dipped his head to step through the low-cut doorway. "Broke her heart to see her family leave, it did."

"Aye," Conn agreed, following him. "She'll be up on the battlements a good while, hoping to catch a glimpse of their galley through the mist. She'll stay at the wall until she's sure their ship has slipped beneath the horizon."

"Is that so?" Roag braced his hands against the cold, rough-stoned wall and lowered his head. Then he raised it as swiftly, whipping about to glare at his sour-faced friends. "You ken women so well, the two of you?"

"Better than you," they answered as one.

His patience gone, Roag hooked his thumbs in his sword belt and decided to remind them of what they'd clearly forgotten, their fool heads having been turned by a bonnie face and a full bosom, the swish and sway of shapely hips. The hint of beguiling lavender that wafted after her wherever she went.

"See here, lads." Roag thrust his own admiration of her charms to the darkest corner of his mind and focused only on the disaster she could so easily call down upon them.

Or could have done had he not taken the measures he had.

"Thon lassie kens my name," he said, amazed his friends could've forgotten so quickly. "She doesnae ken our business, but she is aware that I am no' MacDonnell. What do you think would've happened had she told her father?"

Conn and Big Hughie looked at each other, some of the belligerence fading.

But not so much that they answered him.

So Roag used his most earnest Fenris tone. "If you dinnae ken, or have nae wish to say, take a look at thon sky," he prompted, nodding toward the room's lone arrow slit where nothing could be seen but the day's thick, swirling mist. "When the fog clears, like as no' we'll have a sky of woolly clouds."

Looking back at his friends, he waited to see which one would respond to the coded words.

"Woolly clouds, aye," Conn returned meaningfully. "Today like sheep, tomorrow wolves."

"Humph." Big Hughie gave him another sour look. "She has naught to do with our work here. The lass may be a bit spirited, but I'll no' believe she—"

"I didnae use the code because I suspect she's an English spy." Roag felt frustration clawing at him. "If the Sassenachs are even responsible for sinking the King's ships, much as I believe it is so. Truth is"—he drew a long breath, stunned that his friends couldn't see the danger before them—"I ordered all of you to arm yourselves this morn because she needed to see you that way."

"Aye, and you only upset her," Big Hughie argued.

"The blood drained from her face when she saw us, it

did." Conn shook his head, looking miserable. "I'm no' fond of frightening lassies."

Neither am I, you flat-footed, ring-tailed arse! Roag almost roared the reproof.

Instead, he shoved both hands through his hair. "Only if she believed we'd fall upon her kin would she no' shout my name to them," he explained, sure his men had gone daft for not realizing it.

"So what will you tell her?" Big Hughie posed the question he was dreading.

"The truth." There, he'd said it.

His heart felt lighter and a great weight fell from his shoulders, his relief so boundless the blood rushed in his ears.

"Are ye mad, then?" Conn's eyes rounded, his brows arcing nearly to his hairline.

"Nae, he isnae that." Big Hughie sounded amused, a small smile even quirking his lips. "He's smitten with her, he is."

"I am no'," Roag denied, sure his feelings for her were lust and naught else.

"She's a risk." Conn started pacing in the tiny chamber, once surely a guardroom. "Clever as she seems, it will-nae take long for her to guess why we're here, whate'er you tell her. We should have sent them all sailing the moment the *Valkyrie* rushed ashore. Now that she's here, amongst us—"

"I trust her," Roag asserted, not sure where the words came from.

A tightness in his chest, perhaps. The warmth that wrapped round his heart when she tended her ancient dog or spoke of her family and home. He'd never known such love and caring from anyone, but he'd once desired it. Long ago when he'd been a wee lad, aye trying to hide his resentment and envy of the boys who did have families. In those days, he, too, had yearned for kith and kin, and a home to call his own, and where he belonged.

Lady Gillian had all that—leastways she had before she came to Laddie's Isle.

For the life of him, something deep down in his soul just knew she could be trusted.

He didn't much like her.

She was far too prickly for his taste. Bold and brazen, clever and intelligent, she'd no' be the quiet, docile wife he imagined all men secretly yearned for—aye keeping a home running smoothly, bearing children, and seeing to a man's comforts with a smile and a nod, never arguing or questioning.

Wise men—in his experience—visited willing and eager tavern wenches when certain itches plagued them.

Such women caused no hiccups in a man's life.

Lady Gillian MacGuire would give a husband no peace.

But he did trust her. His gut told him he could and his instinct had yet to err.

"She willnae betray us," he spoke the words aloud, secretly willing it so.

No man was without mistakes and he hoped his belief in her wouldn't turn out to be one of his own greatest gaffes.

If so, it could cost him, and his men, their lives.

Yet...

"She only needs to understand why we're here." He was sure of it, and not just because his honor needed assuaging. "Why I came here pretending to be a dead man."

"So, fine." Big Hughie began pulling on his beard. "You tell her, she's here and would figure it all on her own, anyway. But"—his eyes narrowed on Roag—"what will you do with her when we leave? How will you silence her then?"

"She'll no' say anything." Roag was sure.

"That's no' what he meant," Conn spoke up, glancing from Big Hughie to Roag. "I'm thinking he wanted to hear where you'll be taking her when we're done here."

"Aye." Big Hughie nodded. "Shall we sail a roundabout course, then? Dropping her off at Sway before we head on to the port o' Glasgow and then Stirling?"

Roag hadn't thought that far.

And he didn't want to now.

For some inexplicable reason, the problem annoyed him more than it should. So he did what Conn had done a few moments ago, and started pacing.

And an answer came to him at once.

"We'll find her a husband somewhere in the Highlands," he said, the notion feeling as right as it did wrong. "Women aye love Highland men. Perhaps Alex kens a good man somewhere in his north lands who needs a wife. Or maybe my friend Sorley will ken someone, now that he's wed to a Highland lass and hisself living in the hills."

"Aye, that we could do." Conn and Big Hughie again spoke in unison.

Roag frowned, not caring for how his own plan sounded on their lips.

"Worst case, we can take her to Stirling with us," Big Hughie suggested, nodding vigorously. "There are plenty well-pursed nobles there who'd surely want her."

"She'll no' be going to Stirling." Roag spoke more harshly than he'd intended.

The idea of Lady Gillian on the arm of a strutting, peacock-breasted courtier husband tied his liver in knots.

"We can aye return her to her da," Conn voiced the last matter niggling at the back of Roag's mind. "If he believes you're handfasting her, he'll accept if you claim she didnae please you."

Roag almost choked.

Ye fool! If e'er I lifted her skirts and sank myself inside her, 'tis till the end of all days I'd be keeping her.

Just kissing her has doomed me—already it grieves me to think of letting her go.

Keeping those truths to himself, Roag rolled his shoulders, not liking how tight they felt of a sudden. "She doesnae want to return to the Isle of Sway," he told his friends, perplexed as aye by her wish to journey to Glasgow rather than go home to a family and island she clearly loved so much.

It was a puzzle he intended to solve.

If she would still speak to him after learning that he'd also lied about his threats to her family.

He despised liars.

Something told him she did, too.

If the fates were kind, she'd understand that sometimes love, honor, and loyalty required a slight shading of the truth—for the weal of good men and the safekeeping of kingdoms.

If she didn't...

He'd have to convince her. If it came down to it, he hoped he could.

He didn't want to consider the alternative, and that disturbed him almost more than anything else.

Chapter Eighteen

❧

Gillian knew the moment Roag the Bear approached.

She'd been on the battlements nearly all day and gloaming was nigh, darkness already beginning to cloak the tower and its cliffs. The air was colder and the seas rough, the waves edged with white foam. Yet she'd only left her vantage point once, of necessity. Throughout the day, many men had passed behind her—guardsmen set by her captor to watch the horizon. Men who'd also been ordered to keep an eye on her, she was sure.

Either way, none of them had bothered her.

Their footsteps had come and gone as they'd made their dutiful rounds. Just as the earlier fog had lessened and was beginning to thicken again.

The footfalls coming toward her now weren't Roag's henchmen.

They belonged to him, and no one else.

The fine hairs lifting at her nape said so. As did the

sudden quickening of her pulse, the agitated recognition that sent angry heat to bloom on her cheeks.

She turned and waited for him.

"You're too late if you wished to gloat at my sorrow," she said, her voice as cold as the chill of the blowing mist. "My father's ship is gone from view. My eyes are no longer damp from looking on as she slipped over the horizon."

"You have every right to think the worst of me, lass." He stopped several feet away from her, his tone and the look on his face sending odd shivers up and down her spine.

Something was different about him, and whatever it was made her uncomfortable.

"I didnae come to taunt you," he said, still making no move to step closer. "In truth, I let you be as long as I could, for I knew you'd need time to grieve."

"Indeed." *I do not believe a word.*

"I've seen to Skog." He did take a step forward now, his tone, his expression, like another man entirely. Clasping his hands behind his back, he stared out at the sea and mist, as if he deliberately didn't want to meet her gaze.

She understood—weren't her eyes blazing with disdain?

She hoped so, anyway.

"Skog is not your concern." *He's mine and has only looked on you kindly because he is old and sometimes confused.*

"He is under my roof and so my responsibility," he said, ignoring her reproof. "He's been taken out often enough, and fed as well." He paused, heaved a deep breath. "I just carried him back abovestairs to settle him for the e'en. He has fresh water and a bowl of cold, roasted venison should he be hungry again.

"When I left him, he was asleep." He glanced at her then, his dark eyes seeming to say so much more than his words.

Things that, she was sure, had more to do with the two of them than the welfare of her dog.

"I thank you," she offered, watching him carefully. "For all that you are, I cannot fault you for not caring for animals." *In truth, when I sought my chamber less than an hour ago to see to him myself, I turned back because I heard you in there, speaking to him comfortingly.*

It was a scene she hadn't cared to witness.

Taking sweetmeats from the hand of the devil was never wise.

Even so, she was grateful that Skog's needs had been addressed.

Her own...

She returned her gaze to the sea, drank in chill, briny air; appreciated the whistling of the wind and the crash of waves on the rocks below. Drawing her cloak tighter, she closed her ears to all else, not wanting to hear his deep, richly burred voice, the sudden and unexpected pounding of her heart.

If she kept silent, perhaps he'd go away.

Of course, he didn't.

"I ordered an extra basket of sea coal for your brazier," he said, clearly ignoring her wish to pretend he wasn't there. "The room is too cold for a dog as up in years as Skog."

"It is good of you to think of him, but make no mistake—I'll not be swayed to think kindly of you." She rested her hands on the cold, damp stone of the walling, hoped he'd not dare to touch her. "I am not easily fooled, as you've seen."

"I have nae wish to fool you, lass." His voice was right behind her.

He'd moved, silently and without warning, as was the way with thieves and blackguards.

Gillian stiffened, splayed her fingers across the wall's rough ledge. "If not to ply me with more falsehoods, or gloat over my plight, why are you here?"

"To tell you the truth," he said, his voice deep and gruff.

"I see." She didn't.

She also didn't turn around. "You have yet another name?"

"I have but one and you've heard it."

"You've given me two," she reminded him.

"I am Roag." He stepped around beside her, set his own hands on the walling. "It is my true name."

"So you say." She looked out at the rolling gray vastness of the sea, too aware of his sidelong perusal to risk meeting his gaze. If she glared at him as she wished to do, he might pitch her into the water.

It wouldn't surprise her.

But he sounded so sincere, even troubled. And that unsettled her even more.

He was clearly up to something. Another deception surely meant to get the better of her. Or perhaps he did have a truth to share with her? One that was so unpleasant even he felt guilty telling her. She could only think of one possibility.

She whirled on him. "You have more men than came with you. You've somehow signaled them to chase after my family, sinking their ship and—"

"I dinnae attack innocent men." He scowled at her, his expression darker than ever. "Such cravens—"

"You are the craven!" She lifted her voice above the wind, clutched a hand to the side of her face to keep her hair from whipping across her eyes. "Isn't that what you threatened to do this morn? Fall upon unwary men if I but spoke your name?"

"Aye, so I said."

"You admit it?"

"For sure," he owned. "But they were ne'er in danger. I just would've kept them here, as my guests, had you no' heeded my warning."

"Your guests?" Gillian bristled. "I would say prisoners."

"Howe'er you see it, they'd have been treated well. Supping at my table, sleeping comfortably and warm, and enjoying all freedoms save leaving this isle. They could've sailed away, unscathed, when I leave here."

"Then why keep them at all?"

"I didnae, so it scarce matters."

"It does to me." Gillian lifted her chin. "What you're telling me makes nae sense. If you wouldn't have harmed them, if what you're saying is true—"

"It is, sure as I'm standing here."

"Then why frighten me?" She glanced down at the rocks, the little crescent of the sand and shingle where his ship was now beached. Sea foam shone along the tide line, but it was hard to make out the *Valkyrie*, for the galley was nearly hidden by darkness and mist.

Gillian bit her lip, feeling equally fogged, for she didn't understand his explanations.

"I believed you'd cut down my father and brothers." She turned from the wall, lifting her gaze to his. "Why would you want me to think that?"

"Because you had to," he said, making it sound perfectly reasonable to strike terror into someone's heart.

Which it wasn't and never would be.

Gillian set her hands on her hips. "There can be no reason for what you did."

"Aye, there was." He towered over her, something in his expression making her feel like the guilty one, which was ridiculous. "It was necessary because the alternative was keeping your family here, as I just told you. That needed to be avoided."

Gillian released a deep breath. "Now I understand." *It's as clear as the mist blowing over these battlements.*

"Nae, you dinnae, and that's because it's hard for me to explain." He reached for her hand, tightening his fingers around hers. "I am no' a man of words. I am a fighter, no' a poet. But by all that is holy, I swear it isnae my wont to frighten women and threaten hapless old men who only wish to see a daughter wed."

"Then why did you?"

"Sakes, did I no' just tell you?"

"Not that I heard."

"And you shouldnae." He released her and shoved a hand through his hair. "That's the problem. I risk my death by telling you what I'm about to, but my heart will be lighter. 'Tis a risk I'll take, for I cannae abide deception. Still, there are times when honor demands its use. Especially when doing so serves the greater good."

"Which you do?" She lifted a brow.

"If I do my work well, aye."

She blinked. "Your work?"

"Indeed."

"Is that why you came here, pretending to be Donell?"

He didn't answer at once, his gaze again on the night-darkened sea as if some scaly denizen of the deep would rise and answer her questions for him.

Or perhaps he hoped such a beastie would spirit her away, out of his sight and bother?

That seemed more likely, given the fierce look on his face.

"Aye, that is why I came here as MacDonnell. I did so on highest command and no' to seize the poor dead sod's home." He waited as a gust of stronger wind raced past them. "I shouldnae be telling you any of this."

"Yet you are." She could see his jaw tightening, his struggle to reveal the things he was.

He *was* different now.

She'd been right, and the change was disturbing.

But it wasn't the relief it should have been. Her heart hammered and her mind whirled. She tried to make sense of his explanation, casting aside one thought as soon as it came to her, finding none better.

"Aye, so I am, telling you true. I hope ne'er to regret it." Turning aside, he made a sweeping gesture to encompass the tower and the sea beyond. "There have been attacks on the King's ships and they've increased to an alarming level. Some hold that the English are responsible. Others look to these isles. Such men claim that the Hebridean chieftains are too fond of power and that there's a plot amongst them to regain control of the islands."

"Why shouldn't they?" Gillian felt a need to defend her fellow Islesmen—even if she'd never heard of any such plot.

"I've no' grievance with your chiefly houses"—he leaned in, his eyes narrowing—"so long as they respect the crown's right to sail these waters. Nae man should sink a King's ship. Truth is, nae ship should meet the sea's bottom, no' without due cause."

"I have heard of one such attack." Gillian shivered, remembering. "It was near the wee Isle of Colonsay. Not far from Iona." She rubbed her arms, the night's cold, and the conjured images, chilling her. "But I know nothing of any rebellions. There would be talk, yet there hasn't been."

"Whoe'er is behind the attacks must be stopped." He looked at her, his voice hard now, his eyes glinting in the darkness. "Laddie's Isle is positioned strategically, allowing an excellent viewing field of these waters and the ships plying them. It is in the interest of the realm to have someone here."

Gillian's eyes rounded. "Are you saying the King sent you?"

"I came to observe and, I hope, put an end to the sinking of royal ships." He gave her as direct an answer as she figured he was willing, or able, to do. "To that end, it was necessary to assume the role of this isle's most recent keeper. Once my duties are fulfilled, my men and I will leave. It was ne'er my intent to seize a dead man's holding." He gripped her chin, lifting her face. "For sure, I didnae plan to claim his bride."

"My father gave you no choice." She understood at last.

"So it could be said." He didn't deny it.

Gillian nodded, embarrassment, shame, and annoyance flooding her all at once. The last emotion directed not at Roag, but at her father, however well-meaning his intent.

"I am sorry." She was.

"So am I, lass." He smoothed back her hair, tucking the strands behind her ear. "Most especially because I must keep you here until I leave this isle. Be assured that you shall be treated with all courtesy and that when our work is done, my men and I will see you safely away. Nae harm will come to you. I ask only that you speak to nae one about what I've told you. On that I must have your promise."

"Of course." She nodded as a rather unpleasant feeling took hold of her. She suspected that it sprang from his vow to see her away when he left.

Yet that made no sense.

She'd be glad to see the last of him.

Even if he wasn't the fork-tailed, double-horned devil she'd believed him to be.

In truth, she wished he were.

It was much easier not to fall for a blackguard than a hero.

Sadly, it was too late either way.

Chapter Nineteen

❖

A fortnight later, in Inverness, an ancient royal burgh many miles from Laddie's Isle, two dark-cloaked men made their way along the narrow, rain-slicked alleys that converged on the town's bustling harbor. Shops and alehouses lined the wharves, weathered structures of stone and timber that crouched side by side, vying for trade. Smoke rose from their roofs, its scent blending with the reek of fish, brine, and seaweed. Some of the buildings sagged, as if their great age caused them to fall in on themselves. Their sheer number rivaled the docked ships and even the countless vessels anchored farther from shore in the dark, heaving waters of the Moray Firth.

Alex Stewart, the older of the two, set a hand on his sword as he eyed the traders, seamen, and foreigners who thronged in such plentiful number that the River Ness could hardly be seen behind them.

He flashed a smile, looking round as if the town—rumored the erstwhile seat of Pictish kings—belonged to him.

In truth, many might say that it did.

For sure, those who appreciated breathing would not argue with Alexander Stewart.

Handsome in a fierce, imposing way, he had a shoulder-length mane of auburn hair and sharp blue eyes that missed nothing. Unusually tall and powerfully built, he moved with a sure, purposeful stride that made him stand out against the rabble. And well he should, for he was King Robert III's brother, Lord of Badenoch and Earl of Buchan. Better known as the Wolf, he wore bold Highland raiment and heavy Celtic jewelry of finest make. The silvered flash of his sword, mail, and arm rings warned that he was also a warlord no wise man would dare to counter.

If anyone did, he welcomed such challenges.

Nor did he have qualms about tossing miscreants into the sea after a thrashing. Alex Stewart made his own rules. Any upstart foolish enough to break the King's peace deserved to end as crab fodder.

For good measure, and as a nod to his royal blood, a dozen or more hard-faced, brutish men followed in his wake. Silent and watchful, they deliberately blended into the mass of folk teeming through the harbor alleys. These men were of bullish strength and unforgiving loyalty. For nothing would they disturb the Wolf's course. Should anyone else do so, they'd move in after Alex was done, making certain such fools never bothered the King's brother again, and that their decidedly grizzly end served as a warning to others.

To those he loved, Alex was the best-ever friend.

As an enemy, he was terrifying.

"I love this town," he declared, flashing a broad smile at his companion, a younger man of dark good looks and equally confident stride. "Every time I chance to come here and breathe in the reek of brine, shore mud, and dead fish, I swear I appreciate the peaty moors and pine woods of my wild Highland home all the more! And"—he nudged the younger man with a plaid-draped elbow—"I vow to ne'er again leave my fine, bonnie hills!

"Alas..." He stopped in the road, his gaze on a well-lit, timber-fronted alehouse, still a good distance ahead of them. "Duty demands that we visit the One-Eyed Mermaid. Naught save the need to watch my brother's back would draw me from the warmth and comfort of my own hearth."

"'Tis an odd name." The younger man paused as well, his own eye on the large wooden sign that hung above the inn's door, swinging and creaking in the wind. He was Sorley MacNab, though more often called the Hawk, and one of the Wolf's most trusted men, for he served as a Fenris Guard, a privilege granted to few.

"I hope the food and ale are no' so strange as it's called," he added, sounding doubtful.

"You willnae leave empty-bellied," the Wolf assured him, starting forward again. "The name is no' so common as our friend William Wyldes's Red Lion in Stirling town, for sure." He cast Sorley an amused glance. "There is nae tavern or inn name more rampant in all the realm than the Red Lion. Likewise to the south in England, for their innkeepers are equally fond of the name. Or so it is said, for I have little time or interest in journeying about down there to see if such a claim is true.

"There is a story to the One-Eyed Mermaid's name."

Sorley waited, knowing well that, like all Highlanders, Alex Stewart loved to tell a tale.

"Word is," the Wolf began, "that a previous innkeeper in a century long past had a one-eyed daughter and couldn't find a husband for her." He slowed his pace, speaking as if he'd known the man and sympathized with his plight. "No one rightly kens where this innkeeper hailed from, though many suspect Aberdeen. Truth is, when he arrived in Inverness and took over the alehouse and its rooms, he changed the name to the One-Eyed Mermaid in honor of his poor daughter. He put out word that she wasn't his true blood, but a mermaid he'd found on the beach, saving her from a scaly serpent who'd sought to drag her back into the sea."

"A good legend." Sorley slid the Wolf a smiling glance.

"I tell you true." The Wolf stopped where he was, turned to Sorley in the crowded alley. "Ask Hector Bane, the present ale-keep," he suggested, his tone serious. "All ken the tale hereabouts and nae man who has been long in these parts would dare say that suchlike couldnae happen.

"True, or no', the long-ago innkeeper swore that the mermaid knew of a great treasure and the scaly serpent meant to put out her eyes so that she couldn't lead anyone to the wealth he guarded as his own." He paused, stepping aside as two back-bent women hurried past, the herring-filled creels they shouldered filling the damp air with the reek of fish.

"The innkeeper fought off the serpent, chasing him back into the sea, aye?" Sorley watched the women nip into a small, even darker side alley. When the shadows swallowed them, he turned back to the Wolf. "He spread word that he'd spared the mermaid from losing her sight entirely and that"—his smile now matched Alex's— "with her one remaining eye, she'd still be able to locate the treasure, if a man cared to marry her."

"You have learned our Highland ways well, my friend." Alex looked pleased, and more than a little proud. "That is the tale that was put out, by all accounting. Our storytellers claim the lass wed well and soon bore so many sons that her husband no longer cared about a hidden treasure, or that she lacked one eye. He had sons to man his galleys and work in his shipyard, wealth enough, he believed.

"In gratitude, or perhaps for fear of his deception coming to light, the father kept the inn's name." Alex stopped before the establishment's door, set his hand on the latch. "Now, these long centuries later, legend claims that all who sup, drink, or sleep at the One-Eyed Mermaid shall aye be safe on sea journeys."

"A last blessing from the mermaid?" Sorley guessed.

"So men say." The Wolf glanced at him, not yet opening the door. "Superstitious as Highlanders are and given our reason for being here, we might as well gather in a place known to smile on those who take to the sea. It cannae hurt."

"But the lass wasnae a mermaid."

"Who can say?" The Wolf shrugged, as if Sorley's objection was inconsequential. "Perhaps she was. There is a kernel of truth in every tale, even the most outlandish."

Sorley set his jaw, knowing when not to argue.

There wasn't time anyway, because in that moment, the Wolf pushed the door wide and they entered the inn's

crowded main room, stepping into a swell of noise and
bringing a cold, damp wind with them.

The One-Eyed Mermaid was popular.

Men filled every table and others stood at the long
trestle-bar that ran the length of the room. Fashioned of
hull planks from a long-forgotten ship and topped with
a surface of age-darkened oak, the bar was packed with
men who stood three and four deep, all quaffing or hol-
lering for ale.

Smoke haze and kitchen clatter hung in the air, as did
the smell of peat, ale, fish, and roasted meats, along with
the sharper reek of frying onions. But the stone-flagged
floor was swept clean, and if the whitewashed walls were
a bit smudged from centuries of hearth fires, the tables
that filled the long, narrow room appeared well-scrubbed.
The low ceiling's oak beams glistened blackly, proving the One-Eyed Mermaid was truly as old as legend
claimed.

"Our friends are here." The Wolf started forward,
making his way through the public room to the far end
where three men sat at a corner table near the fire.

A pile of peat bricks glowed on the hearth stones and
the flickering orange-red light shone on the bearded faces
of the rugged, plaid-draped men who now lifted their ale
cups in salute as the pair drew near.

"Ho, Alex, Sorley!" The largest of the Highlanders
stood and came forward to embrace them. Tall, strongly
made, with wild black hair and a full beard, he was clearly
a fighting man. Heavy silver rings lined his arms and
warrior rings glinted in his beard. Mail shone beneath
his plaid, and a silver Thor's hammer amulet hung at his
throat.

He was Grim Mackintosh of Nought territory in the Glen of Many Legends. And although he was a man who'd not die in his bed, and was even known to wield a Nordic war ax with greater skill than any Viking of old, his smoke-gray eyes warmed in welcome and his proud face split in a grin.

" 'Tis good to see you," he greeted them, stepping back after giving each man a quick, crushing hug. "The One-Eyed Mermaid isnae known for festive spreads, but Hector the innkeeper has outdone himself this night. He's served up enough good viands to fill our bellies and warm us."

Taking their arms, he led them to the corner table, already set with platters of smoked herring, sliced, roasted mutton, a large assortment of cheeses, and baskets of fresh-baked bread. "There's plenty of ale," he added, nodding to a serving girl as she hurried past, carrying a tray stacked with empty bowls. "Ellice kens to bring fresh jugs as soon as you're settled."

At the table, Caelan the Fox half-stood, his dark auburn hair gleaming in the light of a wall sconce. "Praise be, you're here—we didnae want to eat without you and my stomach's growling."

"I can vouch for that!" Andrew the Adder slid him a mock-sour glance as he, too, pushed briefly to his feet in greeting. Dark as Sorley and Grim, he was also a Fenris. Only Grim was a nonbrother of the secret order, although he was trusted by all, as witnessed by his presence.

"If you hadn't arrived soon, I'd have changed seats," Andrew added, lowering himself back onto his chair just as the serving wench, Ellice, plunked down two large jugs of frothy heather ale before hastening away to clear another table.

"I swear thon lassie thinks the belly rumbles were mine!" Andrew grinned, already pouring himself a brimming cup of ale, which he tossed down in one swig. "Why else would she cast moon eyes at Caelan when I was sitting right next to the flat-footed, cross-grained lout?"

"Why, indeed?" Sorley and the Wolf exchanged glances, both claiming their own places.

"Truth is it's a wild night." The Wolf stretched his long legs to the fire, likewise helping himself to a cup of ale. He sipped slowly, sent a meaningful glance at the inn's diamond-cut windows where candlelight glistened against the darkness of the thin glass panes.

"There's a fine north wind blowing," he said easily, using the code phrase to warn the others that Fenris matters would now be discussed. As aye, in low, casual tones and secret words so none of the other patrons might guess that anything but the night's rainy gloom concerned them. "Thon wind has been blowing awhile," he added, refilling his cup.

"So it seems." Grim lifted his own ale, nodding almost imperceptibly as he gave the correct response.

His assurance that, as a Fenris confidant, he understood the gravity of their meeting—a gathering held largely because of tidings he'd gleaned on a recent sea voyage from Ireland, where he'd visited the in-laws of his Irish wife, Lady Breena.

"Aye, 'tis a foul wind, by its howl," Sorley agreed, foregoing ale to pile his plate with cold sliced mutton.

"It will worsen before the night is o'er." The Wolf kept his relaxed pose, his legs now crossed at the ankles, his ale cup in his hand. "Such weather will be fierce out in the Isles. Huge seas and black winds are no' good for trade. I wouldnae wish to be plying those waters in such conditions, no' when the currents run so fiercely a ship could tip o'er and sink to the bottom of the sea before a man could blink."

"I journeyed back through such weather." Grim set down his ale, dragged the back of his hand over his beard. "Ne'er have I seen such rough waves."

"How rough?" Caelan and Andrew spoke as one, their gazes flicking briefly to the Wolf before they glanced again at the big, ring-bearded Highlander from Nought.

Grim leaned forward, fixing them with his piercing gray gaze. "So fearsome that the merchant ship I journeyed on lost half her goods when we were hit by steep seas in the dead of night during one of the worst storms. Indeed"—he sat back, his hands flat on the table—"when we made land, we learned of another trader, sailing up near the Isle of Lewis, that sank that night."

Sorley frowned. "So far north as Lewis?"

The Wolf's face hardened—a sign to those who knew that talk wasn't of a trading ship, but a crown vessel carrying men loved and valued by the King.

"Aye, Lewis is what we were told." Grim looked round at all the men, his smoke-gray eyes earnest. "The ship went down with priceless goods onboard. Talk was of a hull filled with Frankish oils and wine, finest leather from Spain, and sack upon sack of rare spices from even farther afield.

"An irreplaceable cargo, lost to the brine." He drew a deep breath, his gaze flicking to Alex Stewart.

"So it was, indeed." The Wolf drew a dirk from his belt, turning the blade in the table's candlelight. "My brother was grieved to hear of such riches disappearing into the sea, gone before they could reach their destination."

" 'Tis a sore loss." Hector Bane, the innkeeper stepped out of the throng, rapping thrice on the table's aged, scarred wood, then once again after a pause.

Another coded greeting, his promise that no men possessing long ears or lingering eyes lurked anywhere near the corner nook where the Fenris men had gathered.

Tall, and with a seaman's weathered face, he wore a long leather apron and had braided his thick rust-gray hair in a thick plait that hung down his back, reaching near to his waist. His eyes were the same color as the ale he served, and lined at the edges as if he was fond of smiling, or had spent years squinting into the sun.

"I'm suffering a loss myself," he declared, setting his hands on his hips. "Though naught so troubling as ships sinking into the sea. My eldest lad, Dougie, has taken himself south to run a friend's inn down Stirling way. The innkeeper is gone to visit his brother who's wed some lass out on a Godforsaken rock of an isle in the Hebrides." He leaned in, lowering his voice, his gaze moving from one Fenris man to the next, significantly.

So tellingly that no one at the table misunderstood.

Fenris friend William Wyldes, who owned and ran Stirling's Red Lion Inn, was on his way—or soon would be—to join Roag the Bear on Laddie's Isle.

Wyldes didn't have a brother.

But he looked on Roag, Sorley, Caelan, and Andrew as the family he never had.

And only one of them was currently keeping himself on a wee spit of rock in the Western Isles.

Roag.

The Wolf leaned forward, his eyes confirming it. "'Tis no small thing when a man takes a bride." He lifted his ale cup, saluting the others, a smile quirking his lips at their astonishment. "Sometimes we're surprised to hear the like, but it doesnae mean the match isnae a guid one.

"Indeed"—his smile broadened—"his friends ought to be there to celebrate with him, leastways a few of them."

"My wife, Lady Mirabelle, is in a delicate way." Sorley put down the forkful of mutton he'd been about to eat. "We're still staying beneath her father's roof at Clan MacLaren's Knocking Tower. Our own home is close by, but no' even halfway built.

"She wasnae pleased I left her long enough to journey here." He glanced at the door, as if he should be heading back to her now. When he turned again to the table, a frown drew his brows together. "I dinnae want her fashing, given that she's—"

"She'll have you back anon, my friend." Alex slung an arm around his shoulders. "My Mariota has given me more sons than I can rightly count, but I worried each time she quickened with a new one! Nae man here would expect you to hie yourself off into the wilds of the Hebridean Sea. No' now, of all times."

He spoke as if it was settled, then withdrew his arm and looked to Caelan and Andrew. "I'd rather send the errant bridegroom a shipload of gifts to lend comfort to his new home. Truth is, that tower is little more than a cold and windy heap of salt-crusted stones. He shall have a well-made bed and proper sheeting, a richly carved laird's chair to suit his new station, and"—he grinned—"perhaps a trusted friend to cook for him so long as he's stuck on such a bleak, sea-washed isle?"

"A cook?" Andrew glanced at Sorley, and then Caelan. All three men frowned.

"'Tis true we were raised in Stirling Castle's kitchens," Sorley spoke for them all. "But we spent our youth chasing after serving lassies and laundresses, no' stirring cook pots."

"That I ken!" The Wolf didn't look concerned. "I had another, much more skilled spoon-stirrer in mind," he added, smiling again.

Hector Bane nodded once, his own expression lightening. "I have heard that a fast-running galley called the *Sea Star* is anchored off the headland no' too far from the town's usual moorings." He leaned toward the table, lowering his voice. "It could be that a certain Stirling innkeeper didnae journey directly into the wild, wind-whipped waters of the Hebrides."

He slid a look at the Wolf. "Chances are he's been using the dark o' the last moon to gather and load gifts onto the *Sea Star.*"

"The sort that went down near Lewis?" Caelan lifted his voice a little, for it was raining steadily now, a downpour that beat hard against the windows.

"Supplies any new bridegroom would welcome." Hector straightened, smoothed down his leather apron.

"Cargo needed in waters where such valuable goods have already been lost." Sorley spoke what all the men were thinking.

William Wyldes.

Before he became an innkeeper, William was a warrior of great renown. Even now, few men were better in a fight, no matter the weapon. He could throw a spear faster, farther, and with more accuracy than the King's own spearmen. If he chose to use his bare hands, wise foes would run.

Outside the storm worsened and a gust of damp wind swept down the chimney, causing the peats to spit and hiss, and a plume of smoke and ash to billow into the room. Hector cursed and wheeled about to tend the mess, while Ellice and another serving lass hurried over to resettle the patrons whose table and meals were now ruined.

The ruckus also gave the Wolf and his friends a bit of much-appreciated privacy, with their nearest neighbors now scurrying to another table, well out of earshot.

Andrew leaned forward, pretending to flick invisible ash from the rough-planked table. "I dinnae care for this," he said, his voice low. "If William is aboard the *Sea Star*, the trouble in the Hebrides is a greater broil than we'd heard."

Sipping his ale, the Wolf nodded slowly. "That is so."

The other four waited, ignoring the chaos in the other corner, the howling wind that rattled the window shutters. Somewhere in the night, a dog barked furiously, but they paid him no heed either, their entire focus on the King's brother, Alex Stewart.

Head of Fenris, and—so many believed—the unspoken ruler of the land.

"We suspect more than one ship is behind these attacks," he said now, the fierceness of his expression proving that kingly blood brought more than silver, women, and song, as many less-privileged men liked to claim. "Lewis is too far removed from the other sinkings for us to think otherwise. Especially"—his voice hardened—"as the Lewis attack happened about the same time as the most recent incident no' far from Laddie's Isle."

"No ship can be in two such distant places at once," Grim spoke in a calm, easy voice, although anyone who knew him would see his anger welling.

Like Alex, Grim was fiercely loyal to Scotland. Any threat to the realm, or her King and those who served the crown, ignited a red rage inside him.

"Well observed, my friend." Alex nodded to Grim.

"So you're sending reinforcements." Andrew took a long sip of his ale and then lifted the cup toward the black, rain-streaked windows. "Men already gathered this night."

"All has been readied, aye," Alex added, keeping his voice pitched so that no one outside their table could hear. "Hector Bane's son will do fine running William's Red Lion. Wyldes will lose nae trade and we shall have our master spearman and a score of expert bowmen joining Roag on his isle."

He smiled then, looking pleased. "You didnae think the *Sea Star*'s oarsmen are just that, did you? They are handpicked from my own best archers—should there be a need for fire arrows aimed at any attacking ship."

"And now you'll have a second ship of your own in place on Laddie's Isle." Caelan returned his smile.

The Wolf reached for one of the ale jugs, topping off each man's cup. "I also want you to keep an eye on Roag's unexpected bride. By all accounting, she's a quick-tempered lass, known as the Spitfire of the Isles."

Grim pulled on his beard, making his silver beard rings clack together. "From what I heard she's an inconvenience, but no threat. She is Lady Gillian MacGuire, daughter of the laird of that clan and keeper of the Isle of Sway.

"Word was, she was betrothed to Donell MacDonnell," he explained, glancing at the other table where Hector stood ordering about the kitchen lads who rushed back and forth with cleaning rags, brooms, and trays of ruined, soot-covered food. "Our friend will have had no choice but to wed her.

"A handfast, if the tales were true." A crease appeared between his brows and he returned his attention to the men at the table. He looked at Alex, lifted a hand as if to give credence to his words. "I cannae believe she is more than a complication."

If he expected Alex Stewart to agree, the King's brother disappointed him. "There was a witness to a recent attack," he said, his smile gone. "The man lived long enough to tell a harrowing tale. His ship's attackers had a woman on board—a pitiful creature they'd tied to the rail. Her cries rang out across the water, drawing my brother's men's galley." He leaned forward, his handsome face now hard, his blue eyes like shards of ice. "The poor lass couldnae be saved and the fates only know what became of her.

"I'll no' have such a tragedy befall Lady Gillian." He sat back, slapped the table with the flat of his hand. "Her father is a scoundrel, but he's well-loved in the Isles. His daughter's peppered tongue is said to ignite tempers, her spirit untamed and wild enough for her to run headlong into danger."

"You want her safe." Sorley spoke low, applying himself to the sliced, roasted mutton before him as if his meal and naught else concerned him.

Hector and his kitchen lads had now cleaned the mess of scattered soot and ash from the floor and neighboring table, and the din from the ruckus was lessening.

Swivel-necked patrons—if any chanced to glance at the Fenris table, would see only men enjoying supper.

"I do, aye." Alex began piling herring onto his plate. "I want her safe at any cost. I cannae stomach harm coming to a woman. But"—his voice took on a steely edge again—"I also want her kept quiet. She's said to be clever. Like as no', she'll ken that our lad isnae MacDonnell. She might raise a fuss, attracting attention we dinnae need on that isle just now."

"The Bear would be furious." Caelan waited as another strong wind lashed at the window behind him. "He cannae bide no' having all go his way when he's out and about."

The other men nodded agreement.

They knew better than to say aloud that "out and about" referred to Roag's Fenris mission.

It was enough that they knew.

"You'll have one other task when you reach thon isle." The Wolf looked past Grim and Sorley to pin his gaze on Caelan and Andrew. "You will stay the night here, in the One-Eyed Mermaid. A room has been secured—two small beds, dry, and a lit brazier to warm you. On the morrow, you'll sleep late and then claim ale-heads when you come belowstairs.

"Before you reach the *Sea Star*, Grim and Sorley will have been there, delivering a great carved bed you'll present to *Donell* and his bride as a handfasting gift."

"They're no' sailing with us?' Andrew flashed a look at Grim and Sorley.

"Sorley would worry himself too much o'er the state of his wife's thickening waist to be much use to you," the

Wolf declared, his smile back again. "Grim is but a friend, as well you ken. His lady wife, too, awaits his return to Duncreag Castle where he still mans the MacNab garrison. Archie MacNab is an older chieftain and frail. He depends on Grim.

"His task was a favor, nae more," he added, glancing at the big Highlander with appreciation. "He let us know what he'd heard about our lad, *Donell*, on his journey home from Ireland no' too long ago.

"Your duty, among the others already agreed upon, is to deliver a bed to Laddie's Isle." The Wolf sat back, looking at them all as if no further words were needed.

But the corner of his lips quirked and a gleam lit his eyes, hinting at more.

"There's something else about the bed." Caelan didn't return his smile.

The Wolf only leaned back, tipped his ale cup to his lips. "I do naught without reason," he finally said, setting down the empty cup.

"I ken what's wrong with the bed," Andrew declared. "It'll be dismantled. We'll need forever to reassemble it."

"So I suspect." The Wolf agreed.

"What else?" Caelan persisted.

Alex Stewart drew a long, deep breath and glanced out over the smoke-hazed public room. "There is only one way to tame a prickly, high-spirited lassie. I'll no' have a temper fit risking a mission. Nor will I have the Bear worsen it by riling her. Truth is he can be kept in good fettle by the same method."

"The bed." Andrew and Caelan spoke as one.

"Indeed," the Wolf sounded pleased. "Your task requires more than delivering and assembling the bed.

You must encourage our lad to use it. Better yet, to enjoy it."

"With Lady Gillian?" Andrew and Caelan again responded in chorus.

"With his handfasted bride," Alex Stewart amended. "Their joinings will be right and proper, blessed by my own good will! See you to it, aye?"

Chapter Twenty

❦

No harm will come to you.

Roag the Bear's vow circled in Gillian's mind, ruining her morning even asit had stolen her sleep. *When my work is done, I will see you safely away,* his other words followed as quickly, spoiling her mood and making her temper rise.

It was a curious thing, his promises to see to her well-being having the opposite effect, annoying her beyond reason.

Yet they did, and they had done ever since he'd voiced them, well over a sennight ago.

Seven full days and nights in which her only true peace had been enjoyed in this cold, wee chamber, sequestered away from him, and with Skog the sole witness to her misery.

"Do you think it is my pride?" She glanced at her dog as she dressed, not really expecting an answer because the aged beast yet slept, his snores filling the room. "Can a man kiss a woman so hungrily and then...

"Feel nothing?" The very notion made her want to go toe to toe with him, possibly even kick him in the shin. "He might serve our good Scottish King, but he is heartless."

Frowning, she blinked back the heat that suddenly pricked the backs of her eyes.

Her great hulking captor didn't deserve her tears.

So she dashed at her cheek, determined not to let them fall. "He is a beast," she announced, glancing again at her pet. "We will be better off without him."

If Skog agreed, he gave no sign.

Not wanting to bother him further, Gillian returned to her lumpy little bed and pulled off one of the older, more worn covers. Carefully, she lowered its softness over Skog, knowing he loved sleeping away the morning hours, and wanting him to be as warm and comfortable as possible.

She didn't care if she froze.

Far from it, she welcomed the shivers that raised gooseflesh on her skin; the chill, damp air that was almost icy enough to make her teeth chatter. Better to stamp about, rubbing her hands and swirling extra shawls about her shoulders, than to spend another moment huddled beneath the bed covers, everything she disliked about Roag coiling tight in the pit of her stomach, occupying her attention, slowly but surely driving her to madness.

But how could he not irritate her?

Aside from keeping her here against her will, he was simply too big, too rugged, his dark good looks much too distracting. His swagger was an affront. She didn't want to consider the boldness of his grin, especially not how a dimple flashed in his cheek each time he employed it. As for his kindness to Skog, the good-natured way he dealt with his men, most notably in moments when he wasn't aware that she was watching him, how they appeared to not just respect and obey him, but to genuinely like him...

None of that mattered.

It certainly didn't concern her.

Nor would she be grateful that he'd somehow gleaned that she had a fondness for honeyed bannocks, and that he'd ordered his cook to make certain they were served in plenty at mealtimes, and always placed near to her.

If his hard-muscled thigh happened to bump against hers under the high table at such meals, there was no reason under the heavens for her to relive the rush of tingles that raced across her skin each time such an accidental touch happened.

So why did such rememberings make her heart beat faster, setting her pulse to racing and warming her cheeks?

Gillian released an agitated breath.

Had she lost her wits entirely?

Hoping not, she went to the window, needing air. But before she could draw a deep, much-needed breath, she spied a ship. At this early hour, the sea and sky were still a seemingly merged blend of gray and black, yet there could be no mistaking that a galley rode the dark waves. Or that its path would bring it temptingly close to Laddie's Isle, possibly offering her an escape.

Gillian pressed her fists against her breast, drew a tight breath, her mind racing.

She fixed her gaze on the ship, squinting to see better in the watery light. At a distance, she couldn't tell for certain, but she'd almost bet the galley was a MacDonald vessel. The Lords of the Isles plied these waters more frequently than any other, and she knew most of their ships well enough to trust that this was one of them. Good men, and friends of her clan, they'd surely help her if she could but catch their attention as they neared.

She cast a glance at the door.

But she dismissed that route as quickly as the notion had come to her.

She couldn't go belowstairs, couldn't cross the hall to leave the keep. Roag's men slept there, and many would be waking now, taking their places at the tables to break the night's fast. They'd question her purpose, preventing her from leaving the tower, thwarting her chances of signaling the ship.

Yet even if she caught their eye from her window, and they came closer, she'd have to shout to speak with them, her raised voice heard by the men in the hall.

She had only one chance.

The drop from her window to the grassy ledge of the promontory wasn't daunting. If she jumped and landed well, she could sneak down the cliff path to the tiny cove beneath her bedchamber. She knew such a path existed because she'd seen it when she and her family had sailed beneath the tower, on their way to the far side of the isle and the more accessible landing beach they'd used. Her father had pointed to the track, claiming only a goat could scale it.

She didn't care.

If she could hail the MacDonalds and they came for her, two of them could surely make a swift ascent, fetching Skog and retrieving her pouch of Viking treasure.

She'd give them a small share for their trouble.

Thereafter...

She'd worry about that once she was safe.

Determined not to miss what might be her only chance, she threw one last glance at Skog, then hitched up her skirts and scrambled over the window ledge, dropping lightly to her feet only a short distance below. Desperation lent her speed and she followed the cliff path with equal ease, reaching the tiny, steep-sided cover even faster than she'd dared to hope.

The MacDonald galley was still bearing down on the island.

But with the time they were making, the ship would soon slip around the shoulder of the headland, vanishing from view if they didn't soon see her.

Not knowing what else to do, she crept out onto the tidal rocks, whipping her shawl from her shoulders as she went. At the end of the rocks, she thrust her arm high above her head, waving the shawl in the air, letting it unfurl like a banner.

She could only hope the ship's crew would see her.

And they did, apparently, slewing the galley her way in a great fanning burst of spray. In a beat, the ship shot forward, oars flashing as it came straight toward her.

"Praise the gods," she breathed, her heart thundering.

But then the ship veered round in the other direction, quickly disappearing into the thick sea mist that seemed to sweep in out of nowhere.

"No!" Gillian stared after the galley, stunned disbelief slamming into her. Grabbing her shawl with both hands now, she swung it back and forth in the wind, trying in vain to hold the crew's attention, to draw them back.

"Please," she cried, knowing no one heard her. "Don't go! Please..."

But only the wind answered, rushing now with increased ferocity. Great gales howled past her, sending cold waves to smack into her and sweep her feet out from under her, knocking her to her knees. Pain shot through her and the world tilted, turning into a strange and dazzling blaze of black and silver.

Then even that was gone, leaving only the cold.

"By the love of Thor, we've lost them!"

Roag stood on the *Valkyrie*'s high prow platform, swearing as he stared into the near impenetrable mist that had swept up out of nowhere. "We were almost upon the bastards!" Drenched and cold, he felt a red haze of anger such as he'd rarely known. They'd been so close to catching the other galley—a many-oared warship disguised as a vessel of the Hebrides' own Lords of the Isles, the MacDonalds. Leastways, he and his men suspected that was so.

Why else would the crew have thrown shields over the dragon ship's sides as soon as they'd spotted the *Valkyrie*? Why yank off their plaids to reveal mailed chests and the glint of so much steel hung about them? And there could only be one reason men had raced to fasten a ramming spear to the prow.

They were up to no good.

And now they were gone.

Furious, Roag shouted to his oarsmen, "Veer about! We're away back to the isle!"

Any other time, he'd have smiled, exhilarated as Conn used the long steering-oar to whip the galley round, Roag himself clashing an expert rhythm on the ship's great gong, and his men obliging at speed, sending up a plume of spray as they lashed down with the strakes, slewing the *Valkyrie* back toward Laddie's Isle and the landing beach they'd left hours before.

Were he alone, he'd race on, chasing the fiends on the other ship until he'd run them into hell.

But he wouldn't risk his friends.

Speeding through such thick mist, across waters filled with reefs, skerries, and submerged tidal rocks, was nothing if not mad. Indeed, it was murderous.

And he wasn't that crazed, or desperate.

"We'll have another chance at them," Big Hughie called from one of the front oar banks, speaking Roag's mind. "Now we ken how they're moving about so easily—guising themselves as MacDonalds!"

Roag frowned, set a hand on his sword hilt. "Did you see the black sail?" He flashed at look over his shoulder, his gaze flashing along the rows of straining oarsmen. "Tell me my eyes didnae deceive me. Did the bastards lower the MacDonalds' raven-painted sail at our approach, raising a black one in its stead?"

"Aye, they did," his men chorused, lifting their voices above the wind, the lashing of their oars.

"Could be they've stolen a MacDonald dragon ship." Roag thought it likely.

"Or they're changing their ship—or ships—to suit them," Conn called from his place at the steering oar. "Mayhap they have more than one ship?"

"We'll soon ken, I vow," Roag swore, anger still beating inside him. "A shame we dinnae have a second galley. We'll have to sharpen our lookouts, watch for a friendly craft we can approach and engage, send a few men to Islay to speak with the MacDonalds, to find out if they're missing a dragon ship."

"I doubt they are," one of the oarsmen countered. "The Lords of the Isles are too mighty. Stealing one of their warships would bring down the wrath of all the Hebrides on the thieving bastards."

"Aye," Conn lifted his voice again. "I'm thinking they dress the damned ship differently each time they sail out."

"Like as no' that is so." Roag felt the same.

So he nodded sharply, turning back to frown ahead, into the whirling mist.

There was something odd about it, he was sure.

The shiver that swept down his spine agreed.

It'd been a cold, clear night when they'd set out on patrol. And not too long ago, the first gray light of the dawn had picked out the horizon, the sun's red edge not hidden by a wisp of fog. Yet even as they'd closed in on the dragon ship, the world had darkened, the half-risen sun blacked out as if it'd never been, their enemy victorious, speeding away unscathed.

It was almost as if the damned mist had aided them.

As if the gods themselves had interceded so that the *Valkyrie* couldn't give chase.

Chapter Twenty-One

✦

Roag heard Skog's howls as he strode across Laddie's Isle's landing beach and made for the cliff path to his keep. Heavy mist still swirled everywhere, but the fog did nothing to dampen the dog's cries. Indeed, the wails only grew louder the higher he climbed. When he reached the tower and threw open the door to the hall, he wondered that his ears didn't split.

He suspected the dog was suffering another of his fearful dreams.

A bad one, by the sound of it.

Frowning, Roag strode deeper into the hall, glancing about at the few men who'd remained on guard at the tower—the ones who hadn't sailed out with him on the *Valkyrie* in the cold, dark hours before daybreak. Not a one of them appeared concerned—or disturbed—by the old dog's wailing.

"Have you lost your hearing, men?" Roag drew up near the hearth and thrust his hands toward the flames, grateful that some good soul had tended the fire. "By the gods! Do the lot of you have bog cotton in your ears, or what?"

"He hasnae been at it long," one of the men hollered, lifting his voice above Skog's howls.

"He'll stop soon, he will," another agreed, then tossed down the contents of an ale cup before dragging his sleeve across his bearded chin. "Hasn't his mistress told us that he aye sleeps late and then grumbles on waking, if his dish isnae filled fast enough? The lady isnae yet—"

"She's still abed?" Roag glanced at the nearest window. Even fog-shrouded, the morn was clearly under way, the darkness edged by a much lighter gray. He could also hear the sea crashing against the rocks and for reasons he couldn't explain, ill-ease coiled in his chest and his gaze went to the shadowed stair tower across the hall. "She's no' yet come belowstairs?"

The man shook his head, happily eating a bannock.

"No' that I've seen," another spoke up, setting down his ale cup. "Brodie"—he jerked his head to a man at the end of the table—"went up to look in on her a while ago, but she was still asleep. She didnae answer his knocking, so he let her be."

"Brodie!" Roag was at the man's shoulder in three long strides. "Was her dog howling then?"

Brodie glanced up at him, wiped his mouth. "Nae, the room was silent. Saving the beast's snores—heard them through the door, I did. So I left."

Roag nodded, the chill inside him worsening, his man's words ringing in his head like hammer blows. He lifted a hand and rubbed the back of his neck, looked again across the smoke-hazed hall to the arch of the stair tower.

Something wasn't right.

Then he knew, remembering Lady Gillian's own words...

He whines and howls if I am away too long.

"By all Thor's fury!" he roared, racing across the hall, dread filling him. Behind him, he could hear his men scraping back trestle benches, leaping to their feet to chase after him. He paid them no heed, almost flying up the few steps to Lady Gillian's bedchamber. Throwing the door wide, he burst inside.

Skog stood on his hind legs at the window, his entire body shaking as he strained to scrabble up and over the broad stone ledge. The dog's barks were hoarse, his howls pitched with terror.

It was clear to see why.

Lady Gillian was gone.

And as Roag ran to the window, he hoped to all the gods he wouldn't see her broken body on the rocks below. Blessedly, he didn't, for mist still clouded the air, blurring the view. But the roar of the sea was loud and its thunder put fear in his soul. Heart pounding, he threw off his plaid, barely noticed two of his men rushing at him to help yank his mail shirt over his head. He unbuckled his sword belt faster than he'd ever done in his life, tossing belt and blade onto the floor. Then he did the only thing he could...

He vaulted over the window ledge, praying he wasn't too late.

The world shook beneath Gillian, the very air quaking around her. And the great shuddering had nothing to do with the icy waves that kept slamming into her. Someone was running along the narrow strip of shore, coming fast, and pounding toward her, yelling her name as he raced ever nearer. Relief swept her as she heard his calls, recognized his voice.

He was Roag the Bear.

And she wasn't going to die here on the rocks, trapped by her skirts and her injured ankle, drowning when the tide rose.

She tried to twist around to face him, but she couldn't. Nor could she answer his shouts, for her teeth chattered too much, making it impossible to form words.

But none of that mattered now.

He was suddenly before her, plunging into the surf, his expression wild as he dropped to his knees on the rocks and reached for her, gripping her by the shoulders.

"By all the living gods!" he roared, staring at her. "Have you lost your wits?"

"A ship..." She couldn't finish, shivering as she was. "MacDonalds," she tried again, pushing the words past her trembling lips. "I thought—"

"I ken what you thought—and be glad you're no' with them." He was scowling at the sodden mess of her gown, pulling a dirk from his boot and cutting away the material, freeing her from the rocks and tangle of trapped driftwood. "Thon men were no' MacDonalds, lass." He glanced at her as he worked to free her. "They were up to nae good, whoe'er they were. We were after them in the *Valkyrie*, but had to give up the chase when the fog rolled in. Forget them, they dinnae concern you.

"Tell me if you're hurt." He threw a ruined clump of cloth into the sea, his gaze flicking over her as he plied his dirk to the last of the material trapping her. "I need to know before I lift you. Have the rocks cut you?"

"No, I don't think so." She shook her head, sure she'd only been bruised. "But my ankle..." She glanced at the pile of half-submerged driftwood lodged between the tidal rocks. "It's caught."

"No' for long, sweet," he promised, following her gaze. "Hold still if you can. Dinnae move your leg until I've seen it," he warned, turning from her to start pulling the waterlogged wood from between the jagged black rocks.

Gillian watched him, sure he could never look more furious.

His face was almost as dark as the rocks, his black brows slashed down in an angry line as he tugged and prodded at the trapped wood, muttering oaths as he worked, freeing one piece of driftwood after the other, tossing each one into the sea just as he'd thrown aside her cut-away skirts. That her legs were now all but fully bared scarce mattered. She hardly felt them for the cold— and she didn't feel her right foot at all, a much greater worry.

Then his big strong hands were on her calf, moving with astonishing gentleness downward to probe and encircle her ankle. She only knew because she saw. And for some reason, the great care he took with her was more troubling than any injury.

"I dinnae think it's broken," he said, flashing a look at her. "But it'll be swelling badly soon. There are some scrapes and cuts that will need tending. You'll no' be leaving your bed for a while. And"—he stood, gathering her up in his arms as he did so—"whether it pleases you or nae, I'll be sleeping in your room from now on. I didnae wish to bother you thusly, but—"

"You're worried about the ship," Gillian guessed, guilt pinching her. "If the men return—"

"We'll hope they didnae see you." He shifted her against his shoulder, was already striding down the beach for the goat track back up to her window.

"I waved my shawl at them," she felt obliged to tell him. "They were heading this way."

"Aye, they veered toward the isle because we were almost upon them." He started up the path, his steps sure, his firm hold on her soothing. "We'd been chasing them for a while, had hoped to run them onto the reefs. Then the wind changed and the mist thickened—"

"They sped away," Gillian remembered.

"So they did." *Praise be the gods,* she thought she heard him mutter beneath his breath.

It was hard to tell because they'd reached the top of the path and the grassy bit of promontory beneath her window. Looking up, she saw his men gathered there, so many of their bearded faces peering down at her that she couldn't count their number. She did see that they all appeared concerned.

Not a one seemed angry, just eager to help.

Indeed, two men jumped out the window and set to work securing a long rope ladder against the tower wall. Others leaned over the window ledge, reaching down to prepare to lift her from Roag's arms once he'd climbed high enough.

She was safe.

She was also beginning to feel her injured foot. Her ankle throbbed and a weird sensation now inched up her calf, much as if tiny white-hot needles were stabbing her flesh. For a beat, she squeezed shut her eyes, steeling herself against the pain, grateful nothing worse had happened. She'd have a few bruises and swellings, but she was alive, and would remain so.

The gods were good.

And so was Roag the Bear, the thought—no, that truth—making her very aware of his big strong arms holding her, the hard, solid comfort of his chest, and the broad shoulder against which she was currently resting her weary, aching head.

Had he truly called her "sweet"?

She couldn't remember.

They were now level with the window ledge and a ruckus ensued, his men making a fuss, each one vying to be the man to take her from Roag's arms and ease her through the window. Skog's barks were frantic, his ancient, age-whitened face suddenly appearing at the ledge, his milky eyes so worried that her heart squeezed. Then Big Hughie had her, carrying her to her bed as Roag hoisted himself over the ledge and then turned to help the other two men up the last few feet of the ladder rope and back into the room.

In a beat, they surrounded her, all of them shaking their heads and asking questions. A few took off at a run, shouting over their shoulders that they would fetch hot water to take her chill, more bed covering and furs to keep her comfortable.

Skog fretted, pacing back and forth until Roag lifted him up beside her.

"Skog…" Gillian tried to rise on an elbow to see him better, but ended up just slipping her arm around his great shoulders, threading her fingers in his scraggly fur.

It was enough.

"Sakes!" One of the men peered down at her as Roag swung his discarded plaid over her, drawing its warmth to her chin. "What befell the lass, down on the rocks?"

"She saw the ship," Roag told him, his voice coming as if from a distance. "Like us, she took it for a MacDonald vessel. Belike she hurried down the cliff to signal it, thinking they'd carry her away from us. Cannae blame her," he added—or so Gillian thought, for his words were now even fainter.

She tried to open her eyes to look at him, but she could hardly raise her eyelids. She did manage to squint enough to see him through an odd, shimmering haze. The room seemed to be spinning and growing dark, but she could tell that he'd left the bed and was shooing the others from the room.

It was hard to tell, but she thought she heard him say something about needing to strip away her clothes and look her over for possible injuries, wounds that might be hidden beneath her cold and sodden clothes. Garments that—she did hear clearly—he needed off of her at once, before she took a chill.

Gillian's pulse quickened.

Despite her weariness, she knew what that meant. He'd already seen her bared legs and who knew what else! Down there on the rocks, in the surf, her skirts had swirled everywhere. And he'd cut away reams of cloth, nearly to her hips. Now...There wasn't a stitch of her remaining garments not drenched. Getting her warm and dry would entail total nakedness, and she was in no shape to undress herself. She barely had the strength to breathe.

Which meant Roag would do the honors.

She should object.

Instead, she sank back against the pillows, curled her fingers deeper into Skog's fur. The truth was there were worse things than Roag the Bear seeing her unclothed.

If she'd understood rightly about the ship, she could well have been in much greater peril now.

Roag and his men had saved her. She had nothing else to fear, no reason to be distressed. Roag had even vowed to spend his nights in this room, guarding her should the ship and its men deign to sail back and seize her, if they'd even seen her.

It didn't matter now.

Only one thing did, and in a way it was much more frightening.

She might be safe from marauders, but who would protect her from her own heart?

She didn't know.

How strange that she didn't care.

Chapter Twenty-Two

❦

It was good of you to bring us up here." Lady Gillian glanced at Roag over her shoulder, her eyes lit in a way that made his heart race uncomfortably.

Concern also pinched him, for it'd been little over a fortnight since she'd injured her ankle. Yet in fourteen days and nights, she'd healed well, the bruising and swelling were gone. Even her slight limp had passed. Besides, fresh, brisk wind and salt air was good for anyone, so he waved aside his worries.

Unfortunately, there were others.

Roag frowned, shoved a hand through his hair.

He shouldn't pay any heed to how glorious she looked here on the crags above his tower, the sea shimmering behind her, the mist whirling around her like a fine, luminous veil.

The truth was...

Rarely had he seen a lovelier sight.

He also knew of no one else who fit better into this

elemental seascape. She belonged here, and in ways he could never hope to achieve. Almost as if the wind, rocks, and sharp sea air pulsed in her blood, a part of her as surely as the beating of her heart and every one of her indrawn breaths.

"I will not forget these hours," she said, turning back to the sea.

"The pleasure is mine, lady." Roag watched as she stood at the cliff's edge, not seeming to mind the afternoon's rawness, or the spit of sea spray that surely stung her face.

Far from it, her shoulders lifted as she took a deep breath and let it out slowly, as if she savored the chill, damp air—which he could tell that she did.

She might not like him, but she loved his isle.

He was sure of it.

Her joy in wild places was evident as she looked out at the sea below them. He also saw it when she turned again, this time glancing past him to peer about Laddie's Isle's highest bluff. Her eyes shone still and her cheeks were red from the wind. Gloaming was nigh and her words— *It was good of you*—were the same she'd offered him so often for more than a fortnight.

He'd heard them when he carried her evening meal up to her room, each time he tended the tiny coal brazier, and whenever he fetched fire-warmed, cloth-wrapped stones to place in her bed, keeping her warm and comfortable as she'd recovered from falling on the rocks.

Just now she delivered her thanks with the same cool politeness. As usual, her gaze wasn't on him, but elsewhere. This time gliding over the wild dark sea and the swirling mist that seemed to never leave this stark, rock-strewn promontory.

Roag angled his head and watched her.

The appreciation on her face was the look some women wore when eyeing a lover.

Then she turned to Skog's carrying basket, the large wicker creel with its leather straps that had once been two of Roag's most prized sword belts. When her gaze lit on it, her expression softened, changing to one that slid through him with the ease of a knife cutting butter. Regrettably, it also plunged straight into his heart, making him feel terrible.

He frowned, sure that he had no reason to suffer the guilt that plagued him.

Much as it cost him, he hadn't touched a hand to her. He might've slept in her wee chamber since the mishap on the shore, the sighting of the enemy dragon ship, but he'd done so wrapped in his plaid and sprawled on the floor. Not in her narrow, lumpy bed beside her. He hadn't even peeked as she'd undressed each night, much as he'd been tempted.

His men also treated her kindly and with respect.

He was good to her raggedy ancient dog.

As if she'd read his mind, she left her perch on a large, flat-topped boulder near the drop-off and went to stand beside Skog's empty carrying basket.

The old dog himself ran hither and thither in the blowing grass that grew knee-high on the moors that stretched from these precarious heights down to the gently sloped landing beach on the far side of the isle from his tower. He'd been bringing Skog up here for days, and the beast already had a favorite circuit. Indeed, he was wearing a track in the grass, for he enjoyed running from one preferred marking spot to the next. If, of course, one could call Skog's jerky, stiff-legged gait a run.

It didn't matter.

Only that the beast took his exercise. And that he enjoyed the brisk sea air and getting out from the cold, cell-like room Lady Gillian had chosen as her own.

"It is especially kind of you to carry Skog up here each day," Gillian said then, still not looking at him. "It is good for me, too," she finished, just as he'd known she would.

The problem was that being with her here wasn't good at all.

Not for him.

It was torture having her so near and desiring her as he'd come to do these last weeks.

When she wasn't near, he felt her presence as if she stood beside him, tempting and enchanting him.

Even now, the truth was, he kept these cliff-top vigils because of his duties. He came up to the headland to scour the waves in all directions, waiting and watching to see if a foe crested the horizon. He wasn't a man to shirk his responsibilities. He demanded absolute dedication to missions from his men. He held himself to the same tenets, always.

Yet Lady Gillian distracted him.

He drew a tight breath, pulled a hand down over his face.

He hadn't wanted to be swayed by her.

But he had been, and so badly that each night when he joined her in her horrid wee chamber, he needed all his restraint not to pull her into his arms and kiss her. If he looked deep into his soul, he wanted to do much more than merely kiss her.

Such were the thoughts that tormented him.

Yet he held back, revealing nothing of his desires.

While inside...

His chest tightened now, a sharp yearning wrapping round him like a vise, stealing his breath and minding him that he had no business wanting her.

For sure, he shouldn't care for her.

Losing his heart to her old dog posed an equally pestiferous dilemma, for aged dogs didnae stay with a soul forever. This one was bound to leave his world anyway— as soon as he and his men finished their work here.

Hoping that would be soon, he strode over to her, not really caring if she saw his scowl.

It served him well if she continued to think he was vexed by her presence.

In truth, he was.

His reasons had just shifted.

"I was glad to bring you, lass," he admitted, just standing before her loosening his tongue, opening his heart. "No one can stay hidden away in a miserable wee cell of a room all the day long," he added, stepping round in front of her to block the worst blast of the cold sea wind. "No' you, and no' your auld beast, who likes it up here."

"We both do." Her gaze went to her dog, now sitting in the lee of an outcrop of broken boulders.

Sheltered from the wind, Skog was panting and his tongue lolled out the side of his mouth. But his eyes were filled with canine joy, and his excitement made Roag's suffering a small price to pay to see the bony old beast so happy.

Skog deserved to remember what it was like to be young, strong, and fast.

"I can see that, lady." *I would deny neither of you such pleasure.*

"The cliffs at Sway are also high," she told him, looking out across the sea in the direction of her home. "In earlier years, Skog used to love racing up and down them. He was quite bold, even dashing along the edges of the crags. His daring frightened me, but he was very sure-footed in those days. It does him good to spend time up here," she said, her words spearing Roag's heart because they reminded him of their eventual parting.

"There's a powerful reason for our time here," he said, hoping the reference to his work would dash the strange magic that always crackled between them when they stood so close, especially now on these huge, soaring cliffs.

"I know." She met his gaze, some of the wonder gone from her face. "You appreciate an extra set of eyes to watch the sea. I've not forgotten that we must stay on the cliffs until the *Valkyrie* crests the horizon, giving us her signal for the e'en." She lifted a hand to shove back her windblown hair. "You bring Skog along because he'd howl if he was left alone. His cries would disturb the men who remain behind to guard the tower and patrol the ramparts."

Roag nodded. "Aye, that is so." *Nae, that is no' the way of it. Leastways no' entirely.*

Keeping his heart's words to himself, he ran a hand through his own hair, secretly enjoying the brisk wind. He found its chill, and even its roar, invigorating as little else. This was a place of rock, tides, sea, and mist, an elemental land. Stirling and his King's glittering royal court seemed as distant as the moon. Much as he didn't want to admit it, Laddie's Isle was somehow crawling inside him, claiming a hold on his soul. He suspected it would break him to leave. Yet sail away he must, for the isle wasn't his.

Neither was Lady Gillian.

"The height of this bluff is one reason this isle was chosen for my purpose here." He locked his gaze on hers, closing his mind to all else. "The horizons are easily watched, in all directions." He glanced at one now, the east where dark clouds were gathering. He willed the *Valkyrie*'s great square sail to pop into view.

The sooner his ship was spotted, her signal given—three fire arrows meant the seas were clear, no trouble met; four fire arrows represented an enemy ship sighted or encountered—the faster he could heave Skog into his carrying basket and escort Lady Gillian back to his hall for the night.

To his surprise and delight, her eyesight had proven exceptional.

It was a reason he brought her onto the bluff with him. At least, that's what he tried to tell himself.

"There she is! Your ship!" Lady Gillian dashed forward, hurrying to the cliff's edge. "Way off to the right, just coming up over the edge of the western sea…" She lifted her arm, pointing. "Not the whole sail yet, but I can tell it is her."

"And so you are right," Roag agreed, joining her.

He could see his ship now, too. The *Valkyrie*'s hull gleamed reddish-purple in the gloaming's soft light, and the fearsome dragon's head at her prow appeared alive, the white water hissing along her sides looking like a sea-beast's seething breath. Roag could almost hear his men's shouts, the rhythmic beat of the rowers' gong as the ship cleaved the waves, coming fast across the current, making for Laddie's Isle, and giving the awaited signal . . .

A lone fire arrow arced high into the low-swirling mist, a red-orange streak that vanished quickly as the arrow sped downward into the dark, rolling sea.

A second arrow followed, and then another in quick succession.

When a fourth arc of flame failed to light the heavens, Roag heaved a great breath and stepped back from the cliff's edge. No enemy ships had been met this day.

What a shame his heart still thundered. How sad that he knew in his gut that, as he had every night since coming here, he'd order his men to sharpen their swords before they slept. He'd send two to stand watch atop the nameless tower. No true ramparts crowned the crumbling pile, but there was a wall-walk of sorts. Enough for a patrol to pace as they kept vigil through the night. A time when the wind often died and the heavens cleared, the stars—so very many of them—seemed close enough to grab by the handful.

Roag frowned, reached to rub the back of his neck.

Such a magnificent, soul-stealing place should bring a man peace, not fill his lungs with the sure scent of war, deadly, bloody, and dangerous.

But wasn't that why he and his men were here?

It was, and how he wished otherwise.

His thoughts were disturbing and traitorous; the sort of fool notions that should bedevil poets and not pester the likes of him. Such nonsense had never before visited him on a Fenris mission, and his work had shown him many places, some quite fine. Not once had he regretted leaving after his duties were done.

Here...

He glanced again at the sea, shining darkly in the fading light. Too easily, he could imagine this rocky, storm-racked isle as his own. For real, and with Lady Gillian as his true bride, loving him gladly and eager to fill his life with joy, to share his table and his bed, warming his nights, and making a home of the wee, windswept isle that he sensed she was also coming to love.

His frown deepened, and even more alarming, the neck opening of his tunic seemed to tighten, cutting off his breath. He wasn't a man to plant roots.

He did not want a wife.

Didn't they aye come with ballast? Weighing a man down with burdens that grew greater with each passing year? He'd seen it happen often enough—had watched the bellies of married friends thicken and go soft, had seen such men lose their battle joy and wanderlust, their hearts beating only for their home hearths, grasping wives, hungry bairns, and ancient, milky-eyed dogs whose bony frames troubled him more than he liked.

Biting back a curse, he strode over to Skog, lifting the beast into his arms for the trek back down the cliff path. Skog turned his head and licked his arm, the old dog's smelly breath rising up to tickle Roag's nose.

"Perhaps the men you seek have gone elsewhere?" Lady Gillian said then, looking on as he settled Skog into his carrying basket and then hefted dog and basket onto his back. "We have seen no sign of any suspicious ships since the day I fell. Only a few clan galleys I recognized beyond doubt and one merchant cog. No warships or black-hulled galleys such as some Viking raiders used in days of yore. Can it be that your King has heard false tidings?" She lifted her chin, almost challengingly.

And that was no surprise, for very few Hebrideans were overfond of Lowland nobility, kingly or otherwise.

Lady Gillian was no exception, as she'd proved time and again.

"Only the most trusted men come close enough to give the King such word, good or bad, my lady. No man wanting to keep his head on his neck would dare lie about a matter of such gravity. Ships have been sunk and good men lost."

She turned quiet as they started down the zigzagging path. He refrained from offering her his arm.

He'd done so more than once these last weeks during her recovery, and each time she'd declined, her proud face tightening as if to show she needed no such attention, or courtesy.

Roag frowned, and shifted her dog's carrying basket to his other shoulder, wrapping an arm around its base.

As such a bony beast, Skog weighed less than a large bird. But the basket was unwieldy and Roag didn't want its bouncing to distress the dog, or make him uncomfortable.

If only his own cares could be quelled as easily.

Enemy ships—or the lack of them—weren't the only worry riding him.

Nor was his undeniable appreciation of the little isle and the inherent wildness of the Hebrides.

Something else about Laddie's Isle plagued him, and he wasn't sure he could keep it to himself much longer.

He paused only a few yards down the cliff path and glanced back the way they'd come. He could still see the moors and he let his gaze skim along the headland, the grassy, rock-strewn expanse that stretched behind. Blessedly, nothing unusual stirred there. Only mist curled across the promontory.

Yet, earlier...

"See here, lass." He gripped Lady Gillian's arm, drawing her to a halt. "Have you no' seen the wee laddie on the cliffs?" he said, feeling hot color wash up his neck. "The ghost boy," he admitted, making it worse. "I dinnae believe in suchlike, but I'd swear the mist sometimes looks like a bedraggled lad pointing a small blue-glowing dirk at the sea."

To his relief she didn't laugh.

Though, truly, the seriousness of her gaze unsettled him as much as if she had—for completely different reasons.

"The laddie who haunts this isle?" She didn't blink. Her earnest gaze and the calm way she spoke of the ghostie confirmed her belief in the boy.

"There are tales." It was all Roag could think to say.

"So there are, and every isle in these waters has its own legends and such." She drew her cloak tighter against the wind, glanced out at the sea so far below them. "Anyone you might speak to hereabouts, in any corner of the Hebrides, will tell you that there are places where strange things happen. Some might mention stones that move or living creatures that can speak, or even change into some other beast entirely, perhaps a mythical one.

"These isles are old, you see." She turned back to him, her gaze as calm and steady as if they sat at the high table and she'd just commented on the tastiness of a round of new, green cheese, or the quality of ale. "Even on a fine, sunlit day you might find yourself watched by something you cannot see. Or, as you seem to be suggesting, you might even glimpse the watcher.

"In such ancient places as here"—she swept out an arm toward the sea, the narrow cliff path rising behind them—"many things are possible. We who live here know not to doubt it."

"I am no' a man of these isles, lady." Roag ignored the shivers her words sent down his back.

The quickening of his pulse and how his heart thumped hard in an odd sense of recognition he couldn't explain. It was a feeling of belonging, almost as if despite his denials, his soul knew she spoke the truth—his heart even accepting it.

"At Stirling there are tales of a pink lady ghost," he told her, growing more uncomfortable by the moment. "She is said to be the wife of a garrison knight who was felled when England's Edward I overtook the castle many years ago. In all my days at that great stronghold, from when I was a lad right up to now, I have ne'er come across that poor woman's grieving apparition.

"Yet castle bards enjoy spinning tales about her late at night before the great hall's fires." He felt better now, relieved to have stated his position—voiced as a man of reason.

He was a town man untroubled by legend, myth, and other such nonsense.

"Why are you telling me this?" She gave him a sharp look.

"If I saw something that looked like this isle's supposed ghost laddie," he went on, "then it was only mist o'er the moors or sea spray."

"If he is here and you've seen him, you are blessed."

She kept her chin raised, seemingly undisturbed by the cold wind whipping her hair about her face. "He showed great trust in appearing to you," she added, a slight note of reproach in her voice. "Ghosts choose carefully when deciding to manifest."

Roag drew a breath, not liking her logic. "Lady, I asked if you have seen the like."

"I have not seen 'the like,' no. Neither have I seen a wee lad who is surely to be pitied."

"He has been on the cliffs each day for weeks." Roag felt his face heating. Not from anger, but from embarrassment, for her gentle reprimand shamed him. "Leastways whate'er it is I've been seeing that might resemble a lad.

"Though I am sure it was only bog mist," he said, willing it so.

"So what was he doing, the poor mite?" She pushed back her hair, definitely challenging him.

"Moving from one side of the headland to the other," Roag told her, remembering how he'd glimpsed the ghost earlier that very afternoon. The see-through sprite had first been on the far side of the promontory from where he and Gillian stood, then, as soon as he'd stride that way, the lad would vanish before his eyes—only to reappear as quickly on the other side of the cliffs.

All that he told her, speaking in a rush, before ending with, "Folk say that he—"

"He warns of danger," she finished for him, looking surprisingly calm.

"And he will surely be here, showing himself to you, because your work here is needed. His appearances prove that I was wrong to think our King was misinformed.

Clearly"—she made it sound so possible—"there is a threat about, as we now know beyond doubt. The wee laddie is trying to alert you of the menace."

She looked away, then back at him.

"I am sure of it," she said.

"Are you?"

She nodded.

"Aye, well." Roag fought the urge to thread a hand through his hair. For two pins, he'd tell her that she was the menace. Even now, listening to her expound on ghosts, his mind wandered where it shouldn't.

He was of a mind to grip her face with both hands, circle his thumbs over the chilled smoothness of her skin. It'd been sō long since he'd kissed her, yet he'd swear he still carried the taste of her on the back of his tongue. A sweetness he'd love to sample again, now.

Instead, he refrained. "Lady, I am well aware of the peril hereabouts."

He was.

She should be, too. Such as how perilously close he was to hauling her flush against him, plundering her lips and ravishing her, here on the cliff path.

Unable to help himself, he gave her a smile—his darkest, most wicked. "I dinnae need a wee spirit following me about, telling me my business."

"Perhaps he fears you will leave without addressing the trouble." She slipped her arm from his grasp and then hitched her skirts, turning back to the downward path. "You have said how eager you are to leave," she added over her shoulder as she started forward, stepping lightly on the steep and narrow track. She moved away briskly, her straight back and her raised head indicating that once again, for seemingly unfathomable reasons, she was wroth with him.

"Are you not going to deny it? That you will sail away as soon as you can?" Her voice floated back to him as she nipped around a curve, disappearing behind the cliff's jutting shoulder. "I suspect the lad wants you to stay. Perhaps he showed himself to the crew of the dragon ship? Mayhap"—she popped back into view, one hand holding her hair against the wind—"he even conjured the fog that rolled in that morn? Bogles have powers the living do not. Had the mist not rolled in, you might've chased thon ship.

"Could be . . ." She let her words trail off, a glimmer of speculation in her eyes. "I might have drowned—had you not returned when you did."

Roag suspected she was right.

The thought chilled him to the marrow. He couldn't have borne her death. He would indeed have felt responsible, and he'd have carried that weight on his shoulders for all his days.

"Then I am grateful to all the gods that I did," he said, and he was.

But his admission was wasted.

She'd already turned and hastened back around the bend in the path.

Her words stayed with him, circling in his head . . .

I suspect the lad wants you to stay.

"And you?" Roag remained where he was, spoke the words into the wind.

It was probably best she'd not heard him. He also didn't care about ghosts and what they wanted. He cared about Lady Gillian. He also wanted to stay here, much as that surprised him.

She was the one who burned to leave.

And the more he thought about it, the stranger her wish seemed. Much as she appeared to appreciate the wee isle and determined as she was not to return to her home, she had to have reasons for wanting off the isle so badly. That could only mean she was keeping something from him. A secret he determined to air, and as quickly as possible.

Chapter Twenty-Three

✣

The hall was crowded that night. Men in mail or leather milled about or packed the long tables, while some stood warming their hands at the hearth where a roaring drift-wood fire filled the air with sea-scented blue-green smoke. Most of the men were newly returned from the landing beach below the tower, and, having secured the *Valkyrie* for the night, they all held horns of ale. They drank gladly as they spoke of what they'd seen—or hadn't seen—on their circuitous journey throughout the isles.

Gillian sat at the high table, trying her best not to listen to the men's talk of swords, spears, and axes; fire arrows, and the blood that would flow when they captured the blackguards attacking the crown's fleet. After each such boast, they'd knock ale horns—or cups—and exchange thoughts on what should then be done to such miscreants.

"If they are English," Conn of the Strong Arm, the *Valkyrie*'s Irish helmsman, waved a hand toward the hall's main door and the dark night beyond, "they shall have their bellies slit open and be tossed into the sea to feed the sharks and then the crabs. If they be Scots," his tone hardened, as if such a betrayal were the most despicable sin in the world, "they shall twist from a rope in a place where all may stare and curse them. Then—"

"They, too, will feed the fish and crabs!" Big Hughie raised his voice above the crackle and roar of the fire. "King Robert will dispossess them of their lands, and their families and servants should be scattered—banished from the realm so that their tainted blood can befoul us no more."

"Hear, hear!" a round of agreement rose from the others.

Throughout the hall, men rapped the tables with the blunt ends of their eating knives, while those standing stamped their feet or shook their swords in the scabbards.

The noise was deafening.

In truth, the racket was no different from the din in Castle Sway's hall in times of unrest and trouble. She understood the need of men to swell their chests, make threats, and swagger. Such posturing was needed now and then, especially at times when a raid or foray hadn't brought the desired results, such as an attempt to run down and capture an enemy ship.

The night's bravura and ale guzzling would help the frustrated warriors to sleep on their too-thin pallets and the hall's cold stone floor.

Gillian knew that well.

Hadn't she been raised in a household of men?

She was also clever, more sharp-witted at times than most men gave her credit for.

So, being of a sound and lively mind...

What concerned her was that none of Roag's men bothered to keep such talk from her listening ears.

That meant one of two things.

Roag could be planning to add her to the diet of hungry Hebridean crabs.

It was a possibility she couldn't ignore, much as she doubted he'd stoop so low. Still, he had gone out of his way to emphasize the importance of his mission and how seriously he took his responsibility to his King. He'd made no secret that her presence was a thorn in his side, a complication he didn't want or need.

She'd be amiss in her logic if she didn't consider he might think to have done with her.

The other likelihood was equally unpalatable, but for a very different reason.

There was a chance he wouldn't release her.

That he'd keep her at his side, even after he left the isle—perhaps as his servant or slave.

Why else would he allow his men to speak so freely in front of her?

They'd only do so if she wouldn't prove a threat.

"My apologies, lass, that the hall is so loud this night." Roag turned to her at the table—for they sat side by side—and touched his big hand to her cheek. "They will quiet soon."

He leaned in, lowering his voice. "You see how much ale they're quaffing. Snores will soon replace their boasts."

"I do not mind." *I would hear why you let me listen.*

"I forget that you have so many brothers." He sat back, his face clearing as his words proved that, like so many men, he didn't have any idea what truly bothered her.

He lowered his hand, looking at her in a way that made

a delicious warmth blossom inside her. It spread through her despite her worries, spilling from somewhere deep in her chest to flow clear to the tips of her fingers and down to her toes.

"You will have a large garrison at your home as well," he went on, the casualness of his observation annoying her, once again revealing that he understood little of her. "I am no' surprised you are so tolerant of warriors. Sway is known to be a castle of men."

"So is yours." *But only one of you interests me.*

"This isle is nae place for a woman, for sure no' this excuse for a tower."

"It is a good enough hall for warriors to tease, laugh, and boast together." She reached for her ale horn, glad that it held warm honeyed mead. Before she took a sip, she gave him a smile, surprised how easily she could. "In days of strife and warfare, men who fight together become close. They love and trust each other as brothers, even if nary a drop of blood binds them. That I learned early, my lord," she added, enjoying her mead. "Do not ever think your men's nightly din disturbs me. In truth, I would be more worried if they were silent."

As you so often turn quiet when you look at me and think I do not see. Your eyes then say things I'd hear from your tongue.

If my heart is listening correctly.

But never you mind, for I already know that it is dangerous to care for you. I do not wish to give my heart—or my body—to a man who would shred my soul as easily as a good wind rips apart the soft white heads of bog cotton.

"It is a poor hall that isn't filled with manly ruckus,"

she said, speaking another truth—one that she didn't mind putting voice to with her tongue.

"You are a remarkable woman, Lady Gillian." He knocked his ale horn against hers, his dark eyes warming.

His lips even curved, his smile making his rugged face disturbingly appealing.

Sadly, the effect was ruined by his use of her formal title.

She wanted him to call her by name.

A mad wish if ever there was one—but for all that she knew how unwise it was to desire him, she couldn't stop her pulse from leaping when he looked so deeply into her eyes as he was doing now. Worse, if she cared to admit it, her heart raced just seeing him stride across a room.

She admired his swagger.

She appreciated his confidence and liked how he treated his men. He was clearly a good leader and fair, qualities any chieftain's daughter knew to respect and count highly. The compassion he showed her beloved pet revealed a different side of him. One that was, perhaps, even more dangerous because it proved he had a heart.

Not all men did, she knew that, too.

Certainly not for the neediest souls, such as the old and feeble, be they two- or four-legged.

Gillian took another sip of mead, now certain she was poised for doom.

She should not think about his good qualities. She shouldn't remember his kisses or think about how his hands had felt on her when he held her to him. She did her best to forget the hard ridge of his manhood and how it then pressed against her, bespeaking his virility. The red-blooded lustiness that surely had more to do with his just being a man than any desire he might feel for her personally.

He would have rescued any woman trapped by rocks and the tide. That he'd stormed down the cliff path and worked so frantically to free her, then taking such fine care of her as she recovered...

He was keeper here so long as he remained on Laddie's Isle, honor-bound for the weal of all.

It didn't mean he cared for her as a woman.

Still...

She couldn't deny that everything about him appealed to her. Even here at his table, in full view of all, every time his arm or leg chanced to bump against hers, tingly warmth raced along her skin. Her pulse even quickened, a shiver of excitement inside her. Yet he made no secret that he had no interest in her—leastways beyond keeping her at his side so that she couldn't ruin his work.

As if she would do aught to endanger the Scottish realm!

She loved her country.

And she wished he'd come to see and accept that in the weeks they'd been together. Striding about the high promontory much of this day and through till gloaming. Spending the evenings in his hall and, since her fall, sharing their nights in her little room, with poor old Skog witness to how little he desired her.

His initial, seemingly eager kisses had been a ploy.

However heated and thrilling they'd been for her, he hadn't felt the same raging passion that she had, much as she'd resisted feeling anything at all.

She had, and still did.

The fates have mercy on her.

He'd only hoped to convince her father and family that he was indeed her newly returned betrothed. Donell MacDonnell come home to Laddie's Isle, ready to claim her, and happy to do so, in the fullest sense possible.

It'd all been false.

As untrue as the bloodied "virtue cloth" he'd presented to her father with such aplomb.

Gillian frowned, carefully replacing her mead horn in its curved metal holder. She wished she hadn't let him carry Skog abovestairs so early. If her dog were with her now, curled at her feet under the table, as was his wont, she'd have an excuse to slip from the hall. She could say she had to settle Skog for the night, and he'd have no choice but to let her go.

Even if he carried Skog to her room, courtesy would demand he leave her be if she said she wished to rest.

Alone.

But he'd seen to Skog as soon as they'd returned from the bluffs.

And that, too, kindled an appreciative warmth inside her that could easily ignite into something more.

She rubbed her brow, annoyingly aware that the tingly flutters she felt in certain womanly regions were a powerful indication that such heat needn't be sparked at all. His strong, hard-muscled thigh rested against hers beneath the table and that simple contact proved her vulnerability, the heady attraction he was to her.

Her blood ran hot, and he'd fired it.

That meant it remained to her to douse the flames.

"I should like to go to my room now." She turned to him, amazed she could speak so calmly. "It was a long day and I am tired."

"As you wish, my lady." He pushed back from the table, stepping away to let her rise. "I shall see you abovestairs."

"You needn't." She nodded her good nights to his men, brushed down her skirts as she made to leave the dais. "It is only a short way."

"That may be," he argued, falling in beside her, taking her arm, "but you are nae longer sleeping in that room, my lady. I have moved you, and Skog, to the topmost chamber. You will—"

"But—"

He didn't give her a chance to object. Turning toward her, he leaned close, bringing his mouth perilously close to hers. "You will be more comfortable there," he said, his breath warming her skin. "And I shall have a greater view upon the sea. You ken now why that's important." He straightened, but not before he touched his knuckles to her face, smoothed them lightly down her cheek, across her lips. "The laird's chamber will suit us well, you shall see."

And she did, as he ushered her from the hall and up the winding turnpike stair.

It wasn't about a more suitable place for seduction.

He wanted a better vantage.

It made perfect sense, she knew. How sad that it also riled her beyond all telling.

Chapter Twenty-Four

❦

My sorrow, lass, that the room is still cold." Roag pushed open the laird's chamber door—if the largely bare room could even carry such a grand name—and stepped aside so Lady Gillian could enter. "The fire has only been lit a short while ago, but its heat should warm us soon enough."

Indeed, he was pleased that his men had brought up the same fine-burning driftwood as in the hall's great hearth. The sea-scented wood gave off a pleasant tang that was already beginning to haze the air, while the flames were a remarkable blue-green and almost iridescent. Such a fire was a startling oddity that fascinated him, but did not seem to enchant or excite the Spitfire of the Isles, who'd stopped just inside the door and folded her arms.

She did not look pleased.

She did glance about the room, her gaze taking in the bare stone floor, the four unadorned window embrasures, each tall arch-topped opening bearing shutters that would surely fall into the sea before Roag's time here was done—if the wind didn't first blow them away, which seemed a distinct possibility.

Lady Gillian's goods, the two crates from Castle Sway that held all her worldly possessions, had been placed in a corner near her bed. And someone had thoughtfully lit the wall torches and even the small brazier from her previous room.

An oil lamp hung on a chain as well, shedding light and a bit of additional warmth. Not far away, a small iron kettle sat beside a wall, hinting that heated water could be had without the trouble of men lugging a cauldron up the tower stair. It was a thoughtful gesture and Roag wished it'd been him and not his romantic-minded helmsman, Conn, who'd had the idea to provide the warming kettle.

The Irishman had also carried up a small stand to hold a ewer and basin for the lady's ablutions.

All that had been done throughout the day while Roag and Lady Gillian had been on the cliffs, and later as well, when they'd supped in the hall with his men.

The chamber was as comfortable as Laddie's Isle could offer.

To Roag's mind, it could have been worse.

For sure, it was an improvement over the dank cell-like room she'd slept in until now.

This chamber had other advantages as well—ones he did not want to think about, and hoped would not be necessary.

If the wee isle should come under attack—something he hoped would never happen—this topmost chamber of the tower would provide Lady Gillian with the best possible refuge.

It was a consideration he couldn't ignore. Not after her harrowing experience on the rocks, and knowing as he did now how easily determined men could climb the tower wall and reach her old chamber.

For that reason, he'd ordered several of his best fighters to sleep there—should the dragon ship they'd chased deign to return.

The lass would be safe here.

This chamber's walls were thick, much sturdier than the half-crumbling room she'd used off the tower stair's first landing. The outer stones would repel arrows, and although the window shutters were warped, these quarters were high above the isle's most daunting cliff. Not even the most skilled climber could scale such a sheer, formidable rock face, eliminating the possibility of an attack from without.

And although there was no secret tunnel carved into the walls to allow a swift escape, there was a fresh water supply, thanks to a rather large stone urn on the roof. A tiny stair granted access to the tower's narrow wall-walk where the urn collected rainwater, and such a boon could prove lifesaving if ever a raid or siege required her to hide away here.

He just hoped she'd never have to make use of the room's amenities in such a dire way.

The rainwater could also provide the luxury of an easily readied bath.

Lady Gillian, highborn lass that she was, would surely appreciate such a nicety.

So he pushed aside his darker thoughts and forced a smile. "If you aren't warm enough, I can fetch a small basket of peat to add to the fire."

"I do not mind the chill." She moved deeper into the room, the reserve in her voice proving he'd not erred in sensing her displeasure. "But I thank you for the fire. I have ever been fond of driftwood burning. My brothers always made sure there was a supply of such wood for my quarters at Sway.

"The scent will also be soothing to Skog." She glanced to where her dog slept soundly on a plaid before the small hearth. "He will recognize the smell and the familiarity will comfort him."

"The bed is the same." Roag strode over to the pitiful cotlike bed, wishing its frame weren't so crudely made, the mattress less lumpy. "My men and I expected nae more than to sleep wrapped in our plaids or on seagrass pallets. This bed"—he reached to straighten the coverings—"was here when we arrived, as well you ken.

"If there were a finer one anywhere on this isle, it would be yours." He looked at her again, her silence unsettling him. "Nae one thought to need more luxurious trappings."

"That I know." She went to one of the windows, set deep in a thick-walled embrasure, and stood looking out at the sea. "I understand why you prize this chamber," she said, turning back to face him. "One can see to the ends of the world and beyond from up here. Such an outlook will serve you well."

"I would hope you will find more comfort here, too, my lady." He drew back a heavy but faded wall hanging, the only tapestry in the tower, and proudly showed her the small, rough-planked door near the foot of the bed. "This opens to a few steps that lead to the roof," he told her. "This tower does not have true ramparts, but there

is a narrow wall-walk. In the corner of it, just above this
chamber, is a large urn that gathers rainwater.

"You will have the ease of bathing as and when you
wish. There is a washtub in thon corner." He indicated a
darker area of the room that, at this late hour, and without its wall torch burning, stood in deep shadow. When
he saw that she'd spotted the tub and the stack of folded
drying linens on a nearby three-legged stool, he glanced
back to her, hoping this luxury, at least, would please her.
"Shall I heat the water for you now?"

She bit her lip, looking from the bathing area to the
little wooden door in the wall to the driftwood fire, and
then again to him. "I would not trouble you, though..."

Roag grinned and strode to the door in the wall.
Throwing it wide, he stepped aside so that she could see
at least six small wooden pails lined up on the narrow
stone steps that led to the roof. "You see, fair one, all is at
the ready. A bath can be prepared anon."

"Perhaps later, after..." She stood straighter, clasped
her hands before her as if she did not want to speak the
words dancing round on her tongue.

Roag figured she'd meant to say "after he'd left her in
peace." A courtesy he surely meant to give her. But he
was not yet ready to go. His own mind was yet troubled
by unspoken quandaries and he'd promised himself he'd
voice them. This night, before he spent another one staring into the night blackness and wondering over what
was beginning to plague him more and more as each day
passed.

Determined, he went to the room's last bit of meager
luxury, a rather large oak table of much sturdier form and
better quality than all other furnishings in the tower.

Just now, the table boasted a small repast of salt herring, cheese, and oatcakes, as well as a jug of ale. Two of the room's torches blazed on the whitewashed wall above the dining niche and the light fell across the offerings.

"You will have dined well at Sway," he said, hoping the humble viands would please her all the same. *If I were able, I'd have set out slices of cold, spiced venison and a whole, roasted capon, along with sugared almonds and custard pasties, rich red wine to enjoy with such a feast.*

As is, my lady, I have provided what I could.

Not about to lay bare his thoughts, he spoke the best words he knew. "You did no' eat much in the hall this night. If you are hungry"—he indicated the victuals— "there should be enough here to keep you until the morning."

"I might have something," she decided, pleasing him.

But she didn't leave the window alcove. Instead, she glanced down at the empty stone benches that flanked the embrasure walls, her brow knitting again. "I think it has been many years since someone sat here and appreciated the view," she said, the sadness in her voice piercing his heart. "I doubt Donell will have dressed the window benches properly. He was not a man to value such things."

She looked over her shoulder at him, her face pensive. "I have heard that the laird before him was a man of similar bent. It is a shame for the tower, don't you think, that no one ever truly cared for it?"

Roag blinked. "The tower?"

"Aye." She nodded, trailing her fingers along the rough stone wall near the window arch. "You know the legend of how this tower came to be. Each stone laid was put down by the men of passing ships, stopped to do honor to the wee lad who'd survived a shipwreck only to find an end alone on this isle.

"Over time, the stones were so many that from a cairn, this tower grew." She looked at him, keeping her hand flat against the wall. "Those of us who live in these isles, places of such wild grandeur, know that the very things that make our world so wondrous cannot be without feeling themselves."

Roag didn't know what to say.

"You do not understand." She spoke his mind for him.

"Can you blame me, lass?" He opted for truth.

"Then let me ask you this..." She came over to him, angling her head to peer up into his eyes. "Have you ever walked along the shore in the quiet time between gloaming and night? If you have done, did you chance to catch the glitter of star in a tidal pool? 'Tis a sight to see, I promise. Those who do are blessed, for we of the Hebrides believe we are then not seeing the twinkle of a distant star, but the eyes of the rock spirits looking back at us."

"A lovely thought, I'll no' deny." *You should be a poet, my lady, for your words are too fanciful to be believed.*

He took a step closer to her, drawn by the freshness of her lavender scent, and—he didn't care to admit—an odd tug on his emotions.

"You willnae be surprised that I have no' spent much time thinking about rock sprites," he said, lifting a hand to skim back her hair. "Nary a moment that I recall, nor even pondering the stars."

How could I when the sparkle of your eyes dims their

glory? Who needs Highland magic when wonder dwells beneath your own roof?

She smiled, her expression warming as if she'd heard his thoughts. "I do not blame you for doubting me," she said, returning to the window and standing with her back to him, once more gazing out at the cold, dark night. "You are a town man and even more, hailing from a court where more Lowlanders walk than any people of the Highlands and the Isles.

"Our ways are different." She stood straighter, her shoulders squaring. "We do believe there are spirits in the wind and fey beasties in the sea. We know the winter is a crone, and that the gods dance across the heavens on the coldest nights of the year, their whirling movements lighting the sky as their colorful veils and ribbons trail behind them. And we are aware"—she raised a hand, lifting a finger—"that stones not only walk and speak, but remember, seeing and absorbing all that happens around them."

"So these stones are lonely?" Roag understood at last, leastways he grasped what she believed.

He just didn't accept such nonsense.

"They have seen much, aye." She lowered her hand, nodding. "And the most of it has been bleak. It could be they are smiling now, though. And that they will weep again when you leave. Something tells me that they like you."

"Why should they do that?"

"You cannot guess?" She glanced at him, her eyes smiling.

Roag shook his head. "Sweet lass, I have pondered the thoughts of stones even less than tidal pool stars."

"What a shame," she said, her tone almost teasing. Her smile spread, curving her lips and lighting her face in a way that just might haunt his dreams. "I would've thought any Scot would know such things as surely as they breathe." She tilted her head and looked at him, searchingly. "Consider this, that since you are here, the hall is filled nightly with men. Good cheer and laughter echo against stones that, perhaps, have thirsted for the like for centuries. I do not believe this was a merry keep in Donell's day.

"It could also be that your hearth missed the joy of knowing it spent warmth to appreciative men." She took a few steps toward him, her eyes shining in the torch-light. "And we mustn't forget the stair tower. How glad the ancient steps must be to know they are again trod by living souls?"

"Indeed." Roag had had enough. He didn't much care if stones liked him. He wanted to know why he was ever more convinced that Lady Gillian loved her Hebridean home—all these isles and the waters around them, not just her own Castle Sway—far too much to even consider leaving.

Yet...

"Lady, you puzzle me." He spoke another truth. "How is it that you bear such devotion to these isles and yet, by your own admission, you would barter your greatest treasure for passage to Glasgow? A city so great and teeming that I know fine you would suffocate from the crush before you'd gone ten paces from the ship that carried you there?"

Her chin came up. "I had my reasons."

"And now?"

"I still do."

Roag leaned in, studying her face for a very long time. "I believe you. But I dinnae think they have aught to do with what's in your heart."

"You cannot know what's in my heart."

Roag almost snorted.

Her feelings were writ all over her, leastways how she felt about her Hebridean home.

"Then tell me this," he said, still watching her carefully. Her smile had faded, and although he couldn't say why, he felt a powerful need to see it again. Truth be told, just the memory of it made his heart hammer. No other woman's smile had ever affected him so strongly, as if he'd been punched in the gut, but in a good way. He might even be persuaded to think her smile brightened the room, making colors more vibrant, the air fresher and sweet. But other concerns rode him, and he meant to air them. "See here, lass," he began, hoping to do so. "As I have refused to take you to Glasgow, I shall make you a different offer. When I leave here, what say you if my men and I return you to your beloved Isle of Sway?"

Her eyes widened—just as he'd known they would. "I cannot go back there."

"Cannae or willnae, my lady?"

"Both," she admitted, the sorrow that flickered across her face making him feel like an arse again.

But at least he had his answer.

Something was amiss at Castle Sway. And it was damaging enough to keep her from the home she loved so fiercely.

Worse, that love was now putting a shimmer in her eyes. Tears that misted her lashes and—to his great horror—began rolling slowly down her cheeks. Lady Gillian was crying and it was his fault.

He'd provoked her. And she'd ripped away the last restraints of his heart, her upset unleashing something inside him. Something that had begun to change the moment he'd landed on Laddie's Isle and pulled her into his arms, kissing her there and then.

It was all he could think to do now.

"Precious lass," he said, his voice rough, "what have you done to me?" Not waiting for an answer, he bent his head and kissed her.

He'd only meant to brush his lips over hers, soothing and calming her. He'd half expected her to reel back and slap him. Instead, she brought her hands up to grasp his shoulders, melting into him. When she returned his kiss, even parting her lips, he slanted his mouth more firmly over hers, sweeping his tongue inside to deepen their kiss.

From somewhere outside himself, seemingly a great distance, he thought he heard her breathe his name. Whether she had or not, she was leaning into him. Her tongue even flirted with his, touching lightly, then swirling over and around his own in a sweet, questing way that steeled him at once. He tightened his arms around her, drawing her closer, his heart hammering as need more powerful than he'd ever known slammed into him.

He also knew that he had to have her. That he'd wanted her all along, regardless of how hard and often he'd tried to convince himself otherwise. More than that, unless he'd fallen into an entirely new world where he knew nothing of women, she wanted him with the same strong, unbridled passion. Whatever happened now would change both their lives forever.

And for his, he didn't care.

Only she mattered, all else be damned.

But for her...

She was an innocent, he could tell. For all that she had such passion in her blood, so much fiery spirit, she was a maid untouched.

And he...

He was ignoring every shred of honor he'd ever possessed.

"Forgive me." He shook his head, spoke the words against her lips.

He broke the kiss, tearing his mouth from hers. Gripping her face between his hands, he locked his gaze on hers, looking deep into her eyes. "Sweet lass, I didnae mean for this to happen. I'd sworn no' to touch you, but you were crying and—"

"You kissed me," she declared, lifting her chin, looking both proud and defiant. "I did not mind. And"—she blinked, lifted a hand to dash the moisture from her cheek—"I do believe it was better than before." She touched her fingertips to her lips, a glimmer of wonder in her eyes. "Much nicer."

"Nicer..." Roag couldn't finish. Her bluntness, the way she looked at him, did something unholy to his insides. He felt as if the sun had risen in his chest and was bursting, sending dazzling golden light and warmth all through him. His heart thundered still, his pulse so loud in his ears he could hardly hear his own words. But he had caught hers.

And he'd been right—for they changed everything.

Lady Gillian enjoyed his kisses.

For sure, he wanted her. But there was more, and

whatever it was, he could feel it humming in the air between them, sizzling and crackling, waiting to be ignited. And when the sparks flew, the flames would consume them.

He wasn't sure anything would remain. Ash and a hint of scorched air, a smudge of soot on the floor where they'd come together, all bound by beautiful memories that would brand them forever.

The heartache that would follow when they parted, the weight of it crushing down on him unbearably.

He didn't care.

For the now, she was here.

And something told him that very soon, she'd be in his arms, and for more than just kisses. Possibly even before the morning light slipped through the window shutters. Here, in this edge of the world place, he could almost believe nowhere else existed. That for a brief time, at least, they could forget the reasons they shouldn't give in to passion.

Dare he deny that he was duty-bound to leave here? That there was no room in his life for a woman? Worse, that he had so little to offer her even if there was. Frowning, Roag glanced at the night-darkened window and drew a tight breath. His heart thundered. Not touching her would be the hardest thing he'd ever done. Indeed, he wasn't sure he could be so noble. The truth was he couldn't resist her.

Surely the gods wouldn't damn him for wanting her?

If they did, so be it.

Chapter Twenty-Five

✦

Gillian felt the change in Roag more strongly than if he'd announced he bore yet another name. He'd tightened his arms around her as he'd kissed her, crushing her to him more fiercely than ever before. She'd felt the hard beat of his heart, her own racing as furiously. Now that he'd released her to stride away from her across this large, lofty room, she was even more certain. She clasped her hands before her, would swear she could still hear the wild rushing of their pulses. She did see dark passion burning in his eyes when he cast a glance at her. She wouldn't have believed it, but her difficulty catching her breath seemed a problem that troubled him as well.

She blinked a few times, trying to compose herself.

She hadn't expected him to kiss her. But he had. And she'd felt desperation in its fury, almost as if the kiss would be their last. That the moment he tore away from her, they'd be ripped apart, never again to share such powerful desire.

And desire him she did.

More than that, she suspected she was falling in love with him.

She'd lost so much already and wouldn't be able to bear bidding farewell to him as well.

"Dinnae tell me I've forgotten how to kiss a lass? Has my lacking put such worry on your face?" His voice startled her, coming from across the room.

"No, I..." She couldn't finish, her face flaming. Hadn't she just told him how much she'd enjoyed his kiss? She had, and she couldn't believe she'd been so bold. "There was nothing wrong with your kiss."

By the gods, now she'd made it worse.

"Aye, well." He grinned at her, his eyes twinkling. "Then I am much relieved."

Gillian pressed a hand to her breast, her own eyes so full of the sight of him that she could scarce breathe. How could any one man be so magnificent? He was kneeling before the hearth, pouring water from one of the roof stairwell's pails into the iron kettle that now hung from a chain above the fire. His dark hair fell down over his forehead, the glossy black strands catching the firelight. The light also played across his shoulders, emphasizing their width. She tightened her fingers into a fist, felt the hard beat of her heart through the wool of her shawl. Her pulse quickened even more when she realized the purpose of his task.

He was heating water for a bath.

"What are you doing?" She narrowed her eyes on him, all manner of possibilities whirling through her mind.

His smile flashed again, as if he knew.

"Can you no' see?" He glanced at the pail in his hands.

When he returned his attention to her, he looked so handsome in the shimmering blue-green glow of the driftwood fire that she almost swayed where she stood.

He could've been a Celtic sea-god risen up from the waves. But his eyes were manly, not godlike. They held warmth and tenderness, and just enough mischief that her knees weakened. A rush of pure female need swept through her, bringing a tide of excitement such as she'd never felt. She did know that no matter what came, if she never saw him again, the look on his face now, this moment, would stay with her all her days, even haunting her dreams.

She took a deep breath, wondered if her emotions blazed bright for him to see.

He raised a brow at her. "I have no' yet seen you so quiet, Gillian-lass," he said, his voice soft, teasing. It was the first time he'd spoken her name without "lady," and the way he'd said it sent warmth spilling into her heart.

"Dinnae tell me nae one washes at Sway?" He held her gaze, a corner of his mouth lifting.

"Of course," she blurted, sure her cheeks were glowing red. "You're making a bath."

"So I am." He pushed to his feet and crossed the room with long, sure strides. Sending her another smile, he ducked into the little stair cut in the wall, returning almost as quickly with two pails of rainwater. "You forget, sweet, that I was raised in the kitchens of Stirling Castle. My friends and I were oft given the task of carrying washtubs and water abovestairs for the fine ladies who'd ordered them.

"Even as wee lads, we had ears and learned fast that the ladies most often wished to bathe when they were troubled." He set aside one pail, already emptied, and began tipping water from the second into the steaming kettle. "Whene'er a scandal broke, or some turmoil weighed on them, they aye felt a need to soak in a bath. The warmth seemed to soothe them."

"You observed much." Gillian's own gaze drifted over him, the fluttery sensations in her belly making it hard to think.

She was powerfully attracted to him, and having him prepare a bath for her was an intimacy that made her shiver. The desire ignited by his kiss spooled deeper now, tingling deliciously in places that should shame her, but didn't.

Instead, she wanted him to kiss her again. Was she turning into a wanton?

She didn't know, so she smoothed her skirts, hoping that by doing so she would ensure that he wouldn't see that her hands trembled—they did, for he was affecting her that strongly.

"I am surprised you noticed such things, young as you were." It was all she could think to say.

To her surprise, he laughed, the dimple that then flashed in his cheek only making her pulse quicken more.

"Aye, well." He stood looking at her, the two pails clutched in his hands. "The lads and I didnae see as much as we would have liked!" His smile deepened, and so did his dimples. "The auld harridan who ordered us about made sure we left the fine ladies' chambers before the women had so much as removed a pin from their hair."

"What a shame for you and your friends." Gillian found herself smiling, her worries of earlier fading.

"So it was!" He disappeared again into the roof stair, and then hurried back with two more pails of water. "I am gladdened to see you amused," he said, filling the kettle. "Did I no' just tell you that a bath settles many woes for ladies?"

Gillian's levity dimmed. "I do not have any woes."

"Nae?" He glanced at her, busy now setting the wooden bathing tub before the fire, arranging a large linen sheet so that its length lined the tub. "You have no' yet told me how you can judge my kisses. No' hearing your answer is a woe of my own," he teased, clearly attempting to coax her into smiling again.

She did have cares, but didn't wish to speak of them.

For sure, not now.

So she drew a long, deep breath and went over to him. "I am not called the Spitfire of the Isles for naught," she declared, tipping back her head to look up at him. "It is not in the nature of a Hebridean woman to deny herself pleasure. Nor do we lie—ever," she added, holding his gaze. "It would be a falsehood if I said I did not enjoy your kiss just now, or the one you gave me when you first landed on this isle."

"How did you ken if they were good or no'?" He looked down at her, his voice rough, and his eyes darkening. "Are you so well used to kissing? Passionate lass that you are?"

"No man has ever kissed me," she told him true, pride ringing in her voice. She would not count Donell's betrothal kiss, mere peck that it was, and loathsome at that. "You were the first. But I recognized with a woman's kenning that your kisses seared me."

"Indeed?" His smile returned, wicked this time.

"That is so," she admitted, now certain she was indeed a wanton.

"Then perhaps we should kiss some more?"

"I'm not sure that's wise."

He laughed, surprising her. "To be sure, it isnae."

"Then we shouldn't." Gillian glanced at the bathing tub, still empty of water, but draped with linen in readiness. "My bath—"

"Dinnae you worry." He lifted a curl of her hair, began twining the strands around his fingers. "Perhaps I shall kiss you as you bathe?"

Gillian stepped back, breaking free. "You wouldn't!"

He grinned again, looking entirely too appealing. "Sweet lass, do you no' yet ken that there is no' much I willnae do?"

"For King and country, I have seen what you're willing to do, *Donell*," she said, trying to lead their converse in another direction, away from the one that sent a floodtide of tingling heat racing across her most secret places. She glanced aside, hoping he couldn't tell. "No one would deny that you will go to any length needed for Scotland."

"I would go even further for you, lass."

She snapped her gaze back to his. "Then take me to Glasgow."

"I willnae do that, nae." He shook his head, his smile fading, the denial unmistakable.

Nothing would persuade him to bend to her wish. And the one thing she desired even more, to remain with him, here or wherever he might take her, was an impossibility as great as if she'd attempt to reach up and pull the stars from the heavens.

He'd made clear that once his duties were done, they'd part ways.

And she knew he was a man of his word.

He'd be rid of her, whether or not he enjoyed kissing her.

"More than once have I offered to see you safely returned to your father's home, my lady." He caught her chin when she tried to look away again, turned her face back up to his. "I can tell fine that you belong here, in these isles and nowhere else."

"All men who know the Hebrides desire to stay here," she argued. "Those of us born and bred here are only half ourselves if we are torn away. The ache that then consumes us eats the soul and squeezes the lifeblood from the heart, reducing us to nothingness. An empty shell is all that remains," she finished, unable to stop the shudder that rippled through her. "I have seen it happen and know that it is a suffering worse than death."

He released her to pace, whirling back around when he reached the table with her untouched repast. "Yet you persist in wanting passage to Glasgow," he said, frowning darkly. "I have told you, lass, thon city is nae place for you.

"No city or town is. No' even a midsized village, I'm thinking." He strode back over to her, gripping her arms. "It's the wild places that stir you, lady. And if it is the last thing I do, I will make certain that you are ne'er banished from these isles."

Gillian swallowed, her throat suddenly too thick for words. Nor could she push a response past the hot lump swelling there if she'd tried. In truth, she could hardly even see him, for her vision was blurring again, tears stinging her eyes.

He knew her soul, had seen into the deepest, truest part of her.

She would die if she left the Hebrides.

But returning to Sway was out of the question. And much as she'd come to care for Laddie's Isle, even with all her spirit and strength, she couldn't remain here alone when Roag and his men sailed away.

Doing so would see her meeting the same fate as the poor ghost laddie who walked the isle.

She pressed a hand to her lips, furious that they quivered. It galled her to admit such a weakness, but she was not ready to leave this world.

She wanted to live, and love...

She yearned for...

She wasn't sure, but Roag's image swept her mind. His dark eyes and his bold, rugged face blotted all else until her only thoughts were of him and how much she wished he loved her. Her hope that he'd do so fiercely enough to never let her go.

Instead, he was scowling down at her, his expression hard and unreadable. The strong hands still gripping her arms felt angry, not loving. Fury and not passion fueled his firm hold on her.

"I can see, lass, that you are in sore need of a soak," he said, releasing her at last.

Going to the fire, he picked up a length of rough woolen cloth and folded it several times, using its thickness to protect his hands as he unhooked the brimming kettle from its chain. Carefully, he then tipped the steaming water into the linen-lined bathing tub.

"I will fetch a few pails of cool rainwater to temper the heat, and for you to rinse with," he said, already making for the door opening in the wall. "See that you are unclothed and wrapped in a toweling cloth before I return. I will stay on the roof long enough for you to prepare yourself.

"I ken, too, that you have a pot of lavender soap somewhere," he added, pausing at the stairwell. "I have smelled the scent on you and appreciated its pleasantness."

"My soap is in my chests." It was all she could manage to say, her gaze flashing to the two crates from Sway—both of them on the far side of the room.

"I will need a few moments to retrieve my soap, and to undress." She was already heading across the chamber, half certain that, shaken as she was, she wouldn't manage to find the little earthen pot of soap. "I will call you when I am ready."

"Do that, my lady." His voice was deep, his tone as unemotional as if he'd ordered his squire to help him remove his armor.

Yet Roag the Bear wasn't a man who relied on servants. Hadn't he prepared her bath himself? And didn't he treat every man in his party as an equal?

He did, and those were all things that she admired about him. They were reasons she'd found herself softening toward him. Why, she suspected, she'd come to feel so strongly about him.

She wasn't just wildly attracted to him, she respected him. And she couldn't bear the thought that he could kiss her, that he could *want* to hold and ravish her, and yet rather than keeping her at his side, he wished to deliver her elsewhere.

It was a truth that broke her heart.

Half tempted to say so, for she was still bold deep

inside, she stopped rummaging in her chests for her soap and glanced over her shoulder, ready to challenge him.

But he was already gone.

The door opening to the roof stair was empty, nothing peering back at her but darkness.

In that moment, her fingers closed over the soap jar, so she pulled it from the crate and stood. She knew he would stay out of sight until she was undressed and then properly covered again, draped in a towel.

For a beat, she considered calling for him when she was yet naked.

But if she did so and he rejected her, the shame would gut her.

No, that wasn't true.

She was already gutted. And it wasn't humiliation or embarrassment that hurt her.

It was the love in her heart.

Chapter Twenty-Six

❧

If ever he was a bastard, he was the greatest one now.

Roag stood in the window embrasure on the far side of the laird's chamber from the hearth and Lady Gillian in her bath. Trying not to think about where she was and what she was doing, he braced his arms against the cold damp stone of the window arch, his heart and mind in turmoil.

Behind him, he could hear the warm, scented water lapping against the rim of her bathing tub. Soft splashing also reached his ear, the sound torturing him, setting him like granite. No red-blooded man should remain in a bedchamber when a lady bathed. Yet, much as he knew he should, he couldn't bring himself to leave.

He had sworn to keep his back to her.

So far he'd done so.

But staring out the window brought torment of another kind. This high up in the tower, no noise from the hall could be heard. Beyond the tall, ancient window with its crooked, weather-warped shutters, a great silence had descended, deeper than any he'd ever known. To his astonishment, he found that the immensity of the stillness filled him with a surge of freedom and wonder.

At Stirling Castle, there was no escape into quiet.

Never, not even in the smallest hours.

Loud and raucous, or muted, the din of many people and the running of the stronghold was a ceaseless accompaniment to daily life.

Nothingness such as this was new and unknown. He embraced it gladly, the night's peace sliding round him like a sweet, soothing balm.

And as he looked out at the open sea, dark now save the silvered path of the moon, he'd swear he hadn't just sailed to a wee Hebridean isle, but had entered a different world. At last he understood Gillian's fierce attachment to her home. Why she could claim that more shimmered beneath the rush of wind or the wash of waves on the rocky shores. From somewhere in the night came the cries of seals, a poignant, almost human wailing that she'd surely ascribe to merfolk, a belief he'd no longer call nonsense.

He finally understood her affection for the isle and its sad, age-worn tower.

Indeed, he was beginning to feel the same.

Perhaps he already did.

Here, atop a soaring black cliff and with the whole of the night-sheened sea beneath him, it was easy to accept that there was more in the running tide than one could see with mere eyes. That perhaps a tower's stones truly did absorb all they'd seen of past lives, the comings and goings of men.

Who was to say that with the passage of countless centuries, stones didn't begin to think for themselves?

Roag drew a deep breath of the chill and briny air, no longer scoffing at the possibility. Gillian believed that the tower held memories and might welcome a caring hand.

And if that were so...

He'd like that hand to be his.

Gillian's touch would be even better.

Yet he'd already offered her all he could. His life wasn't his own for him to be able to give her more. She was a lady, a chieftain's daughter, who deserved all the courtesies of her station. He was a fighting man and adventurer with no wealth or property to speak of.

Court bastards had little to give ladies.

But he could make certain that he left her content and at peace when they parted.

Determined to do so, he turned from the window to cross the room to the bathing tub, taking care to keep his gaze on her face.

Unfortunately, he failed.

"My apologies, lass, but we must speak." His gaze drifted lower, gliding slowly over her and setting her cheeks to flame.

"Speak or stare at me?" Clearly flustered, she grabbed a washcloth and clutched it to her breasts.

"A bit of both it would seem. I'll no' lie."

"You promised to stay across the room," she accused, her brows snapping together.

"So I did," he agreed, glad that the washing tub was deep enough, its water dark.

Try as he might—and he was looking—he could see no more of her nakedness than her bare and glistening shoulders.

Lifting his gaze at last, he gave her a lopsided smile. "I have warned you that I am an earthy, rough-mannered lout, for all that Stirling is my home."

"Is that why you interrupted my bath?" She looked at him, her green eyes sparkling in the firelight. "To remind me who you are?"

"What I am, lady."

"I already know—I have done since you first arrived." She angled her head, the motion giving him an all too tempting view of the soft, creamy skin of her throat, the sweet curve of one shoulder.

His damnable cock twitched then and he scowled, wishing he'd stayed in the embrasure.

But it was too late. All restraint and good sense had long fled. He wanted her, and he did so badly.

Yet there were things he needed to know.

Thereafter...

He swatted at the folds of his plaid, hoped they'd shield his baser thoughts from her.

Apparently that was so, because she was still peering up at him, her face chilly with annoyance. "Well?"

"I would hear why you dinnae want to return to Sway," he said, his tone more brusque than he'd have wished. "Only if you speak plainly can I help you."

"I do not require aid unless you're prepared to take me to Glasgow. If you're still unwilling, you would serve me better now by returning to thon window." She glanced across the room to the embrasure he'd vacated. "I am finished bathing and the water is turning cold."

Roag folded his arms, not budging. "Answer me and I shall go."

"It is none of your concern." She glared at him.

"I am making it so."

"You have no right."

Roag arched a brow. "I am laird of the isle, for the now, anyway. You are the handfasted bride of Laddie's Isle's keeper. I am that man, whether it pleases you or nae."

"We are not bound in truth." She let go of the washing cloth and snatched a length of drying linen from the stool beside the bathing tub, throwing it swiftly around her as she surged to her feet. "Why I do not wish to return to Sway has nothing to do with you," she added, climbing from the tub.

"Even so, I am making it my business." Roag stepped around before her, blocking her path, when she sought to scoot past him. "Speak true, sweet, and I will be gone."

"I know fine you are leaving." Her chin came up, her eyes suddenly blazing. "You have made no secret about your wish to depart, or to be rid of me."

"You dinnae want to know what I wish." *I want only to rip thon toweling from you and scoop you into my arms, kissing and then ravishing you properly.*

"What I want, sirrah, is—"

"You want to stay here—in these isles." Roag gripped her arms, looked down at her, locking his gaze on hers. "I mean to see that desire granted."

It is all I can give you.

She pressed her lips together, her eyes snapping like emerald fire. But then she released her breath in a rush and broke free of his grasp to begin pacing, the linen wrapping clutched tightly about her. Clearly furious, she sailed to the window embrasure where he'd stood and then whirled to face him.

"As you will not give me any peace until I tell you, it is

my stepmother, Lady Lorna, who keeps me from returning home," she declared, high color staining her cheeks.
"It is not just that I fear for Skog." She glanced to where
the old dog slept curled on his plaid pallet before the
brazier. "She is no lover of animals and can be careless in
her treatment of them."

Anger swelled in Roag's chest. "She would hurt a bony
old dog?"

He couldn't believe it, though he should know that all
manner of folk walked the earth.

In his Fenris dealings, he'd seen the worst of men, and
women.

"I have already told you some of this," she said, coming a few steps back toward him, her lavender scent swirling out before her, enticing and irritating him. "I do not
think she would willfully hurt Skog or any pet. But she
forgets to think of them. When a dog is old and frail, he
depends on the people around him to make sure his world
is safe, free of obstacles and possible dangers.

"My stepmother has other interests." She lifted a hand,
pushed her skein of damp and gleaming hair over her
shoulder. "She is careless, that is all."

"I am sorry. I didnae ken—"

"She is also unkind to my father," she added, "though I
have no proof of my suspicions."

"She is unfaithful?" Roag guessed.

She nodded. "I have seen the way she looks at my
father when she thinks no one is watching. Her eyes hold
disdain, not love. Yet she stays abed with him for hours on
end, sometimes even days, and I know that they..." She
broke off, her cheeks brightening. "I know that they are
coupling properly because I have heard the sounds when

passing their door," she finished in a rush. "Her gasps and cries are lusty, easily heard in the passage and even down in the hall. My brothers would say you the same."

"I see." Roag scratched his neck, thinking.

More than one daughter had been known to resent a stepmother, especially if the father was well-loved. Who-ever Lady Lorna was, whatever sort of woman she might be, she would not be the first wife of such tender years to feign passion for a much older husband. There were many such unions at court. And he wasn't the only man who'd taken advantage.

Unhappy, poorly satisfied wives made excellent lovers.

Such women were willing and eager to air their skirts. And they made uninhibited and lascivious bedmates.

They also posed no threats to a man's freedom, asking only discretion.

"There are worse things than a young wife pretending to desire an older husband." Roag spoke as he saw it, not surprised when she scowled.

"It is more than that." She grabbed her night-robe off the bed and swirled it around her shoulders, letting the damp drying linen fall to the floor. "You have not seen—"

"I ken what you mean, lass. You believe she seeks pleasure elsewhere."

"She has a lover who visits her when my father and brothers are away at sea." She began pacing again, another pleasing waft of lavender trailing after her. "I am sure of it, for I have seen her setting a signal lamp in her window. I caught her at it and she denied it, but not before I saw the galley that was beating toward Sway. It flashed round and sped away the moment she doused the lamp."

"Did you no' tell your father?" Roag was sure she hadn't.

"I couldn't," she confirmed. "How could I? He is besotted with her. It would break his heart if he knew."

"If what you say is true, he would be better off without her." He closed the distance between them, took her hand in both of his. "You should no' let such a woman keep you from your home."

"She doesn't." She met his gaze, her voice firm. "It is for my father that I wish to stay away. It was becoming difficult to stay silent, to keep my suspicions to myself. My father is charmed, now. But he is also not a fool. The day will come when he sees through her. It is best that he does so himself. You do not know him. He is a proud man and will stand taller for handling the matter on his own. That he shall, I've no doubt. When that day comes, I will go home."

She slipped her hand from his grasp, stepping away as if his nearness upset her as much as her stepmother. "Until then, I'd hoped to stay in Glasgow. It is a good distance from Sway and—"

"So is this isle." Roag tamped down the disappointment that she didn't wish to be here, a prospect that suddenly struck him as something he wanted above all else.

Until recently, he'd been sure he only lusted after her. Then . . .

He drew a great breath, pulled a hand down over his face—almost as if he could wipe away any trace of his feelings that might show there. His ridiculous belief that Laddie's Isle and its terrible tower needed her. That, as much he'd damned her intrusion, he now couldn't imagine her not being here. Her smiles and laughter in the hall of an e'en, their shared hours up on the bluff each day, the quiet trek back down in the soft light of gloaming.

The wonder she saw in the turn of the tides, the crashing of waves, or the roar of the wind. Her steadfast trust in the fey and the ways of the ancients, how she smiled each time he touched his Thor's hammer amulet.

Her ever-amusing-to-him love of cold and rain.

How many times a day he just wanted to grab and kiss her.

He was sure all that stood on his face and for just as many reasons, he didn't want her to see.

"You still do not understand, do you?" She came close again, going toe to toe with him. "I have nothing at all against staying here. Truth is, I have come to love this isle.

"The problem is you, not Laddie's Isle." She looked up at him, the firelight glinting on her hair, her lavender scent rising up between them, bewitching him yet again. "I would stay here, and gladly. For all time, even. But I have no wish to remain where I am not wanted."

"Och, I want you fine, lassie." It was her scent that pushed him over the edge, making him blurt the truth he'd fought so hard to hide. The blaze in her eyes, a flame he burned to see switched over into the fire of passion. "If you'd know the way of it, I have ne'er wanted a woman more."

He started to touch her cheek, but instead he cupped the back of her neck, thrusting his fingers into her hair. "If I were a fine and courtly noble, I'd no' be so plainspoken," he admitted, aware of the roughness of his voice and making no attempt to hide it. "But I am my own lowborn self and I'll no' lie to you.

"I want you badly, lass." He whipped his arm around her, pulling her hard against him. "So much that I'm ready to cast aside everything that's aye mattered to me.

"Everything, that is"—he lowered his head, kissing her hungrily—"except you."

Chapter Twenty-Seven

✤

"Oh, dear..." Gillian's heart thundered and she clutched his shoulders as she leaned into him. The desperation of his kiss stunned her, making her pulse race and blurring everything around them. Even the room seemed to tilt and spin so that she was aware of nothing except him crushing her to him, his warmth and strength, the wildness of his kiss as he plundered her lips.

He wanted her, burned for her with a force that stole her breath.

It was a revelation that startled her, need, want, and love rushing through her until her knees weakened. She was sure that if he let go of her, she'd fall to the floor. She hadn't expected him to return her feelings, hadn't believed he even liked her.

But there could be no denying the heat of his kiss.

The arousal that nudged her through their clothes—hindrances she wanted done with, eager as she was to feel his naked skin next to hers. The thought shocked her, but she could no sooner banish it than tell the sea to stop crashing against the rocks below. A madness had seized her and she didn't even care if they weren't truly wed. They were handfasted, even if he'd accepted the bond under a different name. He was the same man and he'd sipped from her clan's Horn of Bliss, sealing the union in a way that, to her, and anyone of her kin, was a joining more sacred than any other.

"Sweet lass, I would have you." He spoke the words against her cheek, between kisses.

"Then do." She decided to be bold.

In truth, how could she do anything but acquiesce when he was nuzzling her neck, skimming his lips and tongue along her skin. He murmured Gaelic love words and praise, lit soft kisses to the hollow at the base of her throat. Delicious shivers rippled through her, warm, golden flutters of need that pooled deep in her belly and low by her thighs. Each kiss he dropped on her skin, every touch, all his softly spoken words, stirred and roused her as only true love could affect a woman.

And love him she did, as she'd suspected for long.

So there was no reason not to desire him.

Far from it, she had a fervent need to claim all of him that she could. To brand herself with his touch so that she'd have something to remember him by in the long, cold nights after he'd left her. For that reason, and so many more, including that she simply wanted him, she slid her hands up between them and undid the laces of her bed-robe, letting it fall open.

"You shouldnae have done that, lassie." He drew back to look down at her. He swept one of his hands over her bared flesh, splaying his fingers over the fullness of her breasts as he plumped and weighed them, rolled her nipples between his thumb and forefinger.

Gillian placed her hands on his chest and then smoothed them upward, gripping his shoulders. She closed her eyes and took a long, shaky breath. She was trembling, but didn't care. Wicked sensations raced through her, a spill of tingles that danced across her most intimate flesh, warming and exciting her. She was melting with pure need. Never would she have believed passion could be so crystalline and yet so maddeningly dizzying. Her knees had gone so weak that she could hardly stand, and the more he rubbed her breasts, his thumbs now circling round and over their thrusting crests, the closer she came to screaming out for more. She ached for a desperate, urgent something that whirled tightly inside her, threatening to consume her if not soon released.

"We can stop here, sweet," he said, even as he lowered his head, his tongue now flicking at her breasts—his thumb still working its terrifying magic.

"I'll no' be wanting to end this, for sure." He dropped kisses across her bared skin, his tongue like silken fire. "But I'll no' do aught you dinnae desire. You must tell me, lass. Shall we stop now?"

"No." She spoke her mind, seeing no shame in her feelings. "I would have at least one night of passion, true carnal bliss, with you. More, if the gods are kind."

He lifted his head, his gaze fierce. "Gillian, I would lie with you until all the world's tomorrows, again and again if it pleased you..." Again, he said her name without her title, that intimacy—and his words—spearing straight to her heart, and elsewhere.

"Would it?" he asked, touching her face, his smile

flashing again and in a way she knew she would never forget. Lifting her hand, he pressed his lips to her palm. "I would have your answer, lass."

"I will not keep it from you." She met his gaze, gathered all her strength to answer true.

If she were to spend her life without him, she'd rather have heated memories than cold virtue to wrap around her when she was old and alone.

Feeling most daring, she raised her hand to his cheek, lit her fingertips across his bearded jaw, his mouth. She looked deep into his eyes as she did so, her heart knocking wildly against her ribs.

"There is much that would please me." *A marriage in truth with the man I've come to love and desire, the chance to make a home of this tower, to know the isle is smiling again, if ever it did, and to raise our children here, teaching them to love and care for this world I can't bear to leave.*

Unless it were to be at your side in another place you love more.

"I am not a shy lass," she said, leaving her heart's cries unspoken. "There can be no wrong in a handfasted pair mating. Though, in truth, I would see no shame anyway. Viking blood runs in the veins of Hebrideans. We are strong and proud, a lusty race."

Proving it, she cradled his face and kissed him deeply, letting her robe slip to the floor as she did so. Stepping out of it, she kicked it aside to stand unclothed before him, desiring no more than to feel his hot naked flesh pressed tight to hers. "I've been waiting for this for so long."

"You are certain?" He pulled back, taking her wrists and lowering her hands to feel the hard ridge of his manhood. "I am no' able to resist you, sweet. See what you have done to me."

"I am glad." She curled her fingers around him, gripping tight.

"Och, you shouldnae do that, lass. No' yet..." But he made no move to thrust her hand away.

Instead, he reached to unclasp the large Celtic brooch at his shoulder and then tore off his plaid, flinging it onto the floor. Next, he pulled his shirt over his head, and then bent to tug off his boots. In almost as little time as it'd taken her robe to slide down her body, he stood equally naked before her, his large, swollen hardness leaving no doubt about how much he wanted her.

She shivered, sure she'd never known a greater thrill than standing skin to skin before him, both of them bareskinned and desirous, wanting and needing nothing more than to indulge the passion that flared between them.

Every inch of her thrummed with excitement. Delicious, almost unbearably intense sensations whirled across her woman's flesh, a heated throbbing that made her ache for more. Precious gifts she knew only he could give to her. Things she'd heard of in Sway's kitchens when the serving lasses and laundresses shared tales of their tumbles in the heather with the lads they desired.

She'd always let on as if she hadn't heard. In truth, she'd inched near. She'd hidden in the shadows, listening raptly to the delights they revealed, secretly yearning to know such pleasures herself—though she'd never expected to experience them, betrothed as she was to a man she'd loathed.

Now...

He stepped even closer, so near that his warmth

surrounded her, as if their bodies had already merged. "I doubt that tiny cot will hold us, but I would touch you, lass." He reached down between them as he spoke, gliding his fingers up her inner thighs. "Part your legs for me so that I may caress you properly."

His words took her breath, his intent sluicing her with embarrassment despite her previous declarations of bravura. She could feel two spots of heat blooming on her cheeks. Yet she also loved the feel of his hands on her. His fingers were warm and moved over her lightly, so magically she wondered she could still stand—so exquisite were the pulsing sensations between her thighs. There, where she knew he meant to touch her. It was beyond imagining! How could she deny herself such pleasure?

She couldn't.

So she closed her eyes for just a beat, and reached deep inside herself to grasp the wild abandon of her Norse ancestresses. She was sure that none of them would have hesitated to grant the carnal wishes of a man as naked and glorious as Roag, most especially when he stood before her with his hands on his naked hips, his smile saying he wanted to devour her.

She stole a glance at his hands, so strong and beautifully made. His long, skilled fingers stroking the tender skin of her inner thighs, moving slowly upward...

Her Viking blood heated, all modesty fleeing.

"Like this?" She did as he bid, opening her legs so that she stood before him with her feet about a foot apart. "Is that enough?"

"For the now, aye," he fair growled, staring down at her, his heated gaze almost scorching her exposed flesh. He kept his gaze there as he slid his hand higher, and then lit his fingers over her intimate hair. He brushed softly back and forth a few times, toying lightly with the curls, before he slipped his hand down between her legs and began stroking and rubbing her. "You can do the same to me, sweet."

He wrapped her fingers around the long, rigid length of him, showing her how to stroke him. He kept his hand over hers until she found the rhythm, all the while rubbing her intimately as she squeezed his hot, silken hardness, her hand moving up and down on him.

"Is this right?" She could hardly speak.

"Aye, just so." He sounded strained, but also pleased.

She was, too, for such intense pleasure ripped through her that she didn't know where it began or ended or which sensation was the most thrilling—his fingers moving so skillfully over her or holding him in her hand and stroking him as she was. In truth, it was all almost too glorious to bear.

She could hardly breathe.

And she didn't want him to stop. Didn't want to take her hand off him either.

"This is more pleasurable than I'd imagined," she blurted, rocking her hips against his hand, the sensations whipping through her filling her with wonder. "I'd heard—"

"You have spoken of such delights?" He drew back to look at her, his dark eyes amused.

"I have not," she met his gaze, and the very act of looking into his face as they stood there naked, touching each other so intimately made her quiver and tingle all the more. "I heard whisperings in the Sway kitchens is all."

"What sort of things did you hear?" He kept his gaze locked on hers, his thumb now circling a swollen, aching place that felt under siege by white-hot bolts of incredibly intense pleasure. "Did they say that men enjoy touching women as I am touching you now? Or perhaps that when a woman is caressed by a skilled hand, she will know a greater bliss than much else?"

Gillian bit her lip and nodded. "More or less, aye," she managed, not sure she could stand holding his gaze much longer. But, the fates have mercy on her, it was so delicious to do so! "They said a man with good hands was a prize worth more than gold."

"You believe that?" His voice was low, husky. He looked even deeper into her eyes, his thumb circling slower now, the rubbing deliberate, maddeningly delicious.

"I do . . ."

"Did you also hear that if a man and woman kiss when touching each other this way, that the pleasure increases even more?"

"I did not hear that, no."

"Would you like to try?" He lifted his thumb from that exquisitely sweet spot, trailed his fingers lightly up and down the center of her before he again resumed the thumb-circling. "If it pleases you, we can kiss now."

Gillian couldn't speak.

She did feel a great tremor rip through her, a cresting madness so powerful that she feared she might break apart. As if he knew, he swept an arm around her, drawing her hard against him as he lowered his head and claimed her lips, kissing her deeply in a rough, plundering blend of lashing tongues and a bold sharing of hot, desperate breath. It was like no other kiss they'd yet shared.

Wild and raw and open-mouthed, this kiss was so hunger-filled that only his thumb and fingers moving so skillfully between her legs felt more delicious.

Or so she thought until the world shattered, blowing apart in thousands of colorful fragments that whirled everywhere, leaving her limp, gasping, and so wondrously depleted that she could only cling to him as he scooped her up and carried her a few paces to where he'd tossed his plaid before the fire. He lowered her gently, settling her onto the fire-warmed wool as if she were made of spun glass.

"Dinnae move, precious lass," he urged, kneeling beside her, looking down at her with such intensity that she felt another quick flurry of the same delicious sensations that had just torn through her. "Breathe deep, and lie still. I will fetch you something to drink..."

Standing, he strode across the room to the table with her untouched evening repast. He poured two cups of ale and returned to her, once more dropping to his knees beside her.

"Nae, dinnae sit up." He placed a hand on her shoulder, gently easing her back down when she tried to rise. Instead, he slid an arm around her shoulders, supporting her as he tipped the ale cup to her lips. "Drink, my sweet, the ale will refresh you."

Gillian almost choked. She would never be the same again.

And she'd rather have more of the same than be replenished. But she drained the ale, her breath still coming fast and shallow. "Oh, my," she gasped as he set the empty cup aside and smoothed back her still-damp hair. "That was...I cannot describe it. I have never known such a feeling. It was more than—"

"It was you, my love." He slid his knuckles down her cheek, then trailed his fingers along her neck and over her shoulder, soon tracing light circles across her breasts. "You are beautiful, wonderful, and dinnae e'er think I didnae enjoy every sweet moment.

"I have ne'er desired a lass more," he told her, plucking lightly at her nipples, his touch sending more streams of the same kind of pleasure spilling through her. "Ne'er have I known a more passionate, responsive woman. You, sweetness, are a treasure."

"And your pleasure?" She did push up on her elbows now, her gaze flicking to his rampant manhood, still aroused, and not yet sated. "What of you?"

"My enjoyment is in pleasing you." He traced his hand lower, down her ribs and across her belly, threading his fingers lightly in her intimate curls. "Though it would make me very happy if you will let me just look at you."

Gillian caught her breath, his words sending another bolt of powerful liquid heat arcing through her, right to the swollen little nub that had caused such delicious sensations when he'd rubbed her there with his thumb.

"What do you mean 'look at me'?" She could hardly speak for excitement.

Something told her he meant a most wicked kind of looking. And the thought of it was making her tingle anew.

"I would gaze upon your beauty." He slid his hand between her legs again, began stroking her once more. But very, very lightly now, and using only the tips of his fingers.

"You are looking at me."

"No' as I'd like to." His grin flashed against his beard, the bold, wicked smile that did funny things to her belly.

"I am sure I don't know what you mean." *I do and just can't say the words.*

Go ahead and look, please, whatever you want of me. I am already shivering with need, my desire burning.

As if he'd heard, his eyes lit triumphantly and he moved farther down the plaid. Still kneeling, he placed his hands on her knees. Then he looked up and met her gaze, seeking her willingness.

"Please…" Gillian nodded, biting her lip as he returned her nod. Then, lowering his gaze from her face, he eased her legs apart, letting her knees fall wide.

He looked down at her there, his gaze dark, fierce, and so filled with masculine appreciation that she almost cried out with the sensations that swept her. She did begin rocking her hips. A deep urgent need to do so almost consumed her. It was a wild, elemental urge that she couldn't control and didn't want to.

"Nae, lass, no' yet." He placed the flat of one hand across her lower belly, holding her down. "There will be time for that soon. All you need to do now is keep your knees apart and let me gaze on you."

And so she did, sure that the longer he peered down at her, stroking her so lightly with one hand as he did so, the more she became convinced that his hands weren't just "good," but magical. But then so was everything about him.

Perhaps he was a wizard?

A fae man not of mortal men, but sent here to torment women with his pleasure-spending talents.

Gillian shivered, almost believing it.

"Relax, be at ease," his voice was deep, roughened by what she supposed were the same delicious sensations flooding her. "You're tensing, and I want you completely comfortable. Indeed, if you'll trust me, I know another way to be sure you're ready—"

"I am now." She knew enough of breeding, was aware of what was yet to come. Preparing herself, she tried to rise again, but he put his hand back on her belly, his warm fingers brushing her curls again, and in ways that made her forget wanting to sit up.

"You have magic fingers," she said, not caring if he could tell how she trembled in bliss, or how wet she was becoming. That, too, she'd heard of from the kitchen wenches at Sway. She'd not understood at the time, but she did now.

She'd gone slick and damp with what they'd called the "dew of desire."

"You are the magic, lass." He was looking down at her again.

No, he was *breathing* on her!

"By the gods!" This time she did push up on her elbows, her bravura fading when she saw just how closely he was looking at her! His head was right between her thighs, his dark, amused gaze peering up at her now. "What are you doing?"

"Nothing that you willnae enjoy, I promise," he said, and licked her.

"Oh!" She nearly burst. Her hips rose off the plaid, bucking when he did it again, and again.

Embarrassment sluiced her, but only for a moment. The feel of his tongue on her, licking slowly up the whole of her, then swirling over the exceptionally sensitive spot, was too exquisite to resist. Still, she had to say something...

"Please, you shouldn't—"

"I should, and you need only relax and enjoy." He looked up at her, once again locking gazes with her, this time as he licked and licked her.

It was wondrous beyond all imagining and she started to say so, but then the world tilted again and she gripped his shoulders, holding tight so she wouldn't slide off. But she couldn't have anyway, because in that moment, he'd somehow moved up on top of her, sliding one arm beneath her to hold her as he urged her legs to part even more.

Then he was pushing into her, gently at first, the hard, full length of him gliding into her, filling her inch by inch, until he'd claimed her entirely. It hurt, even pinching her deep inside. But the hot stinging was only a momentary discomfort and then he was also kissing her, taking her lips with the same, deep, open-mouthed kisses that had brought her such pleasure earlier.

Delicious sensation slid through her and she forgot all else except him. How much she loved and desired him, and how beautiful it was to lie with him—as she had instinctively known from the first moment they'd met.

She now suspected that knowing was why she'd rebelled so fiercely for so long.

Because accepting such a potent, powerful love was a total capitulation. It was a surrendering of her heart, leaving her vulnerable. He could shatter her so easily now. For the truth was, he'd made clear that theirs could only be a union for a time, and then he'd be gone.

But those worries faded quickly as he rode her, his smooth, rhythmic thrusts firing her blood, thrilling her.

Then the glory of it turned almost unbearable and she felt him stiffen, his entire body going rigid as he broke their kiss to stretch upward and throw back his head in pure, male triumph.

"Gillian!" he called her name, the sound of it beautiful in his passion.

She couldn't speak, simply clung to him as yet again, the same deliciousness swelled and broke inside her. As before, the pleasure washed through her like a sweet molten tide of exquisite heat and tingly sensation.

Then she knew no more, only that she was lost, both falling and soaring in a glittering whirl of sensual delight. An enchanted place that welcomed her and that she didn't wish to leave.

But even as she drifted, tiny doubts resurfaced. She cracked her eyes, not having the strength to open them fully. Her breath was uneven, her heart beating rapidly. He was still sprawled atop her, his wide, muscled shoulders sheened with sweat. His breathing was as ragged as hers, his thundering pulse as notable. Gillian closed her eyes again, surprised how pliant her body was when he rolled off her and drew her tight against his side, even settling her head on his chest, softly stroking her hair. The sweetest sensations slid through her again, but of a different, more gentle sort.

She felt more than saw his smile as he caught her hand, twining their fingers. He didn't say anything, but he did squeeze her hand.

Then his breathing eased and she suspected he slept. Indeed, a snore confirmed her guess. Gillian remained still, savoring the comfort of simply lying beside him, held so securely in his arms.

She imagined she should feel shame, guilt, or regret, but she didn't.

She only knew an overwhelming contentment, a love she could never deny. And as it filled her, claiming not just her body, but also her heart and soul, her worries returned. They nibbled at the edge of her every thought, reminding her that this joy was only fleeting. And that Roag wasn't truly hers.

Much as she wished he was.

For herself, she was certainly his. He'd wakened desire in her and he'd made her a woman. She didn't want to cling to this memory in her later years, she wanted to spend her life reveling in many such nights. So many that the feel of his big, strong body naked against hers became as familiar as the tread of her own feet on the ground, as dear and natural as her every breath. All that she craved, aware that she'd be an empty shell without him.

He was, she knew, the only husband for her. She didn't want another. Indeed, she'd refuse one, no matter what her father and brothers said or did. She let her eyes flutter open again, watched the slow, steady rise and fall of his slumbering breath. Dear, sweet gods, what was she to do? She couldn't bear the thought of him taking a different wife.

If she must, she'd insist on the powers vested in her clan's Horn of Bliss. No matter his denials, she knew from the hammer amulet at his neck that he respected the old ways.

By whatever name he'd bonded with her, their union was now real.

And whether it pleased him or not, she was keeping him.

Roag the Bear was hers.

Chapter Twenty-Eight

❖

Moments later, it seemed, though in truth it was hours, the blare of a horn shattered the early morning quiet. Roag slit an eye, still deep in the dregs of sleep. The sweet bliss of having slumbered on his plaid before the still-smoldering driftwood fire, Gillian wrapped snugly in his arms, her lush body warm and soft against him.

They'd loved once more in the smallest hours. It'd been a slow and tender coupling. Less desperate than their first, but powerfully intense. Afterward, Gillian had gone limp in his arms. She'd swiftly slipped into a deep sleep, her head cushioned on his shoulder. And he'd known then that he'd never before felt so strongly about a woman and never would again. He'd not wanted to think of letting her go, wasn't even sure that he could.

It was a prospect that chilled him to the bone and filled his chest with a sharp, throbbing pain. But he'd tamped down those concerns and spent the hours trailing his fingers gently up and down her side, over the soft, round fullness of her breasts. He'd not wanted to waken her, but he hadn't been able to stop touching her.

In truth, he suspected he'd never have enough of her.

Holding her through the night had brought him a peace he'd never thought to experience. An almost terrifying sense of rightness, as if she'd been meant for him and they both belonged here, in this high tower room, on this isle.

Not just this past beautiful night, but always.

He'd wanted to lie with her forever, half afraid that if he even moved, one of the ancients or faeries she believed in would swoop in from the morning mist and snatch her away. Stealing her before he'd had a chance to tell her how he felt, if even he should.

He knew fine that a binding with him wasn't good for her.

She was a lady, by all the hounds!

And what was he?

Roag frowned, felt his entire body tightening with frustration, even anger—but at himself for letting this happen. He should never have touched her.

But he had, and now...

He bit back a groan, but couldn't stop his hands from fisting. If he cared for her at all, and he did, powerfully so, he'd do what he'd told his men. He'd find a good husband for her amongst his acquaintances in Highland society. He knew enough clansmen to locate a kindly chieftain or laird needing a wife for himself or his heir. She deserved a man who would equal her in station and treat her well.

He would arrange such a match.

Then he'd spend the rest of his days missing her.

He'd curse himself for the first time ever for his lowly birth—the fate that had never bothered him at all, but tore him to pieces now.

He couldn't believe he'd ruined her.

Yet...

How could he have resisted her? And now these last blissful hours were ending, some weird sea creature taking it upon itself to while away the time beneath his tower, wailing and moaning as only strange denizens of the sea could do.

Roag shifted on the cold stone floor and drew Gillian closer against him, taking care that his plaid covered her. Gods pity him, but he was not yet ready to let her slip from his arms. With luck—if he had any remaining—the whale or whatever it was would swim on, leaving them in peace.

But the blaring came again, this time accompanied by the pounding of running feet.

Someone was racing up the tower stair and—he leapt to his feet, awake at once—the "whale" wasn't a sea creature at all but a horn.

It was a warning that something was badly amiss.

"What is it?" Gillian woke then, blinking as she glanced about the still dark bedchamber.

"My men." Roag's voice was muffled by the tunic he was pulling over his head. "One of our lookouts on the bluffs is blowing a signal. There'll be trouble at sea," he told her, reaching for his heavy mail shirt, donning it with the ease of years of practice, for he'd aye shunned the help of a servant.

"You will stay here, and bar the door after I leave." His words were terse, hard. But she needed to heed him.

"Dinnae open to anyone but me—or Conn or Big Hughie, if I am unable to return."

"Don't say that—of course, you'll come back!" She was already on her feet, pulling on her bed-robe as she hurried to the nearest window. "I see nothing, not toward the west, anyway."

Before she could dash to the next embrasure, a loud hammering on the door brought the surety that something was indeed terribly wrong.

"Heed my words, lass!" Roag ran across the room, buckling on his sword belt as he threw the door wide.

One of his men stood there, his chest heaving from charging up the steps. "There's a sea battle to the east," he panted, his gaze flicking once to Gillian before he rushed on. "Three ships, but we cannae yet see well enough through the mist to ken whose they are. Could be thon dragon ship we chased, returned with friends. By the clashing, we think the ships are ramming."

"Conn? Big Hughie?" Roag felt Gillian clutch his arm, so he reached to grip her hand, squeezing.

"They're down on the beach, readying the *Valkyrie*," Roag's man told them.

"Aye, right! We'll be away at once." Turning to Gillian, he grabbed her face and kissed her hard. "We'll leave enough men here to guard the tower, dinnae you worry. But stay here and do as I said. Bar the door and dinnae answer save for me, Conn, or Big Hughie."

"But—"

"Nae buts." He kissed her again, swiftly. "You ken we must go—I'll no' leave till I hear you've thrown the draw-bar. Do it now," he stepped through the door, joining his man on the shadowy landing.

He pulled the door shut before she could argue. Then he heard the heavy drawbar slide in place. For good measure, he tried the door, but it was soundly locked.

"We're off!" He nodded once at his oarsman, then tore down the tower stair, his man behind him. They didn't slow in the hall, sprinting past the men Conn and Big Hughie had ordered to stay behind and guard Gillian.

Then they burst outside, into the chill, mist-hung morning. The noise of the sea fight hit them at once, the clanging of steel and the knocking of shields, the hiss of water and the great splashing of oars as galleys wended and clashed on the waves.

And as Roag and his oarsman dashed down the cliff stair to the landing beach where the *Valkyrie* already rocked in the water, her great oars raised for a swift launch, Roag knew that his reason for coming to Laddie's Isle was about to be met.

It'd be a resolution that would also end his time here.

Damn all the gods!

High above the sea, in the tower's laird's chamber where she'd lost her innocence and won the knowledge that she truly did love Roag the Bear, Gillian stood in a window embrasure and stared out at the horror unfolding below her. One of the worst ship clashes she'd ever seen. As the morning mist began to thin, she saw that it was also the most terrible.

And she wasn't just worried about Roag and the *Valkyrie*.

Unless her excellent vision had soured, her father's ship was also in the fray!

"Oh, Skog, be glad your eyes are so milky." She

threaded her fingers in the fur of the dog's bony shoulders. "But you know, don't you?" She glanced down at him, sure he could hear the dreadful fight, the shouts of men and the screams, the constant lashing of oars on the waves, the splashing of water.

Skog hadn't left her side since she'd barred the door, and he leaned into her now, giving her the only comfort she could find in a world turned so dreadful.

Why her father's ship, *Sea Dancer*, was involved in such a battle stumped her.

Her father wasn't a fighting man and had no enemies. The MacGuires weren't known for warring. Even her brothers, though protective of her, bore no grudges and had only friends. The voyages her family made were to fish or sail for supplies.

Yet her eyes weren't deceiving her.

Four ships clashed not far from Laddie's Isle. One was the *Valkyrie*, now spinning in a tight circle, churning the water, as she flashed after another ship, a galley Gillian didn't recognize. She didn't think it was the MacDonald warship. *Sea Dancer* and a fourth galley sped round the two other ships, the furious beating of their oar blades whipping the water to a seething froth of white. Great plumes of spray rose everywhere, making it hard to see what was happening in the center of the watery circle. The *Valkyrie* was bearing down on the second unknown ship, clearly intent on racing along her side, shearing away the oar strakes.

It was the swiftest and most sure way to damage a galley.

Destruction sure enough to send a ship to the bottom of the sea, for the splintering of oars usually killed the oarsmen. Either the impact sent them into the water, where they drowned, or the jagged shards of the broken oars ran them through, spearing them like a jouster's tournament lance.

"Oh, dear gods..." Gillian bit her lip, not wanting to watch but unable to look away.

She was relieved that the second unknown vessel seemed a friendly one.

A fine galley manned by mailed warriors who looked as fearsome as Roag and his crew. The ship worked in tandem with her father's, circling round the *Valkyrie* and the other ship so that the enemy vessel couldn't veer away.

The sea boiled and Gillian's heart raced. Pressing closer to the window, she leaned out, straining to see through the whirling mist that was again thickening.

Then she was glad for the lesser visibility, because a terrible shattering of wood filled the air, joined by the screams of men who, from the sound of it, were finding their deaths. The *Valkyrie*—now fitted with a long iron-headed ramming spear—had raced down the side of the other galley, shearing away her oars and rendering the ship useless.

At once, her father's ship and the fourth galley whipped about and shot forward, joining the *Valkyrie* as the three vessels crowded round the damaged ship.

The men would fight now, Gillian knew. She could see the flash of steel, so many drawn swords and axes. She shook her head as she pressed a hand to her breast, felt the wild hammering of her heart.

Beside her, Skog began to howl, his aged body racked with trembles.

"Oh, sweet, please do not worry." She dropped to her knees beside him, gathering the old dog into her arms, pulling him against her. She comforted him as best she could. She needed his warmth and familiarity as well. "It will be over soon, I promise." *And I hope to all the gods that no one we love will be lost!*

She didn't say the words aloud, knowing, as did everyone who ever loved a dog, that Skog would understand and fret the more.

She needed to be strong for him.

The heartache that would come with a defeat was a horror she refused to accept.

She couldn't.

She did force herself to push to her feet again, almost wishing she hadn't when she saw the scene below. The four ships had crashed together and grapnel chains strained between them, holding them bound to each other and making the deck of each galley into an awful, red-slicked fighting platform.

Men from the three friendly ships were pouring onto the damaged galley. They leapt from one bow to the next, weapons drawn and clashing as the warriors shouted and fought, swords and axes glinting everywhere. Unfortunately, the whirling mist didn't let her pick out faces. All the fighting men were huge, mailed, and clearly furious. They attacked in a rage that would've terrified her even more if she hadn't known they were good men. Equally unsettling, the decks weren't the only thing stained red now. She could see the gleam of blood on the men's swinging weapons, and a great film of red was spreading across the water, a ghastly tint that she knew wasn't from the rising sun, because the day was an overcast, misty one.

For a moment, she caught a glimpse of Roag and her heart leapt to her throat. He fought in the middle of the enemy ship, towering above the other men, his sword arcing again and again, the blade shining crimson and terrifying her.

Then something else chilled her to her soul—a woman's scream pierced the mist.

And her cry ended abruptly, hinting at a grisly end.

Gillian swayed, felt her own blood draining. She forced herself to lean out the window as far as she dared, but the wind was picking up and it was beginning to rain. Icy pellets struck her face, making it difficult to see. The mist blew hard now, drifting in sheets past the tower, sealing Laddie's Isle and the ships from view.

But not before she saw the dark shapes of the three victorious galleys wending away from the fourth ship. Pulling back, she knew, to allow the defeated warship to die in peace.

Or perhaps to lend the ship a quicker end, because one of the retreating galleys began shooting fire arrows at the floundering vessel. The sparks must've caught despite the rain, for the ship's square sail and mast ignited in a burst of orange flame, dooming the ill-fated ship.

The sea fight was over.

Relief such as Gillian had never known swept her. "By all the ancients, thank you!" she breathed, sagging against the window arch.

She reached down, stroking Skog's head again and again, hoping to soothe him the same way seeing the three ships beating toward Laddie's Isle calmed her own racing pulse.

She knew Roag would be well—she couldn't make

him out, or even tell which ship was his, for the mist was swiftly turning to thick sea fog. But she knew in her heart that he'd be unscathed, victorious against his foes.

Her father and brothers...

She bit her lip, a shiver of trepidation rippling through her. She prayed to all the gods and ancients that they'd be well. She refused to think about why they were even involved—or that Roag might insist that she return to Sway with them.

As for the wee lad on the shore...

"Oh, my!" Her eyes flew wide, her heart almost stopping. She blinked, sure she wasn't seeing him.

But she was.

Mist rolled along the landing beach, thick and almost impenetrable—save one small area near the base of the cliffs. That spot glowed with a shimmering blue light and a wee lad in a ragged plaid stood there pointing at the sea with a tiny blue-glowing dirk.

"Skog! It's him, the laddie ghost!" She glanced at her dog, but when she looked up again, the wee bogle was gone. Only a faint tinge of fast-fading blue luminescence remained where he'd stood, the landing beach once again completely cloaked in mist.

"He knew." She dropped to her knees beside Skog. "He knew all along that the danger would be here and not far out to sea where Roag's men went sailing each day."

Those men were returning now, the hissing of water on hulls and the splashing of oars striking the waves revealing their fast approach. The *Valkyrie* and the two other ships were almost back at the landing beach.

She didn't care what Roag had said—she wasn't going to wait for him in this room.

Neither was her dog.

Trembling all over, from relief and love, she dressed as quickly as she could and then threw back the door's drawbar. She flung the door wide and then took a great breath, willing herself to have the strength she needed to heave Skog unto her shoulders.

She managed with surprising ease, settling his bony frame against her as securely as she could.

"Come on, laddie," she soothed him, lowering her head to drop a kiss onto his straggly coat. "We're away below-stairs to greet our men. They'll have much to tell us!"

Chapter Twenty-Nine

❧

I knew fine something was amiss with the she-witch!"

Mungo MacGuire thumped Roag's high table with his fist as he scowled round at anyone who'd listen. His eyes blazed and his red-bearded face glowed as bright as his fiery hair. It was hours since the sea battle that had ended the life of his nefarious young wife and her lover, not an Englishman at all, nor a MacDonald, but a Sassenach sympathizer, just as Lady Lorna had been.

"Why do ye think"—Mungo half rose from his chair, lifting his voice as well—"my lads and I made haste back from our supply trip to Islay? No' because the MacDonalds were all fashed that someone had cut the prow off one o' their most-prized dragon ships, even stealing the sail, the thievin' dastards! Och, nay, that wasnae the reason we sped away, soon as our hold was loaded."

He dropped back into his chair, gripping the armrests in an angry white-knuckled hold. "'Twas because of her! My own lady wife! I kent she was consorting with the devil English—or leastways a fiend Scotsman who fancied he'd have a better living south of our borders."

Beside him, Roag placed his hand over Gillian's, squeezing lightly. "I would ne'er have suspected her, lord," he said, speaking true. "Nor have I even heard of Cormac MacCraig. A shame the man will pass eternity feeding crabs rather than spending your treasure in London or where'er he and the lady thought to flee."

Along the table and amongst the men gathered near, growls of annoyance could be heard as they all shook their heads, wondering over a Scotsman who could commit such treachery as attacking the King's own ships and stealing a clan's hoard of treasure with the intent of presenting it to the English king.

"Lass," Mungo leaned around Roag to peer at his daughter. "You should have told me straightaway you'd seen her setting signal lamps in my own bedchamber window."

"I did not want to see you hurt," Gillian said, speaking true. "I did guess she was alerting a man that you and my brothers were away on *Sea Dancer*. But I'd never have believed that, along with betraying you, she was giving him our clan treasure."

"Aye, and it's at the bottom of the sea now." Her eldest brother, Gowan, spoke from the next table, his deep voice more amused than sorrowful. "The ancients might say nae one was e'er supposed to remove that hoard from its hiding place." He lifted his ale cup, draining it. "No good comes of taking what isn't one's own."

"Humph!" Mungo scowled at him. "If the old ones weren't pleased we had that silver, they'd have snatched it back long ago," he declared, tossing down his own ale, but drinking from a horn. "Be that as it may, my true treasure is in this hall." He waved his ale horn to take in Gillian and his sons, half of them at the high table, the other four at a nearby dais table. "I'm grateful for that, I am! There be nae greater wealth than family."

"Hear, hear!" Everyone who heard agreed, raising their cups or thumping the tables with the blunt ends of their eating knives, or their elbows.

Even Skog joined in, his old dog barks a bit thin, but no less enthusiastic.

"I am glad for my friends!" Roag glanced toward the other end of the table.

It was there that his two fellow court bastards from Stirling Castle—Caelan the Fox and Andrew the Adder, his Fenris brothers—sat with William Wyldes, proprietor of the Red Lion Inn in Stirling. William was a big man with unruly auburn hair that he wore tied back at his nape. His beard was just as bushy and wild, and he had light blue eyes that always smiled.

Roag raised his cup in his friends' direction, silently thanking the gods that they'd happened to pass the Isle of Sway just as Mungo's *Sea Dancer* shot out of the island's little bay, giving chase to Cormac MacCraig's ship. According to Caelan, Andrew, and Wyldes, they'd first suspected MacCraig of kidnapping Mungo's young wife, Lady Lorna. She was seen at the prow of the enemy ship as it'd sped from Sway just as Mungo and his sons beat home two full days early from their supply journey to the neighboring Isle of Islay.

Mungo, with his poor eyes, had only been able to tell that his wife was onboard the fleeing ship.

His sons had seen more.

They'd spotted her first—glimpsing her in a heated

embrace with the ship's captain, MacCraig. A man who, they soon learned, had been sneaking in to Sway whenever Mungo and his men were away. Once there, he hadn't just partaken of the charms of the lady of the keep. He'd also carried away the clan's treasure, taking it bit by bit so Mungo wasn't likely to notice.

Wyldes leaned forward then, twisting round to look at the MacGuire men at the next table. "Did MacCraig truly think the English King would grant him lands and a title for sinking our ships and plying him with centuries-old Viking treasure?

"I cannae believe any Scot would be so foolhardy." Wyldes glanced at Roag. "We have seen much in our day. But ne'er such a fiend as this."

"Hate and greed will spur a man to much, my friend." Roag knew it well. "Women likewise, leastways some of them."

"Lady Lorna's face always changed when she spoke of King Robert." Gillian set down the bit of roasted gannet she'd been about to eat. The seabird was tasty, but thinking of her stepmother didn't aid her appetite. "It was clear that she did not like him."

Her brothers nodded agreement.

Gillian glanced at Roag. "Her family had been staunch Balliol supporters in the Bruce's day. Once he took the Scottish crown, many families who'd given their loyalty to Balliol and the English lost their lands and wealth.

"Lady Lorna hails from such a clan, with strong ties to the MacDougalls." She paused, shaking her head. "Apparently, she resented King Robert more than she let on."

"So she sought to repay him by helping an equally grieved soul with aspirations of grandness." Blackie,

Gillian's middle brother and the only one with dark hair and eyes, finished for her. Also her most dashing brother, he wasn't looking happy now. "I do feel bad for killing her," he said, his face still ashen as it'd been since the sea battle. "Who can stomach spearing a woman?"

"Aye, well!" Roddy and Rory, the MacGuire twins, spoke in unison. "Did you have a choice?"

Rory leaned toward Blackie, reaching out to clap his brother on the shoulder. "You were closest to her. If you hadn't stopped her, she'd have run Da through."

"Indeed!" Mungo pushed to his feet again, set his hands on his hips. "Would you rather it was me feeding fish in the sea, laddie?" He fixed Blackie with a stare, his beetling red brows drawn low. "Your da, or the she-witch who'd been ready to skewer him?"

Blackie didn't answer, only emptied his ale cup and then dragged his sleeve over his mouth.

"Aye, well." He glanced round. "There wasn't much else I could do, right enough."

"Taking a life is nae pretty, lad." Roag sympathized, weary himself of all the battles he'd fought. "You do get used to it, if you're a warrior. But few men e'er come to enjoy it, that I say you."

"And what do you say to my gel?" Mungo snapped his gaze toward Roag and Gillian. "Far as I can tell, you're enjoying your handfast, but I'm no' sure what to think of your name!"

"Father!" Gillian sent him a frantic look, shaking her head. "We told you why Roag said he was Donell. No man in this hall can condemn him for aught. Far from it, if it weren't for his friends' coming here this morn, you and my brothers might have been dead.

"You're no' fighters," she added, sending an apologetic look at her brothers. "You're fishermen. Lady Lorna's lover and his men have attacked the King's best ships, sinking every one they chased after."

"We had a fair chance to beat them." The twins Roddy and Rory spoke together again, swelling their chests as they did so.

"'Tis true," Logie, another brother, joined in, tossing a grin at William Wyldes, Caelan, and Andrew. "Roag's friends' ship was so weighed down by cargo she moved like a slug in the water. She only caught up to us after pitching much of her freight into the sea."

Roag frowned, hearing this for the first time. He'd assumed the louts had been passing through the Hebrides on a different Fenris mission, or perhaps on Alex's command to patrol the seas off Laddie's Isle. They could've been ordered to stay out of sight, unless needed. He'd meant to question them later, away from non-Fenris ears.

Now...

He could only puzzle. Any Fenris duty that involved a ship wouldn't call for a vessel so weighed down that she couldn't sail at speed.

"What cargo?" He turned to his friends, not liking the sheepish looks on their faces.

Caelan and Andrew exchanged guilty glances.

William, as always, met his gaze full-on and grinned. "Foodstuff from Alex," he said, his deep voice amused. "Your friend the Wolf worried you'd starve out here in the wilds of the Hebridean Sea. He put together enough viands and ale to fill your kitchens for a year, he did. Good Wolf that he is, he sent me along to cook for you.

Yet"—William spread his hands—"there isn't much need of me, eh?"

"Our work is done, it is true," Roag agreed, the admission causing a sharp pain in his chest. "You'll be wanting to return to the Red Lion, I ken fine."

"That is so!" William grinned. "The Wolf did send a lad down to Stirling to run the inn for me. But you ken"— he leaned back in his chair and patted his substantial girth—"no one within twenty heather miles of Stirling stirs a cook pot better than I do.

"I'll no' be wanting to lose trade because I'm no' there." He straightened and grabbed his eating knife to spear a gannet breast, popping a large piece of the roasted seabird into his mouth as if all had been said and there was no need to discuss more.

But Caelan and Andrew and, surprisingly, Mungo MacGuire kept sliding glances at each other. Roag was becoming weary of what looked like scheming.

He already knew Mungo was capable of trickery.

Caelan and Andrew...

They believed a shared childhood in Stirling Castle's kitchens and years of joint Fenris missions gave them leave to meddle in his affairs.

"What is it?" He narrowed his eyes at them, his suspicions growing.

"Aye, well..." Caelan hedged, lifting his ale cup and studying it as if it were the most interesting thing under the heavens. "It could be that when we were hurrying to catch up with the *Sea Dancer*, we didn't toss all the Wolf's goods into the sea."

"For sure, we didn't," Andrew agreed, his quirking lips worrying Roag even more.

"They kept the best, they did!" Mungo slapped the table, his red-bearded face splitting in a grin. "A bed, see you?" He stood, swelling his great barrel chest. "The King's own brother has sent a wedding bed to my gel," he boasted, his voice ringing with pride as if he—and not Roag and his friends—was a much-loved favorite of Alex Stewart, Lord of Badenoch and Earl of Buchan.

"Ne'er will you see a finer bed!" Mungo roared, his excitement spreading to everyone in the hall. "He sent you a laird's chair." He beamed at Roag, clearly pleased to make the announcement. " 'Tis a glorious piece, richly carved, and surely straight from the Wolf's own Highland lair.

"Your friends"—he looked their way—"did toss it into the water, but my lads and I fished it out as it bobbed past us!"

"Indeed?" Roag didn't know what else to say.

His temples were beginning to throb, his head aching at the evidence of his world crashing down around him. The reminder—in the shape of a bed, no less—of what could have been and yet would never be. He sat back, drew a long, tight breath, half certain he was suffocating.

He wasn't surprised the Wolf had learned of his handfast with Gillian.

Alex Stewart knew everything.

But whatever goodness of heart caused him to send food supplies and lairdly trappings to this wee bleak isle, there was no need for them now.

And that gutted Roag more than it should.

"Where is this bed? The carved laird's chair?" The words slipped from his lips before he could catch them. "I havenae seen—"

"Have you noticed that a few of my lads are missing?" Mungo raised his ale horn, saluting Roag. "That's the good thing about having many sons, see you? You can have them everywhere at once and no one is the wiser. A few of them were down at the ships as we've supped. They carted the bed up to your chamber without any of us even seeing them marching through the hall, so busy were we all railing about the evil deeds of my late wife and her pestiferous lover!"

A strange tightness began to spread through Roag's chest. "Where is the laird's chair?"

"Och, it's oe'r by the fire on the far side of your hall!" Mungo thrust out an arm, pointing at a massive, elaborately carved chair of gleaming black oak.

Beautiful enough to grace Stirling's finest chambers, the chiefly chair was nothing less than a throne, and surely did hail from the Wolf's own castle.

Roag couldn't imagine Alex sending anything so priceless on such a journey, for naught.

Turning to Gillian, he leaned in, speaking low so that only she would hear. "There is more to this than meets the eye. Alex wouldnae risk such goods if—"

"If he didn't think you would be staying on here?" She smiled, her eyes shining in the torchlight.

Roag's heart kicked hard against his ribs. He couldn't think of anything he'd want more. Indeed, he'd been planning to sail to Stirling and petition the King for just that. He'd cite the isle's strategic location as a boon for the crown, emphasize the advantage of having a trusted man to watch the traffic on the seas.

"If that were so, lass, would you remain as my lady in truth? My own bride and wife, and no' as Donell's?"

"I was never Donell's." She leaned in and kissed his cheek, then looked past him to her sire. "Did you hear, Father?" She smiled at him, too. "I am Roag's handfasted wife and, aye, we are enjoying ourselves—as well you knew we would, I'm thinking!"

"So I am, lass," her father agreed. "So I am."

"Then you'll no' have any objections if we hold a more formal nuptial ceremony?" Roag met Mungo's cheeky gaze, not believing he was making such a declaration. Or the happiness that it gave him. "Perhaps toward summer's end after all this excitement has passed?"

"I've only been waiting to hear you say that, laddie!" Mungo could hardly finish before everyone in the hall stood, knocking their ale cups together, stamping feet, and cheering.

Only Roag's smile was a bit forced. Happy as he was to have a secure hold on Gillian's hand, he hoped upon hope that he'd not lose Laddie's Isle.

Taking her back to Stirling with him wouldn't be the end of the world, but it would be a world she'd never truly fit into with the whole of her heart.

And—the realization stunned him—it was now a place that no longer felt like home to him.

Laddie's Isle did.

Even though he'd come to feel as if he belonged here, he didn't really. But he was a man who'd fallen fiercely and fully in love with a wonderful woman he knew he couldn't bear to live without, no matter where their path might take them.

That was a blessing.

A great joy he'd never expected.

It would have to be enough, and was.

Chapter Thirty

❖

A sennight later, seven full days and equally splendiferous nights, Roag toed open the door to the tower bedchamber that he shared with his lovely lady wife and did his best to sneak into the room without disturbing her. She slept soundly, for it was an ungodly hour, and she hadn't heard Skog scratching at the door.

As usual, Roag had noticed. He'd climbed from the massive and magnificent four-poster bed they now called their own and had carried Skog down the stair and out onto the grassy moorland behind the tower so that the old dog could take his late-night comfort.

Roag didn't mind.

In truth, he secretly suspected Skog had come to prefer him to Gillian.

It was a notion he wouldn't dare voice to her.

He did take a moment to stand admiring her. Chiefly daughter that she was, and already more beautiful to him than any woman he'd ever seen or could imagine, she looked even more lovely in the new bed.

A huge, glorious piece that—he'd learned—had taken three of Mungo MacGuire's sons, two of his own men, and also William Wyldes to assemble. Crafted of heavy black oak, the wood was smooth and satiny to the touch. The four bedposts, the headboard, and even the ceiling board were carved with thistles, sheaves of heather, galleys, mermaids, and heraldic shields so old that whatever family they'd once honored could no longer be discerned for the wood was so age-worn.

Roag didn't care.

The bed was grand enough for royalty. And though he'd gladly sleep naked on the cold stone floor, Gillian deserved better.

Stepping closer to the bed, he would almost swear it had been made for her. The mermaids that appeared to frolic about the tops of the bedposts and also across the bed's curved ceiling had bold looks about them. Their tempting eyes, flowing hair, and lush breasts, reminded him of Gillian. She loved to stretch across the covers. Bare-bottomed as the bed's aquatic seductresses, she'd then open her arms to him, and—on nights when he was particularly lucky, she'd spread her legs as well, offering herself to him, invitingly.

His lady, he'd learned, was insatiable.

He deemed himself the most fortunate of men, for he loved nothing more than satisfying her.

He might not have a chiefly name to offer her, or a true claim as the isle's keeper, but he did love her fiercely. And he meant to dedicate his life to pleasing her, keeping her happy in heart, soul, and body.

Just now her body was naked.

And she was on her back with her long, lithe legs

parted just enough to give him a tantalizing glimpse of the tender bits of her that he couldn't sample often enough. Worse, or perhaps better, depending on one's view, moonlight fell across the bed, gilding her silver so that she might well have been one of the sea sirens she claimed sang on the reefs when the waves broke high and white across the jagged, half-submerged rocks.

"Odin's balls," he swore, his own danglers aching as he started forward.

Unable to help himself, he leaned over her and stroked his hands lightly along the inside of her thighs. "I have to taste you, sweetness," he breathed, lowering his head to follow his hands with his mouth. He kissed his way up her legs, making for the triangle of red-golden curls that beckoned him so powerfully.

"Roag!" Her eyes snapped open and she pushed up on her elbows, staring at him through the moonlight. "What are you doing?"

"Can you no' guess?" He gave her a bold smile, summoning all his strength not to pounce on her and sink himself into her, loving her fully.

But he knew she was tired.

Their guests hadn't yet left and the tower wasn't outfitted to host so many visitors.

Wonderful as it had been to have her family and also his own Stirling friends on the isle, he secretly yearned for the return of the deep quiet that usually cloaked Laddie's Isle. It was a tranquility and peace that he'd known nowhere else, and that he'd come to need and appreciate.

"I thought you were sleeping." Gillian's eyes glittered in the silvery light—and to his immense delight, she didn't pull her legs together.

"Skog needed to go out," he told her, skimming his fingers up and down her hip.

"It was good of you to take him." She glanced at the nearest window, the tall, arch-topped opening dark save for the glow of the moon.

"It was better of you to greet me so finely." He looked down at her parted thighs, his arousal hard and heavy. "You are too tempting to resist." He tore off his plaid and then pulled his tunic over his head, tossing it onto the floor. "I've a ferocious need to taste you."

"Roag!" Her cheeks flamed, but she teased him by parting her knees a bit more.

"I see you dinnae mind." Now as naked as she was, he climbed onto the bed, settling himself between her thighs. He lowered his head, opening his mouth over her, kissing her deeply. Then he drew back, using his tongue to rouse and pleasure her.

She lifted her hips and thrust her fingers into his hair, clutching at him, pulling him closer. Her need spurred him on, firing his own passion as he kissed and licked her, taking his time before swirling his tongue round and over the tiny bud of sensation that he knew would send her spiraling over the edge of her release. His own didn't matter, for he really did want her to rest, something she hadn't been able to do in days.

Yet having the tower so filled with family and friends was a pleasure unto itself. It was also one he'd never thought to experience. He wouldn't say he was regretful that he'd been bastard-born, for he'd had a good life all the same, most especially of late, with Gillian at his side.

But he did understand her better.

He admired her devotion to kith and kin, the Isle of Sway that was her home.

He suspected he'd always hunger for the taste of her. Wanting to brand her essence on the back of his tongue, he drew deeply on her, licking the very center of her until she jerked beneath him, her hips rising to press against him. Then powerful tremors ripped through her and she cried his name, clutching him to her.

When she finally went limp, he stretched out beside her, pulling her into his arms. She rolled against him, sliding one leg up and over his hips and reaching to trace her fingers gently through his chest hair. Resting her head on his shoulder, she gave a contented sigh.

"I do believe your kisses are even more magical than your hands, hard as that is to believe," she teased, lifting up to smile at him.

"You, sweet, are the enchanted one. You have brought me more joy than I have ever known." He curled a hand round behind her head, bringing her to him for a soft, gentle kiss. "I am more glad for you than I can say. Dinnae you e'er forget that."

A short while later, or so it seemed, another horn blast woke them. The sound was long and shrill in the morning quiet. Startled, Gillian scrambled from the bed, pulling on her clothes as she ran to the windows, darting into the nearest embrasure.

"Roag!" She pointed as he joined her, still throwing on his plaid. "Another ship—anchored this time."

"Looks to be an Irish galley." He leaned out the window to see better. "No' a warship, but a trader by the fat-bellied hull and the men aboard.

"They aren't warriors." He stepped back from window, ran a hand over his hair.

"Perhaps they slept there and our lookout only now spotted them?" Gillian kept her gaze on the ship, the idea making sense. "Ships often moor off Sway, taking refuge for the night. They move on at first light, doing no harm."

"Aye, like as no' that is the way of it." Roag turned back to the room, making for the door. "I will tell my men no' to fash themselves, though I'm still for taking a look from the shore."

"I think they're already leaving." Gillian watched as the men onboard stirred, oarsmen taking up positions on the rowing benches, others crowding along one side of the ship where, she thought, they might be trying to pull in the anchor. "Come look, I'm not sure what they're doing..."

Roag joined her again and in that moment it was clear what was happening on the Irish galley. Someone had lowered a skiff over the side and a huge man in mail and with a wild mane of black hair and an equally wild black beard was already in the small boat, reaching up to take someone in his arms, helping that person into the skiff.

"Roag..." Gillian gripped his arm, her eyes widening. "That's a woman!"

"So it is." He frowned, staring down at the pair.

Whoever they were, the big man now had the woman in his arms and was settling her carefully in the little boat. He then claimed the other bench and took up the oars, pulling strongly as he turned the skiff away from the Irish galley and toward Laddie's Isle, rowing sure, coming fast.

"It would seem we are to have yet more visitors." Roag glanced at her, his lips twitching.

But when he turned back to the window, his jaw slipped. "By Thor, that's Grim!"

Gillian blinked. "Who?"

"A friend," he told her, his almost-smile vanished as he now frowned down at the sea.

"You don't look pleased," Gillian observed, worried by the way his brow had furrowed. "If he is a friend—"

"He is, but he aye turns up when trouble is afoot." Roag narrowed his eyes, clearly straining to read the big man's expression. "He's a Highlander, a Mackintosh from Nought territory in the Glen of Many Legends. I havenae seen him in a while. He's manning a garrison deep in the Highlands these days, standing up as captain for an aged chieftain named Archie MacNab."

"You know him well then." Gillian looked away from Roag to again peer down at the skiff.

It was closer now, nearly ashore. It was easy to see the big, fierce-looking warrior Roag called Grim. Gillian even caught the flash of beard rings braided into the fullness of his beard. The woman she'd first suspected must be Grim's wife proved older. Maybe his mother?

She appeared to be a slight, somewhat frail lady with hair as dark as Grim's, though the morning light glinted on streaks of silver that fanned away from her brow. Even from a distance, it was clear that she'd once been very beautiful.

Gillian couldn't see more because Roag's men and her family were already hurrying down the cliff stair and crowding the beach, waiting to help the little boat and its passengers ashore.

"I wonder what they want." She glanced at Roag as they, too, quickly descended the tower stair, hastened through the hall, and then down the narrow steps that made a path from the top of the cliffs to the rocky shore. "Did you have business with this Grim?"

"Nae." He shot a glance at her, giving her his hand for the last few steps to the cove. "He is a friend only, no' a Fenris man."

"Well, he seems welcome," Gillian smiled when a great cheer rose ahead of them.

It wasn't possible to see past the crowd gathering round the skiff, which was surely on the beach by now. The friendly greeting had been a courtesy, she knew—her family loved company. And if Roag knew Grim, so would his men.

But as she and Roag neared, everyone went silent.

Eerily so, and their faces were oddly expectant as they turned to watch Roag and Gillian's approach. They also parted, opening a path for them.

Grim Mackintosh stood at the path's end, not far from the skiff. He'd put an arm around the woman, the gesture almost protective although he surely knew that no one here would harm her. Equally interesting, the Irish galley was beating away, leaving them there.

Whatever their purpose, they expected to stay, at least as guests, on Laddie's Isle.

And with each step closer, the fine hairs on Gillian's neck lifted more and more. Far-flung as it seemed, she couldn't shake the notion that she knew why they were here.

Indeed, she was certain.

The beautiful older woman before her had the answer in her dark, shimmering eyes. The worry clouding them was telling. More than that, it was her face that gave her away—it was one Gillian knew well and loved dearly.

"By all that's holy!" She reached for Grim's hand, squeezing tight. "Do you see her?"

"Aye," Roag said, his voice oddly thick, strained. "I do, but I dinnae believe it."

Then, before either of them could say anything else, the woman swayed and pressed a hand to her breast, her eyes flying wide as she stared at Roag.

"Such a big man!" she cried then, slumping to her knees.

Chapter Thirty-One

✤

Roag rushed forward across the landing beach, hurrying to help the woman who'd fallen, but Grim was closer and already had her on her feet again, his arm once more clamped tight about her waist.

The woman's eyes were still round as she stared unblinking at Roag, her hand now over her mouth in shock.

Roag stared back at her, a loud buzzing in his ears. The world around him blurred, swimming so crazily that he almost believed he'd wakened in the middle of a terrible dream.

Gillian and her fanciful notions were getting to him.

Because of her and her ancients and faeries and mermaids, he'd almost seen his own face looking back at him from the old woman's before him.

He did see Grim's ugly countenance, though the lout was just as hazy as the woman and everyone and everything else.

"Ho, Grim!" Roag greeted him roundly, wanting to prove that if his eyes were mysteriously damp and burning, there was nothing wrong with his voice. "This is a fine thing—seeing you here so early of a morn, and your lady mother with you!"

"You err, my friend," Grim spoke plainly. "She is Lady Liana MacLean, late of the Isle of Doon, and she is your mother, no' mine."

Roag's heart stopped, and then slammed hard against his ribs.

He opened his mouth to say that was not possible. That such a claim was as absurd as if the night sky darkened to reveal ten moons and not one. But no words left his mouth.

He could only stare. And his burning eyes now damned him by leaking hot tears down his cheeks.

Beside him, he heard Gillian gasp—leastways he believed so. He couldn't say for sure because, although he was still standing, he felt as if Grim's pronouncement had blown him full off his feet.

He blinked a few times, then shook his head, his gaze still on the woman.

No, the lady.

Roag pulled a hand down over his beard, sure the world had run mad.

"I dinnae have a mother," he finally managed. "She died birthing me, she did."

"Nae, she didnae." Grim stepped away from Lady Liana to clap a hand on Roag's shoulder. "She might well have, for she was young and had you torn from her arms before she could set you even once to her breast.

"That is a terrible fate for any woman," he added, watching Roag carefully.

"I'm no' saying it isnae."

"She was banished, my friend," Grim reached behind him, grabbed the woman's wrist, drawing her near. "Given the choice of hieing herself from Stirling and never seeing you, or even speaking of you, or being made to watch as you were dashed against a wall, killed before you were an hour old."

"That's rot!" Roag broke free of Grim's grasp and scowled at the friends and family who were again closing in around him. He tried not to look at Gillian, Grim, and the lovely, fine-boned woman who couldn't possibly be his mother. "No one at Stirling would e'er have done such a deed. No' now, no' even a hundred years ago. I'll no' believe it." He folded his arms, the matter settled.

"They might no' commit such a heinous act, but there are some who would threaten the like." Caelan was suddenly at his side, Andrew close behind him.

"Remember last year, when Grim rooted out that our own Sorley's father was a Highland chieftain, Archie MacNab." Andrew edged closer, glancing first at Roag and then briefly at Lady Liana. "He told us he'd heard all kinds of tales about the miseries Sorley's mother endured. Sadly, she never lived to meet him."

"Be glad you have the chance, lad." Mungo joined the argument. "Family is everything, I say you."

Andrew and Caelan exchanged glances, went to flank Lady Liana. They'd clearly taken sides, were fair falling over themselves to appear as gallants. Rarely had Roag seen them act so foolishly. Some men weren't meant to be courtiers, and their rough edges only stood out the more if they attempted to be what they were not.

Roag had aye been fine just as he was.

So he frowned at his friends. "The lot of you are crazed, I swear it. Next you'll be telling me old MacNab is my sire as well!"

Silence answered him.

"O-o-oh, it is wonderful!" Gillian spoke first, hurrying forward to embrace the older woman.

Up close she truly was striking, with her raven hair and the sweeping streaks of silver that winged back from her brow. Her skin was clear and smooth, the lines of her face noble, giving testimony to her gentle birth. A few creases at the corners of her eyes and lips revealed her years, but didn't detract from a beauty that would surely stay with her through life. But her eyes were her most remarkable feature—the same thick-lashed, peat-brown eyes as Roag.

"Humph." He couldn't say more. He was having a dreadful time just trying not to trip over his tongue or shuffle his feet like a lad.

"We never thought to see this day." Gillian spoke up, her tone encouraging.

"Nor did I, my dear," Lady Liana gave her a tentative smile. "I always hoped. But there seemed little chance of ever even catching word of my wee lost bairn, sequestered away on Doon as I've been all these years. My clan, the MacLeans—"

"So you're Hebridean?" Gillian flashed a triumphant look at Roag.

He tried not to see and hear her.

The implication—that this Isleswoman was his mother—meant that Hebridean blood flowed in his veins. He might not have been aware of its being there, but it was. Its presence would explain why he'd felt such an inexplicable pull to these isles.

"Aye, I am," Lady Liana was telling Gillian, her voice soft and sweetly musical, just like Gillian's own. "In younger years, I journeyed with my family to court where"—she glanced at Grim, who nodded reassuringly—"I came to the notice of the late King. One does not refuse such a man. So I remained at Stirling, even with the blessings of my family.

"Later, I fell from favor, as also happens so often at court. About that time, a young Highland bard would sing to me, lifting my spirits…" She didn't finish, but there was no need.

Roag knew who she meant.

His pounding heart, the heat inching up his neck, and the awful tightness clamping round his chest, all told him the man's name—as did the glances exchanged by Grim, Caelan, and Andrew.

If Liana MacLean of Doon was his mother, his father was none other than Archibald—Archie—MacNab of Duncreag in the Highlands. That made him not just a Hebridean and a Highlander, but also Sorley the Hawk's true brother.

It was beyond belief.

Looking at Liana MacLean now, seeing his own eyes staring back at him…

He could deny it no longer.

How could he when the truth had just hit him like a hammer blow? Indeed, his heart pounded so hard that he could hear its thunderous beat.

"I dinnae ken what to say." He went over to the woman, meaning to offer her his hand but ending up clutching her to him, crushing her roughly against his chest. "Howe'er did you find me?"

"I didn't." His mother glanced at Grim. "He came to Doon looking for me. We have a rather notorious cail-leach on the island, the great Devorgilla. She'd paid a call to Duncreag where Grim is garrison captain for Archie, your father.

"It was Grim who'd found Archie's other bastard son, Sorley," she reminded him. "When he spoke about Grim's continuing quest to locate Archie's lads, Devorgilla urged him to come to Doon to meet me."

"I have heard of her." Gillian nodded, looking suitably awed. "I should like to meet her someday."

Lady Liana smiled. "Perhaps you will. She travels quite a bit."

"I have heard she's a right meddler," Mungo declared, striding up to them. "I be Gillian's father." He caught Lady Liana's wrist, bowing over to give her a gallant hand kiss. "Seeing as you're here without a ship, mayhap you'll grant us a visit at my own Isle of Sway before you return to Doon?"

"I would enjoy that, but…" She let her voice trail away, glanced once more at Grim. She wrung her hands, then released them only to brush at her skirts.

Roag frowned, watching her.

"What is it?" *I can tell fine something is amiss.*

"Mungo saw rightly," Grim put in again. "The Irish trader will no' be coming this way again." He looked to William Wyldes, Caelan, and Andrew. "I was hoping to sail back to the mainland on the *Sea Star* with you when you depart."

The three men nodded in unison, agreeing.

"Lady Liana will not require passage back to Doon, because"—he turned back to Roag—"she is hoping to stay on here, with you and your lady wife."

Roag's jaw slipped. "She can fine," he blurted, not knowing what else to say. "But—"

"Oh, that is wonderful!" His mother smiled at last—the first true smile to light her face since she reached the isle. "Doon is lovely, and my home, but…" She looked down, perhaps embarrassed, before lifting her face again to Roag and Gillian. "Clan MacLean is a happy one. There are many young families on Doon, more bairns and striplings than a soul can count. I love them all, and have aye done my best to help care for them, but—"

"There be no kin like your own flesh and blood!" Mungo hooked his thumbs in his sword belt, rocking back on his heels. "For sure, you'd be better off here. You can help care for the many bairns my Gillian will soon be giving your fine braw laddie!"

"Father!" Gillian's face flamed.

"Aye?" Her father jutted his bearded chin. "Am I wrong, or what?"

"Nae, we do want children," she said then, her response making Roag's heart burst. "And we would love another pair of loving hands to help raise them." She turned to Lady Liana, hugging her and then kissing her on both cheeks. "We are honored, my lady. You are most welcome—for always."

Roag just looked at her, at the two of them.

He didn't know what to say or think. But his heart was splitting. And somewhere deep inside, hidden away in the darkest, deepest corner of his soul, little hard edges began to fall away, replaced by an ever-growing rush of warmth and sweet, golden love that swept him like a fast-running tide. It wasn't the same kind of love he felt for Gillian, but it was powerful. It was also beautiful, and welcome.

As if she saw his capitulation, Lady Liana then needed to dash at her cheeks.

"You will not be sorry, I promise." She looked from one of them to the other, then up at the tall, stout tower that, though proud, was clearly a ruin.

When she returned her gaze to Roag and Gillian, her smile held something else. It was a look of promise and assurance that hadn't been there before.

"Grim has told me that your home is somewhat bare," she said, once more lifting a glance to the cliff-top tower. "I will not praise myself. We of the Hebrides are a modest folk. But I will tell you that I am not unskilled with a needle. In all my years at Doon, I filled my hours making tapestries and embroidering all manner of linen goods for the castle and the strongholds of the clan and the homes of our friends and allies.

"If you can provide me with needles, threads, and linen, I can make lovely wall hangings and other cloth goods for your tower." She bit her lip then, waiting for their response.

"Then I do believe that must've been yet another reason the great Devorgilla of Doon arranged for Grim to bring you to us," Gillian declared. "I can hold my own on a galley, even manning the steering oar as well as most men. But I am clumsy with a needle. I have already been worrying about how I would make our first bairn's swaddling gowns!"

"Oh, my dear," Lady Liana took Gillian's hand in both of hers, her joy apparent. "It would be my greatest pleasure to prepare everything for the wee lad or lassie, whenever you are so blessed."

"Then all is well." Gillian glanced toward the cliff path, tellingly. "Shall we return home? Break our fast together and begin our first day as a new family in our almost-new home?"

It was her last words that kept Roag from striding after them.

He stood frowning.

Everyone else gathered round his sweet lady wife, his mother, whom he'd just learned he had, and his meddlesome group of friends and in-laws that all crowded his isle. They were now tramping up the cliff stair as if a grand feast had been announced.

"Are you not coming?" Gillian was back at his side, hooking her arm in his. "You can't stay down here while everyone else is in your hall, lifting their cups to your mother and our new home, the completion of your work here."

"Odin's balls, lass, have you run daft?" Roag gripped her shoulders, looking down at her. *Are you so excited about gaining a good-mother that you're forgetting this is no' my isle? Or that finishing my work here means we'll surely have to leave?*

"Not at all." She lifted up on her toes to kiss him.

"I see it differently."

"'Tis you who are not seeing everything," she argued, her smile taking the sting out of her words.

Roag stepped back and folded his arms. "Then tell me what I'm missing—save wishing it was night so I could sweep you off to our grand bed and ravish you!"

"See?" She wagged a finger at him. "That alone proves what you're overlooking."

"Oh?"

She nodded, beaming again. "Your friend Alex Stewart sent you more gifts than our bed and your new laird's chair, and the viands that your friends sadly had to pitch into the sea."

"He is a good man, aye." He wouldn't deny that.

The Wolf of Badenoch treated his friends well.

"He is more than good." Gillian stepped closer, slipped her arms around him. "I was just speaking with Grim—"

"I knew he was behind this." Roag flashed a look round the landing beach for the big beard-ringed lout, but he was already gone. Vanished up the cliff stair with everyone else, perhaps even now claiming a seat before the fire of Roag's hall.

A fine driftwood fire that was only borrowed.

A truth that ripped his soul.

"Grim cannae keep his nose out of others' affairs."

"You should be glad that is so—I am." Leaning into him, she rested her head against his shoulder, took a deep breath. "You have said that you've come to love this isle. That you would rather stay on here than return to Stirling. Is that still so?" She drew back to look at him.

"You know it is." He didn't hesitate. "Indeed, as soon as our guests leave, I want us to sail for Stirling so I can speak with King Robert. I shall petition him to allow me to remain here, as his guardian of this isle. The location is a good one. There is always a need for someone to keep an eye on sea traffic, in time of war and in peace."

"You have been planning this?"

"I have." Roag was rather proud of the idea. "I will convince him that I am that man. The guardian he needs—"

364 Sue-Ellen Welfonder

"What if you could stay on here as Laird of Laddie's Isle?" Gillian's smile widened, and a tear caught on her lashes and then rolled down her cheek. "What would you say to that?"

"I would fall onto my knees and kiss the ground." He meant it.

"Then, Laird of Laddie's Isle, I greet you!" Two more tears leaked from her eyes.

Her smile wobbled as she dashed them away. "Laird," she repeated.

"What are you saying?"

"Only what your friend Grim told me." She grabbed his hand, pulling him toward the cliff stair, the tower where so many dear souls waited for them. "When Alex Stewart learned that we'd handfasted and then also heard that Grim had found your mother, a Hebridean woman, he suspected that, now that your work here was finished, you'd rather stay on. Grim said that, as a Highlander himself, the Wolf understands the pull of wild places.

"Knowing you as well, and all that's transpired, he told Grim he believed you'd be a fine man to watch this corner of his brother's kingdom.

"Not," she added, pausing at the start of the cliff stair, "as a keeper, but as laird. This isle and its tower are now yours, my heart." She swept out an arm, taking in the sea and the cliffs and the tower, the cloud-chased sky, and the ever-racing wind. "He had only one stipulation, and Grim swore to him that he'd see it done."

"Alex tied string to it?" Roag's heart sank.

"He did." Gillian didn't look troubled at all. "He insisted that the tower bear your name. From now and ever onward it shall be known as Roag's Tower."

"Nae..." Roag just looked at her, the strange buzzing back in his ears.

His fool eyes were also stinging again.

His heart split wide. In truth, he wasn't sure it could expand enough to hold the love and happiness welling inside him. Indeed, he might burst with it!

He did drop to his knees.

"What are you doing?" His sweet lady wife's eyes rounded.

"Only what I just said I'd do." He grinned and bent low, pressing a kiss to the rocky ground.

Then he leapt to his feet and crushed her to him, kissing her even more soundly. When at last he broke away, it was all he could do not to pull her back into his arms for still more kisses.

But their guests were waiting.

Still, he bracketed her face, looked deep into her eyes. "I love you so much, lassie. I dinnae want to think what would have come of me if you hadn't been waiting for me the day I arrived here."

"You needn't worry about that," she said as they began the climb to Roag's Tower. "Even if my father hadn't brought me here, we'd have found each other, somehow, somewhere."

He cocked a brow. "Is that so?"

"It is."

"More of your ancient ones and faerie notions?"

"Not at all." She leaned in to kiss him. "It is a matter of the heart."

Epilogue

❖

Laddie's Isle
In a hidden place beneath Roag's Tower
Several months later…

Hamish Martin didn't think he'd ever been so happy.

Leastways, he hadn't been in all the endless years he'd spent on the wee isle that living men had given his name. Yet the Laird of Laddie's Isle and the lovely lady that was his wife stood just outside his hidden place deep beneath their tower, and what he'd just heard them say filled Hamish's small, insubstantial breast with so much joy that he feared he might burst.

Hoping that wouldn't happen—he didn't think bursting would be good, even for a bogle—he wondered if he dared to sift himself out of the small round chamber where he now hovered so excitedly. But the pair's words echoed around the low-ceilinged sea cave and he couldn't resist listening to them again and again. They were so wonderful even his ears were smiling…

You are certain, my love? The Laird of Laddie's Isle

had asked his wife, setting his hands on her shoulders and looking at her with so much love and wonder that Hamish almost forgot to keep himself unseen, so greatly did he share their delight.

His wife, Lady Gillian, as Hamish now knew she was called, had nodded, smiling. Then she'd lifted a hand, dashing sparkling tears from her cheeks.

As sure as I can be, aye, she'd told him, stepping back to place a protective hand on her middle.

Hamish was sure he'd never seen a living soul shine as brightly as the lady did in that moment. But then the other lady, the older one he knew to be the laird's mother, joined them and as she'd slid her arm around Lady Gillian, she'd beamed just as brightly. Then she'd said the words that Hamish would remember always...

My dear son, your lovely lady wife is so certain that she's even decided on a name for your child.

He will be called Hamish.

The laird had grinned then—Hamish had noted that he smiled a lot—and agreed that the name was a good one. Then he'd wrapped his arms around both ladies and hugged them tight. He'd just released them and now stepped back to glance up at the tower, its walls glistening from a recent rain and, somehow, looking proud.

But not near as much so as the laird.

"Hamish it is then!" He nodded once, his gaze going to his wife. "Is Hamish a MacGuire name?"

"No," Lady Gillian said, looking puzzled for just a beat. "The name just came to me." She smiled and glanced Hamish's way, though he knew she didn't see him. "It just felt right."

"So it does," the laird agreed, still grinning. Then he

lifted a hand to rub the back of his neck as if a chill had prickled his skin. "So it does, indeed."

And then they were gone, the three of them talking excitedly as they headed back toward the cliff stair. Hamish didn't linger at the opening of his little sea cave.

He didn't want to watch them disappear.

He didn't like being alone. Worse, something was wrong with his hiding place and much as he tried to think, he couldn't decide what he'd done to cause the difference.

The blue was gone.

He knew the bright blue light that often hovered around him frightened many living men, but he'd grown used to shining. And sometimes, when he was lonely and feeling sad, he'd watch the walls of his wee cave shimmer and shine, the dancing light and sparkles keeping him company.

Now his little hiding place was only cold and dark, the cave's walls black and damp, no different than the rocky cliffs just outside on the beach.

I can't bear it, I tell you.

A woman's voice floated to him from the shore, soft and sweet, hauntingly familiar. *We must go in there and fetch him. It has been too long, we have waited enough.*

He can only leave with us if he comes out hisself, a man countered, his voice just as known—and dear—to Hamish as the woman's. *I dinnae mind if you sift his wriggly new puppy here to draw him out, but we're no' going in there.*

If we do, he'll be lost to us.

Hamish's eyes rounded. His heart started knocking so fast his entire body shook and quivered.

His parents were outside his hidden place!

And not just them—the blue light was out there, too. He could see its shine through the small cave opening. It was beautiful, dazzling, and a much prettier shade than he'd ever seen, the shine of it brighter than the stars and sun.

One more heartbeat, his mother warned his father, her eagerness to see Hamish making his eyes leak. *At the least, I shall count the waves, and when the ninth one rolls ashore, I will go in there and—*

"Mother!" Hamish ran from his cave, glad that he knew the rocky beach so well, because his tears almost blinded him. "Father!" he called, his wee legs moving faster than they ever had. "I am here! See me, I am here, with you now!"

And then he was, their shining arms reaching for him, hauling him hard against them in a hug so tight he again wondered if he might burst. He'd also never felt as much love as now rushed through him, filling him with so much warmth he doubted he'd ever be cold again. Not now, with his parents come to collect him.

That they were here to take him away, he knew.

Ghosts were smart, he'd learned long ago.

Some things were just clear to them.

Yet...

He drew back from the embrace, his gaze lifting to Roag's Tower. Lights blazed in the windows and the sounds of pipes and fiddles, and merry laughter, drifted on the wind. The good folk who dwelled there were celebrating, it was clear.

Hamish knew why, and for a moment, he wished he could join them.

"They need you nae more, lad." His father followed his gaze, approval on his face. "You did us proud these years, my boy," he added, his voice roughening as he ruffled Hamish's hair. "But it is time for you to come home."

"We have missed you so!" His mother dropped to her knees, pulled him into her arms again, raining kisses on his face, his brow, and his hair.

"I missed you, too," Hamish admitted, again blinking back tears.

But they were happy ones. And when his mother at last released him, straightening, he gladly let them take him by the hands and lead him down the shore. Not toward the cliff and its steep stair carved of stone, but toward a beautiful moored galley that shone a brilliant blue and glittered as if all the stars in heaven had swept down to grace its hull and sail, to light the way.

"Are we truly going home?" Hamish looked up at his parents as they reached the surf's edge and started sifting across the water, drawing near to his father's ship.

"We are, laddie, aye." His father smiled down at him.

And this time Hamish's heart did burst.

At least, he thought so. But it was with happiness and there was nothing frightening about it. Then, as was the way with those of other realms, the three of them were aboard the blue-shining galley and in a blink, they were away.

Hamish cast one last look at Laddie's Isle, dashed a hand across his cheek.

He was ready to leave.

His work there was done.

To keep from marrying her odious suitor, Lady Mirabelle MacLaren must turn to his sworn enemy, the one they call "Hawk." But as they set about the task of ruining her reputation, Hawk and Mirabelle soon learn that rebellion never tasted so sweet.

❦

Please see the next page for an excerpt from

To Love a Highlander

Chapter One

❦

Stirling Castle
Summer 1399

Sorley the Hawk slept naked.

His bare-bottomed state was glaringly apparent, even
to Lady Mirabelle MacLaren's innocent eyes. She should
have known that a man with such an inordinate fondness
for pleasures of the flesh would take to his bed unclothed.
Still, it was a possibility she should've considered before
sneaking into his privy quarters. She hadn't expected him
to be in his room so early of an e'en. She'd hoped to catch
him unawares, surprising him when he strode inside.

Now she was trapped.

She stood frozen, her heart racing as she glanced
around his bedchamber. Even in the dimness, she could
tell his quarters were boldly masculine and entirely too
sumptuous for an ordinary court bastard. Exquisitely
embroidered and richly colored tapestries hung from the
walls and the floor was immaculate, the rushes fresh and

scented with aromatic herbs. A heavily carved and polished trestle table held the remains of what had surely been a superb repast. Several iron-banded coffers drew her curiosity, making her wonder what treasures they contained. Above all, her eye was drawn to the large curtained bed at the far end of the room.

There, atop the massive four-poster, Sorley was stretched out on his back, one arm folded behind his head.

That he was nude stood without question.

What astonished her was her reaction to seeing him in such an intimate state.

Her mouth had gone dry and her heart beat too rapidly for comfort. She couldn't deny that she found herself strongly attracted to him. Yet to accomplish what she must, she required her wits.

Unfortunately, she also needed Sorley.

Sir John Sinclair, an oily-mannered noble she couldn't abide, was showing interest in her. Worse, he was wooing her father, a man who believed the best in others and didn't always catch the nuances that revealed their true nature. Castle tongue-waggers whispered that Sinclair desired a chaste bride, requiring a suitable wife to appease the King's wish that he live more quietly than was his wont. Mirabelle suspected he'd chosen her as his future consort.

She knew Sorley loathed Sinclair.

And that the bad blood was mutual.

No one was better suited to help her repel Sinclair's advances than Sorley the Hawk.

Time was also of the essence. Mirabelle's father's work at court wouldn't take much longer. As a scholar and herbalist, he'd tirelessly seen to his duties, assisting the royal scribes in deciphering Gaelic texts on healing. Soon, the MacLaren party would return home to the Highlands.

Mirabelle didn't want to remain behind as Sir John's betrothed. For that reason, she summoned all the strength she possessed to remain where she stood. It cost her great effort not to back from the room, disappearing whence she'd come. Harder still was not edging closer to the bed, then angling her head to better see Sorley.

He was magnificent.

Blessedly, the sheet reached to his waist, hiding a certain part of him. The rest of his big, strapping body was shockingly uncovered. Mirabelle's face heated to see the dusting of dark hair on his hard-muscled chest. She felt an irresistible urge to touch him. Well aware that she daren't, she did let her gaze drift over him. Light from an almost-guttered night candle flickered across his skin, revealing a few scars. His thick, shoulder-length hair was as inky-black as she remembered, the glossy strands gleaming in the dimness. Even asleep, he possessed a bold arrogance. Now that her eyes had adjusted to the shadows, she could see from the bulge outlined beneath the bedcovers that his masculinity was equally proud.

The observation made her belly flutter.

Unable to help herself, she let her gaze linger on his slumbering perfection. His darkly handsome face and oh-so-sensual mouth that, if all went well, would soon play expertly over hers, claiming her in passion.

The only problem was she'd rather make her proposition when he was fully clothed.

Confronting him now would only compound her troubles.

So she pressed a hand to her breast and retraced her steps to the door. It stood ajar, the passage beyond beckoning, urging escape. Scarce daring to breathe, she peered from one end of the corridor to the other. Nothing stirred except a cat scurrying along in the darkness and a poorly burning wall sconce that hissed and spit.

Or so she thought until two chattering laundresses sailed around a corner, their arms loaded with bed linens. A small lad followed in their wake, carrying a wicker basket brimming with candles.

They were heading her way.

"Botheration!" She felt a jolt of panic.

Nipping back into Sorley's bedchamber, she closed the door.

It fell into place with a distinct *knick*.

Before she could catch her breath, Sorley was behind her, gripping her shoulders with firm, strong fingers. He lowered his head, nuzzling her neck, his mouth brushing over her skin. She bit her lip as he slid his hands down her arms, pulling her back against him.

He was still naked.

She could feel the hot, hard length of him pressing into her.

Almost as bad, he was now rubbing his face in her hair, nipping her ear. His warm breath sent shivers rippling through her.

She gasped, her heart thundering.

"Sweet minx, I didnae expect a visitor this night." He chuckled and closed his hands more firmly around her wrists. "Followed me from the Red Lion, did you?"

"To be sure, I didn't!" Mirabelle found her tongue at his mention of the notorious tavern, an ill-famed place frequented by rogues and light-skirts. She jerked free, whirling to face him. "Nor am I a minx. I'm—"

"You are Lady Mirabelle." His voice chilled, his eyes narrowing as he looked her up and down. He stepped back, folding his arms.

He made no move to cover his nakedness.

"I'd heard you were at court." His gaze held hers, his face an unreadable mask. "Indeed, I've seen you in the hall a time or two. I didn't think to find you here, in my bedchamber."

"Neither did I." Her chin came up. "I lost my way."

"You're also a terrible liar." He angled his head, studying her. "You wouldn't be here without a reason. My quarters are no place for a lady." A corner of his mouth hitched up in a smile that didn't meet his eyes. "So tell me, to what do I owe the honor?"

Mirabelle drew a tight breath, the words lodging in her throat. The explanation, her carefully crafted plea for help, had slipped her mind. Vanishing as if she hadn't spent hours, even days and nights, practicing everything she'd meant to say to him.

"Sir, you're unclothed." Those words came easily. They also caused her cheeks to flame.

"So I am." He glanced down, seemingly unconcerned. Turning, he took a plaid and a shirt off a peg on the wall, donning both with a slow, lazy grace that embarrassed her almost as much as his nakedness.

"Now that I'm decent"—he placed himself between her and the door, crossing his arms again—"I'd know why you're here."

"I told you—"

"You told me a falsehood. I'd hear the truth."

Mirabelle wanted to sink into the floor. Unfortunately, such an escape wasn't possible, and as she prided herself on being of a practical nature, she kept her head raised and flicked a speck of lint from her sleeve. Her mind raced, seeking a plausible explanation. It came to her when the wind whistled past the long windows, the sound almost like the keening cry of a woman.

"I thought to see the castle's pink lady." She didn't turn a hair mentioning the ghost. Everyone knew she existed. Believed the wife of a man killed when England's Edward I captured the castle nearly a hundred years before, the poor woman was rumored to be beautiful, her luminous gown a lovely shade of rose.

Mirabelle had quite forgotten about her until now.

But she did believe in bogles.

Her own home, Knocking Tower, abounded with spirits. She'd even encountered a few. Not a one of them had disquieted her as much as the man now standing before her, his arms still folded and the most annoying look on his darkly rugged face.

He was entirely too virile.

He also had proved a much greater threat than any ghost.

"The pink lady walks the courtyard, last I heard." Sorley spoke with the masculine triumph of a man sure he knew better than the gullible female before him. His tone left no doubt that he didn't believe in the bogle. "You would not have met her in my privy chambers.

"Come, I'll show you where folk claim she prowls." He wrapped his hand around her wrist and led her across the room to one of the tall, arch-topped windows. "Look down into the bailey. Tell me if you see her."

"I won't. See her, I mean." Mirabelle tried to ignore how her skin tingled beneath his touch. "She's elusive. She doesn't appear simply because one peers out a window."

"Even so, I'd hear what you see." He stepped closer, so near the air around her filled with his scent.

Mirabelle set her lips in a tight, irritated line, doing her best not to notice how delicious he smelled. It was a bold, provocative mix of wool and leather, pure man and something exotic, perhaps sandalwood, the whole laced with a trace of peat smoke. Entirely too beguiling, the heady blend made her pulse race.

Furious that was so, she straightened her back, determined to focus on anything but him.

She failed miserably.

Awareness of him sped through her; a cascade of warm, tingly sensations that weakened her knees and warmed unmentionable places. His near-naked proximity also made it impossible to think. Never had she been in such a compromisingly intimate situation. She certainly hadn't experienced the like with a man so brazen, so devilishly attractive.

As if he knew she was uncomfortable, he placed his hand at the small of her back, urging her closer to the broad stone ledge of the window. "I'd have your answer, Lady Mirabelle. I am no' a patient man."

"Very well." Mirabelle leaned forward, pretending to study the darkened courtyard below. A hard rain was falling and the bailey stood empty, the cobbles gleaming wetly. Torches burned in the sheltered arcade circling the large, open space. A few guards, spearmen, huddled in a corner where a small brazier cast a red glow against the wall of a pillared walkway. Nothing else stirred.

She drew a tight breath, wishing she hadn't mentioned the ghost.

She turned to face her tormentor. "The pink lady is not down there."

"I didnae expect she would be, prowling—"

"I'm sure she drifts or hovers." Mirabelle held his gaze. "She's had her heart torn and is searching for her husband. Such a soul wouldn't—"

"She wouldn't drift, hover, or prowl, because she isn't real." He came closer, gripping her chin and tilting her face upward. "The pink lady's existence is as unlikely as a flesh-and-blood lady letting herself into my bedchamber. Even women who are not of gentle birth only enter this room at my invitation." He looked at her, his gaze steady and penetrating. "I do not recall extending such an offer to you.

"So I'll ask again." He slid his thumb over the corner of her mouth, then along the curve of her bottom lip. "Why are you here?"

Mirabelle shivered. She didn't know if it was because of the way he was looking at her or if her body was simply reacting to his touch.

Without question, he was the most dangerously handsome man at court.

She suspected in all the land.

He was also the man most suited to aid her.

So she stepped back, summoning all her courage. "You know women well," she owned, her heartbeat quickening. "I do have a reason for this visit. It has nothing to do with the castle ghost."

"So we near the truth at last." He sounded amused. "I'll admit I am curious."

"I have a business arrangement for you." She couldn't believe the steadiness of her voice.

He arched a brow. "Now I am even more intrigued."

"You shouldn't be." She made a sweeping gesture with her hand, taking in his room in all its opulence. "You are known as a man of many skills, greatly favored at court. I am in need of one of your talents."

"Indeed?" He narrowed his eyes, no longer bemused. "And what might that be?"

"I require your amatory skills." Mirabelle kept her chin raised. "I want you to ruin me."

"Lady, I surely didn't hear you clearly." Sorley held her gaze, hoping his cold tone and steady stare would unnerve her into retracting her ridiculous request. "You wish me to despoil you?"

"Take my virtue, yes." She didn't turn a hair. Far from looking embarrassed, her lovely lavender-blue eyes sparked with challenge and determination. "I shall pay you well for your trouble."

Sorley almost choked.

He did his best to keep his jaw off the floor. It wasn't easy, so he went to the door, crossing his bedchamber in long, swift strides. He didn't want her to see his shock. Worse, how tempted he was to accept her offer. Not that he'd take coin for such pleasure. A shame he'd have to decline. Even one such as he had honor, his own brand of it, anyway.

Still, he was stunned. Her suggestion was the last thing he'd expected.

It was outrageous.

He could find no words.

Certain the world had run mad, he unlatched the door, flinging it wide. With surprising agility, Lady Mirabelle fair flew across the room and nipped around him, closing the door before he could stop her.

"A word is all I ask of you." She put out a hand to touch his chest. "Only that, and—"

"Do you believe maidens are ruined by words?"

"I meant just now, as well you know. Later…" She lowered her hand, giving him a look that was much too provocative for a virgin. "You will be generously recompensed."

"So you said." Sorley didn't say how much that offended him.

He also wished he could tear his gaze from her.

Regrettably, he couldn't.

A softly burning wall sconce limned her in glowing golden light, making her look like an angel. Her rose scent drifted about her, bewitching him now as it'd done so many years before. The heady fragrance was hers alone, an annoying intoxication he remembered well. A temptation he was determined to never fall prey to again.

He frowned. "I dinnae want or need your coin. I might be baseborn, but I'm no' a man in need of funds. And"— he let his gaze drop to her breasts, her hips—"the only trouble I wish is the kind I make myself. For naught in all broad Scotland would I touch you, a gently born lady."

A hint of color bloomed on her face. "Do not think I came here lightly." She drew a breath, her shoulders going back as she struggled to keep her composure. "It is not every day that a woman seeks to blacken her reputation."

"You've already damaged your good name by coming here, assuming someone might have seen you."

"No one did."

"Think you?" Sorley cocked a brow. "Are you so well-practiced at sneaking through the night, then? How many times have you crept down empty corridors, slipping into a man's bedchamber?"

"Never before, but—"

"You'll no' do the like again, if you're wise." Reaching around her, Sorley cracked the door and peered into the darkened passage. Seeing no one, he turned back to her, needing her gone before he reconsidered his options. An irritating twitch at his loins was making a damned persuasive argument.

He was also tempted simply because her remarkable eyes held nary a flicker of recognition.

She'd forgotten him.

And the knowledge annoyed him almost as much as the slight she'd shown him at her uncle's celebratory feast all those years ago.

The memory dashed the pleasurable stirrings at his groin.

With slow deliberation, he shut the door and leaned back against its solid, unyielding wood. He crossed his ankles and folded his arms, letting his stance show her that he was prepared to remain there until he had the answers he desired. He was a stubborn man.

Nor did he tire easily.

"So-o-o"—he gave her a slow smile, careful not to let it reach his eyes—"I'd hear why you came to me with such a fool request."

"Seeing you now, sir," she returned, her own voice as chilly, "I almost regret my folly."

"You should." He studied her face, feeling a scowl

darken his own. If anything, she was even more fetching than he remembered. Her silky red-gold hair gleamed in the light of the wall sconce and her sparkling eyes were still the widest, loveliest he'd ever seen. Her small, upturned nose gave her an irksome air of innocence, while her mouth, so full and lush…

The pestiferous twitch at his loins returned.

He willed the stirrings away before she noticed and took advantage.

Praise the gods she wore a cloak that only hinted at the ripeness of her womanly curves.

She was no longer a girl.

And for sure, he wasn't a cocky, full-of-himself lad.

"You haven't answered me." He put just enough arrogance into his tone to prove it.

Her chin came up again, showing her own mettle. "I say I did. I am troubled by a matter of some delicacy and require a man's aid in—"

"Creating a scandal that will soil you," Sorley finished for her.

To her credit, she blushed. "It could be put that way, yes."

"That I understand." He knew exactly what her wish entailed. "I'd know why you'd give me such an honor?"

"Because it is rumored you are one of the Fenris Guards." She didn't blink. "Men the King employs when his noble, more fastidious warriors fail him." She tilted her head, her gaze bold. "Word is men of the Fenris will do anything. They are known to be fearless. Formidable fighters who"—her eyes took on an entirely too determined glint—"are also known for their legendary skill at seducing women."

Sorley laughed. "The Fenris *are* legend, my lady. Such men dinnae exist."

"I have heard you are one of them."

"All I am is a bastard. Though"—he flashed his most roguish smile—"I'll admit I enjoy tumbling comely, willing lasses. That includes ladies of quality so long as they are wed or widowed and looking for mutual pleasure. I do not lie with virgins."

"You speak bluntly." She glanced aside, the wall sconce revealing the high color blooming on her cheeks.

"I told you the truth, no more."

He was also damned glad to have shocked her. In his experience, just a hint of a man's baser nature was enough to send ladies running. Their fear of carnality filled their innocent minds, chasing all else. She wouldn't mention the Fenris again. And when he discovered who'd dared to breathe his name in connection with the band of secret warriors, there'd be hell to pay.

"Then I shall do the same." She looked back at him, now calm. "You spoke true and so you deserve to hear my fullest reasons." Her head high, she went back to the window arch across the room. When she turned to look at him, she might as well have kicked him in the gut.

Rarely had he seen a woman more bent on having her way.

Regrettably, he also hadn't ever gazed upon a female he found more desirable.

She clearly knew it, and she meant to take advantage.

Proving it, she moved to the small oaken table by the window where a ewer of finest wine and a jug of excellent heather ale waited almost conspiratorially amidst the remains of his evening repast. Equally annoying, as he truly did enjoy entertaining amiable women in his quarters, a half-score of ale cups and wine chalices stood at the ready, each one gleaming softly in the candlelight.

"You'll surely join me?" She glanced at him as she lifted the ewer, pouring two measures of wine. When he didn't move to accept her offering, she set his chalice on the table. Her gaze locking on his, she took a long, slow sip of the strong Rhenish wine.

"I think no'." Sorley frowned and pushed away from the door. "Drinking my wine is no' telling me why you're here, seeking a man to—" He snapped his mouth shut, his scowl deepening when he was unable to finish the fool sentence.

He did start pacing, taking care not to stride too near to her and the cloud of disturbingly enchanting rose perfume that wafted about her.

"Not any man." She touched the chalice to her lips, sipping slowly, provocatively. "I wish your aid, no one else's."

"Any man could perform such a deed." Sorley glared at her.

"Could, I certainly agree. But would they? I believe not." She set down the wine chalice. "Most men at court would decline out of respect for my father. Those of less noble birth would refuse because they'd fear the repercussions. My sire is a scholar, not a fighting man, but he employs a garrison of formidable warriors."

"I see." Sorley did, and her explanation riled him unreasonably. "You chose me because I'm known no' to stand in awe of my betters. And"—he couldn't keep the anger from his voice—"because it's rumored I'm wild and crazed enough to fear no man.

"Lastly, for the reason you already stated." He crossed to the table and tossed back the wine he'd refused. Setting down the empty chalice, he deliberately let his gaze slide over her from head to toe. "Everyone at court is aware of my appetite for comely women."

"Your appreciation of ladies was a consideration." She held his gaze, not flinching.

"I said women, no' ladies. There is a difference."

"I know that very well."

Sorley studied her with narrowed eyes. "Yet you wish to explore why that is so?"

"Would I be here otherwise?" She angled her head, her gaze as sharp as his. "I think not."

"I say you dinnae ken what you're asking." His temper fraying, Sorley stepped closer and braced his arms on either side of her. He splayed his hands against the wall so she was caught between him and a colorful unicorn tapestry. "Sweet lass, I am no' a weak-wristed, embroidered tunic-wearing courtier. A passionless man who likely beds his wife beneath the coverlet, all candles snuffed. If you had even the slightest idea of what it's like to couple with a man like me, you'd run screaming from this room."

Her chin came up. "I never scream. Nor do I cry. Not even when I wish I could."

On her words, Sorley felt like an arse.

But his pride cut deeper.

So he leaned in, wishing his every breath wasn't laced with her intoxicating rose scent. He touched his lips to the curve of her neck, nipped lightly. "I could make you cry out in pleasure, Lady Mirabelle.

"A pity I have no desire to do so." He stepped back,

folded his arms. "I learned long ago that dallying with highborn lasses brings naught but grief."

Rather than color with indignation and sail from his room as he'd expected her to do, she simply lifted her hands to the jeweled clasp of her cloak and undid the pin so that her mantle fell open to reveal the outrageously provocative gown she wore beneath.

Surely designed to singe a man's eyes, the raiment's rich, emerald silk clung to her every dip and curve. Threads of deep bronze were woven into the fabric, an intricate pattern that glittered in the firelight. Her glossy red-gold hair shone to equal advantage, annoyingly lustrous against the jeweled tones of her dress. Worse, her bodice dipped low, offering tantalizing glimpses of her creamy skin and full, round breasts. A braided belt of golden cord circled her slim waist, the tasseled ends dangling suggestively near a very feminine place Sorley did not want to notice. More gold glittered along the delicate border edging the top of the gown, drawing his attention back to her lush bosom.

She looked like a living flame.

And damn if he didn't feel a powerful urge to be burned to a crisp.

Instead, he frowned, ignoring the heat spearing straight to the swelling hardness he was sure she could see.

Secretly, he now hoped she did.

He was that angry.

For truth, he could see the top crescents of her nipples! They were a lovely pink and puckered, peeking up above her bodice's gold-edged border.

"I'll no' deny you're lovely, my lady." He could hardly speak. "Though along with erroneous judgment, I suspect your hearing is no' what it should be. I told you I am no' the man to fulfill your request."

"I did not err in coming here. You are the only man who can help me."

"You will easily find another." Sorley turned his back on her to stare out into the cold, wet night. He didn't like the way just looking at her did funny things to his chest. Elsewhere, he was setting like granite, curse the lass. "You found your way in here. You can leave by the same door."

"I thought you were a man who courts danger." She joined him at the window. "Was I mistaken? Are you not as daring as everyone says?"

"I am that and more, sweetness. What I am no', is a fool. And I'm no' of a mind to make myself one by tearing that fine gown off of you and initiating you in the pleasures of carnal passion.

"I'll leave that honor to a man less wise." He fixed his gaze on the misty drizzle, the darkly gleaming cobbles of the bailey far below. "There's nothing you can say to sway me otherwise."

"Not even if I told you helping me would enrage John Sinclair?"

Sorley stiffened, the name chilling his innards. He closed his eyes and took a long breath of the cold, damp air. Lady Mirabelle's mention of the much-lauded, sneakily treacherous noble struck him like a fist in the ribs.

Sinclair was his greatest enemy.

Even if the dastard didn't know Sorley was aware of his crimes. That one of the innocent young bastard women he'd once raped and tormented had been a lass Sorley loved as strongly as if she'd been his sister. Now she was no more and hadn't been for many years. The courtier's twisted pleasures had caused her to drown herself, ending her shame in the cold waters of the River Forth.

It was a death Sorley meant to avenge.

He was only waiting for the best opportunity.

"I see I guessed rightly." Lady Mirabelle touched his arm. "You do not care for Sir John?"

"There are some who dinnae admire the man. I am one of them, aye." Sorley tamped down the revulsion surging through him. He turned to meet Mirabelle's gaze. "What does he have to do with you?"

Sorley had a good idea, but wanted to hear the words from her.

"He's been making overtures." She spoke plainly. "Enough so that I believe he intends to ask for my hand. As my father is"—she paused, drew a tight breath—"more accustomed to peering at his precious books than into the character of men, I fear he will accept such an offer. I am determined to avoid his bid at all costs."

"So that is the way of it." Sorley now understood why she wanted to be rid of her virginity. "You are hoping Sinclair will no' want soiled goods?"

"I am certain he will not." She looked up at him from beneath thick, surprisingly dark lashes.

"There are many ladies at court who welcome his interest." Sorley wished it wasn't true. "The King has aye held him in high esteem."

"With all respect, the King is a Lowlander. I am Highland born and bred." She lifted her chin, her pride unmistakable. "With some exceptions"—she blushed, clearly thinking of her scholarly sire—"we are not easily fooled. I also put out discreet enquiries."

"Many women wouldn't have bothered." Sorley went back to the table, helping himself to another measure of wine. "They see only—"

"I am not 'other women.' I am myself, always." She followed him across the room, boldly putting herself in his path when he would've started pacing again. "I am not blinded by golden torques and beringed fingers, raiments adorned with jewels.

"Nor do I care for arrogance." She put her hands on her hips, her determination and wit beginning to delight him as much as her other, more obvious charms. "I do not trust Sir John's smile. I'm also not fond of his eyes.

"Such things are more telling than words." She flipped back her hair. "That is why I asked a trusted servant to befriend those working in the castle kitchens. Such people often know more about a person's true nature than anyone sitting at the high table."

"Is that so?"

"I believe you know that it is."

"Indeed, I do." Sorley squelched the smile tugging at his lips.

The last thing he wanted was for her to guess how much he admired her good sense. Most ladies at court fawned all over Sir John Sinclair.

It scarce mattered that the noble's underhanded dealings and treachery had cost him lands and wealth. Or that he'd also lost esteem in the eyes of a few. Those worthies who looked beyond Sinclair's slick, oiled hair and handsome face; the shining mail and lavish clothes he favored. Somehow he managed to dress himself extravagantly even when reputed to have lost much of his coin.

Despite it all, he stayed within the bounds allowed him, craftily avoiding royal wrath.

By comparison, Sorley wasn't half as skilled at self-preservation.

He rubbed the back of his neck, uncomfortably aware that he couldn't possibly keep hiding how appealing he found Lady Mirabelle.

He wanted to despise her.

As if she sensed his approaching capitulation, she came forward, her bewitching perfume floating with her. The fragrance swirled about him, teasing and tempting him, the delicate rose scent forming a trap more inescapable than bars of hot-forged iron.

"So you agree?" She stopped right before him, so near he couldn't breathe.

"I share your opinion of Sinclair." He regretted the words as soon as they left his mouth.

She pounced, the flare of hope in her eyes almost persuading him. "If he believes I am no longer—"

"Sweet lass, I regret spoiling your plans, but they won't work. No' with Sinclair." His voice hardened just thinking of the man. "A woman's purity matters naught to him. He isn't a fastidious sort. No' in that regard."

"Perhaps not," she agreed. "But he is fiercely proud."

"No' that proud." Sorley let his gaze again dip to her breasts. Looking up again, he smoothed the backs of his fingers down her cheek, brushed his thumb over the corner of her lips. "If he wants you, which isn't surprising, he'll no' leave you be until he's had you.

"And there'll be hell to pay if you resist him." Sorley knew it well. "John Sinclair is no' a man you'd wish to rile, my lady."

"If you help me, that won't be necessary."

"Have you Heiland bog cotton in your ears, lass? Sinclair won't care a whit if you're soiled or pure. Not that lecherous bastard."

To Sorley's surprise, she glanced aside, color once again blooming on her cheeks. When she looked back at him, he could almost feel the embarrassment rolling off her. But she stood tall, her shoulders straight and her head raised. Whatever her faults—and he knew she had them—her courage delighted and fascinated him.

She moistened her lips. "My servant also asked around about you."

Sorley's brow went up. "Is that so?"

"It was necessary." She held his gaze, her voice strong. "I learned there's bad blood between you and Sir John. If you help me, you'd benefit as well."

Sorley almost choked. "Any man would enjoy taking you to his bed."

He just wasn't that man.

"Aside from the obvious"—he gripped her chin, his gaze fierce—"how would such an association favor me?"

"It is known at court that Sir John reviles you as much as you dislike him." She spoke as if she'd rehearsed her arguments. "He considers any woman touched by you as tainted goods. They are no longer worth his esteem.

"You've never been in a position to challenge him before his peers." She looked at him with those sparkling eyes, speaking easily of his lowly birth. "Now you have the chance to thwart him, spoiling his plans."

For a heartbeat, Sorley was tempted.

Greatly so.

But he knew Sinclair too well.

So he went to the door, setting his hand on the latch. "Sir John's fury would be terrible, my lady. I dinnae care for myself, but he would—"

"He won't lay a hand on me." She joined him at the door, touched his elbow. "I'll be home to Knocking Tower before he'd have the chance. Besides"—she gave him a smile that went straight to his heart, almost convincing him—"the Highlands are no place for a Lowland noble. He wouldn't find me there if he tried.

"So, please…" She squeezed his arm. "Will you not agree to help me?"

"I will consider it." He wouldn't, but she needn't know that. "Meet me in the castle chapel tomorrow e'en and I'll give you my answer. If anyone questions you, you can say you're hoping to catch a glimpse of the pink lady. That's where she is most frequently seen."

"I will be there." She lifted on her toes and kissed his cheek. "Thank you."

"I've no' yet agreed." He was determined to say no.

Placing a hand on the small of her back, he urged her out the door. Once it was closed again, he leaned his back against the wood, a smile curving his lips. Perhaps there was a way he could assist her and scratch an itch that had plagued him for years.

Sometimes the gods did favor a man, and who was he to refuse their gifts?

Pushing away from the door, he went to the window and braced his hands on the cold, damp stone of the ledge. As if the fates truly were tempting him, he was in time to see Lady Mirabelle crossing the bailey. A thin drizzle still fell and an enormous moon drifted in and out of the clouds. Wind blew sheets of mist across the courtyard, but Mirabelle strode through the rain as if she was made for such weather.

His smile deepened as he watched her.

She paused before the sheltered arcade on the far side of the bailey and tipped back her head as if she savored the misty damp on her face. Sorley's pulse quickened, a whirl of heated images filling his mind. In his experience, women who appreciated rough weather were equally wild and passionate in a man's arms.

He'd enjoy discovering if the same was true of Lady Mirabelle.

His blood ran hot at the thought, pure masculine anticipation surging through him as she disappeared into the shadows of the arcade. Rarely had a woman roused such an intense response in him. And never had he been more inclined to ignore such yearnings.

What a shame he knew he wouldn't.

Fall in Love with Forever Romance

A TASTE OF SUGAR
by Marina Adair

For fans of Rachel Gibson, Kristan Higgins, and Jill Shalvis
comes the newest book in Marina Adair's Sugar, Georgia series.
Can sexy Jace McGraw win back his ex, pediatrician Charlotte
Holden, with those three simple words: we're still married?

Fall in Love with Forever Romance

"Lovable men and lovable dogs make this series a winner."
—JILL SHALVIS, *New York Times* bestselling author

Ever AFTER

Great Series! Great Price!

RACHEL LACEY

EVER AFTER
by Rachel Lacey

After being arrested for a spray-painting spree that (perhaps) involved one too many margaritas, Olivia Bennett becomes suspect number one in a string of vandalisms. Deputy Pete Sampson's torn between duty and desire for the vivacious waitress, but he may have to bend the rules because true love is more important than the letter of the law . . .

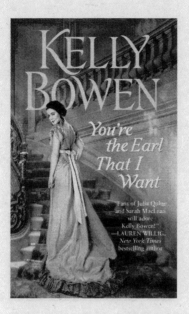

YOU'RE THE EARL THAT I WANT
by Kelly Bowen

For Heath Hextall, inheriting an earldom has been a damnable nuisance. What he needs is a well-bred, biddable woman to keep his life in order. Lady Josephine Somerhall is *not* suited for the job, but he's about to discover that what she lacks in convention, she makes up for in passion.

Fall in Love with Forever Romance

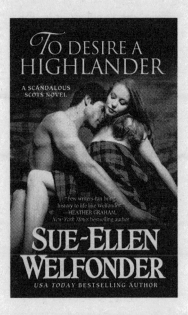

TO DESIRE A HIGHLANDER
by Sue-Ellen Welfonder

The second book in *USA Today* bestseller Sue-Ellen Welfonder's
sexy Scandalous Scots series. When a powerful warrior meets
Lady Gillian MacGuire—known as the Spitfire of the Isles—he's
shocked to learn that *he*'s the one being seduced and captivated...

Find out more about Forever Romance!

Visit us at
www.hachettebookgroup.com/publishing_forever.aspx

Find us on Facebook
http://www.facebook.com/ForeverRomance

Follow us on Twitter
http://twitter.com/ForeverRomance

NEW AND UPCOMING TITLES

Each month we feature our new titles
and reader favorites.

CONTESTS AND GIVEAWAYS

We give away galleys, autographed copies,
and all kinds of exclusive items.

AUTHOR INFO

You'll find bios, articles, and links to personal websites
for all your favorite authors—and so much more.

GET SOCIAL

Connect with your favorite authors, editors, and
other Forever fans, and share what's important to you.

THE BUZZ

Sign up for our monthly romance newsletter,
and be the first to read all about it.